BABYLON REVEALED

THE BEGINNING OF SORROWS

JOHN JOHNSON

Paperback ISBN 978-1-945169-72-4
eBook ISBN 978-1-945169-73-1

Orison Publishers, Inc.
PO Box 188
Grantham, PA 17027
717-731-1405
www.OrisonPublishers.com
Publish your book now, marsha@orisonpublishers.com

Printed in the United States of America

Other books by John Johnson
The Byzantine Chronicles series
    The Blade – ISBN 978-1945169-29-8
    The Brothers of the Blade – ISBN 978-1945169-40-3
    Sons of Light – ISBN 978-1945169-45-8
The World Chronicles series
    In the Shadow of Babylon – ISBN 978-1-945169-55-7

For many shall come in my name,
saying, I am Christ; and shall deceive many.

And ye shall hear of wars and rumours of wars:
see that ye be not troubled: for all these things must come to pass,
but the end is not yet.

For nation shall rise against nation and kingdom against kingdom:
and there shall be famines, and pestilences,
and earthquakes, in divers places.

All these are the beginning of sorrows.

Then shall they deliver you up to be afflicted, and shall kill you:
and ye shall be hated of all nations for my name's sake.

And then shall many be offended, and shall betray one another,
and shall hate one another.

And many false prophets shall rise, and shall deceive many.

And because iniquity shall abound, the love of many shall wax cold.

But he that shall endure unto the end, the same shall be saved.

Matthew 24: 5–13

CHAPTER 1

Tim Johnson and his family stepped up on to the long, narrow, railless porch of the old farmhouse. They huddled before the back door, their closeness an instinctual attempt to hide from the forceful gusts of cold early spring air. The travel bags, holographic books, toys, purses, document computers, sweaters, and a doll baby were, with great relief, dumped on the porch. The sound of the wind buffeting the corners of the wood-clapboard home heightened the perception of cold. Distracted by his weariness, Tim mused at the stubbornness of winter's release upon the Northeast, since the western lands had turned to desert years ago. In his youth, this month had seen greening grass and budding trees. No time to think of the past. Where was the key?

Mary had quietly positioned herself behind him. He was aware of an apartness from his wife of twelve years, an incompleteness in his soul—an ache. Eight-year-old Katie crouched in the shelter of the parental windbreak, scuffing her shoes on the worn, painted porch boards. The boards were eroding in long splinters. With a child's joy Katie devoted her attention to accelerating the process with the tips of her shoes. Ten-year-old Matthew hung at the back of the group, where freedom from parental authority was at a premium. He used his mother as a barrier to the wind as he studied mud wasp nests in the rafters.

Tim hoped that the old farmhouse of historic architecture, his grandfather's home—*Gramps's* home—would provide stability for his family, rest for his wandering soul. Now, his family needed an end to the long trip from upper New York State to southcentral Pennsylvania. The entire trip done by rail, the few necessities of life, changes of clothes, toiletries, document computer lugged along. He fumbled in his pockets, searching for the large antique key. A frustration and anger surfaced then dissipated as he rummaged.

He bent toward a day bag, thinking he had at some point on the trip moved the key to the bag. For ten years they had lived on a college campus, in a single dwelling home of age, status, reserved for professors of geology. Only 5 percent of the American population lived in single dwellings in 2241. The home had given them self-worth, a feeling of importance, uniqueness, stability. The only home they had ever known as a family. Then, the troubles had come, and his job and home had been lost.

Mary noticed her husband's frustration; her emotions did not join nor react to his. Without movement, quietly, patiently, she waited, studied the outside of the house. She had only seen wooden homes in magazines, wondered if rodents roamed freely within. Were the two chimneys, noticed when she crossed the wide lawn, a design element or functional? A certain amount of prestige came from living in a State-designated historical home.

Prestige was of less importance than modern conveniences. Would she be allowed to add those conveniences? Gramps had liked his home primitive and simple, except for his state-of-the-art computer. She had liked Gramps. Think of other things, she told herself. No neighbors for miles, the land zoned agricultural—ag was the slang. The commuter line was a quarter of a mile away, no vehicle of their own. The walking would be good for them. She didn't believe in inconveniences—they were only opportunities for self-improvement and self-awareness. The past troubles would soon be behind her family, and life would again bless them.

Katie began to jump. Unlike other surfaces she had experienced, wood had a bounciness, a hollowness.

Tim glanced back at Katie's antics. She vibrated with cold and anticipation. Two pairs of tights and her long legs still appeared thin. You had to coerce her to eat. Was she thinking of their new home? Like her mother, she preferred the new from life's offerings. Her face was set in simple determination to achieve as much enjoyment from the floor as possible. Her mind was at peace, no worries; Mom and Dad took care of everything.

A continuation of Tim's backward glance revealed Matthew poking the rafters with a broom handle. Tim turned away from the day bag, back to the lock.

Matthew continued his probing. He had studied wasps in science class, the order Hymenoptera. Mud wasps were of the family Sphecidae. His prods turned to systematic destruction, the dirt fell on his family and their baggage. He stopped quickly, thankful Mom had not noticed. He listened to the wind rushing through the distant woods. He had never heard such a sound. He had never seen a yard so big—easily room for a game of soccer. They had never been this alone before.

The rummaging of the day bag complete, Tim revisited his coat pockets. A pang of sadness came over him as he grasped the key through lozenges, candies, a pocket knife, a doll's dress. Gramps was not in the house—Gramps had been murdered. Tim's only sibling, his younger brother, John, was not in the house—disappeared! John had escaped from prison or had been murdered—or had been carried up into heaven, if you believed John's interpretation of the times and the Bible. Enough! Feelings of guilt, confusion clung to the memory of John. Tim had not betrayed his brother; John would have died out in the desert alone. John *had* to be given to the authorities.

Tim inserted the heavy key into the lock. You had to listen for the unlocking; that was the trick to antique locks. The kitchen door window had been replaced by sheet metal. Why? It wasn't important to know. The window would have to be replaced—money out of his account—or would the preservation society pay? They could live with sheet metal for now. Damn it! He had turned the key in the wrong direction.

No subtle gestures of impatience or complaint from Mary as he quickly reversed direction with the key. He loved her; she was his harbor in the storm. Matthew and Katie were exuberantly crushing or stamping on something. He noticed dirt under their feet. Childhood was for having fun. He loved his kids.

No job, a strange city, his family depending on him. Funds shrinking. The last six months had been extremely rough. Traumatic—why hide from the truth? The mystery John and Gramps had uncovered, hidden micro-dots, was the source of the troubles. The microdots that one part of the Church wished to expose, and another part wished to destroy. He and his family caught in the middle. His stomach tightened as he remembered his family held hostage by the subhuman killer named Cain. Thank God John had killed the man. Being in limbo, placed on a high-security estate, waiting for a trial that never occurred had been as rough as facing Cain.

During that wait, Gramps was killed by a commuter train. Murder? Every train had collision sensors; Gramps was old but alert. Then, it had been necessary to turn John in to the authorities so the original microdots could be used in the proceedings. John's accusing eyes, staring. John, so forsaken, empty, devastated by the murder of his friend and confidant, Diana. Where was John now? In heaven?

The door opened stiffly, the edges swollen with dampness, balked. His impatient pushing only aggravated the problem. The door stuttered along the uneven kitchen floor. Tim felt Katie's small hand pushing him in the back. Her touch dissolved his impatience. The family surged in, gasping with cold and relief. Matthew, who had dutifully picked up their luggage and without being told, dropped the day bags heavily, roughly placed the computer on top of the softer items.

Dampness, dust, the overpowering smell of wood smoke in curtains, rugs, furniture, cushions. The bitter, fungal smell of old coffee grounds in an otherwise empty trash can tanged in their sinuses. Flat clods of dried mud, stamped with heel and sole impressions, littered the tile floor. Pensively, Tim wondered if any of the imprints could have been made by Gramps or John. Without thinking, exhausted, Tim sat in the nearest chair.

If only their faction of the Church had won the power struggle. He would still be a noted geologist, a professor, a reputable man in the community. His family secure in the home of age and status. Oh, the months trapped in that prisonlike estate for nothing—for nothing. Thirty-five years old and all that he had accomplished had brought him to this, a dark, smelly, cold home in the midst of dreary ag fields. If only John and Gramps had not sought his help. No, they had that right, that expectation. They were men who would have done anything for him. A man who didn't help his family was no man. You didn't count the cost.

The "Harlot" Church had won. Harlot being John and Gramps's term for their adversary. During his confinement at the high-security estate, Tim had the breakdown, the mental collapse caused by his belief that the "Rapture" had occurred. The Rapture being that event, as described by John and Gramps, when God's chosen, dead and living, were lifted from the earth prior to the seven-year period of God's wrath upon the earth. A good psychologist had helped him through. Any man would have sought help under the same circumstances. Coincidences distorted by stress had created a false reality.

John had been reported missing from his cell. Another man of the same religious beliefs, too. Not escaped; just missing—on the same day as a newscast reporting mass hallucinations on a global scale. The story had only aired once, and then it disappeared. The printed word never mentioned the event. These events occurring immediately after the two factions of the Church had fought so desperately for the microdots. Microdots allegedly containing a Satanic bible, plans for the usurping of the Church, a timetable for the coming of the Antichrist.

Any man, whatever his strengths, would have crumbled. Now, he understood, John had escaped or had been murdered. Mass hallucinations had occurred before, were a historical reality. The authorities, no doubt, had hidden the story to prevent panic. Plots, machinations, intrigues were common wherever great power and wealth resided. Hierarchical squabbles within the Church were nothing new. These were better interpretations of the facts.

The afternoon light coming through the worn curtains was cold, brilliant. The light suddenly faded as the clouds thickened, casting the interior in a stark mood. Tim stood wearily, dazed. Mary had begun an inventory of the kitchen cupboards. Nothing of Gramps's had been removed; plates, silverware, cooking utensils all in place. Matthew and Katie had been rummaging in one of the bags for some object to enhance their newest desired tangent of play. Tim sat down again, realizing he had nothing to do and nowhere to go.

Impatiently, Matthew turned to the door, wishing to explore the woods and fields. He had no interest in the interior of the house.

Tim sensed Katie's predicament, torn between her curiosity about the interior, in her mother's presence, and her desire to be adventuring with her brother.

Matthew's roving gaze caught an object in a recessed corner of the kitchen. "Dad! Look! A woodstove! I read about them in social sciences. Ski resorts have them. I saw firewood on the porch. Can I build a fire?" He remembered the past injunctions associated with most requests. "I'll clean up any mess."

Now he was eager to remain inside, the woods and fields forgotten. His body posture was calmly expectant, though his face was expressive with desire. The calm body came from his mother, the expressive face from his old man.

Katie rubbed her hands together, imagining the warmth of a fire. Maybe she could cook something? Her eyes sparkled with excitement. "I'll get the firewood, Matthew. You get the lighter." She knew the barrier to the operation was the lighter, which could only come through parents. Matthew was older; he should handle that problem. She began moving toward the door, hoping quick action would thwart her father's objection.

"Hold on." Tim grabbed Katie by her hood, gently exerting pressure so her head would not be jerked backward. Katie laughed at being caught, momentarily strained against the invisible force.

Mary read Tim's worn face, felt her own fatigue, and spoke. "Not now. Maybe tomorrow. We need to look around, unpack, call for the rest of our clothing to be delivered. Why don't you two go out and explore."

"Yeaaah…" Katie's voice was low. Her eyes, mischievous, bored into Matthew's gaze as she sought confirmation, a partner in adventure. Matthew turned away, grumped in anger and disappointment as he reached for the door.

Tim bellowed, "Don't go out of sight of the house."

Matthew heard the order as a faint whisper, one he wished to escape, as he leaped from the porch. Katie slammed the door in her haste to catch up to her brother.

Tim stood, flicked on the lights, went to an easy chair, burrowed his hands in his coat pockets, his head in the coat's collar, and sat. The house was cold, the heat set at the barest minimum. The place so old fossil fuel was used. Gramps had received his fuel through some antique auto club that had access to petroleum-based products. Was there a heating bill for the last six months waiting for him? More pressure.

He had to secure a high paying job and soon. He wanted to teach again, at the college level. A deep, annoying suspicion said that the way had been blocked by the power of a vindictive Church. The resumes he had placed on the world net had gone unanswered. The suspicion, almost a paranoia, was like a demon clinging to his mind.

***

Mary located the thermostat, a knocking and clanging came from somewhere, then silence, and warmth flowing out of iron units—radiators, she thought was the term. She opened her traveling bag, pulled out her favorite picture, a six by nine, living picture. In the image: Tim, herself, three-year-old Matthew, and infant Katie in the living room of the professorial home.

She pressed the back, activated the scene. Such pride, contentment in Tim's eyes as he gently rocked his daughter in his arms. Tim had a good tan at the time, having just returned from the field. His bare forearms—it was summer—bulged with wiry muscle. His broad shoulders filled the picture. He wore his hair short when in the field. He looked like a soldier. Such a strong physique, resilient more than powerful, but the power was strikingly evident. That dichotomy of strength and gentleness gave her a hunger for him, for it was with gentleness he held his daughter.

Katie cooed. Tim's eyes gleamed in happiness, his lips pursed, and he cooed in return. Mary smiled as she led Matthew into the scene. Tim bent down, and Matthew kissed his sister gently on the forehead, then attempted to return to his play, till Mom steered him back.

Those two kids still loved each other, were best friends, even for all their squabbling. She and Tim had spent much time preparing Matthew for the coming of his sister, gave him responsibilities, made him her guardian. He had taken it all to heart. This love between them was truly amazing.

In the living picture, she scooped Matthew up, faced the camera. There they were, the perfect family, so full of love and pride, content in each other's being. She would gladly die for any of them—that's how much she loved them. Her little family was an oddity in this world. She had seen figures once, 10 percent? Most children were raised in orphanages, or by same-sex marriage partners, or polygamists, or lost, ignored in the serial marriage confusion. Yes, her family was odd, but they had something special.

She studied her young husband's face. God, he was handsome. Was? Still! Now, some gray along the temples—distinguished. Some wrinkles along the mouth, the skin a little looser. The same man, only deeper in heart. She set the picture on the fireplace mantle; all would be well. She began a tour of the house. Gramps had invited them many times to his home, but there had always been something, soccer tournaments, pre-paid vacations, special classes for the kids.

***

"Snap out of it, Tim! Life will be good again." Tim smiled at his silent words. Yes, life would be good again. Despondency wasn't a part of his nature, never, not once, even in his childhood, did he know depression. God, his partner, was raising him up from these current defeats and setbacks. Society, the American system could not afford to hinder men such as himself. He was fully a product of his culture, an achiever, a conqueror. He was of the mold, the pattern; to deny him success was, in a small way, to lessen the whole, to deny the validity of the American ethos.

Thirty-five is not old, he told himself. He had advantages that most men, of any age, did not have; he was above average in physique, appearance, athletic skills. Perfect health, intelligent, persuasive—people liked him immediately. He had an incredibly supportive, intelligent, caring wife and two talented, obedient children. A break was bound to happen, and he would capitalize upon it. If he maintained a confident spirit, one ready to seize the moment.

Despite the confidence of his will and intellect, a belief, a doubt, an unsettledness lingered in a broken and empty part of his soul. The disturbance said that he and his family were not of God's chosen. The Rapture had occurred. The restraining force of the Holy Spirit upon men's thoughts and actions was leaving. Hell was about to consume the earth. John and Gramps had been adamant in their belief that the world, as men knew it, was coming to an end. They had been sane men, however strange their beliefs. They had met mysterious deaths. Gramps had foretold the splitting of the Church. Both men, and even Diana, John's friend, had insisted that he had not belonged to Christ. Was it plausible that these three had possessed reality, truth, while the world lived in a daze, ruled by a lie?

Think of it—seven years of hell on Earth; the world ending! Totally destroyed! The end of history and existence as mankind has defined the terms. So preposterous! Life continued as it always had. Civilization was at its zenith. Yet, what if John and Gramps had been correct?

What man entering an aircraft thought that craft would never reach its destination, fall from the sky, killing all on board? What man left his home in the morning, thinking two commuter cars would pin him, crush him to death? Two incidents just in the news. A man entered an aircraft or walked the streets, thinking of work, duties, pleasures, of the coming day, thinking he would live to a ripe old age.

Death took people without notice, despite their confidence in life. Why should the world—the corporate group known as humanity—have confidence all would continue as in the past? Scientists, environmentalists, fiction writers had all predicted the end either through evil men, interplanetary aliens, or natural phenomena. Historically, what Jew in nineteen-thirties Europe thought he would be incinerated in an oven like a piece of trash? When would God's disappointment in the evil of men cause Him to react? Why was the death of the world by a cognizant God unthinkable?

He knew God existed. God had helped him in the past. Not as a direct, miracle producing presence, but by dispensing confidence, nerve, patience, the awareness of opportune moments, breaks in his life. He believed God had made the world. If God made the world, then He had the right to do with it what He wished. Tim suddenly wished to believe God hadn't made the world. Had man strayed so far from God that God was angry to the point of closure? Or was it as Gramps had described God's mind: mankind had strayed so far, so long that man was unwilling to come back to God. Gramps's reality seemed absurd. He knew God existed, and that is why this topic hurt so much. Tim Johnson wanted to be liked by everyone, even—and especially—by God.

CHAPTER 2

Mary returned from her inspection. She could work with the house, make it a home. She was now glad they had sold their furniture, inappropriate for a country home. Would the Historical Commission give aid, advice in restoring the home? Tim was still buried in his coat, hadn't moved from the easy chair. He looked like a mannequin propped in a pose. He was in the half wakefulness of restless sleep. At some point in the immediate future, she might be forced to kick him in the behind. For now, she would remain with the gentle, understanding approach.

She stood behind her husband's chair, bent close to him. She placed one arm over his shoulders. Her free hand rubbed his sternum through his coat. Unconsciously, she sought out his large chest muscles. She turned to study his face. She never tired of looking into his blue-gray eyes. She was overwhelmed with a sympathy for her worn man; she must comfort him.

"I like this house. I really do. The country living will be good for the kids, expose a side of life and develop their character, in a way that may be beneficial to their futures. This experience is nothing but an opportunity."

She was extremely grateful for this home. She was thankful for the shrewdness of their family lawyer, who had found that Gramps's home could not be claimed by the State as an historical site if a legal heir was destitute and homeless. When the court proceedings had ended, the Church withdrew the use of their temporary residence and simply threw them out on the street. Like Tim, she believed the Church had manipulated the termination of the professorship.

This vindictiveness from an organization once so central to her family's life had not shocked, nor created bitterness. She was a realist. Organizations were to use, and organizations used. The malignant or benign nature of the organization was dependent on the people in power at the moment. It stung that her close Church friends had just stopped calling. She decided she would never abandon anyone for any reason. She never had and wouldn't.

Tim searched her blue eyes for sincerity, became lost in the beauty of her face, the clear white skin, the firm jaw, the understated fullness of her lower lip. The black lashes and eyebrows, made darker against the ivory skin, highlighted her eyes. The black hair, pushed back from the forehead, by an occasional sweep of the hand, was thick, retaining the imprint created by her fingers. Hidden by the black hair were the small delicate ears.

His desire for her was overwhelmed by the return of the despondency. She saw the remoteness spread on his features; his soul was far away. She was losing her hard-loving man. He needed to confront his fear and conquer it. Time to firm up the gentle approach. Perhaps, even get under his skin, raise an anger. They had a chance for a new start here; the past couldn't be dragged along.

"You don't think there is a future?" She spoke in a duality, part statement tinged with accusation, part question traced with mockery. Confusion remained in his eyes, no glint of anger. She pulled a chair in front of him and sat. She should have confronted him months ago. "You've been holding out on me for some time. Playing your manly game, 'protect the wife and kids.' I know what beliefs John and Gramps held. I paid attention to all the pretrial talk, the court proceedings. I read the books you read from the library at the estate, and those given to you by Gramps.

I studied the notes you were compiling. I know what the Rapture is! I know you think John just flew into space. I was given some information by your psychologist. Why don't you just come out with it, Mr. Tough Guy? You believe the world has seven more years, then God judges us."

"I thought I could handle this. I was certain the psychologist had resolved the issue. I was wrong," he said. "I apologize for holding back."

His voice held a whining quality. In his eyes she saw a weakness that frightened and disgusted her. This momentary disgust, bordering on loathing, repulsed her being. Where did such a thought come from? She loved him; yet, she had never seen him dependent, weak, almost begging. His emotional independence and strength had been the initial attraction in their courtship and a constant in their marriage. Weak men sent shivers of disgust through her. This abnormal behavior was only temporary. Everyone had a crisis at least once in their lives. She spoke forcefully, hoping to encourage forcefulness from him.

"Was John raptured away? We could debate that till the end of time. Do the events, the facts mean this? Or do they mean that? Interpretations are dependent on our mood swings. Let's assume the worst scenario: we weren't raptured. We get a second chance…don't we? A God of love would give us a second chance."

She knew the answer to her question. He had underlined "second chance" repeatedly in his notes, with corresponding scriptural passages. She had formulated a strategy months ago, one she did not wish to use because it was time consuming, distracting, and potentially dangerous to her family.

"Yes," Tim said. "Yes! He has given us a second chance. 'He that shall endure to the end, the same shall be saved.'"

She had never seen him in such anxiety or heard his voice quiver in dread. This, from a man who feared nothing. He had delivered lectures before audiences of thousands, answered questions extemporaneously. He had lived and worked in alien cultures of semiprimitive tribesmen, among men hostile toward—if not defiant of—his missions. He had been submerged in tiny exploratory craft on the ocean's floor. He had flown in flimsy portable aircraft in remote regions.

This man had been a national karate champion through his teens and early twenties. She had seen him subdue troublemakers twice. The first, a mugger, had nearly died from injuries received. The man had made the mistake of confronting Tim while the children were present. The second time, he had taken apart a group of white toughs who had been beating an Asian man. She had heard from a colleague how Tim had stood his ground against a charging polar bear to protect his coworkers. He had withheld shooting, bears being on the endangered list, till the last moment. The bear slid twenty feet onto his boots, stone dead. What did this man fear?

A sadness came to her at the plight of her husband. The Bible quotation was an indicator of just how far he had fallen. He had lost his manhood in some unfathomable, mysterious way. He was using religion as a crutch. The quotation was so out of place, unnecessary. Why hadn't he simply answered "yes" or paraphrased. Words out of context frightened her. The next sentence had to be delivered naturally.

"I knew He would give us another chance," she said. "We might not be in God's will. I can entertain that thought without fear."

She could entertain the thought but never imagine it to be true. She was very spiritual, more so than others, as proven through her conversations with friends and relatives. Among her circle of friends, she was noted for her kindness. Her mind was always turning to thoughts of God. God's goodness was shown through the many blessings in her life; healthy intelligent children; a handsome, virile husband; a high standard of living.

"Let's study the Bible, Tim. Find out what we need to know. Here, in our home. We will attend Church functions as has been our habit. We don't want to be labeled cultists."

She knew the Bible was the ball in this game—not Church doctrine or common sense. All of Gramps's and John's crazy interpretations came from this original source. During the study he would see the error in the logic of Gramps and John. More importantly. he would feel in control of his life again. That is all he needed—to feel in control. His conscience would find justification and peace in the fact that he had made an effort to find God. He would have done his part. She knew God would remain silent. The Bible study would fall away, the world would not end. The entire incident would become a self-effacing anecdote brought out at parties to amuse their new friends.

The Bible study would put her family in jeopardy. The Bible, whole, without modern commentaries, was not a book you would admit to reading. Few pure copies, like Gramps's copy, existed. To possess a pure copy was to invite trouble, be labeled an "Enslaver," a "believer in bondage"—antisocial, antihuman rights, and against the welfare and interests of mankind. The Amendment of 2100 gave the State the right to deal harshly with such people.

Tim smiled faintly. Mary had almost lifted the presence of doom and regret that had lodged in his soul the day John had been reported missing. Did she truly understand the import, the consequences the times had thrust upon their family? He knew she wasn't truly serious about this Bible study—she saw it as a tool of healing. She was a clever woman, who gave deep thought to the problems of her family. She knew the workings of their minds and she was willing to enter those minds to shape, mold.

"Mary, if John and Gramps are correct, do you know what is going to occur in the next seven years?"

"Vaguely." She had skipped those notes and the chapter in the one antiquated paper book addressing the subject.

"Christ calls it 'the time of sorrows' or 'the great tribulation.' He says that no period in history, singly or collectively, will match it in ferocity. Suffering, wars, famines, pestilence, earthquakes, governmental authority shaken. People without compassion or love will attempt to satisfy every lust, no matter how perverse."

His eyes narrowed as he stared into a dark place within the soul.

Her hope returned; he spoke with authority, like the college professor he was.

Tim swallowed with difficulty - his throat dry with anxiety. "Meteors. Poisoned waters. Dead oceans. Demonic creatures. Mass executions.

The order of the heavens shaken. Symbolic or literal or both…I don't know…I know I am afraid." He thought back to that street in Nairobi where he'd seen a pile of severed limbs from political rivals. His rare-earth exploratory party was just passing through. They had ignored an embassy warning of violence and political unrest. The pile had been the height of a man. He shuddered.

Mary clenched her teeth in anger. How could a man believe such things? Tim had totally fled his senses, the teachings of the Church, the wisdom of man. Afraid? She hated that word. She would kick him in the pants like he had never been kicked. Then a patience came to her; the time was not yet.

"I thought I knew God!" Recrimination, betrayal, strained passion overwhelmed his voice. "How can I be different than what I am? No Bible study is going to work. As if John and Gramps were different than us because of something they read, and we didn't?"

She wondered how a man could suddenly lose heart. Whatever had undergirded Tim in the past had collapsed in a mighty heap. No cause for this, none at all. She had spent the last twelve years with a different man. The psychologist had assured her that Tim was sane. She believed in his sanity. What was the essence, the origin of this problem? What flaw within his mind had been exposed by recent events? Remain calm.

"Maybe it isn't knowledge that made John and Gramps different and therefore acceptable to God. But it seems the process has to begin with knowledge. Let's find out who God is, then we can rightly know what He wants."

Tim knew she had to understand the immediacy of the problem to understand his dread. Her calm and common sense aggravated him. This was a time for action, not calm. She was calm by nature, sure, but it seemed casualness now. Her tone was one used for Matthew—not a man, her husband.

"Mary, there are signs already happening. There is a progression. Total peace, the first horseman, has come. The Antichrist rules the European Federation. The man with the strange name, just elected. He will make war. War is the second horseman, then famine, plagues, more war, more famine…"

He talked gibberish. Calm him with a soothing tone. His emotionalism and passion, usually an endearing trait, the perfect stimulant to her stoicism, was now too much, hysterical in nature, annoying, unmanly.

She spoke slowly, calmly. "Let us read the Bible Gramps gave you. Let's find out who God is. We have control over ourselves—not the world or these coming events. Our focus should be on our family."

Tim fumed. She hadn't given credibility to the prophesy, the future coming. She had simply ignored his words. So condescending, so certain she was right, and he was wrong. He would penetrate that calm.

"You don't understand. This isn't a game." His stare bored into her eyes. "You don't just play, lose, shake the winner's hand, and say, 'You were better than me today.' And life goes on. This is war, honey! The winner gets eternal life, and the loser gets eternal damnation."

She pulled back from him, folded her hands in her lap. *Honey*? Tim knew how she hated that word, dripping with sweet patronization. "Pleease! Stop this crap!" she said. "Have you lost your mind? No one believes in a literal hell. The Church hasn't taught it in centuries. You can see why you've put yourself in hell just thinking of it. Hell is the condition of a man's heart. God is love, Tim. God is love. He loves everyone, not judgment. He can't pour out his wrath on the world; that would be a violation of His nature. Hasn't the professor picked that up in thirty-five years?" She knew how he disliked the term *professor*; it was payback for *honey*.

In such moments, he always marveled at her poise, lack of facial expression or animation, even, as on this occasion, when her voice held a rare passion and anger. He placed his arm over her shoulders, his free hand upon her folded hands. He had learned the value of touching in moments of anger early in their courtship. The information picked up in some forgotten book.

She sighed and hoped he hadn't heard.

Tim knew, of course, that God was love. But how do you reconcile a God of love with punishment and wrath? Gramps or John must have told him, but the logic had been lost. Punishment for the sake of chastisement, he could comprehend. Wrath, he could not fathom. What had he and his family done to deserve God's wrath? Angry at Mary, he could still appreciate her wisdom. Find out who God was, and then you would know what He wanted.

They both knew this was not the time for an argument. Two tired, disappointed people, their lives in shambles, the good things in life temporarily missing. Logic hidden by the stress of responsibility. Nothing good could come from argument. He moved onto her chair and scooped her up to nestle within him. So damned manly he could be gentle, she thought. He rubbed her neck, shoulders with his hand; she sighed into him. They both knew the conflict was not yet over. They would battle the night away upon their bed.

The kids burst into the house, Katie laughing her throaty chuckle. The door flew into the corner of the table. The odd behavior of the door, they had never experienced hinged doors, provoked more silly laughter. Their cheeks were ruddy, their shoes covered in mud. The cleanness of the outside air hung on their clothes and in their hair. Mary noticed the muddy shoes of her children but had no heart to scold.

"Shoes off," she reminded.

Katie began moaning as she laughed. Tim's eyes gleamed. Katie was in her silly state, which was always amusing to him. With a father's love and care, he ran his eyes along her thin body. An athletic build, straight, tall, with an understanding of its own movements. Her light-brown hair, rarely combed, reached for her shoulders. She had the straight, strong jaw of her mother, the model's lips and cheekbones, and narrow eyes of constant merriment.

"It's good out there, Momma," Matthew said, sitting beside his mother on the armrest, with no intention of resting. Katie remained standing, spread her arms, signifying space, freedom.

"The creek is so nice, and there are no people anywhere." Her voice was purposely soft, lilting; her eyes dreamy. Her arms remained outstretched as if waiting for a wind to carry her away. She was a fairy, a nymph of the woods.

"Come here, precious." Tim held out his arms. Katie jumped into his lap without warning, watching his eyes for shock, surprise. She laughed at his grunt of discomfort, then cuddled in his arms. Matthew's fatigue drew him into his mother's side as his mind began to calm.

Tim proudly, contentedly gazed upon his son. Matthew had the same athletic build, straight bones, tall, lean, the same strong chin, narrow eyes. He had the hair of his mother. His hands were large, his balled fist delivered a noticeable impact in their wrestling, sparring play. Tim believed the arms and shoulders of Mat would be his defining physical quality. He had slightly above average speed. He did have a calm in tight situations, an aggressive spirit, and a belief in himself. Sometimes these qualities were worth more than raw athletic gifts.

"I'm calling a family meeting."

Disapproval flashed on Mary's face. Neither of the kids complained; it was one of the rare times they knew their own tiredness and were content to sit. Mat noticed Mom's disapproval. Tim held Katie's wrists, so small and delicate. He felt her pulse, rapid, pounding. Life was good when he held his daughter.

"What's it about?" Katie asked as her head turned toward her father. Daddy was so warm and comfortable. She liked the smell of his hair, the calmness and warmth of his hands. She kissed him upon his lips. Tim sighed as he snuggled Katie into his arms, gathered his thoughts.

"It's about why we are here, and what the future might hold."

Matthew's mind was drifting, while Katie became alert. Katie spoke.

"We're here because you helped Uncle John and Gramps and that girl."

"Diana," interjected Matthew.

"Oh, yeah. Diana. And some people in the Church, like Winkie and Archbishop Gilroy, just couldn't live with the truth." She finished in a matter-of-fact, sophisticated tone, then added. "Remember that moron, Cain?"

Matthew shuddered in comedic revulsion. Katie mimicked her brother, only her display revealed a true dread. Mary remembered her own fear. Matthew spoke. "Uncle John killed him." His Uncle John hadn't been afraid of anyone; Cain had been the bigger and stronger. Uncle John was special; he often thought of him. Uncle John had been a soldier. He was always calm. He believed in Jesus. In fact, Jesus was his friend. Uncle John said Jesus was always with him.

"Yaaay!" Katie cheered as her arms went into the air. "No Cain to worry about anymore!"

"Yes, that is all true, but there is more," said Tim. Katie had mentioned Winkie—Father Winkler—once his best friend and Archbishop Gilroy—Satan's child. Winkie was probably still climbing that ecclesiastical ladder, using friends and acquaintances along the way.

Mary tensed. She hoped Tim would conceal the Bible study within a harmless lie.

"Tell us," demanded Matthew, now intensely interested after noticing his mother's subtle tension.

"You know John is no longer in prison and no one knows where he is," Tim said.

"He escaped," Matthew said firmly, not wanting to believe death a possibility.

Mary shifted in her seat; her posture tightened. The course of the conversation was wrong. Just tell the kids they planned on studying the Bible. Why burden them with the end of the world? They'd spill it in school and be labeled cultists. Then they would have real problems. But interrupting Tim might force an emotional tirade that would be even more upsetting to the children.

"Yes, he could have escaped. But if he did, it might not have been by his own power. I think God might have taken him alive, to heaven," Tim said.

"Gosh!" Katie's voice was an awed whisper of incredulity. "Dad, you're joking." She had uncovered his humor.

"No."

"Was he the only one?" Matthew asked shrewdly. He would show neither skepticism nor surprise.

An anger seized Mary. Why was Tim burdening impressionable children with such foolishness? He had forced her to speak. An icy glare had already met her intention. The Tim of restraint had vanished. This was not the time, so she remained silent.

"Remember that day on the news of sightings of people in the air?" They had not seen the report, only heard his shout.

"Sort of," said Matthew, twisting his mouth to one side in an attempt to drain the remembrance from his mind.

"Kids," Mary interjected forcefully, "do you think God could do that— take people away?" She thought her tone held neutrality.

"I guess He could." Katie spoke without much conviction.

Matthew shrugged his shoulders, was aware of the cynicism in his mother's voice. He spoke. "Highly unlikely." That statement would make her happy. He saw Dad's disappointment. "But possible." He would call it a draw. "Why would God do that, Dad?"

"That's the difficult part to understand. I think some bad things are going to happen, and He didn't want certain people to go through these bad times."

"Why do we have to go through the bad times?" Katie asked, perceiving an unfairness. Her voice remained even, nonjudgmental. Her mother used this tone all the time.

"Maybe it's like a commuter train. If you're not at the station when it arrives, you're left behind. It's my fault we didn't make the train, not yours. I should have had you up early, dressed, and waiting. The good news is that another train is coming. This one we won't miss."

"While we're waiting for the next one, bad things will happen?" asked Katie.

"Yes."

"Like what?" asked Matthew. Uncle John caught the first train. He was smart.

"People will be stealing, lying, fighting, calling us names. Food might become scarce, and diseases will come."

Matthew jumped up, assumed a karate stance. He had been taking lessons since the age of six. "I'll protect you, Katie!"

Katie clapped her hands and whooped as Matthew began fighting imaginary assailants.

"That's enough!" Mary scolded harshly. Just when they seemed to be calming. Tim was her true irritation. Matthew didn't intend to obey. She grabbed his arm roughly, brought his face to hers.

"Listen to me. There will be no woods after school for a week if you don't stop."

He calmed immediately. How did she know about the woods?

"What time's the train coming, Dad?" Katie asked innocently. Her tone seemed to indicate she believed a real train was coming for her family.

"In seven years."

Katie and Matthew looked at each other. Matthew pulled down his jaw, lengthening his face. Katie grunted at Matthew's antics, not deeming the face worthy a laugh. Tim continued.

"We are waiting for Jesus, not a real train, Katie."

"Oh." They had been talking about God, and it was Jesus—the guy who healed people and said things that angered everyone—who was coming. She remembered that He hadn't died, so He could be coming back.

"To get ready for Jesus, we must read the Bible, study it, so when He looks into our hearts, He knows we're ready to go."

Matthew had returned to his mother's side, rested his head against her shoulder. Matthew wondered what they needed to know. Evidently, there would be a test. How else would you know that you knew?

Katie sighed, her eyes narrowing in sleep. Their concentration had vanished. Tim spoke firmly, loudly.

"So, it is decided? We will study the Bible and be ready for Jesus."

Nods came from Katie and Matthew.

"I can't hear you."

"Yes," said Katie.

"Yes." Matthew spoke in a deep tone. Katie studied Matthew's expression, searching for enthusiasm for the study. She liked the idea, whether he did or not. She liked being with her family in group endeavors; she liked classes in school, reading, studying. Mary spoke.

"One important reminder." Mary paused after her deliberately spoken sentence. "This is just for the family. Don't mention this to anyone else. We don't need other kids wanting to join."

She hoped Tim would let her explanation stand. He did not.

"Besides, we'd be labeled as weird. The Church might get involved. You know the troubles we've had with the Church." Tim watched Mary's displeasure grow with his words.

Sometimes Tim could be the biggest ass, she thought.

Matthew wondered why the Bible study was "weird." To Katie, "troubles with the Church" meant losing their home.

"I want to stay here," she said. Katie already liked the coziness of the home. The absence of people made her feel free and secure. She wouldn't miss her old friends. Dad, Mom, and Mat were the only really important people. Matthew was her best friend. Come summer, the creek would be fun to wade in. The back porch had possibilities for play.

"So do I," said Matthew. He intended to begin a scientific collection of the insects and animals in the woods and fields. He'd have to buy nets, traps, preservatives. He wanted to make a bow and arrows or a blow gun. His mind wandered into the endeavors. He'd go along with the Bible study; he'd have an audience for his antics.

"Then it has been decided by unanimous vote: we study the Bible." Tim realized no one was listening.

***

Mary gazed at her two sleepy kids. Yes, they would do well here. Tim would have no problem finding a job, the Harrisburg area, like the ag fields, was burgeoning. Maybe, he would not be a professor of geology, but work was plentiful. She had a degree in geriatrics, she wanted to work. In no time, they would have a proper home in the suburbs. He would be promoted at the workplace, have people under him who respected him, equals to keep his brilliant mind sharp, and superiors to praise him. Mom and Pop would watch Matthew and Katie grow, marry, have careers and children.

The Bible study would last a month. Now, she must give everyone a hot meal and check on the cleanliness of the bedding. They had brought enough food for tonight and breakfast tomorrow.

Tomorrow, she would enroll the kids in school and buy food and cleaning supplies. The kids were asleep. Tim had fallen into a nap. Mary's eyes closed.

CHAPTER 3

The commuter car was crowded, no vacant seats, people pressed together in the aisle. At the final stop, the end of the line, he would be alone. A pleasant physical weariness held Tim still, made him appreciate his seat. The fat lady beside him smelled sweetly hormonal, sexual. She radiated an inclusive heat. He glanced up at the newscast on the electrascreen. No mention of armed conflicts or wars, the signs of the second horseman of the apocalypse, as of the moment. The first horseman, peace, rode with that rising star, the political newcomer to the Federation, who was featured in several stories. He had gained ascendancy over the Federation. He was the Antichrist. He had to be. He had brought peace to the Middle East and to the world. Tim's eyes turned toward the window. He watched the movement of people, cars, commuter trains on the streets.

It was a "one briefcase" day on his scale of crowd density and quality of movement. You could fit the length of one briefcase between each person, or groups of people. A good day was two briefcase lengths; a bad day, less than one. The majority of days in the three months since his arrival in the Harrisburg area had been bad. Once, he had been forced to go into the city in the evening. Katie had needed cough medicine, and the courier service had a lengthy backlog. The crowds had not lessened.

The city had a twenty-four-hour schedule, many shifts began and ended at staggered times. No business or office ever closed. He was happy to be working again, even as a waste disposer. He wasn't making much more than welfare but at least he was occupied and not anxious about welfare terminating. The walking, the manhandling of fifty-pound bags of waste, and the maneuvering of the truck through traffic was physically and mentally draining. The compensation: hands and fingers as hard as steel, with a grip that could crush any object; a lightness in his torso and thighs that spoke of gravity-defying strength. He had shed fifteen pounds. His body was near the end of the adjustment cycle. In another two weeks, he'd be sitting on this commuter with energy to spare.

He felt fortunate that the collections were varied. Each household or business signaled the main office when their precompacted bundles weighed fifty pounds. Each morning, on a map, he traced a route between the calls, always a different route. At the end of the day, he was free—no take-home work, no meetings, no papers to present, no student's personal problems occupying his mind. His self-worth was protected by a change of clothes. No one on the street knew he was a lowly incinerator man.

He was certain he would never teach geology or work as a freelance corporation geologist again. The Church had ruined his career. Since his confinement and his coming to Harrisburg, he had put seventy-five resumes out globally, and all had returned rejected. He was the best in his field, had presented papers, was well known and respected in the highest circles of business and academia. The Church had his identity number, traced his resumes, and with lies or political pressure, closed the doors.

He had a simmering rage within him, a rage at the evil in men. This obstacle of spite, vengeance, he could not fight. He had no political connections, no money to hire lawyers. His impotence only deepened his hostility. Thank God he had this job to occupy his mind. While unemployed, searching for work, he had imagined dark, ugly scenes of revenge at those who had ruined his life. He could think of no greater crime than to keep a man from what he did best.

Maybe God was working through this seeming problem with employment. From the family Bible study, he remembered Joseph being sold into slavery, then the twists and turns that were not fate but the plans of God. Maybe it was best that he was not in the field of geology at this time. Maybe something better was planned. Here, he had a home in the country—a very rare occurrence that offered security, peace. He could remain close to or with his family when the disasters came, unlike a field geologist. Central Pennsylvania had less chance of drought or earthquake damage than many locations where professorships were open. His job offered security; even in the rough times waste would be gathered.

His job offered another advantage that might be important in the years ahead—unrestricted access to the city and surrounding suburbs. He was learning the location of major food warehouses, police headquarters, precinct boundaries, water pumping stations, reservoirs, power stations, electric grids, armories, rail lines, highways, streets, and alleys. He was becoming familiar with barge, truck, rail terminals; air-platform pads and airports. He was learning strategic points, hills, traffic bottlenecks, places of ambush. He knew the territories of every gang.

He knew more basic information. Where large deer herds roamed on the ag lands. Where bear could be found in the forest reserves, where coyotes were thickest, what areas of the river held large concentrations of fish. He knew when the fishponds were harvested, where other stocked ponds and lakes were located. He knew what was grown in the ag fields, what fields were irrigated, where the orchards were located. He knew what buildings housed the cattle, buffalo, hogs, chickens, turkeys, emu and where the dairy herds were milked and the livestock were slaughtered.

The fat lady beside him brought him out of his thoughts. Her leg was now pressed up against his. She had a cute face and breasts that could smother. The hormonal odor—human female hormones, bought at the cosmetics counter—had worked into his flesh as it was designed to do. Most men would have taken her to a rest booth or a sleep cubicle and had the desire resolved. His fellow professors had often told him stories of the women they had met on the streets, in restaurants, on the commuters. He was different—devoted; Mary had everything he needed. Good sex was the product of time, of exploring a woman's mind. He knew himself to be a sexual oddity and was not disturbed.

He shifted his eyes from the woman's breasts to the looming concrete heart of the city. The ample lady snarled at the rebuff. He searched for the tops of the buildings. Lines of rectangular windows reflected light from the sun soon to be hidden. The shadows grew. The safety lights began premature blinking on the communication towers perched, crowded, on every building. His eyes caught on the wing-shaped pedestrian walkways that tied the buildings together from all directions and heights, like strands of a molecule. He glimpsed sky where an old building had been demolished. Clouds, thin and feathered, moved swiftly. Air traffic was thick, the pulsating lights seeming frantic. Living in a new city had brought back some of the excitement of life.

His eyes returned to the streets. Escalators spewed people up from the depths, the city one-third as deep as the buildings above ground were tall. For a moment the people from the subterranean city seemed like molten rock running out of a fissure. He pleasantly remembered a field excursion, with selected students, to Hawaii and Indonesia to study volcanic activity. One student, Deborah, came to mind. He shook his head sadly at his indiscretion. Mary had never suspected. He wasn't as different from others as he thought.

An equal number of people—evening workers—were coming into the city as were leaving. Streetlights would, within an hour, be snapping on, bathing the city in pure white light. The city had become incredibly prosperous with the resurgence of agriculture on the East Coast. Most of the western grazing lands and farmland had been destroyed by volcanic ash and changing weather patterns over the last twenty years or made useless by dried-up aquifers. Government had grown in the city, bringing wealth and work, a trend in all state capitols. Communication and transportation industries, expanding with economic growth, had added their money to the area.

He watched a gang of forty or fifty white toughs dressed in black— Odin's Men—move down a street in columns. Aggressively polite, they forced their way through the crowds. Most people were eager to remove themselves from the line of march. A policeman, formerly a storm trooper, bred for size and strength, vigilantly and alertly trailed behind them. He was easily four hundred and fifty pounds of well-proportioned muscle. In the mixed-race eyes, favoring the Negroid blood, was the desire for conflict. Aggression and strength were visible within his movements. The body armor shown a dark blue.

The men and women of the gang, in their late teens and early twenties, sneered in derision through white face paint as they glanced at the threat behind them. The Bible had said nothing of race wars in the final days. Yet, if man's love grew cold, wouldn't society crack along proven fissures? Nationwide, gangs had been moving in larger bodies in the last year. The number of gang members killed and maimed in the past decade was staggering. Soon, laws would be passed, the problem resolved.

Gangs! Odin's Men (white), Voodoo Disciples (black), Jihad (Middle Eastern and black Muslim), Muerto (Hispanic), and the Masonic League (mixed races forming the militant arm of the Church, yet outlawed from the Church) were the dominant forces in the area. Each of these main groups had clustered about their ideology and race concepts tens of lesser groups, sometimes allies, sometimes enemies. All would be fighting when food became scarce and the government lost control.

Tim needed to arm himself—a difficult task whether done legally or illegally. His arms license had been revoked when his professorship had ended. He had carried both pistol and rifle in the field at various times. Both arms registered to the university. Laser weapons were still only for the military and law enforcement. The university car had gone with the job. Mobility would be very important, a car a necessity.

The Susquehanna River, straight, narrow, deep was visible through the stately trees of River Front Park. On the far side of the channel of black, cold water lay the recesses of the barge port. Scores of barges sat in the bright lights, mechanical arms lowering and raising cargo containers. One deep sitting barge slid up the dark water. Tim could see the pilot in the navigation booth. Beyond the leveed channel, the square fishponds glimmered from the flatness of the old riverbed. He knew the catfish and bass were thick in the waters. The geometric pieces of water were held together by dark levees, and the whole appeared to Tim as the terraced rice paddies of China and Indonesia.

The river must have been impressive when it flowed on its natural course a hundred years in the past. A wide river with billowy islands and houseboats, from the pictures he had seen in the State museum. Ahead, he saw the first mountain and the advertising banners from a clifftop restaurant. The food was good at the restaurant, and the view was excellent over the river, city, west shore. Twice they had eaten at the restaurant: a breakfast and sunrise, a supper and sunset. Both days cool, windy, and with a hollow yearning in his soul.

The commuter stopped at the last transfer station on the run. He watched people spew from another commuter across the tracks. A pregnant woman tripped, stumbled, fell as she exited. The people behind her stepped over, on, around her. A crowd of waiting commuters surged around her onto the emptying car. Only when the car was full, the platform clear, could she rise. As a young man, he had seen a woman fall. Men had immediately helped her to her feet. Had the Holy Spirit as a restraining force begun His release of mankind? John and Gramps had sworn His departure had begun.

Nervously, anxiously, he glanced up at the electrascreen. A drought on the South American savannas, where once rain forests had stood. No deaths of any significance, the World Food Bank had adequate resources. Few people were watching the screen. The troubles would begin with wars and rumors of wars. He felt no heat beside him; the fat lady had exited. A new crowd entered.

He studied their faces as they settled in. Dull, bemused, tired, expectant faces going to their homes just as he was, to begin their other lives. He had a sorrow for them. He believed in their goodness. He couldn't imagine great evil coming from them. Everyone lied on occasion, said an unkind word, or exhibited selfish behavior. Why hadn't these people been taken by God?

Looking at them, understanding their normality, their humanness, he began to believe that maybe he had a touch of madness. These people should have been taken. Who was perfect? Gramps and John hadn't been perfect. You tried to do more good than bad while you lived—what other standard could there be? What kind of God would condemn these people? Not only condemn but, in a sense, torture them for eternity?

The standard, from what he could understand of the old religion, was that you had to belong to God. Like a son belonged to his father. He knew his affection was for these people and not for this strange perception of God. He had lived among these people all his life. He had taught their children, visited their homes, worshiped with them in church. They had been spectators at his karate tournaments, applauded him at his graduations, sat smiling at his wedding. They listened to his lectures, read his articles. They shared their hopes, lives, dreams with him, and he with them. These were intelligent, good people. Something didn't add up, and he was beginning to believe it was himself losing touch with reality.

The pregnant lady who fell. The people stepping over her had had no time to react to her plight. If they had been aware, the surging crowd had pushed them past her before they had time to react. It wasn't evil to be caught in the rush of a crowd. The people waiting for the commuter to empty had only seen an open door. Why should they be looking at their feet? None of them had been uncaring or selfish; they were just caught in the surge of a crowd. Nothing had left the earth. People were as good as they had ever been. What was the verse in the Bible? "Love your neighbor as yourself." Well, before that came: "Love the Lord your God with all your heart, soul, strength, and mind." Maybe that was the catch. Tim had never thought of actually loving God—only His creation and the good He did for Tim Johnson.

The supplies he had been storing in the basement—army surplus meals, waste containers pilfered from work and filled with water, blankets, sleeping bags, stoves, camping supplies, and military equipment—all seemed so foolish. The Bible study they had every night—what a waste of time. A history of the Jewish people with lessons of faith embedded within. Anger and confusion as he attempted to comprehend the nature of God. The commuter lurched forward, picked up speed, and crossed the river with Tim oblivious to his surroundings.

This God of the Jews was demanding and harsh. Yes, you were richly rewarded when you obeyed. But disobedience brought brutal consequences. Should such a God be seen from a historical context? How could such a God bring forth a loving Messiah? This God had no qualms about destroying tribes, nations, his own chosen people. If the story of Noah was believed, God had destroyed all of the people of the earth but a handful. No one was able to live up to his perfect standards. If this was truly the nature of God, then the world was doomed.

Tim was pulled out of his musings, oblivious of recrossing the river, as his car slid into the final station. He was alone in the car, except for a teenage boy, who had missed his stop from honest confusion or a drugged mind. The boy showed no signs of evil purposes. Tim stepped from the car onto the cobblestones of the platform. A raw country air made him aware of the human odors his clothes and hair had collected. The car doors closed; the commuter slid silently into the darkness. It was sheer luck that the line ended at the beginning of the ag lands and only a quarter of a mile from his home. He moved from under the canopy roof, past the station lights, into the darkness. He breathed deeply of the emerging greenness of the fields.

When land was zoned ag, the towns, villages, homes, roads, and all that had been made by man were either reconsolidated or destroyed—hauled away or buried. Ravines, gullies were filled; stream beds straightened; and, if need be, hills flattened, and slopes terraced for the efficient, hungry ag machines. Nothing would ever be built again on the ag lands unless that object served agriculture. Only a site like Gramps's home, judged historical, would be allowed to remain.

The trees showed small new leaves. He longed for summer. The mountain, one long, steep ridge, blocked light from the city at night. The mountain was delineated by the distant sun's light in the west. In the shadow of the mountain, he felt hidden, safe. He had a mountain ridge at his back as well, running straight and long. Truly, the farmhouse was a blessing! God was watching over his family. The farmhouse would be their salvation when the evil times came. Christ had said to flee to the mountains. Tim shook his head in bewilderment. What was he thinking? Believing, again, in the end of the world!

He walked at a brisk pace. His walking during the day was slow and not of constant duration. Without a fifty-pound bag of waste on his shoulders or a bag grasped in each hand, his step was springy, powerful. The motorized dolly, standard equipment on the trucks, was never used, an impediment to his speed and efficiency. He had done sit-ups and push-ups in the morning at home. He would construct a chin-up and dip bar and add those exercises to the morning routine. He would still have time for his cup of coffee while he watched the deer browse in the yard.

He should buy a weight set and electric stimulators. The entire family needed to be strong. Training together would bond them more closely. Steroid supplements were a possibility—they needn't worry about long-term effects. Three-quarters of the male population took supplements at some point in their lives. He had to be equal to the competition. Believing again! What had happened to his mind?

Truthfully, he liked thinking of social upheaval, catastrophes. Was he bored with life? Filling an inadequacy left by his work and social standing? Were fantasies of destruction an outlet for his impotent rage against the Church? Or did these imaginings fluff up his ego? Did he dream of surviving, of being a hero because he was more clever, intelligent, better prepared than everyone else—the superior being? Because he knew the future? Because he was wise? Because he was above the average man? Whatever the reasons, the time had come to snap out of the lunacy.

The dark shadows of forest and mountains lay upon the road. Strange, most people feared the shadows and darkness. He liked shadows around him and the blanket of night coming. He heard the fall of his feet, smelled the hemlock trees, the fields further up the valley. Water had collected along the road. Damp and sweet, it mingled with last year's leaves, branches, hemlock cones. He saw the porch light on—caused by the mountain shadow that hid his home. In the evening darkness, the white structure reflected starlight, stood out against the blackness of the mountain. Mental note: paint the house a dark color this summer.

Mary and the kids had arrived home an hour earlier. They came home together, the kids meeting her at the geriatric center where she worked. His legs stretched out, pulling in the roadway. A road that only saw the passage of farm machinery or sightseers seeking country scenes. Nothing suspicious this evening, nor had there been any night since they moved to the farmhouse. He turned off the public road, onto the private drive. His shoes scuffed on the arch of the stone bridge over the creek. His calves pushed him up the narrow macadam lane.

From across the wide expanse of yard, his eyes were drawn to the light in the kitchen, the figures moving before the windows. A probing, thoughtful warmth overcame him. He loved his little family. They were his, he was responsible for them, accountable. To whom? God? Yes,

God. Whatever Mary thought or said, and sometimes her words could be emasculating, he was the head of his household. He took the title seriously. This was not a quaint phrase from antiquity, a meaningless label, nor a joke.

He had created this family. He had wooed and won his wife. His passion had created their children. His work had provided sustenance, his leadership order and purpose. He protected his creation from the world's dangers. He taught his children the intricate balance of belonging, being compassionate, caring, and yet remaining separate, true to themselves.

This sense of family responsibility, of protecting of your own, of manhood was, he believed, instinctual. His mind had often wandered to the subject, due largely to his contacts with more primitive cultures. Raw force, subtle, gentle, open, harsh, sometimes violent, permeated the laws, institutions, social customs of primitives and was readily apparent. A man's physical power, his ability to persuade, to bind others to himself were the basis of order. Benevolent or malevolent men decided the course of society. Women, children, the old, the infirm, had no more power than what was given to them.

If John and Gramps had been correct, life would return to primitive beginnings. The inherent power of men would dominate, set free from God's truths. As God's restraining hand pulled away, the kind and gentle rules would crumble. This realization had been the impetus for his return to basic thoughts and actions of survival. Store water, food; buy weapons, a car; find likeminded friends. This planning would give his family a chance, time to discover what God wanted from them.

Strange, his cultured world had never attempted to teach him how to be a man. He never had a course on manhood, never read a book on the topic. Never had the media made him aware. If anything, he had been taught how *not* to be a man, equal, at best, with women; men were to blame for the flaws, problems, inequalities of the world. Yet the instinct, the realization of his true position and authority could not be extinguished. He had remained true to this inner course within himself. He was the strength, the foundation of his family—whatever his weaknesses.

He stepped onto the porch, peered through the steamed, recently in-stalled kitchen door window. He saw Mary moving busily. He entered the warmth of his home, threw his jacket onto the easy chair in the den. He kissed Mary as she placed the last serving dish on the kitchen table. She smiled calmly at his kiss. She felt his love, satisfied and deep, pass into her. In his eyes she was the greatest woman who had ever lived, none was superior. He possessed her. She allowed him to possess her. A power came from him that created a submissiveness. Knowing her own headstrong will, she continually marveled at her weakness. She returned the kiss softly.

The kids bolted from the electrascreen in the living room to the kitchen when they heard the door close. At this hour, their hearing was keen for the sound of the kitchen door. With Dad home, the family was complete, their sense of security assured, the pleasure of eating imminent. They had an eagerness to hear Dad and Mom talk about their workdays. Dad always had information, a lesson, an observation to impart. He asked of their schoolwork, their friends, their thoughts. He loved them.

Katie spoke as she squiggled into her chair. The chairs were heavy, large, didn't slide easily on the floor.

"There's talk about a war, Daddy."

"In Africa," added Matthew calmly.

They had discussed at length what evil might befall the earth as the Bible study had unfolded. The story of Noah, the tower of Babel, the destruction of Sodom and Gomorrah, the famines that had come upon Egypt in Joseph's day, the plagues that Moses pronounced upon Egypt, the desert wanderings of Israel, and Israel's wars with pagan nations had given substance to their talks. He had bound their excitement and glee by explaining the terror and heartbreak that could befall them. Matthew retained his excitement, while Katie's emotions sobered.

He wasn't certain he believed any of the stories completely, in a literal and historical context. Literal interpretations aroused anger and confu-sion. Matthew and Katie, free of his logic and experience, accepted the stories as credible, if not fact. He saw no reason to dissuade them. Yes, there were strange—even miraculous—events portrayed: the plagues of Egypt, rods becoming serpents, the ark of the covenant, the miracles of Elijah and Elisha, and more. His strategy was to keep reading and thinking until the book was done. He knew disparate and incongruous facts, statements, events would join together into more cohesive explanations. Learned men had studied the ancient writings for thousands of years. He would find their thoughts and meditate till answers were produced. He would not trust the Church's doctrine, ideology, or pronouncements. John, Gramps, Diana he could trust.

Mary encouraged the figurative, remained silent on the literal. They had a heated discussion the first night, out of hearing of the kids. He had accused her of blatantly using her motherhood to sway the children into accepting her interpretations, though they had agreed to allow the kids to seek their own truth. Her anger at his reproof had been intense, more so than had been experienced in their marriage to that time. Uncharacteristically, her anger had lingered for days.

Tim moved to the newly purchased sterilizer; washing with water, as Gramps had done, wasn't sanitary. He assumed the kids had cleansed their hands earlier.

"Yes, this could be the beginning of the troubles." He must have missed the news accounts while musing on the ride home. The bright light bathed his hands sterile. Katie was already eating from a plate heaped with food. She had acquired a healthy appetite since arriving at the country home. Due to the fact she played outside often? Or was it the lack of stress in country living? She was still thin. Tim sat with his already seated family.

"Prayer?" asked Mary, seeking volunteers.

Katie bowed her head, seemed about to bless the meal. "Matthew, you say it." A sudden shyness came over her.

Mat was quick to seize his opportunity. "Dear Father, Bless this food for the use of our bodies, and us in your service. Thank you for helping us through this day. Please tell us whatever it is we need to know to belong to you. In Jesus's name we pray, Amen."

He was thankful for the food and for getting through the day without trouble. The bully at school hadn't sent any comments his way. It was only a matter of time before he would have to fight a moron two grades higher, two years older, and big. Dad said it was okay, if he was pushed or struck or even if the verbal abuse was too much, to fight back. They had practiced how to bring down the big moron. They had gone over where the fight could take place. Dad said God was on his side. God wanted him to use his martial arts training, and Mat believed.

CHAPTER 4

A brutal, insistent knock sounded at the door.

Tim swore under his breath. Why hadn't he heard the approach? Who would come to their house at this hour? Had someone been watching the house from the woods? He had just come in! Had someone been watching him? John? Was his brother at the door? He begged God to allow it to be John. If John were at the door, no crisis existed. If John were at the door…apologize, beg forgiveness for the betrayal. Let it be John!

Tim grabbed the child-sized baseball bat propped by the door. He saw figures through the steamed window. Two men? He held the bat against his leg to hide it from the view of the men. John would not have knocked so violently. He pushed the curtain aside, rubbed a clear spot in the plexiglass. Some type of badge was being presented to him. Mary turned on the porch light. Two men; one heavy, a thick torso, robust; the other thin. The robust man spoke.

"I am Inspector Simmons and behind me is Mr. Smith from the Historical Commission. Open the door, now!"

Simmons's face was snarled in anger, even as Smith pulled an identification card from a black carrying case. The card was placed against the window. Simmons was pulling violently on the door handle. That Simmons's crude, imperious, even intimidating behavior had to be tolerated because of the power of his position—inspector—rankled Tim. Simmons cursed under his breath as he gave the handle one last shake. Simmons had no concern for breaking the handle. He was enjoying his rudeness.

"I left a message on your compuphone." The tone accused those in the home of stupidity.

Tim looked to Mary for confirmation or denial. Mary spoke.

"I haven't had time to check. The automatic reminder isn't on." Her eyebrows rose in doubt as she spoke. She moved quickly into the den and returned with a printout. "Let them in." He obeyed her, though annoyed she hadn't handed the printout to him. He should make the final decision.

Simmons, first through the door, strode to the kitchen table, his eyes scanning the interior. His aggressive entry had forced Tim to move suddenly to the side to avoid a collision. Tim studied the eyes of Simmons. What was he searching for, or was this just a detective's habit, an eye for detail?

Tim's dislike for Simmons was overpowering, visceral. Simmons was a crude man, enlivened by self-importance, boldly arrogant, intimidation and violence a part of his being. Tim came upon these men with a distressing frequency on his job—at the collection terminal, the incinerator, on the highway, at homes and businesses. As a professor, he had moved among a more refined group, his coworkers, the people within the university environs and neighborhood. Harrisburg had a frontier quality, a rapid influx of workers, jobs for unskilled and semiskilled labor. He was confident in his ability to handle such men. Physically, he could subdue any man or hold his own. His weakness was that he had no desire to become involved in the courts, whereas they, it seemed, had no fear of legal entanglements. Restraints seemed to be missing in these types and the inability to project the consequences of their actions on their future lives.

He had always hated bullies as a child. Here was a grown bully in his home, with the authority of the State behind his swaggering ways. How had such a man been made an inspector? Or was his type now the norm? He remembered the inspectors from his brother's troubles, one good, one bad. Smith remained at the door, definitely embarrassed by his temporary partner. The embarrassment revealed Smith's standards—Smith was a good man. Simmons spoke.

"I will make this brief. Your banking account shows you found employment. This means you have thirty days to leave this house. Your status here was dependent on your being destitute and homeless."

"*What?*" Tim was dumbfounded.

Simmons voice revealed the habits of alcohol, tobacco, mind expanders; the tone was deep, rough, words at once dry and phlegm choked. The tone allowed for no compromise. Tim would obey or suffer consequences. Simmons seemed delighted in Tim's confusion, uncaring of the plight of the family. "The legal papers will be placed in your compuphone tomorrow."

Simmons brushed past Mary, his forearm pushing her aside. A sudden rage propelled Tim before Simmons. Tim's fists balled, he studied the face of Simmons, who gazed at the children sitting at the table. Simmons was blocked from leaving. Tim realized Simmons had no awareness that his actions had crossed the bounds of decency. Katie, glancing at the square-faced man of cold eyes, looked at Matthew in fear, searching for support. Matthew's face had taken on a deadly seriousness. He didn't like this man. He would strike his groin first, and when his head went down, his face would be pummeled just like Dad had taught. Tim waited for an improper word to the children from Simmons. Simmons would be ordered to leave. A lawyer would have to be hired, court proceedings. He would push Simmons out the door but would not incapacitate him. He would not strike the inspector unless a weapon was drawn.

Simmons released his eyes from the children and studied those rooms visible from his position. Simmons glanced at Tim Johnson, saw the suppressed anger and fear. Johnson might be man enough to hit back. Simmons turned his gaze back to the den, smiling as a man who has uncovered an advantage.

"I see you have a Bible on the table."

Simmons's eyes bored into Johnson. He liked to see fear come upon a man. Instead, Johnson's eyes turned steel hard. Simmons smiled bemusedly from his inspector rank. A real tiger, this Johnson, thought Simmons cynically. He could pound Johnson into the floor in a heartbeat, though he was older. Johnson looked in shape but hesitant, a restraint holding him that would be his defeat. He should have pulled the dossier on the man immediately upon hearing of the Church's interest in the family.

Matthew noticed the tensions rising. That's all they needed: Dad killing an inspector. "I'm doing a report for school," Matthew volunteered with cheeriness on his countenance.

Simmons's eyes bored into Matthew.

"What class?" His eyes smiled though his voice held doubt and accusation.

An intense, flushing rage and fear overcame Tim as he linked Simmons to the Church. Had the Church motivated the State to send an inspector to harass them? Did Simmons know of the Johnson family's past? Blocked by the Church from a professorship. Forced to take the lowliest job in society. Goals, self-esteem frustrated, and now they were being harassed by this goon.

"Reading class," Matthew said.

Where was his son going with this? If the lie was uncovered, their situation would be even worse.

"In what respect?" Simmons's tone was harsh.

Tim bit his lip. Simmons was damn determined to find *something*. He was dogged. Simmons sought Enslaver tendencies. Keep your head, Matthew.

"To show how much English changes. Do you want me to explain?" Matthew smiled eagerly. He saw himself as a young student wishing to impress with his newfound knowledge. He believed his own story, the words flowed, buoying him like a rush of water.

"No, just tell me where you found a paper book. That one has to be over a hundred years old." Simmons bristled with accusation.

"It is!" Matthew's voice rose happily. "My great-grandfather owned it." Pride welled in his voice. "His father was a pastor. Gramps had lots of paper books."

Simmons strode to the coffee table, picked up the book roughly. Pages loosened from the spine as he leafed through the brittle paper. With the book still in his hands, he studied the room.

"Inspector! Do you have a search warrant?" Tim couldn't keep the emotion from his voice. He had attempted to disguise his indignation and rage with a tone of matter-of-fact curiosity. His words came choked, stifled, almost apologetic. He knew Simmons heard weakness in the attempt at restraint. Simmons looked blankly at Tim, grunted.

"Are you worried I might find something?"

"That's an antique book, worth money. You've manhandled that and my wife."

Mary knew the signs of violence in Tim, the chest puffed up, the eyes steel hard, the trembling muscles. Mary pressed against Tim's chest with her small hands.

"No, no, no…" she whispered calmly. "Think of the kids."

Simmons pretended not to notice Johnson's aggravation. He would have liked to have taken the book, but no law allowed confiscation. He had come across Enslavers in his thirty-year career. The Church had requested a diligent search of the home, pressure applied to this man. Johnson was correct, an inspector couldn't search the home. Smith was to perform that function. The boy was clever; Simmons couldn't tell if he was speaking the truth. He could ask for the teacher's name and the school, watch the eyes, the lie would show.

"What's your reading teacher's name?"

"Barnhart."

"The school?"

"Reed Middle School."

Simmons turned to Johnson. The boy was a blank—no child could lie so well.

"It is the right of citizens to be free of harassment, persecution, discrimination from religious, moral, ethical beliefs which are in excess of or impugn civil law. All such religious organizations which express said beliefs are lawfully restrained from the promotion of said beliefs in any way, means, form."

The amendment of twenty-one hundred had been recited. For the first time, Tim understood the absurdity of the amendment. This was a carte-blanche law used to crush potential troublemakers or condone the behavior of allies. A religious organization could be interpreted as a family or a grouping of friends. It contravened the first amendment. The amendment assured a social cohesiveness controlled by the State. Why should the State control the culture of a nation? Mary remained in her characteristic stoicism as Simmons searched her face for fear. She wondered how a law could be so vague. A home could be entered, lives disrupted on the slightest pretext.

Simmons bored into Matthew. He wanted the boy to crack.

"Know what Enslavers are?"

"No."

"They tie you up in knots inside. Afraid to do this, afraid to do that. All that is fun is said to be bad. They deny the goodness of life, make you miserable, and then tell you to make others miserable."

Matthew crinkled his nose as if sensing an obnoxious smell, puckered his cheeks in distaste. Simmons was the cause of the reaction, not the definition of Enslavers.

"Stick with the Church."

"We all go to church," Katie said meekly, innocently, understanding nothing of the conversation, except that Simmons was an evil man.

Simmons grunted disbelievingly. Mary noticed Smith had been watching Tim's face closely, as if searching, since entering the home. Smith's expression had been one of sympathy and something else. What was it? Shame? Embarrassment? Both were odd emotions, ones you associated with antiquity, like the house.

Simmons voice, thick with anger and confrontation, bellowed. "Mr. Smith is here to give your house an inspection, so that he can assure the Commission you have been abiding by the antiquities law and have not made irreversible or destructive changes to the structure." Simmons jerked his head from Smith to the house. "Go."

Simmons did not notice Smith wince at the command. Tim and Mary noticed. Smith moved quickly, his eyes scanning ceilings, walls, furniture. Tim wondered what reaction the stored supplies in the basement would elicit. Reasonable suspicion for cultist activities? Tim wasn't certain of the law. He remembered a newscast from a year in the past, when a group had come under suspicion because of their hoarding of supplies. He was already under suspicion. Were his actions illegal?

His self-possession began to return. Maybe Simmons was having family problems, a divorce, or children in trouble. Perhaps he had been passed over for promotion. Perhaps he had been ordered to rattle the family. He had made Simmons his enemy from the beginning and probably had aggravated whatever tension already existed.

"Mary, let's sit down and eat." Diffuse the situation. "Care to join us, Inspector?"

Simmons needed to be preoccupied. Most people had difficulty being obnoxious, cold to someone who extended friendship. Not most people—people in the circle he once lived within. The family heard Smith upstairs.

"No, I am working. I don't eat or socialize with strangers while working." The words carried the tone of annoyance.

They heard Smith go down the steps into the basement. An eternity seemed to pass before Smith's footfalls were heard coming up the cellar steps. It was times like these when a man needed to believe in a loving God. Helpless, powerless, his fate in another man's hands. Tim had seen the glee, the loathing in Simmons's eyes produced by the offer of hospitality. In Simmons's mind, Johnson was kissing the old rump and hating every minute of it. Simmons gave a disdainful humph, took a position by the door. What would come from Smith's mouth?

Smith entered the kitchen, spoke. "Thanks, Mr. Johnson. Sorry to inconvenience you. The sterilizer must go with you. We will replace the plexiglass in the kitchen door window with antique glass. You're welcome to the plexiglass. Here's my card, should questions arise."

Smith placed the card on the edge of the table. Smith turned to Simmons. "They're in compliance."

Smith was out of the door. Simmons stared into each pair of eyes as his mouth smiled crookedly. Without a word, he turned, exited. As the door slammed, a communal sigh of relief came spontaneously from the family.

"Quick thinking, Mat!"

Matthew beamed at his father's praise. Tim wondered if the inspector's curiosity and hateful zeal would lead to a call to a reading teacher?

"What an actor." Mary grabbed her son by his wild tangle of hair and shook gently.

"You're good, Matthew." Katie referred to his acting. It didn't occur to her to be jealous; she liked praising and encouraging other people, especially her brother.

"Dad, are we Enslavers?" asked Matthew.

"No, and they're not like the inspector said, either."

He had to say no. John, Gramps, and Diana had been Enslavers, and he in turn had to be following their trail to Christ. He was admitting that he might be seeking the title *Enslaver*, and if this was revealed, the weight of government would crush him and his family. That thought sobered Tim. A painful clarity for the possible consequences, risks, and losses overwhelmed him.

The time had come to either believe wholeheartedly or deny the course of action he had set. The entire Tribulation idea had become ludicrous. Remain with his country, humanity, within the law, that was life and prosperity. Why aggravate the State for a fuzzy, blurred notion of God? God would understand. The God he knew from the past would understand. This new perception of God would not. This new God wanted loyalty whatever the cost. Daniel being thrown into the lion's den—that captured the essence of the new understanding of God. He had no faith that God could control the lions of the State. The Christians of Rome had been devoured by the lions.

On the other hand, where was *his* prosperity? He had lived by the rules and had been crushed by a system he had so slavishly served. Where was his professorship? Would he even have a home? What was the value of life if you couldn't do what you were meant to do? Pushed around by the Church. Pushed around by scum like Simmons. He was damn tired of being pushed. Yes, soon a decision would have to be made. He couldn't straddle the fence forever.

Tim picked up, flicked the card over between his fingers. Why had Smith made no comment on the stored goods? No curiosity? In a hurry to get home? None of his business? Had Smith relayed the information to Simmons outside the home? On the reverse side of the card, a handwritten message said, "Call at home." A phone number was underneath.

Was this a used card? The message written at some other time, then forgotten? Had Smith written the message while in the basement, so as not to arouse Simmons's curiosity? Did Smith know or suspect the supplies might be illegal or suspicious and wish to blackmail? Was Smith an Enslaver or a cultist? Tim handed the card, message side up, to Mary.

She read, spoke. "I don't think we should make anything out of this. Maybe he spends more time at home working than in his office. Maybe he's conscientious and wants to give us more latitude in our calling time. This note could have been added to all his cards. There's no reason to call. If he wants to speak to us, let him make the first move. I'm leaving a message with our lawyer this evening.

Matthew quietly removed the card from his mother's hand when he saw her attention absorbed in conversation. The message meant nothing to him. Katie leaned over her brother's shoulder, read slowly, her lips moving. Matthew began to whine, as he forced tears.

"Just when you find a place you like…they take it away from you… it's not fair…"

Katie watched her brother's face as his eyebrows knit. Her own face wrinkled in sympathy. It was sad, but the next place might be fun too. Still, she had just gotten her bedroom the way she wanted it, and she had yet to wade the creek.

Tim's voice came gruffly. "They haven't taken it from us yet!"

His son's defeatism annoyed him. Matthew was in his whining phase, the emotional prelude to puberty. This knowledge didn't help the annoyance. Matthew was not a defeatist; he had brought many of his soccer and baseball teams back from deficits. The annoyance was that Tim Johnson couldn't provide a home for his family.

Mary spoke. "Matthew, stop your whining. We don't know for a certainty we are leaving. If we do, perhaps a better home awaits us. Remember how Abraham was told to leave his home and he received a better one?" In the past, through every experience of failure, setback, and uncertainty, victory and success had followed. Letting go of one thing had always led to something better. She had never known absolute defeat or failure. Her optimism and faith were strong, and many times she created success simply by her positive thinking. Matthew was making a mess of his food with his fork. "Go to your room if you're done eating."

Matthew pulled away from the table sullenly. Katie was about to follow, wondering why her brother was acting so moody. She decided to sit and eat. She couldn't react to his every mood, no matter how much she loved him. Mom and Dad were always right. She would trust them.

Tim studied the face of his wife. After all these years, he could not read her thoughts—a face of the purest texture of stone. He resented her optimism. Why? Did her hope seem flippant or arrogant? His anger and confidence had melted into weakness, emptiness, and finally total helplessness. What if they had to move from this house? What could they afford on their combined salaries? An apartment in the rundown high-rises of the lower class.

Trapped in a tiny apartment when the troubles came, likely without water or electricity or the ability to forage for food in the countryside. Surrounded by people of low morals and education, made worse by lack of any restraining influence. His neighbors' only desire would be to take from, use his family. How could he withstand the power of the gangs?

His son would either be constantly fighting and struggling to retain his integrity, or coerced into a gang, where he would lose his soul, his spirit, the values that made him a man. His daughter would be harassed by sexually active ten-year-old delinquents till she had been corrupted, raped, or he had fought every so-called parent or gang member in the building. A burst of reflective thought gave him understanding as to why God had wanted the Jews to separate from the pagan tribes surrounding them. His mind connected to the tower of Babel story, a puzzle until now. The Bible had been telling him that man, society knew only evil when God was forgotten.

Their lawyer *had* to come through so they could remain in Gramps's home. A well-paying job *had* to be found.

Katie's plate had been emptied. Tim watched her as she began squiggling out of her chair, holding the plate. Understanding the mess that was spilled food and fallen silverware, she placed the plate back on the table.

She freed herself, stood, picked up the plate, walked with eyes on the plate, deposited it on the kitchen counter. Tim smiled at her succession of tasks learned, her concentration given to the level plate. The smile faded to a sadness as she ran to join her brother in the living room. He spoke quietly, determinedly to Mary. "We must hold onto this house."

"This home isn't everything," she replied. "You act as if it's our salvation."

The thought came to her that God was their salvation, but the thought didn't fit the occasion. Belief in God couldn't take the place of a home. Every family needed a physical home. The Abraham reference had been mentioned to show that a good outcome could come from an uncertain future. Had she twisted the meaning of the story? God hadn't asked them to move; the State was forcing them. God had not promised a better home, and they were certainly not the progenitors of a new chosen race.

Where in the Bible had God promised them a good home? Proverbs or Psalms? She could only remember Christ's words about foxes having dens, birds their nests, and Christ himself having no home. Thank God that had been Christ's burden and not her family's. Christ had his life of suffering so her family could have a life of goodness and blessing. Somewhere in the Bible must be the promise of a good earthly home. She knew for a certainty they would be forced to move. Moving was a wearying process to be dreaded, but she was not so enamored of the house as to be torn emotionally. The cold hard fact was that the State always won. Determine the future on facts, make decisions on facts. Use God and the spiritual to interpret those facts in the most positive light. Never make a decision based on the spiritual, hoping God is on the other side of a misguided leap of faith.

Tim detected Mary's underlying desire to leave the farmhouse. He would leave this issue alone, leave their separation of desires alone. She had her own mind, her own life, even within theirs. The farmhouse was essential if the Tribulation was truly coming. Even if there were to be no Tribulation, a free home and country living gave them a quality of life they could not, on their salaries, have in the city. He would contact Smith, ask for a break, offer a bribe if necessary, if their lawyer could not help.

He shoveled the remaining food on his plate into his mouth, complimented his wife on the meal, went into the living room with the kids to watch the electrascreen. The uncertainty of the future goaded his calm, gave him an irritability. What if they lost the farmhouse? He had been certain that God gave them the house—was He now in the realm of imagination? Imagining a God that didn't exist and depending on His warm feelings? What was the advantage to Gramps's and John's God?

CHAPTER 5

Tim stood on the passenger platform of an unfamiliar station. He wasn't returning home after work as usual; instead, he was headed to the south side of the city, where he was to meet with Smith, the Historical Commission employee. A mass of expectant and anxious commuters hemmed him. He was a stranger not only to the station but the route as well. The aggressive jostling of the crowd pressed the limits of civility. He assumed the regulars knew the seating capacity on the arriving train would be strained, and people might be left behind to battle for a place on the next train.

Their lawyer had filed for and obtained a sixty-day extension—that was all—and then the house would revert back to the State. He had called Smith, and an awkward conversation ensued in which he had asked for a break, a loophole, possible options, imploring, almost begging. He was about to suggest a bribe when Smith mentioned the stored goods in the basement, the reasonableness of such actions, given the times.

Smith alluded to a group. His conversation had turned philosophical, touched on the condition of humanity and its inherent spiritual needs. Biblical phrases were unobtrusively interwoven through the discourse. Smith's politeness, understanding, sympathy seemed genuine. Smith encouraged this meeting. What could be lost by meeting? Smith could be an agent of the State searching for cultists! He would allow Smith to do the talking. Tim felt confident in his ability to obscure and evade. He would not be entrapped—the recording program in his pocket phone would be on. Mary had thought the risks too great. He had not made this appointment with her blessing.

The commuter trains must run at half-hour intervals, given the insistence, determination of the now shoving and pushing crowd. He had positioned himself toward the front of the mass, but others had boldly crowded into the unsafe area between the safety line and the tracks. Men and women cursed, some quietly, some loudly and aggressively. Feet were being trampled, equilibriums momentarily lost, elbows prodded into flesh. He had a detachment from the others; his own problems absorbed his concentration. He felt someone pulling their hand out of his coat pocket, the hand catching on the corner of the flapped pocket. He kept his pockets empty. He couldn't have turned to confront the would-be thicf had he wished. Pickpockets had been in existence since pockets and crowds.

He didn't mind being taken out of his routine and enjoyed the prospect of seeing the south side of the city, having only passed through once before. He felt good physically; he had energy, strength. He had adjusted to the bodily demands of his work. The possible loss of his home was balanced by having twenty job applications out, all for higher-paying work. He had hope. The meeting could be seen as an adventure.

The emotions within the curses of the mass were comical in a pathetic way—to be so upset over catching a commuter. Judgmental? Who, but they—and God—knew their schedules? He didn't intend to give up his place on the long slender car and he could afford a delay. Still, he wouldn't be cursing if he missed this commuter. The curses were extremely raw, crude, and seemed to come from a hatred in the soul. People had cursed since Adam and Eve; this was a part of the human condition.

The public electrascreen cast three-dimensional scenes above the station's throng. News, always news. Africa had two wars; Central Asia, one. The second horseman, on his red steed, was roaming the earth. Wars and rumors of wars were nothing new. What would he give to remain in the farmhouse? He denied the import of the world situation and yet planned for a course based on an affirmation of what he denied. Would he even need a bargaining position? The employment records he had uncovered while investigating State computer files showed Smith to be a minor official without much influence. Would the Johnsons be asked to join a cult? Mary had begun a search for a new home; there was no need to feel pressured.

Heads turned to the left; bodies tensed in anxiety. A single commuter car rushed in and then eased fluidly to a stop. Three cars were needed for the size of the crowd gathered. The outgoing passengers spewed from the doors in a massive rush, pinning people against the doorframes. The crowd on the platform tightened, pushed. One old woman at the rear of the outgoing rush lagged. He believed she had dropped a package, stooped to retrieve it. She hurried to rejoin the body of the outpouring crowd. An unevenness marked her movements.

Suddenly, the crowd on the platform rushed to the open doors before all had exited. Tim was swept up in the surge. His physical helplessness caused an anger to seize him. The old woman was shoved back into the car as the impatient boarders moved past her. The old woman had been too slow, like a sick caribou lagging behind the herd, devoured by a swarm of wolves. He had seen such a sight on the tundra during an oil field exploration, back when he was important, his expertise respected. The wolves had torn hunks of living flesh from the caribou's flanks. The caribou collapsed under the weight of bodies and sat, dumbfounded, watching itself being devoured. The old woman had been pushed into a seat, dazed. He wondered if she would ever arrive at her destination. People had behaved badly all through the course of human history.

The pressing bodies annoyed him, he wished to strike out. The remembrance of the exciting, life he had lived compared with his present state created an anger within him. He wouldn't need to be at this commuter station, pushed around, if he had a car—professors could afford or were given cars. He was a nobody now, couldn't hold onto a drafty farmhouse as shelter for his family. Thirty-five and a failure. He attempted to shake the negative thoughts.

The car was rapidly filling, many people would be left at the station. He had two bodies between him and the car door. A mental relief, a bodily relaxation came upon him as he realized the car would hold him. His luck still held.

A violent shove pushed him sideways, away from the door. Three tall, large black men stood in the gap created by his departure. The two farthest from him smirked. The man nearest him, the man who had pushed him, glared in loathing. Anger, superiority, aggression exuded from his body. Instinctually, Tim measured his opponents, three to six inches taller, on the average fifty pounds heavier, men in their mid to late twenties. They were riding the crest of their bodies' hormonal surge of aggression, their minds keen.

He was physically smaller, confused, stunned; his flesh was calling for flight. With a will trained through his martial arts experience, he fought the natural tendencies of his body. He studied their faces as he regained his composure. The small linear scars on the balls of the cheeks told him they were high-ranking members of the Voodoo Disciples. Their fifty pounds of extra weight appeared to be alcohol- and/or opioid- or marijuana-induced. It was just fat and skin that would tax the heart and slow their reflexes.

Tim's mind began to seethe in anger; these men were more evidence of his powerlessness. His anger was magnified by his low self-esteem, all the stress of the last year. His body began to feel the seething anger. But he knew when not to be a fool. Police record, trials, lawsuits, hospitals, damaged health, fear of death restrained him. They had the advantage and the power at the moment. He wasn't hurt. He would say nothing. Do nothing. Inwardly prepare the body and mind for possible confrontation.

"You got any problems with us, trash man?"

The words were spit into Tim's face. How did this man know of the waste-disposing job? This man with the Middle Eastern hook in his nose, the light skin, the crisp delineation of the thin lips. The man read his victim's puzzled expression. "I can smell the ash, ash hole!"

The two others laughed at the joke. Why would they know the odor? Had they been trash men or had known waste-disposal workers? Tim sensed their hormonal surges were dying even as they believed they had mastery of their victim. Hormonal surges couldn't outlive another man's determination. Tim did not respond; he averted his eyes, stared at the ground, lowered his head, gave all the signals of appeasement. He trailed behind them; the remaining commuters had backed away.

He could still make the commuter. His confidence had returned. He would not fight unless physically attacked. He hadn't been aware of any odor upon himself. He had noticed an odor from the bundles within the truck on his white overalls while at work. Mary had never mentioned an odor. Yes, once, when he hadn't showered before coming home. The odor wasn't foul but distinct, acrid.

Was it the odor that had made him the target, an object of scorn? Or his skin color? Why not the man ahead in the suit? Strange that men would judge your self-worth, importance by your clothes, your work. No, that wasn't odd; he had always done so. Now, he was the little unimportant man. The world saw him differently. He could be trampled on with ease. Such an incident was to be expected. He entered the car, the last man on. He saw the old woman who had been pushed back in suddenly dart out the side of the doorway. Good for you, lady, he thought. She had kept her head in the game. His line of vision was purposely away from the men, though he closely monitored their movements in his peripheral sight.

"Blanched man! Ash hole! I'm talking to you."

Upon hearing the words, Tim understood his submission had fed the man's ego instead of appeasing him. The man wanted to degrade and probably would use violence. Tim had hoped they had only wanted a place on the car. Why was this man flirting with the power of the law? Police had been freed of lawsuits when he was a child; necessary force issues were reviewed by a board of their own. This man didn't believe he was taking a chance; it was a certainty that no reaction would come from the cowardly Tim Johnson.

Tim smiled devilishly, assumed a fighting position. This enraged his taunter. A fist came toward Tim's head. Tim blocked the punch, answered with combinations to the body. The solar plexus, then up under the ribs, then a lower blow under the belt but above the crotch.

The punches brought grunts; the torso was flabby, the muscles loose. His assailant bent at the waist and appeared ready to vomit. Tim and his attacker sent the packed bodies scrambling, falling. He heard gasps, grunts; a woman swore, men shouted, bodies compacted behind the combatants.

The years of karate training decided Tim's movements. His legs were useless in the crowded space. He had cross-trained as a boxer and wrestler. His punches were solid. The height advantage of his adversary was lost when his midsection doubled over. Tim's fists began to work the head and neck and throat. The punches inflicted pain. His friends had been caught with their hands in their pockets. The man's fury quickly turned to fear—the fear of losing.

Tim backed away. He would never make a man desperate, even those he loathed—unless it was to be a fight to the death. "Want more?"

His voice was dispassionate. His own rage had been expended in the first punches; his attitude became one of business, calculating, serious. Had someone pressed the police emergency button? His opponent glared in pain, shock, hatred. His two friends had pushed their way to his side.

"You got to pay now! You trammeled our brother." Words but no punches.

Tim said nothing. Talk had no relevance now. In the narrow aisle he was certain he could keep all three at bay till helped arrived. The car came to a sudden stop. The gang members lurched forward as Tim stumbled back. He heard the door behind him open, then an angry bellowing voice. The gang members attacked; he blocked the fists. He was picked up from behind, spun around. He had been deposited behind a police officer, a black storm trooper, who caught a blow meant for him. The attacker's knuckles popped against the police armor.

The three gang members, seconds before enraged, were now cowering, begging for forgiveness. An unending torrent of accusations were directed against Tim. The police officer, after a moment of silent study of the participants, grabbed the belt and coat collar of the man who had accidentally struck him and slammed the man to the floor. In one swift movement, a downward heel stroke bearing full body weight struck the prostate man in the area of the kidneys.

"Never strike a police officer!" The voice resounded in rage, contempt.

As the downed man groaned in agony, begged for mercy, pleaded for help, the two remaining gang members were shoved out the door. The trooper forced them to the ground, even as they were attempting to comply, and expertly cuffed them. With one hand, the officer dragged the moaning, prostrate man across the aisle, threw him out the door to the street, and cuffed him.

"Follow me," he demanded of Tim.

Tim moved with an alacrity motivated by thankfulness even as he was handcuffed.

"These handcuffs contain an explosive force that can be detonated at my discretion. Cooperate." The officer pulled a scanner from his belt, moved the device across the forehead of Tim in silence. The invisible number had entered the police files. The passengers on the commuter had uncoiled, picked themselves up from the floor, and watched through the open doors and the closed windows. A crowd gathered on the street. As the officer scanned the foreheads of the gang members, a beeper sounded a panicked warning. The ex-storm trooper pointed at Tim. "You. Get back into the car." The officer unleashed the cuffs.

Tim moved quickly. As he climbed the steps, he felt a pain in his hip, a twinge as if his leg were out of joint. Grasping the handrail, he felt stiffness in his knuckles, a burning rawness on the skin. The upper layer of skin had been peeled back and was bleeding—nothing serious. In the car, a man, white, late fifties, beamed at him. Pride, amazement, respect was in the gaze.

"You held your own, had a coolness. We could use a man like yourself."

Tim did not resist the admiration. He had done well. He thirsted for praise, appreciation. In a small way, he was somebody again.

"Who is *we*?" Tim asked for the sake of conversation and in hopes of more praise. The commuter car pulled away from the forms of the three prostate attackers and the street crowd. A police department criminal-containment vehicle known as a CCV pulled up on the scene.

"A fraternal organization. Good men."

"Why would you need a man with the talents I just displayed?" Tim asked.

"I don't know that we do at the moment. Times, circumstances change. We have many men of your caliber..." The older man saw a younger man hungering for praise, affirmation. The questioning gaze within the need was good; skepticism had virtue; gullibility was for fools. Test every word out of a man's mouth. The wedding band said the young man was married, a father, by his demeanor. Intelligence hung on the man and a brokenness, a sadness, even through the elation of victory, that evoked empathy. Carl Stasic had been broken by circumstances many times. "They're decent, law-abiding men, who only want peace, a safe environment for their children. Men who realize that destroyers, malcontents are pulling down the greatest country and society the world has produced."

Carl rummaged in the pockets of his rugged all-weather jacket. Tim noticed the jacket—handmade—and studied the man's clothes and shoes—quality leather. Within the clothes was a strong physique. Time was spent in physical training. The skin had a tan—health club. The hair had been blacked with the new, in-vogue method that lasted months. The eyes radiated brightness. The stranger had done well in life.

"Here. Here is my card. Carl Stasic is my name."

Carl extended his hand. Tim's hand was engulfed by the large, warm, powerful hand of Carl. Tim placed the card in his pocket.

"Tim Johnson." Tim winced when his knuckles were squeezed. Carl was unaware of the discomfort.

An organization that didn't trust in the goodness of the future. So many people thinking as himself. Why? They surely had no knowledge of Bible prophecy, Enslaver doctrine. What was it about the times—so prosperous and with limitless freedoms—that had people frightened?

"What is this organization centered upon, Carl?"

"The spirit, values, that made this country great. Come to a meeting."

"Someday I might."

They gazed into each other's eyes, maintained contact with a calmness and trust that amazed both. Carl could see gladness in Tim's eyes at being respected, wanted. Tim saw in Stasic's eyes admiration, respect, a joy in a treasure found. Carl smiled broadly; this Tim Johnson had something—a quality that lifted him above other men. Tim could have been one of his sons. Carl resumed the conversation.

"Don't say someday. Say, 'I will come.' You wonder who I am—and you should. I believe in decency, honesty, hard work. Raised in a State school. Never met my mother or father. All I had was life. I developed a will to succeed. Joined the marines the day after I graduated from high school. Worked in demolitions. Started my own company after my tour of duty. Physical work with iron crowbars, then wrecking machines, lasers, explosives, whatever it took. My company went international. Made a fortune. Lost a fortune. Remade a fortune.

"I've seen men blown into vapor, just a mist on your safety goggles. I've seen men with reinforcement bars protruding through their skulls, talking coherently, as if nothing happened. I've seen men lose limbs; seen men crushed to death, the blood gushing out of eye sockets. I've seen bloody riots in Africa, Indonesia, Myanmar, Australia.

"I've killed a few men, blackmailed some, ruined the careers and lives of dishonest men. Not for myself, but for the good of my company. God still loves me, and life is still good. On my seventh wife—twenty-five years old, a beauty, with all the good parts in excess." Carl winked, his eyes burning brightly. "I'm seventy years old and just had a daughter."

Boasting was absent from Carl's tone, except during the mention of his daughter. Tim smiled in simple amazement—if only *he* could look so good at seventy. He had guessed Carl to be twenty years younger. An assessment of Carl was a simple matter. He could admire men because he was secure in his own self-worth. He did not admire possessively, nor envy others for what he lacked; for lacking nothing, he saw a part of himself in each man. Carl was a man who conquered life and took what he wanted by rules he was convinced were fair, and he had no remorse. Carl lived for life; probably life and God were synonymous in his mind, and why not? They were men of the same beliefs.

"I've rambled on about myself." A mild disappointment clung to Carl's sentence. "What's your story, Tim?" Carl had a genuine interest and eagerness to know.

"Once a geology professor. Did some consulting work for corporations. I've been to Indonesia, Myanmar, both poles, South America, Middle East, Central Asia, Siberia. Australia, Pacific Islands."

Tim stopped, seeing Carl anxious to jump in. "Ever eat at Lucky's in Yangon?"

"Yes, as a matter of fact. Breakfast, lunch, dinner for almost a week." The odors of the restaurant flooded his mind like a subtle light through bamboo shades. The downtime had been caused by a government official seeking a bribe. The entire project had stopped till the man could be paid.

Carl laughed. "Small world. What are you doing now?"

"Incineration collections."

"Why? With your education, abilities?"

"Crossed the wrong people." Tim pursed his lips.

Carl understood the freshness of the heartbreak, the reticence to speak further. "Look! Life will turn for the better. Keep the faith! All the more reason to attend a meeting. Make job contacts."

Tim smiled hopefully through his reluctance. He liked the idea. One of his goals was to find men of common beliefs. No man would be able to stand against the Tribulation alone. Most likely Carl's spirit was indicative, representative of this fraternal organization. Carl was the kind of man who could flourish in the hard times. He would take care of his own. Would he sacrifice for others at his own expense? This, Tim could not ascertain. He had always thought that quality—personal sacrifice for others—differentiated common men from great men.

Carl turned toward the door after a brief glance out the side windows. "My exit's approaching." He extended his huge, strong hand and gave Tim's hand a shake. He saw Tim wince. "Ah, the knuckles! Sorry. You did well, Tim, very well. Unawares, at peace, you rose to meet the challenge! Nothing more difficult than to defend yourself when unsuspecting—at peace—and your attacker has his muscle on the rise. Call me. We'll get your life back on track." Carl eyes beamed in merriment and sincerity. The commuter stopped; the door opened. Carl was carried out on the rush. "I mean that! Call me!"

"Certainly." Tim waved, chuckled to himself. Carl's appreciation of life was contagious. How could God destroy the world when men such as Carl came from His creation? Man was good, not evil. If anyone should have been raptured it should have been Carl. Words of encouragement and praise to a total stranger, willing to help a stranger in need. Carl blended into the crowd as boarding commuters blocked Tim's view. Why hadn't God taken Carl? That question arising again, haunting him. What did God want?

***

Tim exited his commuter at the southernmost edge of the city, where the commuter line looped back into Harrisburg. He saw Smith, standing gawkishly within the bustling masses of the station. Hands in jacket pockets, shoulders slumped, Adam's apple protruding, chin recessed. If you could believe impressions, Smith was a lackadaisical bumbler of stolid mind and mundane interests, who happened into a job above his minor abilities.

Smith, gaping at the incoming cars, waved stiffly upon recognizing his guest. Tim was touched by the simple pleasure in Smith's eyes and the warmth of the handshake upon meeting. Tim felt a guilt for his unkind appraisal—judge a man's heart, not his appearance. Once, that rule had been automatic with him. Where had he lost that search for the heart? Smith began walking, with Tim close at his side. An awareness came to Tim that mystery and danger were a part of this meeting. Could Smith's simpleness walk the two of them into the hands of the authorities?

"This decision to meet with us is a milestone in your family's life, Tim." The words seemed to verge on self-importance while equally weighted with the gravity of truth. Tim was encouraged that Smith addressed him informally, even as he was to call Smith by his first name, Bill. This had been decided in their compuphone conversation. Tim activated his recorder app. Bill continued. "You're preparing for a bleak future. I don't know how you know it is coming, but it is."

"How do *you* know it is coming?" Tim attempted to keep a humorous tone to his words. Tim tensed mentally from his relaxed state. The freedom of his wife and kids might be at stake here.

"We are led by a man who knows the future."

Tim smiled as his thoughts were affirmed: cult. He must be wary. Smith's use of the word *we* brought relief—in one sense. Smith was a genuine soul but perhaps guileless, simple, common, without energy, initiative, or the cleverness to survive what might be the future—or to help the Johnson family. Smith, on his own, wouldn't take a bribe, lie, or risk his job for another. Maybe the cult was Smith's excitement in life.

"By the way—you've angered the Church." Smith averted his eyes from Tim's face when he saw the terror his words had produced. "Simmons told me to look thoroughly for cult material, violations of the building code, anything that he could use to arrest, detain, or harass. He said the Church had made the request."

"What did you tell him?" Tim struggled to project a casual tone.

"Just what I told you while he was present. I'm glad you didn't take a poke at him. He had a live stun stick in his pocket."

"Why are you telling me this?"

"To show we can be trusted, to warn you, to make apparent to you the risk we are taking in seeking you."

They walked in silence through a development of singles, expensive, sitting on spacious lots of detailed, abundant landscaping. The fragrance of thick green turf, exotic trees, shrubs, flowers came to them through the cool early summer air. In utter disbelief Tim realized how wrong his character assessment of Smith had been. Smith was risking much in this contact and likely had sold this meeting to the leader of his organization. Smith was gambling against the power of the Church.

Or was Smith lying about the Church and Simmons? No, Simmons's behavior, at the time and now scrutinized in retrospect, had been excessive, confrontational. Smith had no leverage for blackmail, as he had withheld information from an inspector. Smith was guilty of a crime, if he had spoken the truth. The question then became: Why was this cult so interested in Tim Johnson? The farmhouse? In sixty days, Tim Johnson would have nothing to do with the farmhouse. Smith must know a way to hold onto the house! The cult wanted the farmhouse for storage? As a place of refuge? Or was the cult seeking members?

Smith stopped before an empty, nondescript parked car. They entered; Smith drove. The development of singles gave way to ag fields and a distant line of trees. Tim saw tall light poles against the line of trees. Playing fields? Smith seemed unnaturally placid—a chemical high? Elevators or serenities? Most people were mentally floating, but Smith stood out.

"Is there anything you can do for me through your office, Bill?"

"We believe that in a few months, ejecting occupants from an historical home will not be on the minds of the authorities. Especially if the complainant bureau loses the records."

Tim smiled broadly—how wrong he had been about Smith. The peace the man possessed certainly had not crushed his daring. A few months? The troubles were to begin in a few months? This leader of the cult certainly had boldness to predict a time. Credibility would be zero if he was wrong.

"Will the records be lost in sixty days?"

"We're not sure; timing is critical. You should search for an apartment. We could help."

"What exactly do you want from me in return?"

In the momentary silence, Tim stared out at the countryside. They drove down a lane lined with massive oaks. The trees must be well over a hundred years old. Amazing that a lane could have survived such a length of time.

"A base of operations in the country will be important in the future. An escape from the ravages of the city, gang warfare, starvation, disease, earthquake damage. A place to store supplies, perhaps to farm or forage. Good men joining our congregation is important. Our pastor has predicted many events that have occurred. The Church leadership changing, the new leader of the European Federation, the peace treaty in the Middle East, the rebuilding of the Jewish temple. He has predicted small events within the congregation that have come to pass. Marriages, sudden windfalls of money, births, deaths.

"You will like him," Smith said. "You are meeting him tonight. He has a peace. We have a peace."

Smith chuckled softly as that peace became real within him. Tim saw the peace, like an aura, surround Smith. Mind control techniques, chemicals, self-hypnosis were possible explanations. John and Gramps had had a supernatural peace; Smith's was not supernatural. This pastor, predicting of the world situation, sounded like Gramps. Predictions of a biblical nature. Gramps had been adamant the temple in Jerusalem was the key to future events. The predictions within the congregation could have been manipulated. He was meeting this pastor tonight—directness he liked. He would judge this pastor's authenticity. Tim's tension increased; was this a setup?

CHAPTER 6

The lane seemed to be reeled in by the massive European manor house before them. The extensive additions to the main structure gave the conglomerate the appearance of a massive, looming cliff. The stone walls, slate roof, gables, chimneys that seemed homes in themselves were made deep, mysterious by subtle landscaping and ground lighting. The large narrow windows revealed most rooms in darkness; some had the glow of night-lights. Only one well-lit room appeared occupied. The main door consisted of heavy oak and iron. Acres of manicured lawn surrounded the home. A high perimeter fence began where the oaks stopped.

"Your pastor has done well." Tim pondered how this wealth was made. The house and grounds with massive trees reminded Tim of movies with haunting specters and murders.

Smith laughed unaffectedly. "No, the home does not belong to our pastor. He works here." Smith reservedly came out of his laughter. "We prefer you keep this meeting to yourself. Persecution will be coming soon. Talk to your wife, but not to your children. Children talk without thinking. Mine do."

Persecution in the future had always been accepted by Tim. Now, hearing the word from another man, fear swept over his flesh. Persecution!

From his own people, those of his nation, city, neighborhood, workplace? Being hated, hunted, killed for something you believed? Persecution is what happened to people with no political power, people outside the mainstream. Persecution knew no laws, no standards, no protection from harm. You could be harried and harassed by unkind shouted comments or anonymous texts. You could be, denied access, refused service, belittled, stripped of dignity, pushed, shoved, struck down without warning, spit upon, or doused in chemicals. Your children could be kidnapped or hurt. There were no time-outs to persecution, no safe havens. Unrelenting fear and apprehension stalked the mind as paranoia made a home in your thoughts. He was of the mainstream, in the very center of it. He would do nothing to take himself out of that center—yet he must. He was being forced to choose between a jumbled notion of God and a comfortable, secure life among his fellow citizens. Smith had children. Smith had the weight of fatherhood upon himself; they shared that bond. Tim had an empathy for Smith, even as he wished to distance himself from a man who might be persecuted.

Smith lowered his window, extended his arm, placed his thumb on an unobtrusive black pad that extended from a gate pillar. The gate opened; the thumbprint checked against a file. Tim studied the high fence, noticed the sensor relay boxes. A pack of Doberman pinschers trotted across the lawn midway between the fence and the mansion. A mechanical dog watched, cameras and hearing sensors activated, jaws snapping, head turning. The pack glanced at the vehicle. The entire pack had electronic control collars; two of the dogs had equipment strapped to their bodies. He couldn't guess the purpose of the devices. The gate opening had sent a neutral signal through the collars. The fence being breached, the gate being forced, would send an action signal.

"What are those devices on the two dogs?"

"Vehicle neutralizers. What that means, I don't know."

It means they carry bombs, thought Tim, or electronic disrupters to stop an engine. "Is the owner of the estate a member of the congregation?"

"I've never seen the man. I understand your curiosity. With a man of such wealth behind a group, they could do almost anything." Smith laughed ambiguously. Tim sensed a wealthy man would keep his distance from a cult, though nurturing the cult's growth might have an appeal. He doubted if Smith had any knowledge of the owner's involvement. The owner of the estate certainly controlled more than one global business. With such wealth came great political power.

They turned onto a road branching off the main drive and leading to the rear of the house. Directly parallel to the house, they encountered another fence and touch pad. Inside the fence, a wide veranda, thick with fountains, statues, umbrellaed tables overlooked three swimming pools. He saw tennis, basketball courts, playing areas, a soccer or football field encircled by a track. He saw garages, stables, hangers, an air platform. What lay beyond his sight? Equestrian courses, polo fields, a skeet range? High light poles were spaced around the grounds.

On the very edge of the grounds, the road ended in a parking area flanked by two rows of townhouses. Each home had a two-bay garage. The servants' quarters, guessed Tim. They were better than most upper middle-income people's homes. Could he secure a position here? At an end townhouse, Smith rang the doorbell.

The door slid open automatically. Tim's eyes went to the movement in a crowded corner of the living room. A man, dressed in shorts and muscle shirt, lay on a weightlifting bench, pressing out the last repetitions of his set. Weights, racks, weight machines, benches, a rower, a small whirlpool bath crowded the corner. Tim followed Smith inside as the man gave a slight kick of his feet, curved his back, assumed a sitting position.

The man stood, his mouth set in a smile, white even teeth on a tanned face. His demeanor and appearance pierced through the average, etched into the memory. Deeply tanned, heavily muscled and defined, a solid jaw with a dark shadow of a beard, brown hair of shoulder length. One might judge him the perfect man. Woman would call him handsome. Early thirties, thought Tim. The man had a calm, a subdued happiness, and he projected an empathy—less of emotion than of knowledge.

"This is our pastor, Dave." Smith's voice held pride as he brought Tim into Dave's presence. The hand offered Tim was tensed with muscular strength, warm, with no desire to crush and overpower. Tim felt no discomfort from the bruises on his knuckles. Dave's smile widened as he looked into Tim's eyes. The dark eyes held a softness, a kindness. The body posture held a good will—a trust in the one before him. Dave's voice resounded.

"This is the man trying to hold onto his home." The sentence was delivered as a certainty imbued with the righteousness of Tim's cause.

"Yes," said Smith.

Dave's voice lingered in Tim's mind. The voice carried authority but only asked for attentiveness.

"Let's sit, talk." Dave moved to the living room amid sofas, chairs, coffee and end tables. The furnishings were not expensive, most pieces worn. The gym equipment had a secondhand look of heavy wear. Dave didn't appear to be making money from his congregation. Some men preferred power or sex. Why the shoulder-length hair? That style hadn't been popular in decades, though the style was still well represented. Uniqueness, free spirit, earthiness, naturalness, wildness? The body builder's physique? Hiding an insecurity, a love of health, a celebration of manliness, desire for power, domination?

Tim eased into a worn sofa. Dave sat across from him, his legs extended to the side, propped on a coffee table. Inexpensive shoes, well worn; shorts and muscle shirt ready for incineration, noted Tim. Smith, his peace seemingly increased, sat beside his pastor. Tim was struck by the definite presence of a charisma emanating from Dave—from body magnetism, hormonal subscents, heat auras artificially induced? Or did the charisma come from a mind looking through eyes of humbleness and warmth and an aggressively positive spirit?

"Have you determined who I am yet?" Dave smiled.

Tim smiled in return, noticed the marriage band on the ring finger. "A general theory."

"I married my childhood sweetheart at the age of eighteen. Fourteen years of marriage, and each day is better than the last. Three children—ten, eight, six."

Tim sensed Dave was addressing the thoughts that had arisen at the sight of the wedding band. The ring had been seen in a general sweep of his vision, no glance or protracted stare. How had Dave come to address the subject of marriage? A definite field or aura was between them. Dave continued.

"As a child I watched my uncle lift weights. He began training me. Life is better when your body is strong and healthy. No steroids, though I take enhancers, which focus, encourage the natural steroids in my system. I sometimes leave the weights for weeks or months, for running, swimming, or agility phases. Dave paused, smiled. "The hair? I allowed it to grow when as a young man I dedicated my life to the Lord. It is a symbol of my separation."

"Like Samson?"

"Yes, a Nazarite vow. Do you know of this?"

"A little." Better to hide his Bible knowledge.

Dave became absorbed momentarily, inwardly, then seemed mildly jolted. "Forgive my manners. Would you like a drink?"

A deep thirst had been building in Tim for a German beer with the customary high alcohol content, a mild painkiller for the pain returning to his hip. His thirst had become so great that he had intended to ask if not offered.

"Yes." He would be satisfied with whatever was brought. Dave moved easily, with agility, from the chair into the kitchen, talking as he went.

"My wife is working late. We keep the kids in the afterschool program. She brings them home."

Tim waited for a list of choices to come. Dave returned with a heavy bottle topped with a ceramic cap in his hand—a German beer. Tim smirked in amazement. Dave extended the bottle to Tim, his face showing no signs of an extraordinary act.

"I don't drink, of course—my vow. I keep these for guests. Put it anywhere, the table, the floor. The kids and their constant spills have taken the formality from our furnishings and carpet." As Dave eased back into his chair, he said, "You had an exciting incident on the way here?"

"Yes." Had Dave's men had him under surveillance, or had his memory been read? Tim, chagrinned, realized a slight limp might be noticed, but surely the bruised and brush-burned knuckles were evident—Dave could have noticed at the handshake. The incident on the commuter had not been at the forefront of his thinking, though the hip pain, basic and physical, might easily project itself into another's conscience. Dave seemed content with the single-word response. How much could Dave discern of the incident? Were there limits to his power? Tim had no consciousness of probing or of Dave glancing at hands or hip. He would play along. "When did you realize you had this power?"

"As a child—age seven."

How many times had Dave been asked this question? Weariness, boredom overcame Tim—these were Dave's feelings! Had this recognition of Dave's state of mind come through facial expression, body posture, tone of voice? These visible signs would account for recognition, but he had felt or internalized those states of mind of Dave. Could Dave project his mind to another? "Tell me about your group and what you believe."

"We believe in God, his only son—Christ, and the Holy Spirit. We believe in the goodness of God. We are here to share that goodness with each other, by word and action. We know the world has become an unloving place, a place where God is ignored. The world is sterile, a place of little interest to God, a world to be rooted up like an unfruitful tree."

Dave's confident voice was tinged with sadness. Tim thought it wise not to think upon anything that was said. He would only ask questions, keep his mind moving forward. Out of Dave's presence, he would analyze. The power must have spatial limits. "How do you differ from the Church?"

"We are a family. The Church is an organization. We are here to serve each other as we serve God. The Church serves itself, or rather, its hierarchy—those men at the top think themselves gods. Our path to God is narrow; the Church's way is broad. We believe in sexual purity, one mate for life, no lesbianism, no homosexuality, pedophilia, or pseudo families. Though we forgive those who are divorced or who once were contrary to our way in any area. No drugs except medication for the body. Do unto others as you would have them do unto you. People aren't victims to be exploited or tools to use. We know God is interested in our lives, finds joy in His relationship with us, and we with Him."

"Are you adversaries of the Church?"

"We do not speak against the Church. We believe what we believe. You can clearly see the differences."

"Does the State consider you Enslavers, cultists?"

"Yes, to the State we are cultists. That is why we are secretive. They might classify us as Enslavers because we believe that certain lifestyles, beliefs, attitudes are wrong."

"How do you differ from Enslavers?"

"We do not believe man is totally depraved. The original goodness put into him by the Creator is not fully tainted by evil. Good remains; we simply peel away the bad. Man is inherently good because that is the nature of God."

"Have you written down your beliefs?" Contemplation, thought should be brought to bear, in a quiet place.

"No. In this age, the visible word draws trouble. God makes our beliefs real in our hearts. You must come to our meetings to learn, discuss."

"How do you know the world's future?"

"I could ask you the same. You have the basement filled with supplies."

Dave's tone had held an undercurrent of tension. A hint of fear? Dave was human. Was his security in proclaiming his faith based on the knowledge of the hidden supplies? Was Dave reminding him they were both conspirators against the beliefs of the State? Tim answered in his voice from childhood.

"I asked you first."

The tone of voice carried the three men back to their childhood experiences. They chuckled, as men in collusion in absurd times, acting as fools. A tension lifted, they trusted each other. When the humor had faded, Dave spoke. "The book of Revelation has been studied by many. I have read the old texts. I see the prophesied events that mark the future course of history. This would be all that is needed, but because of my God-given ability, I have corroborating evidence. I sense deeply an upheaval coming, the power of the earth and the heavens soon to be shaken."

"Do you think the Rapture has occurred?" Tim knew the word *Rapture* was not in the Bible. To concede to its meaning was to admit to reading commentaries of the Protestant radicals—the forerunners of the Enslavers. The Church had banned the word hundreds of years ago.

"No, it *will* occur. You have in mind those sightings months ago. A trick of the Church to create doubt, confusion in its adversaries. Our group remains, formed before that day. None of us has gone. You have not gone anywhere."

Was the last sentence a subtle compliment? Genuine? Or of a probative nature? Dave had prior exposure to the Rapture concept and knew Tim's fears. Cut off thought, allow Dave no more access. Tim watched Dave's eyes narrow imperceptibly. No, not as much a compliment as a key into anxious places within the mind. John, Tim's brother, entered Tim's mind and was quickly dispelled. Dave's curiosity, upon touching Tim's hurts, backed away humbly, respectfully.

"Tim, following God isn't a formula for a life without struggle, nor is it a covenant where man dictates the terms and results, and God fulfills those terms and outcomes. Many people think of God as their supernatural helper to a life of riches, health—a genie as it were—and that is not God's purpose. Because people think they have done something for Him doesn't mean He's obligated to hand out rewards."

Dave's eyes were distant, as if listening to words not of himself coming out of him. Did he know of the Bible study? Or of the bitterness at losing one and possibly two homes, or the good life that had gone bad? Was he a conduit, unaware of the source of his revelations? How did he sense the need to make sense of all this? Tim spoke. "The Old Testament makes one believe this is the way it works: Do good—be rewarded. Do bad—be punished."

"Have you read Job? He doesn't fit that perfect model. Though in the end, God did reward him. But, yes, you have identified a prominent theme in the Old Testament, and it is valid because principles of living are the guides within this society's cultural and environmental givens. If you work hard, the chances are you will prosper. The system rewards hard work. If you have a good attitude about those around you, treat people fairly, chances are rewards will flow from such behavior. Who wants to promote a man they don't like on a personal level? Who will mention a business opportunity to a man who has been unkind to them?

Such principles only work when the hearts of men are responsive. You can work hard on some jobs, pour out your life's blood, and you won't be rewarded because the leadership has no concern for you, might even see you as a threat. You must live the principles, expecting nothing, just because they're true. Just because they please God. You have had setbacks in life, caused by the evil in men, not by an unfaithful God."

Dave felt Tim's hope fade into a resentment even as he watched the body slump and the eyes dim. He would say no more; a seed had been planted. Tim took a long pull on his bottle, decided to finish the remainder, tilting his head back. The alcohol broke through the tensions and rigors of the day, settled peacefully into his mind and body.

He was among friends. This might be the group. Dave had powers, was no charlatan. Love seemed to be the guiding principle. How could you go wrong with love? He snapped out of his peace, almost as if hearing a crackling in his mind, like the clapping of hands. Dave was probing his mind, gently, with kindness. No offense was taken, but a wariness returned. Tim spoke as he stood. "Time to go…have a long commute. I will begin the search for another home, but I would like to keep in contact with you." Tim realized he and Dave had never discussed Gramps's home.

Eagerness clung to Dave's voice. "This Sunday. Here. A meeting. One in the afternoon, then a picnic. Bring the family and swimsuits. Our help to you for remaining in your home is not dependent on your joining the congregation. Be prepared to leave your home for a time."

"Thanks for the foreknowledge. I know you don't do business like the world does." Tim offered his hand, and Dave shook gently. "I noticed your limp and your knuckles when you first walked through the door."

Tim laughed in amusement: Dave had purposely resolved that puzzle. Tim spoke softly. "Good night, pastor."

"Good night," was returned as softly.

Tim turned and walked out the door.

Bill was beside Tim as they stepped out into the cool air of the night. Bill said nothing of his pastor or his church as he drove Tim to the train station. No hard sell, no bragging about his pastor, content in his peace. The talk was casual—the pointing out of good restaurants, his kids' schools, where a man was murdered by a gang, and they hilariously chopped him into pieces. At the station, as Tim was readying to exit the vehicle, Bill said, "Can you find your way back to us?"

"Yes…but…" How would he enter the estate? Dave interrupted. "Just write with your finger the number twelve on the pad. Someone will pick you up. Good for Sunday only."

Tim laughed. "You read minds too?"

The smiles had yet to fade from their faces as Tim exited and was absorbed by the mass of commuters. His mind, which he had purposely attempted to keep blank in the car, as a precaution, was now set free. Dave could not pull out one thought pattern from so many people, even if his powers could reach this distance. Tim entered his commuter, only half filled, he chose a seat beside an old man. No gang members present, no obviously mentally deranged riders, no prostitutes—male or female—to annoy him. He settled into his mind and mused on the probing thoughts of Dave. How much did Dave know of him? Had Dave researched him on the web? A few hours of immediate memory? Days? Years? A lifetime? Hard facts? Emotions? What could block Dave's probing? Where was the limit? A spatial distance? Knowing the future was an entirely different matter than reading other peoples' minds. The future had a script, if it could be read? He had always assumed he would be defensive, offended by any intrusion into his mind. Such feelings had not occurred.

The women of the congregation probably adored Dave—handsome, muscular, caring. Strong morals were professed. Dave had the wisdom and the discipline not to use his admirers for sexual gratification. Once a woman had been used, Dave's hold over the others would be gone. Mary would be drawn to Dave, though she disdained men who attracted women. He supposed her ego saw her above the average woman, the swarming masses. He had been the exception, according to Mary, because he possessed humility. This really meant she thought she could manipulate him. What every woman wanted deep down—a man who lived life her way. Whatever she decided "life" was at the moment. He chuckled to himself at his cynical humor.

Who owned the estate where Dave worked? Did he support the group? If he did, then finding a home in the country wouldn't be a major problem—money was influence. Why would the group be interested in an antiquated Pennsylvania farmhouse? Maybe he overestimated the power of money. Strict laws applied to ag zones; the State's enforcement of ag laws was uncompromising. Perhaps, the farmhouse was less important than having Tim Johnson and his family as members of the congregation. That term *congregation* left him uneasy; he didn't know why. Yes, he did. Congregation meant *follower,* not *leader*; it meant being an ant amid a swarming pile of ants. Ants? He had seen a spring ant war on the ground beside Smith's vehicle at the mansion. The vagaries of the mind; better stick close to God, Timmy boy. Only *His* mind could you trust.

***

Dave awoke from his brief nap; probing new people was mentally exhausting. He had been interested in Tim Johnson the moment Bill had told of the Church's dislike of the man. The meeting had affirmed initial hopes. Tim was necessary for the group. Bill had the only leadership-caliber personality in the congregation, was the only trusted adviser. Given the size of the congregation, a second man was imperative. He wondered at Tim's injuries—from a confrontation in which Tim had done well. He knew this with certainty. Was it discipline that kept Tim from seeking praise or solace or simply fear of revealing too much of himself? Dave knew that 99 percent of the population would have shared the incident. Tim would probably overshadow Bill's leadership.

Bill's intellectual abilities and personality had grown; he had becoming daring, bold. Unbelievable when you saw his slouched appearance and gawking eyes. Could have been a fighter pilot—if not for that complaisance that might make enemies friends. Once in a system or a group and motivated, he performed, even had initiative, protective tendencies that were aggressive when necessary. Left alone, without a group, he was average man. Now he was a man hard to contain. That energy could be used to train Tim.

Tim had a keen mind, pragmatic values—the man was focused on surviving the future troubles. At the same time, he had a blindness, his hands reached out for God but could not find His form. Tim thought he was seeking an answer, a specific concrete fact, a key that would open the right door. There in the doorway would be God. Would Tim embrace God, or simply sneer? Dave smiled at the simplicity of the goal, yet all goals should be simple. Tim revealed his intelligence in his simple goal.

Tim's emotions were woven into the fabric of his family. He knew how to love, and he would be loyal. Dave longed to meet Tim's wife; she was quite a woman, judging by the emotion given her. This love that Tim had was not like the world's love, not possessive, not a support of his ego, it was giving love. Half the congregation was absent of such love. Tim was not living from his body as most did, for the gratification of self. Food, sex, ease, power—all were becoming muted in him. This disturbed Dave. Was this dying body a cause of depression, an absence of focus? This death force seemed almost like a person grafted to Tim. Dave understood that in himself he had no desire to take from the world, but he looked forward to life's pleasures even in the hard times coming. Tim was losing this desire. Very odd.

Admiration. Tim needed admiration, but he was wary of flattery. Tim wanted to be wanted. Self-worth? Strange that a man so much better than average needed such self-affirmation. Dave shook his head as if to scold himself. He knew he clung to his special ability—that was *his* self-worth. Without the ability, he would be a nobody as needy, as hungering as Tim.

***

Tim, vaguely aware he was on the commuter, sat quietly, without movement. The theology of Dave seemed sound. He doubted persecution by the State when more radical and troublesome groups existed. Yet, Pastor Dave, on the key issue, differed with Gramps and his brother. His brother and Gramps had said the good in man initially given by God had no purity. In fact, it was so tainted that it was worthless. Nothing good remained in man from God's original creation. Man, in his natural state, might want spirituality but not obedience, subservience to God. This was the big issue with them—the biggest. Basically, it was the dividing line between an Enslaver and everyone else. This reasoning was why John and Gramps insisted that Tim did not belong to Christ. Man needed to be born again—remade. Is that why Pastor Dave and his congregation had not been raptured? Just like all the other seemingly worthy people within the world, such as Stasic or himself and his family?

On the Rapture question, Dave's argument seemed fallacious: The Rapture hasn't occurred because God's people are still on Earth. We are God's people. Dave said the Church had perpetuated the hoax. Why? To scare up a few radicals from the general population? But Tim's knowledge of the inside politics was scanty—perhaps Dave was correct. Tim slipped into a mild sleep.

He exited at the main station. People packed tightly, so many smells—tobacco, marijuana, perfumes, talc, aftershaves, perspiration, leather, wool, synthetics. Noise. Another commuter, another seat. Dave had solved a spiritual problem, this idea that God owed him something. He had been wrong. God owed him nothing for the Bible study, nor for any other behavior. What was the advantage of knowing God? Perhaps there wasn't any. Or was the advantage a place in heaven, eternal life? Why did he always forget heaven, eternal life, as if they had no value? He didn't care for the philosophical sweets. Science, facts were his bread.

What did God want from him? Obedience—just obey. He was a good person. Back to square one. No, he understood God wasn't a genie, and you couldn't make up contracts and assume God signed them. If you followed God's principles, you probably would have a better life. Because of men's evil, such principles and the blessings flowing from them might be thwarted, postponed. He dozed again.

The bottom line was that he liked Dave and Bill, and what was told him was not radical, not outside his belief pattern. Love was the most important thing—love of life, your family, those of your group. Strong morals were second; the rest was theology, philosophy. Here was a group of people who would strengthen his family through the difficult times coming. Very little risk was attached, less than had been taken when he helped John and Gramps. He was safe as long as he kept a back door open, a way out. Eventually, he would have to make sense of this inherent goodness issue.

He walked dazedly into his house. The workday, the fight, the conversation with Stasic, the meeting with Dave had left him exhausted. The kids had finished their meal, their homework and watched the electrascreen. Mary had received his message on the compuphone as to why he would be later than expected. As she placed food on the table, she ranted about not joining a group of people just to remain in a farmhouse. He ate, showered, felt no more revived, went to bed. His hip still hurt. He had begun to limp by the time he had reached the house.

As he lay in bed, he thought upon the attack on the commuter. His fitness and martial arts training would have to begin in earnest, with his family participating. He needed weapons. He smiled at Stasic's admiration. Good to be admired again. Yes, he had done well. Carl…he would contact Carl Stasic. He must explore all options. Thank God tomorrow was Saturday. He slept.

CHAPTER 7

Tim awoke without the aid of the alarm. The light of the just-risen sun passed through the woods, broke into beams, penetrated the master bedroom window. The far wall soaked in the light, as did the covers over his feet. On the spacious lawn around their home, the robins were singing or aggressively forewarning territorial rivals. How many people had the luxury of sunlight streaming through their windows? Few. High-rises, the predominant architecture, blocked sunlight from smaller buildings and each other. Their professor's home in New York had been overshadowed by surrounding buildings a quarter of a mile away.

He would miss this home. No sounds of traffic or of the affairs of men. This morning, not even the sound of an ag machine in some distant field. He wished the sunlight's heat to penetrate the covers, bring warmth to his feet. The sunlight, the robins promised summer, life, hope. His hip pain seemed to have subsided if not disappeared, and this too raised his spirits. Mary lay across from him, curled up, her habitual sleep position. Her dark hair, eyebrows, and eyelashes contrasted against the white of her skin and pillow.

She had always reminded him of an angel in sleep, untroubled, pure. Would she have any residual anger from his meeting with Smith? She was by nature forgiving, but it seemed lately an irritation had developed. Why shouldn't the stress of their unsettled lives affect her? He flicked the electrascreen on to the news channel, kept the sound off. The scenes of riots, insurrections, wars in city and countryside; in tropical, desert, and temperate climes sped by his eyes.

When had Katie and Matthew mentioned a possibility of an African war? He remembered one in Africa and two in central Asia. Now, the entire world had erupted in war, wars between nations, wars between ethnic groups, wars of religion, wars of politics, wars for natural resources or access to the sea lanes. Peace, the white horse of the apocalypse, had been the first horseman, a peace so brief few had noticed. Now, the second horseman, the red horse of war, galloped over the earth.

Pulsing through the rapid, hectic scenes of destruction and misery was the unchanging stock footage of the Federation's capitol building. The hope for an end to all this conflict was tied to this building and the leader within. Each day new pronouncements were made and new footage of the world's hope, the president of the Federation, was shown. Humanity and war were inseparable. He turned the screen off, listened for his kids still sleeping. Pastor Dave had said some catastrophe would be happening soon, within months. Was the time really upon them? He moved quietly to the window. A twinge of pain coursed through his hip. The dark-green grass on the spacious lawn sparkled in dew. Genetically uniform in height, the grass never had to be cut. A herd of deer fed near the wood line. The sunlight's warmth felt good on his face. How many times had Gramps watched the deer from this window, felt the early morning sunlight on his face?

"Show me the way, Gramps?" He spoke under his breath. Gramps couldn't show him the way; no one came back from the grave, though many had claimed as much. Christ came back, gave the Holy Spirit to mankind, before again leaving for His place by the Father.

"Holy Spirit," he said softly, tickled with appreciation and wonder by the idea of the cosmic ghost, yet wishing for God's Spirit to be real and to infuse him. "Show me the way." Gramps had decidedly pointed in a direction while he had lived, a direction buried in uncomfortable memories of many discussions and arguments.

Yes, the Holy Spirit must be the key. How many times had he been told the Spirit was not within him? His brother had said, "We must die with Him and be raised with Him." Christ had to impart wisdom within a man and give him the drive to live it. He had been greatly affected by Proverbs and the Psalms—their power and wisdom were undeniable and constantly intruded…no, *appeared* within his thought processes. But where was man and what was a man if a rebirth was necessary? This fact, that a man must lose himself, irked him. Diana, his brother's friend, had said, "The Lord presented me with choices, my life or His life. I kept following Him till I had left me behind." Why did Christ have to fill him when God's guidance was enough? God's guidance wasn't enough was the obvious answer.

Tim moved quietly from the room. The Bible study, after Isaiah, had bogged down in the prophets, would need to be revived. Go directly to the Gospels—that's where the Holy Spirit was expounded upon in profusion; then Acts and the rest of the Epistles, where He worked in the new believer's lives when Christ returned to heaven. Tim looked in on Katie. The thumb was not in the mouth; one little victory. He moved down the hall to Matthew's room. Matthew was propped up in bed, listening to something through headphones. His thick, black hair was wild, curling, looping in all directions; his eyes still heavy with sleep. Mat pulled the headphones off. "We're still going?"

"Yes, after breakfast, so just relax."

"Okay." The headphones went back on. They had planned to go into the city to check on military items offered for sale. Matthew enjoyed these forays immensely.

Mary was sitting up in bed, watching her morning show of weather and news, when he returned. Her lips and cheeks always appeared puffy in the morning; the lips seemed to pout. The look never failed to stir his passion. He propped his pillows up beside hers, lay close. He loved the smell of her skin and her breath. She cuddled beside her husband, placed her hand on his hard chest. She sensed deep thoughts upon his mind.

"Talk. I know something is bothering you."

He shook his head, perplexed. "How do you always know?"

"That's my secret." Her hand slipped to his stomach, began a slow caressing.

"The group Smith belongs to is not a cult; it's more like what the Church might have been hundreds of years ago. They are Christian. Their pastor, Dave, does have uncanny powers. I'd like you to meet him. If you think he's unsafe, we won't have anything more to do with his congregation." He knew Dave would win her over.

His acquiescent attitude gave her a wariness. "Sure." She answered just to confuse him. "Will they help us keep the house?"

"They will try, but they think we should be searching." Tim felt Mary's sigh of relief. She had never liked the house. The electrascreen hypnotized him.

"Well? What else? You've got more on your mind."

"I met another man, by accident, on the commuter. Carl Stasic. I think he is a man of influence. Met him after an ugly incident on the commuter with gang members."

"Are you alright?" Her voice revealed no emotion. She hadn't noticed any external damage. His emotional state last night and this morning seemed steady.

"My hip hurts a little; it's nothing. My fists are healing nicely."

She gently placed her hands upon his and moved his fingers, examining. Why hadn't she noticed? She waited for more information. Silence. He was a tough guy, and she liked it. "So, what else?"

"Why do you think there is something else?"

"Because I know you, stupid."

"You think you do." For the first time in his life, her affectionate *stupid* hurt; life seemed to be proving the term true. His hand reached under her armpit, she jerked wildly, grabbing his arm.

"Okay. Okay. I don't…I don't. I don't know you." Her words came quickly; she had an extreme ticklishness.

"That's more like it," he said. "Show me respect, let me remain unfathomable, and I'll tell you the rest."

"I knew it," she whispered.

He cherished the fact she knew him so well. "Dave, the pastor, mentioned they weren't Enslavers. This is good for us, as his group won't be on the State's prosecution hit list. They don't believe in anything but one-man, one-woman marriages, but they don't write their beliefs out or attempt to proselytize. We will need the support of a group."

She let that thought alone. Better for him to think they were in agreement as to the future.

He said, "You just want to safely buy time till my theories prove false."

"Yes, and *safely* is the key." She sensed a brooding frustration building within him.

"At one point I made a list of the differences I and the Church had with Gramps, John, Diana. I have it somewhere…the desk."

He began to lift himself out of bed.

She held his waist. "Don't look now. Just tell me what you remember."

He settled back into bed.

"Enslavers believe the world is Satan's kingdom…usurped from God. The Church believes this world is God's kingdom, and an annoying force of evil is present upon us. Enslavers believe man's inherent evil is held in check by law and conscience. Which, by the way, convicts and confronts us with our sin nature. That is how we can know our true state. Enslavers believe in archaic laws; the Church, in rational thought. The Church believes evil is held in check by knowledge and will. Humanity's evil is controlled by the environment, social or genetic, and can be controlled, altered, or eradicated by reshaping the environment. Enslavers believe guilt is a reflex action to evil behavior. The Church believes guilt is a product of self-hatred, to be rid of by lessening condemnatory laws, by understanding the forces that control us. Enslavers believe God is King, Master of their lives, and they are servants, slaves. The Church believes God is our partner in life, aiding, helping us with our goals. He serves us."

A stillness came upon the room. He was amazed that his little list, made the first week after his brother's disappearance, had taken root. Mary pondered the Enslaver doctrine as presented by Tim. A discomfort clung to her. She wished to speak, comment, but could not utter a word. For every argument or question she wished to present, she saw the counter argument or answer. What was this about law and conscience proving estrangement? Nonsense.

Enslaver doctrine was so alien—they lived in a world upside down to hers, if what Tim told her was correct. How could you function believing such things? Gramps had been a kindly old man, lived a lifetime with such beliefs with seemingly little harm done. Tim's brother had been different, though she hadn't known him well. His beliefs seemed to have led to a course of action that could only bring unhappiness and death. His girlfriend, Diana, another unknown, had clung to him and met the same fate.

Tim spoke. "From what I understand, law and conscience create guilt, a disgust at one's own imperfectness, which leads to a loathing of one's life. This loathing leads to a death experience of self, whereby Christ can come and live within, recreating you through the power of the Holy Spirit. Christ the Master, you the slave. You follow meekly. Whatever this invisible force tells you to do, you do. That was their complaint with me—that I had not let Christ in, did not allow the Holy Spirit to work within. I remember a Bible passage Diana quoted to me, 'But as many as receive him, to them he gave the power to become the sons of God, even to them that believe on his name: which were born not of blood, nor the will of the flesh, nor the will of man, but of God.'"

Mary rose from the covers, propped herself against the headboard, sat with a straight back, fully attentive. Tim had himself and her totally mired in his rambling knowledge. Her hand grasped his forearm, her fingers applied pressure. "Slow down, Tim. You remind me of Mat in his first soccer game. Remember when he stood unmoving as the ball and the players swarmed past him. His mind flooded with what he should and shouldn't do—and the coach yelled out, 'One step at a time, Mat. Keep your position. Get the ball back and pass it to someone down the field.' Forget all this Enslaver talk and theory. Forget what you think John and Gramps were thinking or you thought they were thinking. Listen to the coach who, in this case, invented the game."

"I need knowledge."

"No, you need to listen to the voice of the coach. Find out who God is, His character. Let's move straight to the Gospels—straight from the coach's mouth. You use the past and this Enslaver theology as if it were a clue. We don't need a clue. We have the manual." She had scanned through the New Testament prior to the Bible study. Enslaver beliefs were likely built on misinterpreted passages. Christ telling the rabbi he must be born a second time. Take that out of context, make it the center-piece of your philosophy, and skewed results were inevitable. She had simplified the intellectual mess through a sports metaphor—sports he liked. Tim liked having objectives to fulfill, and he liked results. Do what Christ tells you to do and be happy. Period. Tim was not an intellectual; he would snap out of his funk and confusion as long has he had concrete plans. Whether these were sound plans really wasn't the issue, as long as they were safe plans for her family. Who could really know the mind of God? Did He even have a mind like ours?

Tim continued speaking. "The process has something to do with con-trol, with letting go of ourselves. I can't give God more than I have giv-en, so it must be beyond will. I just can't grasp it."

She heard his frustration, an intellectual puzzlement. She spoke.

"The key issue here is: Are we seeking God's control over our lives, His will instead of ours? Has a nebulous quality to me, like holding onto the deeper brain waves in meditation or the highest levels of Buddhism.

Seeking some unconscious state where God lives or where He can live within us. We should be asking: Are we listening to the coach and following his directions?"

"There was nothing subconscious about Gramps or my brother—no blank stares, no repetitious phrases. They had full use of their faculties. They were just on another plane of reality."

Her husband thought it necessary to grope through a psychological maze with no destination. God was a force in place called heaven, somewhere in your mind and in space. You belonged to Him or Her or It at birth, and if you remembered that fact through the course of your life, you would be happier. In turn God placed good things before you, both emotional and material. You had to have the proper attitude to take the good from life; God wasn't casting these things down from heaven. God didn't want anything from you but for you to enjoy life and know He or She was the giver. Enslavers said the world wasn't good, nor was life on Earth. They said people weren't good, and you must run to this strange god and be a slave. Enslavers said her world, her life, which she loved, was a lie. They seemed to be negative, fearful people, lacking confidence, full of self-hatred. But she would remain silent; Tim must reach his conclusions on his own.

"Tim, how do we know when we've reached this other reality or destination in our relationship with God? Feelings? Emotions?"

"I don't know how we will know, but we will know."

He hoped his voice projected confidence, certainty.

He felt nothing but confusion. His concentration was drained by the nagging possibility that the troubles were soon to begin in their city.

***

Tim and Matthew sat at the rear of the empty city-bound commuter. Matthew enjoyed his father's companionship, liked the absence of Katie and his mother. He felt secure with his dad and strangely free, though Dad didn't let him get away with anything. With his mother or Katie, he felt a protectiveness that he was unsure he could provide. He was in the male world when he was with his father. Dad protected him, and so he was free from those responsibilities. He only had to obey Dad. They could talk of sports, the outdoors, guns; he could ask questions about life or just watch his father and learn. On this trip, Mat knew Dad was interested in food rations; he was hoping for a canteen.

At the first stop, a suburban station, the car was inundated by drowsy mothers with their gifted and precocious children. Saturday was the day of classes, practices, and tournaments—swimming, gymnastics, archery, ad infinitum, and every game played with a ball, from golf to soccer; of lessons on musical instruments, in art, singing, acting, and dance. These children would enjoy life, contribute, find that special niche where they would excel, and perhaps find fame and riches. Scattered among the crowd appeared to be those merely on shopping adventures or attending appointments with physicians, dentists, or specialists.

Four teenaged girls, engaged in animated, coarse conversation, sat in front of Tim and Mat. The girls' high-pitched laughter and giggling, their rapid gushes of words, well laced with curses, described coitus, male sexual members, their sexual partners. Tim sat calmly, wondering why the conversation goaded his peace. He had heard such talk all his life; why now did it seem rude, filthy? Was it because his son could hear? Was it because he remembered a time when the public place was considered off limits to sexual content? He no more wanted to hear their talk than he wanted to see them squat and defecate on the public, open-air commodes that passed his view. Matthew showed no interest in the conversation. His head and body were in constant movement as he looked out the window. The sun had disappeared, replaced by heavy rain clouds. In another hour, the car would have commuters standing in the aisles.

Tim thought upon Mary's coach analogy and Matthew's first soccer game. She had been correct—he was overthinking. He had to trust God with the big picture. He needed to concentrate on his little steps. He needed to know the heart of God, his coach, and thought back to his first assessment of Bill Smith, Pastor Dave's man. God likely was searching Tim Johnson's heart, his assessment already formed—hopefully with love and kindness. Probably God saw a man clinging to Himself because he was afraid to die. No, he needed to see his family live with God into eternity. God was good. With God is where they needed to be.

At the second stop, Tim noticed a familiar figure enter the car—a man, perhaps ten years older, who took the commuter into work on weekdays. The man had, from the first, greeted Tim with a glare. One morning, Tim had greeted the man with a "good morning," wishing to explore the man and his motivations. The man had smirked, a smirk containing loathing, superiority, repugnance, contempt. A stare of unyielding hatred always followed the smirk.

Tim hoped the man had not seen him. Eventually, his patience would break, and he would confront the man, even if only with his own long, loathing stare. Not today, not with his son along. The possibility of violence was great with the undiagnosed mentally ill. Before sitting, the man gazed down the aisle and spotted Tim. The eyes beamed with surprise, loathing, then rested on Matthew. Matthew, seeing the gaze, felt the evil and squirmed uncomfortably.

"What's his problem, Dad?"

"Hopefully, he has a psychiatrist who knows. He's invented some hatred against me. I see him every day on this commuter line."

"Why does he hate you?"

"Feelings of inferiority or superiority? I might look like someone he's hated in the past. He's sick, doesn't see me for who I am. Just ignore him. You can't be respected by everyone."

Matthew had heard that line often from his father. His school experiences had taught him the truth of the statement. Some people at school disliked him. Why? He didn't know, but it was a fact. He had believed people matured out of such weirdness when they became adults, but now he knew they did not. Matthew shrugged the man's stare from his mind. His dad didn't even seem bothered.

Matthew turned his attention outward, through the rain-streaked windows. Men, dressed in yellow rain gear, were harvesting one of the fishponds of the old riverbed. A crane lifted a huge net. Fish bellies flashed white, silver; water gushed from the net. The crane leaned forward under the weight. The clouds were low over the flatness of the riverbed. The clouds, firm, gray had a beauty. It was good to look out at the wet land and be warm and dry.

Huge barges moved on the river. Before he could think upon the barges, the commuter was in the chasm of high-rises. So much movement—pedestrians, traffic; so much light—signals, advertisements. He read the movie promos over the subterranean theaters. He marveled at the three-dimensional words and the moving images hanging in space.

Matthew's eyes were pulled to a rapidly moving object, a pedestrian dashing across the street. A car struck the man, the car bumper folded up, the plastic body crunched loudly and buckled. The car had automatically slowed when the sensors were activated, but the man had moved at incredible speed. Or maybe the sensors had been defective. All he remembered was the car stuttering as if trying to stop, the man flying over the hood, and the car body reacting, then popping loudly back into form. The man lay motionless on the street.

"Dad. Look!"

Tim followed Matthew's pointing finger as the commuter slowed to a stop at an intersection. The vehicle involved in the accident moved quickly into the current of traffic activity. The throng of pedestrians flowed, uninterested in the prone, motionless man. A rapidly moving man darted out of the crowd to the victim's side. He bent down beside the victim, took an object from inside the victim's jacket. Standing, he stared only for a second, then savagely kicked the prone man in the groin. Matthew winced as the man melted into the throng. Vehicle traffic parted around the form, barely slowing.

"Nobody's helping him, Dad! Nobody!"

Shock, fear, betrayal, sadness clung to Matthew's quivering voice. Matthew held his gaze to the victim as the commuter picked up speed and moved away.

"Can't we get out here?"

Tim agonized at Matthew's plea. Those other people should have been helping the man or at least calling for help on their phones. Why weren't they? The person nearest the scene was legally responsible for contacting help. No one had moved toward the emergency box on the far side of the intersection. The boxes took the caller's ID, and no one wanted to get involved.

"By the time we get back there, someone else will have helped. Someone has probably already called the police. The crime cameras for certain caught it."

Matthew continued peering out the window, his hands cupped on the glass and around his eyes. "No one has stopped yet, Dad."

"We're too far away. Believe me, someone will help."

Tim didn't believe anyone would help. Police officers, yes, that was their job, and they were paid well—their payrate was equal to that of federal judges. Was the man dead or dying? The kick to the groin had probably broken the pelvic bone. Cruelty—no other word fit. *Cruelty* was a word only used in sermons at church. On the street, the term *justice* replaced *cruelty* and was common place. What could he have done to help? Maybe he wasn't any better than those who'd passed by. If he had been on the street, he would have at least made the emergency call.

"This is part of the bad times ahead, Mat. People not caring about each other."

"That man robbed him, kicked him for no reason."

"Maybe there was a reason. The two men knew each other, one was fleeing, an old score was settled. Maybe both were criminals. Maybe the one kicked was the bad guy."

Incidents like this had happened all through man's history and did not prove that the restraining influence of the Holy Spirit was leaving Earth. Matthew now sat back in his seat, visibly disturbed. Tim pondered his son's disturbance. Matthew was a good kid, a kid who believed you helped others in their time of need. If the adults had not stopped, then certainly they were not teaching their children to stop. Matthew was, in essence, a freak, an oddball in his generation. Holding such archaic beliefs, he could only come into conflict with society and suffer the consequences. Tim wondered whether he had done his son and daughter a disservice by teaching them such values. How could his children cope with the seven years that might be coming?

"Why did you think it right to help that man? Civics class? Did your teachers tell you it was right? Did Mom?"

"Dad! You helped that man back in New York, remember? When he broke his leg on the ice. Mom helps old people all the time at the supermarket. Remember that story about the good Samaritan?"

No mention of school, teachers, or civics classes. Only the Bible story—learned when they belonged to the Church and by the example of his parents. Tim searched his own memory. Yes, the good Samaritan story, Sunday school, Church sermons. They had just read it in their Bible study. Only 5 percent of the population admitted to attending Church services. Social responsibility and the character of love was waning rapidly. Tim shook his head in amazement. How much of their culture had been influenced by the Bible? Their laws, their ideas of right and wrong, the subtle everyday ethics they all used and expected and accepted as given? Or rather, *some* used. It was an archaic story, but it offered truth about man, his relationship with others, a building block of humanity and civilization.

From a story told by Christ. A story!

If everyone decided this story no longer epitomized the standard, then you were a fool to continue using the story as your code…an utter fool. Though the Church had worldwide influence and power, the people who belonged to the Church were few, and fewer still were those who sought standards of truth. Was it preferable to be a righteous fool or an uncaring wise man? Don't decide, let the situation decide, and hope there was no situation. Deep in his heart, he knew he preferred to be an uncaring wise man, untrue to his convictions. What if God asked him to act upon what he knew to be the truth, knowing it would bring heartache or trouble? Even inconvenience?

But if he didn't obey the truth, his conscience would ache. He would just be an animal in human form. He didn't want that ache; didn't want to leave what he knew to be true—and he didn't want his children to live a lie. He knew that this one thing—living the truth—would separate them from people, make them the oddballs, the hated ones.

"Yes, I remember the story of the good Samaritan. It is good to help others, and it is disappointing when people don't. But from now on, think first of yourself and your family. Be careful who you help. People are already acting differently; you might not be able to trust them or anything you see."

A noble thought: a man must cling to what he knows is right, even if no one else does, even if there isn't anything in it for him. In the future, such noble thoughts would get you killed. The pragmatic approach would work—you must know in your heart what is right but must not act upon it unless you are certain of reciprocal behavior.

"Why?"

"Because people will be out to take, to use you. What if you helped that man and then he sued you because you did something wrong? Or he accused you of something? What if that man had just robbed the other man of his wallet, and both were criminals? What if they were working together to rob someone who would help? Know what *right* is in your heart but be very wise if you intend to act upon it. I said there would be wars, and aren't there little wars all over the globe?"

"Yes."

"Didn't I say there would be famines, and haven't the famines grown?"

"Yes."

Matthew understood; his father could see the outcome of events, his father had wisdom. They continued in silence. Famines were growing to alarming proportions. The World Food Bank was nearly empty. The famines had created no problems in the United States. The Eastern lands were producing heavily, sending out a surplus, but not enough. In South America, Asia, Africa there was drought; thousands were dying. With governments unable to cope, small armies were forming, warring. When *hadn't* these parts of the world been starving?

Smirk man was still in his seat when it was time to exit. Anger coursed through Tim. He wasn't sure why—because something ugly had been revealed about his character? Because he was frustrated with philosophical meanderings? He would ignore the man, but he hoped for one untoward word, one caustic phrase, even one smirk. He wanted a confrontation. He could take him. The man was heavier, big shouldered, moved and walked like synthetic hormones had him pumped. This was a man who used his body at work. Perhaps he was stronger than Tim. Strength meant nothing against martial arts training and discipline.

The man was looking out the window; they passed. Tim looked back as he stepped off the commuter; the man had not noticed their departure. Tim cursed. When you want to confront evil, it turns away; when you are weak and vulnerable, it seeks you out. The confrontation would occur another day. He would only grow stronger till that time.

CHAPTER 8

The apartment building they sought was beside the commuter stop. They entered the foyer, which was dimmed by broken light fixtures. The tile floor was dirty, the air humid and unmoving. Tim and Matthew were whisked upward by the elevator. The building was middle aged. Tim noticed maintenance problems, a dinginess to walls and carpeting, water leak stains on floors and ceilings. The rates, posted on the elevator wall, were higher than average. He guessed the tenants to be retirees of slightly better-than-average means and working families living above their means.

On the top floor they took the time to look out the east and west windows of the hallway. A thick layer of clouds had torn apart over the building as if parting to avoid being raked over the sharp concrete. Underneath the clouds, showers passed over the land. The land was lush beyond the confines of the city, where the ag lands began. The fields, striped in various shades of green, depending on the crop, followed the contours of the earth. The river appeared as a narrow straight band of gray on which black barges slid. Along the river, within the old bed, the fishponds, geometric in precision, shone dully like dusky glass. Tim and Mat could see the first mountain ridge, hundreds of feet lower than their elevation, before the clouds closed their view. They discerned the square patterns of reforested land on the mountain sides, planted with different species—oaks, pines, bamboos, hemlocks, and hybrids, each with a distinct texture and shade of green.

The lush greenness softened the immense heap of concrete that rose from the east shore of the river and spread out upon the west shore. The crowded high-rises, interlinked by support spans and walkways, were streaked by the rain—some dark, some gray, some almost white, depending on the original color and the severity of rain. Below, people swarmed on the streets, in their vehicles, on commuters and passenger trains. The bridges spanning the river knew no cessation from the movement of traffic.

Matthew studied the trees in the city parks, along the roads, around buildings, and even atop flat roofs. The trees seemed few at ground level. From this vantage, the branches hid much of the work of men. When the light-spilling rip in the clouds passed, the land grew dark. A steady rain beat against the windows blurring the scenes below.

They walked the halls, searching for the apartment. The hallway's night-lights had activated. The air was humid and smelled of old carpet. They heard a woman cursing viciously. A door opened. The woman's face was contorted in anger, and she dragged a child, pulling him by his arm. The door, in a silent glide, closed. The cursing was unabated as she entered the elevator and was dropped to ground level. Tim and Matthew remained still till she had gone. Tim checked the number on the door where she had exited.

"Unfortunately, that's the apartment we want. Maybe not unfortunate. Let's suppose he's getting divorced. He needs money badly and in a hurry. That can work to our advantage."

Matthew listened and learned.

They were let in by a white man in an undershirt with a thick roll of fat circling his waist. He did not speak. The apartment was cool, the man sweaty. The eyes were bleary, glazed, weary, distraught. The man had drug problems. The military gear was scattered around the living room, even chamel—chameleon combat uniforms. Tim wondered if it was legal to sell such high-tech uniforms. In one corner sat boxes of rations stacked higher than a man. Matthew was among the gear, examining knives and wraparound canteens, when the man finally spoke.

"It all goes for the right price."

Tim perused the gear. Flak jackets, night scopes, rucksacks, web gear, winter and summer clothing, boots, shoes, sleeping bags, entrenching tools, water filtration bottles and systems, a tent, all in good condition. Turning to the man, he noticed the thick white arm held a tattoo of his military unit's crest. A second dark tattoo showed a skull and cross bones.

"Four hundred," Tim said.

The man hesitated, tensing momentarily, knowing what he had was worth hundreds of dollars more. "Go up a hundred and it's yours."

"Five hundred. Done. Weapons?" inquired Tim.

"I know better than that. I don't need a fifteen-to-life jail sentence."

Tim studied the eyes; the man was lying. He was being divorced, he had a drug habit, he needed money. A drug rehabilitation officer would find the weapons, or a divorce lawyer. The man had to sell.

"Matthew, gather up the gear. Put as many of the smaller items in the large bags and rucksacks as possible. We are going to talk in the kitchen."

Tim walked into the kitchen, the man following nervously.

"Look I know you have weapons. I'll give you a fair price. I've got a family; I'm not going to risk them by talking."

"How are you going to pay?"

"By bank card, the same as the other gear. We'll just print out a phony receipt."

"What if your records are scanned? How are you going to account for all this military gear?"

Accounts were routinely scanned by the local banking board under police order. The purchase of military items could be questioned, as the authorities were attempting to curb the power of gangs.

"Let's say you did work on my car." The man didn't know there wasn't a car, and neither would anyone scanning his account, unless they cross-checked motor vehicle registrations. He was certain vehicles weren't entered on the standard personal spreadsheet. "If that doesn't work, I am a geologist. I work in the field, in remote places. And my family takes outdoor vacations—camping trips."

The man studied Tim's eyes and then walked into the adjacent bedroom and closed the door behind Tim, who had followed. An aluminum army chest was pulled out from under the bed, the locks opened by code. Within, on top, embedded in a form-fitting soft plastic, was a machine pistol of the cartridgeless system, outdated twenty years ago by the laser. The cartridgeless or powder systems were still used by recreational shooters and security guards; the military and police used lasers. In poorer parts of the world, the military used the powder guns. The man handed the pistol to Tim. Tim felt the balance immediately, a quality weapon.

Underneath the pistol lay a double-barreled shotgun in two pieces, barrel and stock. The man snapped the pieces together with finality, as a man who knows weapons.

"Mint condition. Used for skeet."

Tim placed the machine pistol into the chest, after examining the barrel. He held the double. Both fine weapons. The sense of power was overwhelming. The man saw the glimmer of desire in Tim's eyes. Now he was dealing from a position of strength.

"No lasers?"

The man shook his head. "I ain't no fool. Selling illegal lasers is life. Even these arms will give you fifteen."

Tim studied the bleary eyes; he believed the man was being truthful. He had been hoping for a laser rifle. A rifle would give him a broad perimeter of defense around his home, necessary if attacked by a large group. A laser was silent; individuals separated from the group could be killed without the knowledge of the others. A laser would have been perfect for the night poaching of deer. With a laser, he would never be outgunned or out of ammunition—at least for a very long time.

"How many rounds?" He thought it unlikely he would be able to replace the ammunition, especially the machine pistol's, though it was a military caliber. The shotgun, a sporting weapon, would have more accessible ammunition. He could cultivate sportsman friends who could purchase or give him munitions. An owner of sporting arms had to have no criminal record, undergo psychological testing, be accepted into a registered sporting club where all weapons were kept, and pay a very unreasonable and discriminatory license fee. He wanted his weapon in his possession.

"Twenty-five shells for the shotgun, buckshot. Fifty rounds for the pistol."

"How much for both plus ammo?"

"Two thousand."

"Too high." Who used buckshot in a double for skeet?

"Make an offer."

"One thousand."

"Fifteen hundred."

"I'll never be able to get ammo for the pistol. Eleven hundred."

"Many collectors would like that pistol." The door alert resounded through the apartment. "Hold on."

The man left nervously but hopeful that another buyer—a man of lesser bargaining powers and greater need—was at the door.

Tim knew that a collector would like the pistol, a classic in mint condition, the rifling in the barrel still crisp. Yet, this seller was increasing his risk level by dickering with many buyers. People talked. Personally, Tim thought it unwise to show the weapon to more than two potential buyers. Through the partially closed bedroom door, Tim saw Stasic enter the living room. Tim moved into the living room, warily. Was this simply chance? Stasic's eyes lit up in happiness and surprise. Yes, just chance.

"We do have some things in common," Stasic said. "Buy anything yet?" Why would Tim Johnson want military gear?

"Bought all of it."

"Ah, well," he said remorsefully. Stasic glanced over the gear not yet loaded into rucksacks. "I probably have most of it."

Tim knew even now Stasic could place a higher bid and take it all. That was the way of business; an item wasn't legally yours till it was removed from the building of the former owner, or you had signed a bill of sale. Stasic watched the young man loading gear, assumed the kid to be Tim's son—the likeness was in the eyes, the cheekbones, the stance.

"Are you sure you won't make an offer?" The seller stood erect, puffed out his flabby chest. This was meant to assert his right to renegotiate and perhaps to intimidate Tim. He knew Tim wanted the arms badly, and this equipment deal would not impair the arms deal. Stasic saw Tim's dismay.

"No. You sold to a good man. I don't need any of this."

"Do any shooting?"

Stasic was surprised by the boldness of the question. This man must not have much to lose, must be desperate. Again, he saw the dismay in Tim's eyes. His organization had all the weapons needed; they owned a shooting club. He had his own collection, there would be other guns, he didn't wish to destroy Tim's happiness or potentially lose a promising member to his organization. Why did Tim want illegal guns? Had the incident on the commuter created a fear? Had Tim awakened to the truth? Did he already belong to an organization?

"No, none at all. But a word of advice. Sell to this man and be done with it. For all you know, I could be a State inspector." Stasic's tone was that of fatherly advice. His hand had gone to the shoulder of the man in sympathy and warmth. Stasic knew how to play people, thought Tim. No, Stasic was genuine, said another thought.

"Why don't you two conclude your business," Stasic said. "I'll help your son take these things down to your car."

"Thanks."

Stasic heard the sincerity of the thanks. This Johnson had the capacity for loyalty in addition to a cool head. What did he see in the future? Where did his intel come from?

When Tim emerged from the bedroom with the metal box firmly in his grip, Carl and Mat had made one trip down and had the remainder in their arms or upon their backs. As they entered the elevator, Tim confessed to Carl.

"We have no vehicle, Carl. That will be another day's purchase."

"Let me help you. To my car."

Carl was a man you couldn't refuse, an order both a suggestion and a pleading, held together by a promise of mirth, luck, excitement for all who remained in his aura. Carl smiled at Mat. Mat had directed the gear be placed in the foyer behind the welcome counter, never mentioning the absence of a vehicle, even when asked where the car was parked. Mat had slid the question easily. What were his words? "Let's put it here for now." The kid was smart, gave nothing away, but hadn't lied. Most kids would have volunteered that no vehicle existed. Might have been orders from his father; but why? Stasic smiled. The nonexistent vehicle might have been used as billing for the illegal weapons. He spoke.

"This isn't a free ride; you must accompany me to my home first. I have something important that must be picked up, delivered later today. A wise man would come along. No urgent commitments this morning?"

"None." Tim was flattered by Carl's inclusiveness. He had dreaded carrying illegal arms on the commuter—even though they were hidden. The bulk of the other items would have been problematic. He sensed by Carl's phrase, *a wise man* that something more was in store, something beneficial. Carl had proven he was out to help, not hinder, when he aided in acquiring the weapons.

"Then it is settled."

***

As they drove to the eastern outskirts of the city, Carl encouraged Tim to talk of his life. His professorship, John and Gramps, the problem with the Church. Carl listened attentively, asking short, pointed questions throughout the narrative, interjecting exclamations of surprise, support, indignation. When Tim had finished, Carl spoke.

"A man of your education, ability—collecting trash! I know the feeling. I was the president of my first company and principal stockholder, till I outbid a company with close ties to the Church. Then misfortune came—men quitting, men intimidated. Supplies and equipment not arriving, lost in transport. Demands being made that weren't on the contract. Lawyers holding work up in court. Within a month I was bankrupt, my company gone. The Church's favored company took over the job. I located the man who had caused the problems, a big man. Got him alone, beat the crap out of him."

"Did you go to jail?" asked Matthew incredulously. He had become fascinated with fights, violence, self-defense within the last year. Matthew liked Carl; Carl made him feel alive, important. Carl wanted to help. Carl was interesting.

"No, though I was attacked by a gang within the week, escaped serious injury. Getting that guy alone had been worth it," Carl said. "For the next year I was a laborer, back where I started, eating dust. I rose again, like your dad will rise, Mat.

104

"You see Tim, I am for God, for life, for the belief system, once espoused by the Church, that makes men something other than animals, raises them up. I am for the United States, our unique history and place in the world. That is the focus of my organization."

"You mentioned destroyers, malcontents in our first meeting." Tim wanted more.

"Yes, this country, the world, consists of two parts—the lawless and the law abiding. You can be rich or poor, of whatever race or nation or educational background, and there are only these two types. The people who want to make their own rules, the people whose personalities are bent on destruction are pulling everyone else down. Do you know you have a better chance of a physical confrontation with another in the streets of our cities than a soldier does with his enemy?"

Tim believed Carl's facts. What did Carl see in the future? Why was he interested in buying military gear?

"Why are some people lawless destroyers, Carl?" He wondered how close Carl's philosophy would come to that of Enslavers.

"A certain and large segment of society wants to hurt others simply for the pleasure it brings them. You understand that. Your place in line was taken, yes, but why weren't your antagonists satisfied? Why did they attack you?"

"Dad? You were attacked?" Matthew was off his seat, leaning into the front of the vehicle.

"Yes, on the commuter."

"He fought valiantly, Mat—held them off. Your dad has grit."

Mat sat back into his seat, awed and proud. He didn't know the word *grit* but knew it was good. Carl continued, "Some people are bored with life, imagining themselves disadvantaged and wronged, and only violence, criminal activity fill the void. Most like the power that comes when another is made to cringe. People who have no concept of love, social responsibility. Perhaps, they have been unloved, bullied themselves."

"Why can't we give them love?" Tim realized the impracticality of his words.

Carl snorted. "The other branch of our organization tries—free psychological evaluations, counseling, scholarships, loans for business ventures. No one wants these things. It is more satisfying to destroy, to hate. It comes naturally."

"Do you think that is the natural state of man, Carl? Hate and rebellion against authority?"

"I don't look that deep. I deal with what is."

"The future looks grim for us, then."

Carl smiled broadly. "I think you have come to that conclusion. I gather that idea has come from your brother and grandfather, though you didn't go into any detail, and I respect your right to privacy."

"Yes, it came from them. They felt as you, that humanity is no longer striving—men are becoming worse. The unalterable future is catastrophic."

"A social breakdown?" asked Carl.

"Yes, a breakdown."

"That's why you need the weapons?"

"Yes."

Carl laughed, turned his car to the open highway.

Tim tensed. "Aren't we going to your place?'

"No, that was an excuse. I really wanted to buy time to talk to you, to find out who you are. You belong in my group. With us, you will be taught what you need to know to survive. Interested?"

"Yes."

They drove east, along the first mountain, speeding down a narrow corridor flanked by green fields. Clouds, mist, fog clung to the green, puffy, forested slope of the mountain. Matthew watched as the wind currents, disturbed by the mountain, pushed the gray shreds of mist and clouds erratically. A torrent of rain engulfed the car. The headlights reached out, though it was late morning. Then the rain was gone.

To his left, the slopes recently had been harvested, and they looked brown and bedraggled. The erosion cover had not yet sprouted, nor had new trees been planted. A turtle was on the road, and they ran over it without a disturbance in the air cushion or the turtle. They came to a crossroads where ag buildings were clustered. They saw one enclosed tractor working a field, then they were gone, moving through the tunnel of green. At some point they turned off the macadam road onto gravel and headed toward the mountain.

"This was once a military base, hundreds of years ago. We still find artifacts, mortar rounds, powder casings, foundations to buildings."

Matthew's face was pressed against the window. The rain had stopped, the clouds were lifting. Carl put down the windows, and they moved slowly over the rough road. Matthew breathed deeply of the wet woods, so damp and cool. They came to a gate; Carl pushed a button on his dash. The gate opened.

"Dad. There are people hiding along the road."

Carl laughed. "Kids your age in war games, Mat."

They passed men in shorts, shirtless, wet, running in formation. The road ended in a wide clearing of carpet grass. Rain lay as droplets on the thick, spongy, short-bladed turf. A huge log structure, the first Matthew had seen, dominated the clearing. The American flag hung limply, waiting for drying breezes.

"Let's stretch our legs." With a finger push, Carl opened the car doors and deftly pivoted to a standing position. Tim and Mat exited and stood beside him. Across the expanse, in clusters, men, women, youths gathered around teachers and watched, learned, received instructions. Matthew saw people throwing knives, shooting laser rifles, building fires, running obstacle courses, rappelling from a tower. Suddenly the blast of shotguns echoed from the mountain. Tim noticed Matthew's eyes were alive. The faces were mostly white, but Blacks, Hispanics, Asians, and people of mixed races seemed to be half of those present. Carl, studying Tim's reaction to the scene, sensed Tim's thoughts.

"No prejudice here by race, color, nationality, ethnic origin, or ability. By character, values, content of the heart? Yes. We have orphans from State schools, and we have two-parent families with incomes of six figures. These people here…" Carl extended his hands to encompass the clearing. "Are those who want to live by the rules. It is strange; a person would rather belong to those who look like him, or dress like him, or have the same size home than those who think like him. The truth has little value today."

"What is truth, Carl?"

"Ultimate truth? Only God knows. But for us, here, I think it is enough that we live as if life is a miracle from God. We do all tasks to the best of our ability. We treat others as we would want to be treated. We believe in equality of opportunity. Then, when it is over, you can look your maker square in the eye without fear."

Tim understood that Carl's words had been memorized, he had given his personal code, the foundation of his life.

"Is there reason to fear God? Do you think He will judge us?"

Carl looked to the ground, thinking deeply, and then his head rose. "I know it."

"That's not a popular thought anymore, Carl."

"To each his own, but I know it to be true."

How close Carl was to Gramps and John, and yet he had no knowledge of their ideas. Carl was different from his brother and Gramps, taking the best life had to offer for himself, not searching to serve God or even needing a God or asking of Him, yet seemingly thankful to God. He certainly fulfilled the "do unto others" admonition. Tim had been correct in his first appraisal: God and life were the same to Carl. Tim realized that Carl, like himself, failed with "Love the Lord your God with all your heart, soul, mind, and strength." The revelation caused deep concern.

"Can we look around, Dad?"

"Carl?" Tim asked for his son.

"Certainly; follow me." Carl wondered if Tim was the man. Did he believe in a final justice? Carl longed for the day when all those who had been his enemies—the good people's enemies—received their just compensation.

As they walked, Tim spoke. "Carl, I'm going to be evicted from my home in sixty days. Do you know where I could find a place to live—inexpensive, isolated?" He wanted to test Carl's motives. Would Carl help, even though he had not expressed a desire to join Carl's organization? Carl smiled.

"Yes, amazingly, yes. A man came to me last week. He runs a warehouse, of which I am co-owner, in the warehouse district. Needs a security man he can trust. Actually, two, which means you could pick your shift, as another man has yet to be found. An apartment is built into the corner of the building. A pistol permit comes with the job if you pass the background check—which I'm sure you will—and take the course. We'll drive past it on the way back."

Someone was watching over Tim Johnson, thought Carl. What a coincidence that isolation was a requirement. Tim Johnson believed whatever social upheaval was to occur would be happening soon. Why did Tim think this? Carl's own intelligence arm saw only increased gang activity, riots; nothing more severe. An untraceable rumor persisted, like a subtle paranoia, among the population at large that bad times were coming. Tim Johnson had a hidden side that could remain his own. He was honest, decent, and would be a valuable member.

CHAPTER 9

With his legs spread wide upon the floor, Tim pushed his chest toward the carpet. His hamstrings barely complained, his hips felt loose, agile. The last stretch of the daily routine. Matthew and Katie, directly behind him, were eating breakfast. Mary, in the bathroom, was giving orders and admonitions to the kids for the coming day as she put on her makeup. The nearness of the kids broke into his peace. He didn't need a chair in his back, a foot on his fingers, breakfast in his hair. The cramped apartment would soon be only a memory.

He looked behind him when the quiet from the table grew prolonged—quiet sometimes meant trouble. They were contentedly eating, seeming hungrier than usual. A half day of school, then Katie had her soccer match and Matthew, an obstacle run at the Camp—the headquarters of Carl's group. He breathed in the smell, the texture, colors, of the homey little apartment. Three months at the most and they would have a proper home. To think it had been six months since Carl had mentioned a security job in the warehouse district!

Within a week the job had been secured, his family moved into the apartment. He worked security during the night, his incinerator job during the day. He had bought a car, had a pistol license only to have it revoked when weapon licenses, for political reasons, were revoked for what were deemed nonessential functions. Within weeks his friends, through Carl's organization, had found him a teaching job, earth sciences, at a private school. He quit the incineration job.

He kept the security position, Mary's part time job in geriatrics helped, they had saved. They would buy a condominium either on the outskirts of the city or in a satellite community within commuter rail distance. He had been back to the farmhouse; it sat empty; the restoration had not begun. The old location now seemed isolated, the home drab. To think that he had once believed that home to be his salvation. Life was good again, the anxieties of the past forgotten. The world situation was not good. What did he have to do with the world? God was on his side, the peace he felt was proof.

He could see Katie's long legs under the table. She was growing tall; the legs held a springiness and speed. She had above-normal reflexes, and in tight situations remained true to her training. She would win a soccer scholarship if she kept her health. Matthew had not developed speed, didn't have exceptional stamina. He had average strength, reflexes. He did have quickness and situational awareness. He had the respect of his teammates. He was a leader without effort. He had a lazy streak; yet, when others quit, he became energized. He made the right decisions at critical moments; he was a strategist. His physical gift was a strong, fast arm that could throw a football, a baseball, a soccer ball, a javelin. The object didn't matter—he could throw. He had grown tall, muscular, but still with the wiriness of youth. Both had good grades, with no weak subjects; they could be whatever they wished. But what could they wish if the world was ending? Anxiety and confusion returned.

Tim turned back, faced the electrascreen and the morning news. The world, at this moment in history, was in a sad condition. Famines were prevalent—caused by droughts and pestilences; the World Food Bank was empty. In the States, the situation had tensed when the European Federation had demanded a greater contribution to the Bank. Only a sickening compromise had averted war. Half of the US surplus was politically—and some believed militarily—forced to be given to the World Food Bank. One prolonged drought in the United States, and Americans would be feeling hunger.

A plague was ripping through Africa and the Middle East, followed by desperate wars between dictators. Travel bans and quarantines had been established globally. It was estimated that one-quarter of the earth's population would die from famine and war. He watched in horror footage of a pride of lions attacking a group of refugees in a tent camp. The lion pride broke necks, carried carcasses away. One lion sat down with its prize and tore chunks from thigh and buttocks. Tim turned away in revulsion. He had an instinctual hatred for carnivores that perceived humans as prey. His heart rate and anger would rise when the natural order had been perverted. Thankfully, the electrascreen's sound was off. The carnivores and scavengers had lost their fear of man, seeing so many bodies everywhere, unburied or dying. Truly, the vast herds of grazing animals had been devasted by their own plagues; the carnivores had no choice but human flesh.

Tim jumped up from the floor—the bathroom was open. Brush teeth, comb hair, check face for toothpaste, wild hairs on ears, or within nose. He closed his mind to the sufferings of others—foreigners. His life was good. He had worth in the community again, friends through Carl's club—the Order—and Pastor Dave's congregation. Dave and his wife, Noreen, had become close friends. Mary seemed to like Noreen, and Mary wasn't typically noted for hanging out with the girls. Dave had taught him less about God and more about his or mankind's willingness to make God in their image. Tim had strayed from his search for the character of God, but he did have money and therefore, hope for the future. His kids were healthy, physically strong, intelligent. His wife loved him.

Mary raced from the bedroom, out the door, the kids by her side. Tim wiped his face with a warm washcloth, speedily joined the exodus. They piled into their used car. They waved to Doug, the day security man coming to work, as they exited the warehouse-district gate. Outside the warehouse-district fence, across a wide grass field, sat the high-rises, occupied by those on the lower economic scale.

Tim noticed only two men outside the entrance, both sitting, their backs against a wall. He surmised they had slept in that position, too drugged to return to their apartments. Later in the afternoon, the gangs would form outside the buildings. Out of work men and women, seasonal workers or part-timers, or those who worked the night shift congregating to half-heartedly play sports, kick or throw a ball, play games of chance, talk, argue, share drugs, food, fight, have sex. He thought it a matter of time before an incident would occur between him and the gang members, who had yet to ask for money or a ride.

The traffic was heavy on the highways, the sheer numbers causing slowdowns. The faces in the vehicles were angry, frustrated, impatient, strained, bored. The pedestrian traffic was no less thick in the downtown corridor when he kissed his family good-bye. Mary took the kids to school, then to her workplace, where she had secure and free parking. A half briefcase day; he entered the crowds.

He felt a bag poke into his back, smelled the colognes, perfumes, soaps, fabric scents, hair conditioners, sprays, talc, body odors of the crowds. No prolonged conversations could be heard, just grunts, gasps, exclamations, directions, names. The vocabulary of the crowd was *get out of my way*, *move*, and curses so vile and potent they seemed a physical violence upon the mind. He knew these vile words came from forethought, from minds dwelling, festering in their flesh, their hurts. The words: *please*, *excuse me*, *pardon me* were no longer heard.

So many people with dark-brown faces, jet-black hair, in tattered clothes, on the fringes, in the quiet eddies. The refugees from South and Central America escaping the droughts and famines. No governments really existed below Mexico, only warlords who lasted a few months before a coup. Mexico existed as a country because of lavish American loans, which were in reality bribes. Many of the refugees coming across the border were aggressive, violent, swelling the prison population, but being fed. Why wasn't the government doing something? These people would find no work, they would drain food resources.

Unintentionally, Tim had allowed himself to be moved to the outside of the crowd. A dark-skinned man thrust out a worn hat. "Senor, Senor. Por favor." The eyes were angry, bloodshot, the words not pleading but demanding. Tim ignored the man. The man was behind, the crowd pulled Tim along. He jostled back into the center, looking through and over those bodies around him. He sought open spaces, used knots as interference, predicted the patterns ahead, the turnoffs, underground escalators, popular building entrances.

He went down into the subterranean city. He used overhead markers, advertisements to steer his course to that place on the commuter platform. He heard yelling, shouting to his left, the crowd surged back toward him. He glimpsed men fighting, white and Hispanic gangs? He saw terror in the eyes, hatred, blood on faces. The bodies, feet, arms moved at blurring speed toward their targets. Through the crowd he continued to forge ahead. All was still on the platform—no movement from the expectant passengers.

He entered his commuter car in a civilized manner, not pushed or shoved. Everyone found a seat. He was by the window, looking out as the cars departed. In a dark corner, around a pillar, in a small space some architect had wasted, he watched as a man spasmodically thrust himself into a transvestite. Her skirt raised, his hands on her waist, pressing into the flesh. Then the tunnel grew dark.

He sighed deeply. Maybe he did miss the peace of the farmhouse. Something had broken down in society. Gramps and his brother had said it would. He looked over the people in his car. His saw distrust, bitterness, paranoia, flights from reality, blankness, and fear; fear was hidden in everyone's features. Nonsense. Living in a large urban center was stressful, that is what he saw on the faces: stress. Good came from the city that made up for the stress—the material wealth, jobs, good and varied foods, clothing, people with stimulating work and lives, educational opportunities for the kids. Besides, here, you were a part of something, of humanity, of a society reaching for a goal. What goal? His mind went blank. Yes, what goal?

He was ready, his family was ready if the end came, or another Dark Age. Carl's group had taught them how to survive. Dave's group had brought them closer to God. The home Bible study had just completed the Gospels. He liked the Gospel of John. He looked for the magic tricks in Christ's miracles—not magic, but the altering of the physical to conform to Christ's desires. He was shocked at Christ's demanding tone for service. Pastor Dave attempted to smooth it all over, explain it away. But he didn't. To Mary's analogy—the coach, Jesus—was strict where Tim had been taught He was relaxed and relaxed where Tim had always been taught He was strict. All that he knew of Jesus from others—priests, pastors, scholars, knowledgeable laypersons—had been wrong. The Jesus he had discovered was angry. Why had everyone softened His words or concentrated on His mercy? The kids had little time between homework and their participation in sports. God would take them, or they would live through the bad times and create a better world. They were living right. He guessed the pale horse was riding the earth. He had forgotten the rest of the scenario.

The commuter car door opened, a gang of Caucasian men in white face entered—teens, twenties, a few in their thirties. They made no announcement. He watched as they began at the back of the car, talking to the passengers. The passengers calmly handed over personal items, cash, some even entered their account cards into a scanner. He wondered what the going rate was. These white-faced clowns were stealing. He had heard of such accounts on the news, now he would experience the thievery. He looked at the police cord at the end of the car, just as a gang member passed and stood guard by the cord. The same man was programming his phone, probably blocking calls to the police. Tim rummaged his pockets; he'd give his pocket knife to their cause. Certainly not his account information, he had no change. He had nothing else—no computer. He always transferred his daily lesson plans created at home to his work computer.

They gathered before him; he looked into their faces. The faces weren't hostile. They held out a hat, he placed his item within, they moved on. Someone must have appreciated the knife—handcrafted in Myanmar—as there were no complaints he should have given more. Like it was a regular job, like this was the way it was supposed to be. Who would resist, who would become violent? A watch, a personal item wasn't worth the effort. The white-faced men exited, and the last man from the car said, "Thanks." No one bothered to pull the cord once the group had left. Pull the cord, you had to wait for the police. Had to testify, make an appearance at court, risk retaliation. Life was too fast for such distractions and worries.

The commuter stopped. Off he went into the crowds, into the building, middle floors, the home of the Academy, his school. He could relax this morning. No classes scheduled, some lesson preparation, student profile cards, homework to look over, and counseling for anyone who wished.

The security device scanned his eyes, the doors opened, he entered the hallway. Students moving to their classes greeted him. He smiled as he heard the desirous tones in some of the girls' voices and realized with a start their desire should not be appreciated—various proverbs came to his consciousness. He entered his office, sat in his easy chair. A note on his computer, Jeremy Lines had taken a counseling time. Jeremy, what could he want? Good student, B+, big, strong, well proportioned, athlete, military academies anxious for him. Had a superior, arrogant air, or maybe just confident. Didn't they all, this generation? He supposed he had been the same.

He slipped into his worn sweater, made a pot of coffee. A pipe would go well with the coffee—reflective thoughts. He really wanted to smoke a pipe. He would look into this next week on his lunch break. He had noticed a tobacco shop on the building's ground floor. Carl smoked a pipe; the odor of burning pipe tobacco crawled into his mind and wouldn't leave. The smell of pipe tobacco was good, would fit his image perfectly.

He eased back into his chair, stared at the computer, the student's disks, couldn't make himself work today, half a day, Friday. The events for the afternoon and evening crowding his mind with pleasantness. First, the athletic events with his kids at Carl's Camp. Then a swim and supper at Dave's with the entire congregation. Perfect late-summer, almost-fall events, and the weather was cooperating, cool, dry, but warm in the sun. The pool was heated, the kids could swim into the evening. Should he be so content?

Life was worsening in the city; or was it? He saw fights daily, or squabbles, rudeness, coarseness on his commutes or if he ventured out at lunch. But his schedule had changed once he left the incinerator job. In that schedule, he had risen early, not worked with people, and his focus had been driving a truck and maneuvering the vehicle or himself around obstacles—no time to notice the world. Maybe he had been isolated from events, maybe everything was as it always had been.

A remembrance intruded—from a month ago—on the streets of the subterranean city, a parade celebrating bike week. He had left his office for a soft pretzel from his favorite vending booth. All the riders nude— men, women, children. A band of nonriding celebrants engaged in sex with the watching crowd and each other. Not a look of horror or shock upon any in the watching crowd, just delight and lust in their eyes. He remembered as a kid when his parents had stumbled across the bike week celebration and hustled him away. In those days, there was nudity but no sex.

Even as a professor in New York, he had been isolated on the campus, dealt primarily with students, not moving, working with the general population through the city. Maybe things were worse, but only due to overcrowding, the pace of life. No, the human mind was worse—barriers had fallen. How was public sex good? He knew in his heart the majority of people would retort with How was it not? When he was a kid growing up, he didn't have the memories of unremitting gang wars of extreme violence, open street sex, thievery, famine, drought. He was right with God—he could relax. Dave had said so, Dave taught inner peace. Dave had not talked about the angry Christ.

His door opened; the solid form of Jeremy filled the doorway. Jeremy smiled.

"I've got a free period," he said. "Could we talk earlier than scheduled?"

"Certainly. Come in. Coffee?"

"No thanks." Jeremy sat.

"What's on your mind, personal or business?" Tim looked at the solid, square jaw and face, the skull of thick bone, the small ears, narrow eyes, shaved haircut. The archetypal alpha male.

"Business. Particularly, my grade in your class." Jeremy's voice was confident, expectant. "It's not high enough, Mr. Johnson. If I am to make a mark in the military, I have to hit the service academies with a reputation."

"I can see where that's important." Tim sipped his coffee hungrily. He was dieting—too many soft pretzels; the coffee helped quell the hunger. "I assume you have already thought about longer study hours or a tutor?"

"I've got no time, Mr. Johnson. Every moment I'm not engaged in athletics goes to study. I don't even watch the news in the evenings. I have no friends, no social life."

"I see." Jeremy was a hardworking student, probably deserved a break. "So, as a favor to you, you want me to raise your grade?"

"Yes. That's a small favor. My parents help pay your salary, as do all the parents. If your students do well, you do well on evaluations—the teaching record."

"Have you asked this of others here?" He might not mind doing Jeremy a favor—if others had not. But for everyone to be raising his grades would be a travesty of the system. Jeremy would appear to be something he was not.

Jeremy smiled broadly. "Now, *that* I won't answer."

Others had raised Jeremy's grades. He had been approached like this before in his teaching career. In private meetings with students, parents, or guardians he had been offered sex with male and female, offered money, rare gifts, vacations in exotic places. Daily, his students publicly joked, in seriousness, for him to raise grades. He had never given a grade a student didn't deserve. Society, civilization couldn't exist on a sham. However unfair the standards, standards needed to exist.

He didn't think it crude that Jeremy mentioned salary and parents. The kid was groping for leverage. Tim knew Jeremy's parents to be on the school board. Threatening a firing or dismissal, through the power of his parents, would have been offensive and a stepping over the line of right conduct.

"Jeremy, I would like to help you, but I have a code I must live by. If it is done for you, it must be done for everyone. Then we are all lying about ourselves. What good can come from that? What good can come from you pretending to know what you don't know?" He wished to see how Jeremy would answer. He could still be convinced to change the grade—he wanted to change the grade.

"I'm not interested in everyone else, Mr. Johnson. Most of life is pretending—acting. I know I have a career ahead of me, and I must dominate. No doubt, the majority—probably all—of my future classmates will have inflated records."

The voice was angry, confident, without any understanding of wrongness. Jeremy gazed haughtily upon the stooge known as Mr. Johnson, Johnson lived in a world of rules and thought rules gave order. It was only the size of your nuts in your sack and your willingness to follow the power that ruled. Jeremy knew his sack was the biggest. Tim allowed silence. If Jeremy had been humble, had suggested writing an extra paper, he would have gotten the grade. What could he say to make Jeremy understand? Suggest the paper. Jeremy broke the silence before Tim could offer the suggestion.

"I'm sure you know my parents are on the board."

"Have you discussed this situation with them?"

"Again, that question I won't answer."

Tim, knowing Jeremy's parents, thought it highly likely they would back their son. This job was too good to lose. He didn't need the aggravation with everything else happening in his life.

"You're so well liked here, Mr. Johnson, and with a salary far above the others."

How did Jeremy know his salary? This was confidential. Had Jeremy's parents talked? Still, he said nothing, waiting to see what other stratagems Jeremy would use.

Jeremy's eyes narrowed, they held hate and arrogance, the waiting was playing on his patience. "Well? It's apparent what you have to do."

The tone of voice was calling Tim stupid, a moron, a man who didn't know who held the power over him. This boy, yes, boy's arrogance irritated him. Still, he kept silent. Jeremy rose from his seat in a rage, leaned over the table into Tim's face.

"Can I help you understand?"

"I suggest you sit down in your seat before I help *you* understand." Tim realized his error immediately: a latent threat of physical action had been introduced by his words.

Jeremy pushed the desk into Tim, lunged for Tim's sweater collar with his hands. Jeremy the wrestler. Tim kicked the desk with both feet and rolled out from behind the desk on his wheeled chair, turning away. Jeremy's hands caught the back of his sweater, stretching and ripping it. Tim stood in the center of the room. Here, there was room to kick, to maneuver. Common sense, restraint, propriety had snapped. He wished to destroy this young, arrogant punk.

"Come on, Jeremy. Come on…" Tim's hand gestures, hands extended, fingers ridged, snapping back to the palm, invited a closing of the gap.

Jeremy stood erect, began to chuckle—the old stooge thought he was a man. Delusions. "Okay, okay. I apologize. But you see how much it means to me. You've got a comfortable life here. Why ruin it?" Jeremy moved toward the door, was halfway out before turning. "Think it over, Mr. Johnson. Give me an answer on Monday." Jeremy smiled and left, as if nothing but a pleasant conversation had occurred.

Tim ran to the doorway and called down the hall. "Jeremy come back, there's more to say." His voice was pleading. Not from fear of reprisal or embarrassment for the actions that had just occurred. But because Jeremy was a child in a man's body. Jeremy had no understanding of how conflicts were to be resolved. The one man who could have taught Jeremy had overreacted and become an adolescent himself. Through this failure of knowledge, Tim glimpsed the lostness of Jeremy—perhaps of Jeremy's entire generation.

Jeremy stopped, turned, began walking back with a smile on his face. It was all about cock, and his cock was the biggest. Mr. Johnson would concede—a little force always worked. "Yes?" Jeremy said, approaching within feet of his teacher.

"Let us sit and talk calmly, just for a moment." Tim's outstretched hand offered the doorway into his office. He reflected upon the many times in the past when he had been involved in these types of meetings. This meeting felt different; his soul—or was it his persona—seemed in a different place.

The two men sat in their respective seats. Tim's mind was filled with a sadness, not for the events of just minutes before, but because within these he felt sadness for a world about to perish. The thought of the world's end was crushing down upon him. "Jeremy. We don't know what the future holds. You have chosen a career where death will always be a real possibility. We should not hold grudges, and we should demand integrity from ourselves through and by the grace of our God, who wants the very best for us." Tim stopped and gazed upon Jeremy, who was smirking. Tim sensed Jeremy's death would be soon. An overwhelming compassion overrode his common sense. "Do you have a commitment to God, Jeremy?"

"I don't know where you're going with this…but I suggest you stop. There is no God, and therefore God is irrelevant to this and all situations. It is not your duty or place to talk of this." The weak and the stupid always turned to their imaginations. He had halfway respected Mr. Johnson until now.

"Suffer my remarks, as I do care about you and your future. You must find this God you don't believe in for the sake of your character and decisions—"

"I'm out of here." Jeremy rose with contempt in his motions and disgust in his tone and walked out of the office.

Tim straightened the office, began to write a letter to the school board about the incident, then stopped. In his college professorship, he had never had a student press the limits to physical assault. He'd had the law on his side until he had mentioned his personal creed. No, that was allowed. His offense was that he had mentioned God. Proselytizing. Why had he mentioned God? Why had he spoken those words that he felt but were not his? For whatever reason he had spoken, and it was done. Own it, Tim.

Was Jeremy's attempt caused by his youth or something deeper as to the state of the country? Tim did have a comfortable life, and that life may soon end—along with the world. He was shaking with rage, energy brought to his muscles but not dissipated through release. His day in his office was ruined. He needed physical movement to bring equanimity to mind and soul. He placed his sweater on his chair back, closed and locked his office door. He exited the school, found the tobacco shop on a subterranean floor, chose himself the perfect pipe. He would take the commuter to Mary's workplace, instead of her picking him up.

By the time his commuter had reached Mary's workplace, the geriatrics center, he had decided to give Jeremy the grade—for a paper on any topic. Jeremy would be gone in a few months. Why risk everything over one person of questionable character? He saw his acquiescence as a microcosm of the fall of humanity—society; once the collapse began you could only get out of the way and watch it fall. Critical mass. He walked up the steps, through the parking building, ignoring the elevator. The exercise helped calm him. Mary's car was not in her allotted slot. She had no reason to be anywhere but work.

He sat in the little park used by the oldsters for exercise. Well landscaped, with a flowing stream and fountain, and sound barriers around the perimeter. If it weren't for the buildings towering on all sides, blocking the sun, he would have thought himself in the country. The park was without a breeze. Though the sky was hazy, the heat brought perspiration. He took off his shirt, sat in the sun-reflector section, tanned and smoked his pipe—turning on the hidden mini exhaust fan for the carcinogenic smoke.

He forgot to ask Mary where she had been as they drove to pick up the kids. She seemed distressed as he recounted the events of his day. It would all blow over. He didn't want the weekend to be ruined, or his life. Jeremy would have his higher grade in exchange for a paper. The paper would salve the conscience, keep honor intact.

CHAPTER 10

T his meeting will come to order." Carl's voice held authority and a reverence for the order of the fraternal club known as the Order. The men gathered in the room responded, pulling in their chairs, making one last run for a beer. Throats were cleared, coughs sounded, postures straightened. Tim took a seat in the circle, amazed at the number of men present—over one hundred. Men who had come singly, whose families were not involved in any of the events occurring that day. He had known nothing of the meeting. Carl had called him in from the soccer match almost casually. He had expected to see ten or twenty men gathered to discuss mundane business.

Though his mental equilibrium had been disturbed, distracted by the incident at work, he sensed that here, too, a moment of importance was building with as much power as the thunderstorm he had seen down the valley. Outside, Katie was engaged in her soccer match, Mary watching Katie and the sky. Matthew was somewhere on the mountain running the obstacle course with his age group. The weather warning system at the Camp tracked lightning strikes in real time. The men in charge were capable and would seek shelter in the numerous grounded lean-tos, if the electrical disrupter field could not handle the wattage of the storm. Carl seemed to wait for Tim's thoughts to return to the meeting, holding the attention of the men by staring into their eyes.

"For this meeting I invoke the pledge of secrecy of the third order." Carl's emotion caused his voice to crack. Men glanced at each other nervously, surprised, shocked; murmurs arose in the stillness of the wide room as bodies stiffened. These were men of high standing in the community, law enforcement officers, men of the judiciary—judges, lawyers, court officers, prison officials—businessmen, corporate executives, professors, teachers, school administrators, health professionals, doctors, surgeons. Secrecy of the third order had never been called in any of their lifetimes. The penalty for breaking secrecy under the third order was death.

"Such a motion cannot be presented until a statement of intent is given." The secretary, a bald man, a lawyer, intoned dryly, knowing that Carl knew, and had, by presenting the third order first, wished to establish a tone to the meeting.

"So be it. I wish to detail a plan to reestablish order within the city." Carl studied the faces of the crowd, searching for dissenters.

"Are there objections to sealing this statement with the third order of secrecy?" asked the secretary.

Tim had been jolted from his introversion. Reestablish order. Then others *did* believe the city had been digressing, no, falling into chaos. He had heard stories, complaints from everyone but just thought it was the norm for life in the city. Was the situation that bad? Carl had real power, these men around him had power. These discussions could get them in deep trouble with the State. Perhaps, Carl meant that by using political means, order could return through the offices of these men and their acquaintances. Why would the third order be needed for talks on politics? Carl was planning subversion, insurrection, some illegal act. Carl had been his friend, helped him in so many ways; he owed much to Carl, and yet he wasn't going to watch it disappear through an ill-conceived, unnecessary plan. Carl should have discussed this with him in private. Tim was jolted into the realization that he was not one of Carl's innermost circle—though he seemed to rate the second layer of friendship, for he was at this meeting. They—the men of the Order—had been playing the survival game too long, and now they wished to force life to conform to their illusion? Tim raised his hand.

"Speak," said the secretary.

Tim stood, spoke cautiously, respectfully. "I have great respect for Carl and his ideas. I don't have any problem with Carl's presentation—if no one else does. But couldn't we avoid trouble, inconvenience, heightened anxiety if we would lay aside the third order? I'm sure Carl doesn't want to present a course of action that is illegal—so why the third order?"

Carl did want to present something illegal. Tim looked over the faces of the men, heard no assents to his proposal. He saw few faces struggling with any moral dilemma; most expressions were of eagerness. Everyone owed Carl, or did everyone have that same belief? The secrecy must be appealing to the bored and the boyish. Carl was not a foolish man; he had been certain of his audience. What risks he was taking with his future! Even with secrecy, the threat of death, the possibilities this talk would find the ears of loyal men of the State was guaranteed.

"Our city is falling apart!" came an impassioned cry from one member.

"So is every city in the United States. Can't the duly elected authorities deal with the problems? We represent a large voting block; we have political power," Tim pleaded, determined to stand till he knew no one supported him.

Carl spoke. "Society is too fragmented for us to ever gain a majority—and that was done purposely—to destroy our voice in our democracy. The elected officials don't want to take the tough measures necessary to heal our country, they'd alienate their voters. The truth is, the good people are a minority and the evil, a majority. The original Constitution of the framers—which was that of a republic—was destroyed long ago. There is no protection from the self-interest of the masses—the urban dwellers—most of whom are unemployed, or the workers in government or high tech or the media. Or our educational system. They have been instilled with hatred for our economic system, our history, and our faith and ideals for generations. The old America is on her deathbed—her patriots are mocked and shamed, and the overwhelming majority of voters are bitter. The most brilliant political system ever devised is dead. It can't even be comprehended by the intellectual morons who now rule, for they don't understand who and what people are. The European Federation—as sick as our majority—will absorb and destroy what little is left. Is that what you want, Tim?"

Carl's thoughts continued, flowed like a river in force and majesty over the audience. Surging power ran through the historical precedents that had led to this moment, beginning with the first tampering of the Constitution—the voting away of the checks and balances system of the Electoral College, hundreds of years ago. The addition of territories, which should have been set free, as states. The packing of the judiciary with bogus ideological judges. The destruction of American history and its uniqueness and goodness. Citizenship to anyone crossing an open border. The constant propaganda of the media created a living deception—lies that became truisms.

"Shouldn't the battle of good and evil be played out through education, discourse?" Tim asked honestly but naïvely.

"The battle has been played out. Truth and all that was good lost," Carl bellowed angrily.

"If everyone else wants to live with the problems, why can't we?" Tim was dazed; he heard his own words speaking the opposite of what he truly believed.

"We're intelligent enough to know where these problems lead. Society is heading for a crash—one which will be permanent. This is the decisive moment. Let's hear what's occurring in our city. Anthony, you speak first." Carl pointed to a portly man of dignified bearing.

Tim realized Carl probably had a long line of speakers ready. It came to him that Carl had purposely not informed him of this meeting, and that Carl welcomed, if not planned on his opposition. Anthony, serene, with great presence, rose and spoke.

"I am the commander of the downtown precinct. Last week, unknown to the news media, a police officer was killed. He was set on fire, his burning body dismembered by machetes, by fifty to a hundred gang members. They chanted, shouted, laughed, hacked like fiends upon his flesh. Attack dogs were let loose on the still pulsing, twitching flesh to devour the pieces of what once was a man. All this on a major street in the middle of the day." Anthony's body was still, without emotion; only the words had emotion, power. "The State deemed the information too distressing for the public. Prior to this, oh, since last year, we've averaged one assault on an officer per day. Ten attempts at poisoning; one attempt through electrocution; one a hit and run with a desensored vehicle; five, I believe, were bomb attempts." Anthony sat; another man rose.

"I'm a judge in the third district. Half the cases involving gangs have been thrown out because witnesses would not testify or security-camera footage had been destroyed, even while it was in police custody. Rape, of men and women and children, is 200 percent higher than it was a year ago, as are homicides." He sat; another man rose.

"I'm a detective. Three-quarters of our City Council is involved in graft, codes violations, illegal drug selling, illegal prostitution, illegal gambling, unfair labor practices, code of business ethics violations." The man sat; another raised his hand.

"I second the invoking of the third order."

The secretary looked at Tim and no one else. "Any further discussion needed?" The secretary gazed upon the gathering, waiting for the cessation of turning heads and whispered conversation. "All in favor of invoking the third order, raise your hands." Everyone, including Tim, raised his hand. The secretary's voice boomed. "The third order is invoked. The subsequent conversations can only be communicated to members of good standing in only this local chapter. As I see that nearly three-quarters of our members aren't present, I would suggest no communication with those members until a grand forum is held."

The secretary established eye contact with chamber security. "Lock the doors. No one enters. All recording devices must be inactive." The secretary again studied the gathering then looked at Carl. "Go ahead, Carl."

Carl cleared his throat and spoke. "No one fears the law anymore, and there are so few laws to fear. The decent person carries the responsibility of their decency—no law is there to support them, to create an environment of safety and order. We must bring back fear to the criminal element. Only fear will cause criminals to curb their evil desires. Fear can only be achieved in two ways—mutilation or death. Incarceration is no deterrent to crime, and the funds for such an enterprise nonexistent. Taking away property, money, rights, and privileges has failed—cases get mired in appeals and we have insufficient funds to accomplish the work. Banishment from the Unites States is no option, for no country would take them."

Carl measured his audience. "Maiming, mutilating leaves the victim alive. We expose ourselves to recognition or to a victim whose desire for vengeance is stronger than his fear of further punishment—in effect, a desperate man would be more deadly than he was before being maimed.

"Dead men send a message to others of their kind. Dead men perpetrate no more crimes. We begin with the weakest gangs and move up the pyramid of power. Whom to kill comes from our intelligence squads, who have access to files. Calm, dispassionate weighing of the facts to determine who must die. Our hit squads must come from within our organization. They must be nerveless men whose passion for justice erases all emotional qualms.

"From buildings, vans, or the street, intelligence men identify the victim. The hit man on the street doesn't know who the victim is. He is told kill the man in the gray coat to his left. He does so. He is told to walk down the street, enter a white van. He does so.

"Gang members will soon seek safety in numbers. We will have justice squads of three men only, a communications man, a demolitions man, a marksman, all cross-trained. Groups of threes may be brought together for larger assignments. We have the men and firepower to annihilate gangs."

Tim realized that most of the men present had helped formulate the plans or knew of the desired goal; only a few of the hundred were hearing this for the first time. Had Carl had this idea in his head for years? Is that why Carl had so actively sought him? Had Carl seen the makings of a hit man in Tim during that commuter-car fight? No one was objecting, no one was angered, all were enthralled. Reality had suddenly changed. Tim was in confusion, unprepared. His grandfather, his brother had told him. He had seen society changing with his own eyes and had explained it away. He had believed the world was coming to an end, and he had not believed there would be an end. What illusionary world had he lived within?

Carl's voice echoed through the room. Dazed, Tim sat. Dazed, he rose from his chair at the meeting's end. Dazed, he shook Carl's hand and wandered off to find his wife and kids. He never digested the ending summation of Carl's speech—where this course of action would lead.

***

Tim and Mary shared a lounge chair within the informal gathering near the pool. Tim could see the roof of the manor house, the thick chimneys, the weather vanes towering above the ornamental trees. A slight but consistent wind played with the greenness of the swaying leaves. Pastor Dave and his wife, Noreen, were a part of the loosely formed circle of parents, children, grandparents. The younger members of the congregation were in or by the pool; adults were lifeguarding. Mat and Katie had both done well in their sporting events held at the Order's Camp. No other parents or children shared membership in both organizations. The kids still had plenty of energy for the swimming pool. Mary seemed distant from him—or was that caused by his own lingering state of shock and puzzlement? He could smell the chlorine, the water, the grass, the warmth that hovered in the air, though the sun had set. He smelled the hamburgers, steaks, chicken—fully half of the meat was genuine animal protein—cooking on the grills. The trees, over by the servant quarters, were full and billowy. Bats were cutting up the sky, lightning bugs flashed.

Dave was engaged in conversation with the others. Tim had discovered that Dave couldn't explore one mind while being occupied with another. Dave's powers with people were spatially limited, though powerful emotional surges could intrude upon him and seemed to have no spatial limitations. All this, he had learned on his own. Dave was disciplined when it came to talk of his powers, even under constant questioning, even when appealing to his ego. Dave kept the secrets of his powers tightly locked. Why? So that his power couldn't be manipulated or duplicated? Or from modesty? Or hidden so that no one would truly understand how much he knew or didn't know?

Dave had foretold of Tim's new teaching position, announcing it to Tim two weeks before it became official. All Tim had given Dave was that he had applied to an unnamed school. Dave, at that time, knew nothing about his involvement with Carl's group. Dave had not predicted Tim's warehouse job or the corner apartment that went with that position. At that time, Dave was predicting some upheaval that had never happened. Dave, when hearing of Tim's involvement in the Order, tried to persuade Tim to leave Carl's group, predicting trouble. Dave's complaints had been that Carl's group ignored the deeper aspects of a relationship with God, was political and power-centered, and would resort to aggressive behavior when passive restraint would win the day. Tim mused on this forewarning that had proven itself to be real. But was Dave's assessment that passive restraint should be the desired course correct? Tim knew action was necessary. Dave had never demanded, ordered, or pressed Tim to leave the organization.

Tim, watching Dave, sensed an unease. Was Dave picking up that unease from Tim? Was Tim seeing himself reflected back? Dave turned to Tim as if at an unconscious level he heard Tim's thoughts on the morning events with the Order. Tim spoke first. "Whatever you uncover, keep to yourself. Life and death are there."

Dave nodded in agreement. "Life and death will soon be everywhere." Dave moved his chair over to Tim, Noreen followed. Dave spoke sadly. "A time of persecution is near. It might be better if we leave this place."

"All of us?" Tim was shocked.

"All who have the faith."

"Why would we be persecuted?" Mary asked in disbelief.

"We shouldn't be. We are not enemies of the State, nor of anyone. The nature of persecutions is that the stated limits are always surpassed.

Once violence begins, it spreads. Tim, as a geologist who once traveled, certainly you know of remote places we can go, live in peace."

Tim squirmed in his seat. He was reminded of his brother, John, whom he had directed to a place in the dead zone. "Travel abroad has ceased under the quarantines. That limits us to the continental United States." Had Pastor Dave uncovered the memories of that time in the desert? This was a constant tension in a relationship with Dave, that he would see those things that should remain hidden. "One particular place was excellent for temporary safety. How long must we live at this site?" Tim used the inclusive "we" and wondered if Dave knew that "we" might be a lie.

"Years."

"More specific, if you can."

"Two or three years."

"Seven years is the number Gramps and my brother, John, said the world had left. They divided the seven in half for three and a half years of really horrendous living conditions at the end. This place I was thinking about is not self-sustaining, and the authorities know of it."

"His brother used it. I told you about that, Noreen," said Mary.

Tim was mildly displeased that Dave knew of the location. Noreen and Dave discussed everything. Mary had been the snitch. Dave had asked a question he knew the answer to. Dave had tested Tim. Tim showed no reaction.

"That it isn't self-sustaining is a problem now, but not later. Any other places that can support us for one or two years? Or supplement what rations we bring?"

"No. No other places. The place my brother stayed is it. There—that location—it depends on what you mean by support. Eke out a living at starvation level? Yes. If the land bureau people don't round us up as they should."

"What shelter and heat source would we need?"

"Tents year-round, though the winters would be nippy, if not rough. Unless habitable caves were found, or we dug into the ground. Regular camping gear, solar stoves or fuel."

"Could we take the entire congregation, 180 people?"

"The satellites would pick us up, the authorities would come. Unless we went underground."

"What would we grow?"

"Beans, corn, melons, peppers. The water is there, untapped because it was too little for commercial exploitation. The soil is good. But green fields show up from the air." Tim finally understood that Dave had no concern for the authorities knowing. Dave knew something else of the future he had not shared.

"Not all of the congregation have cars. We have large quantities of supplies to move." Dave was deep in thought, as if seeing the place.

"You wouldn't have any maps?" Dave asked.

"I might…I might." It was apparent the maps could be found on the internet. Dave didn't want to leave tracks on his computer for authorities to trail.

The group began breaking apart, as someone had announced supper was ready. A food line had already begun forming. "Let's eat," Dave said as he rose.

"We'll be along," Tim said softly. Dave's talk was frightening. The second frightening talk of the day. This sane, intelligent man was going to take more than a hundred people, including children—even infants—into the desert. Life was good. Why the sudden move? They had plenty of food stored. Persecution? His camping days were over; dirt, flies, every move or task an inconvenience. It had no appeal. He had a good job, friends other than in the congregation. He would be buying a condo soon. Carl was planning assassinations, street battles. People were acting strange. Something else bothered him about Dave, something said casually, something that sent a foreboding through him.

"Let's get something to eat, Tim," Mary insisted.

"Yes…yes…," he said distractedly.

***

Not until they were walking into their apartment, and his thoughts turned to the isolation and hominess of the farmhouse, did a realization emerge—a completion to his previous foreboding. Why had Dave appeared interested in the farmhouse years ago and now was ready to move the entire group away from the area? The answer: Dave had uncovered new information. Dave was totally reliant on sensing the future, not knowing the future. Dave, through his supernatural ability, picked up clues from his surroundings. Other men were the initiators; Dave simply reacted—and reacted so quickly that it appeared he had advance knowledge. Gramps hadn't sensed the future; Gramps *knew* the future, the future as told to him by the Bible.

Dave had said there was no reason for the group to be persecuted, but that it would be incidental to a general uncontrolled persecution. The Bible said the saints would be persecuted purposely, that group now known as Enslavers. He and his family should be persecuted. Persecution was a sign that he was on the right spiritual track.

He went into the bedroom, lay down. The stress of the day had taken a toll, he felt drained of strength. He had not really believed he would come to this point in time. As he planned for trouble, he had never really believed it would come. Two groups of average people, with spiritual or cultural leanings, reacting to trouble on the horizon. Gramps and John had told him of the troubles, told him of the Restraining One leaving. Now it seemed His leaving was causing concerns in the lives of ordinary men. Carl and his group knew the effects and even to a degree the causes but not the core reasons. Dave, through probing the minds of others, sensed the disturbance coming and a vacuum caused by the absence of restraint, though he gave it no name. Man wasn't going to conquer the troubles ahead.

Tim was no closer to finding that elusive knowledge or experience that would make his family acceptable. Where had he gone wrong? The search for God had been lost in the search for life. A home, a job, the raising of the kids, a search for friends. Carl's group was not evil; they were good men, who in their way honored God by believing in godly values, in order and rules, in their love of life. Like him, they lived for life not for God. How could you separate the two? How could you know God except through life? If life was not good, then how could God be good? How could you know God outside of life's experiences? Even the Bible was God manifesting Himself through life.

Dave's congregation was not evil; they were good people. Dave was a good person with a special gift, he tried to use this gift for good. But what had he and his family learned about God—who God is—from this group? Nothing of worth. In a sense, even falsehood. The Jesus in the Bible was preaching the end even as He walked the earth, and He was angry. He told of the narrow way leading to life and the cost of following. Why had the Church and everyone else turned their back on Jesus? Why had he? Because he was a follower, and he had joined the wrong team and followed the wrong coach and now they, his family, were going to lose the big game. How do you like that, Mary? He laughed to himself, for he truly loved his wife. The sports analogy worked. The group existed for the group—in seeing God in each other, in doing good things for each other, in meeting emotional needs. Pastor Dave knew God more than any other man he had met besides Gramps and maybe his brother, yet they were not alike.

Pastor Dave seemed to accept the world. Gramps had railed against it. Gramps's God told people what they didn't want to hear. Pastor Dave's God was supportive, encouraging, nonconfrontational. Dave's God wasn't a magic genie, but neither was He a boss, a commander. Dave's God didn't seem to have any goals or aims, no historical agenda other than for people to live and know He was God. There was no battle in Dave's cosmology, even as there was evil. There was no confrontation with a person's nature, only a gentle peeling.

Tim knew he had to confront himself; his stupidity seemed to warrant a battle. He had no idea of how this should take place. What was God's purpose in all this? This thing called life; this globe called the world? It was easy to lose sight of such questions when there were so many diversions, pleasures, needs, desires, so much time spent just reacting to the immediate. Excuses? Was he lying to himself again?

He was stuck, spiritually stuck in the mud, with no way to freedom as the times closed in upon him with the weight and the speed of finality. He forced himself off the bed, to his knees, his face to the floor. He did this because somewhere within he felt this need to humble himself, even as his mind laughed at his foolishness, even as his body felt comical in such a position. He prayed to God even as a small voice repeated over and over again, "Ridiculous! Ridiculous! He can hear you when you are lying in bed."

"Dear God of heaven and Earth. Creator. I am wrong; somewhere in my thinking, I am wrong. Something is missing in me, something that I barely discern. Show me where I am wrong. Please show me where I am wrong."

Mary walked past the room, shook her head in disgust. Her strong husband, lost again. Tim remained kneeling, unaware of her presence. He admitted to himself and God that he was a lout, a fool, not what he should be as a husband and a parent. He did not know what the Creator wanted from him, but he wanted to obey with all he possessed. He wanted to be a better man. "Father, my God. Help me."

"Whatcha doin', Daddy?" Katie had skipped by the door and intrigued, had stopped and entered.

Tim smiled through his tears. To think that this little cutie, full of sweetness and goodness, was his! His to nurture and protect. That she cared enough to inquire why Daddy was on his knees spoke of her goodness. She knelt down beside him. "Matthew and I do this every night before he goes to his room."

"Pray?"

"Yep. We tell Jesus everything. Then sometimes I lie in bed and pray some more."

"Why pray to Jesus and not God?"

Katie rolled her eyes in merriment. "Jesus *is* God, begotten of the Father. Remember? Besides, He's the one who lived through this mess called life." Katie placed her arm around her Daddy's neck and looked into his eyes. "What's botherin' you, Daddy?"

"Remember back when I told you we missed the train because I didn't get us to the station?" Katie knew life was a mess; Tim pondered this.

"Sure, I remember. But there is another train coming, and Matthew and I are ready."

"How can you be ready, young lady, when I attend the same Bible study and I'm not ready? When Pastor Dave doesn't seem to have a clue, when the whole world seems to be colder and uglier?"

"I trust Jesus, Daddy, and so does Mat. All you hafta do is trust Him. He won't let us down."

Tim didn't see Matthew standing at the door listening. Tim wanted to say it was not that simple, the situation was complex, the motivations of people unclear, the evil overpowering, the future grim. The theological arguments and demands tangled and twisted. He wanted to say those things and would not. He would not pull her into his despair and confusion even as his ego cried out for him to chain his daughter to his own misery.

"Is that where I went wrong?" He looked into her trusting eyes.

"High probability."

From the doorway Mat spoke. "Listen to the coach. That's what you always told us."

Tim looked at his son as he placed his arm around his little girl. "It must start with knowledge."

"Dad, it starts with the knowledge we know nothing, and even what we know we can't comprehend or understand. Jesus has to reveal it to us," said Mat.

"So what do I do?"

"Put your listening ears on, Daddy." Katie placed her hands by her ears and wiggled her fingers. She laughed.

Tim smiled, remembering that when Katie was much younger, that was her favorite get-a-laugh act.

"She's right, Dad. Admit you're not the brains, you've got no knowledge, and listen. God's Spirit does the rest. Remember in the Gospel of John, Jesus promised us the Holy Spirit."

"Pray with Mat and me. You need our help," said Katie.

"Okay, I will." Why not? he asked himself. Mat knelt beside his father. Katie began.

"God, time on Earth is getting shorter. My Dad doesn't have a clue as to who You are. Please let him see Your Son…so he knows…it will all turn out okay. In Jesus's name, Your Son who died for us, we ask this. And with the help of Your Spirit, our friend and teacher, Daddy will learn to relax and trust. Amen."

"Amen," said Mat and Tim.

CHAPTER 11

Tim read through his lesson plan for the day as the commuter carried him into the heart of the city and the Academy. He didn't remember saying good-bye to his family when they had dropped him off. Reluctantly and with a twinge of nervousness, he anticipated the meeting with Jeremy. The look of smugness, victory, dominance would surely light up the boy/man's face. If that look came, he would state emphatically that Jeremy's extra-credit paper must be quality work, and he would reject the paper if that was warranted. Such a maneuver ought to take the arrogance from Jeremy. He was certain Jeremy would tell no one of their meeting or their confrontation. Then he sighed; the lesson in character was pointless. Soon, all upon the face of the earth would be dead. His nervousness, seen in the light of a world soon to be gone, elicited a laugh. Another laugh came as he thought of the foolishness of Jeremy's premise of hitting the academies with a reputation. Still, life must be played out to the end. Maybe Jeremy would be one of the redeemed.

He glanced up to look at the electrascreen. He hadn't seen the news at home. His stretching routine had been placed on hold, and he had read the Bible instead. Taking his son's reminder, he reread the Gospel of John and the promise of the Holy Spirit—wanting to see, to know Jesus at a deeper level. War, plague, deserted cities in the Middle East, North

Africa, the Asian Muslim countries. Talk of an Islamic war with Israel, not just involving immediate neighbors, but the Islamic nations to the north and west. Something about religious riots in Jerusalem. A new party of believers, hated by their fellow Jews. Among these world events, the European Federation and its leader consistently appeared.

He glanced out the window, saw an incinerator truck from his old company on its route. Already near the end of the driver's early morning shift. No stress. The pay wasn't good, but you had freedom and were kept physically fit. Perhaps he should not have left that job. Wishful thinking, an attempt to escape the stress caused by the coming Tribulation?

Stress? What should he do about his membership in the Order? Stay on and become a partner in assassinations? Perhaps it would buy time for Christ to gather His people. A commotion on the street caught his attention. A woman running, men pursuing. The woman's clothes were torn. She looked dizzy, bumping from person to person, glazed terror in her eyes. She was at the edge of a walkway, looking down at commuter tracks. The men were upon her. She jumped. He could not see her landing; the commuter continued, the people aboard didn't squirm or gasp. He knew the height of the fall. She was dead. He knew she was dead. The look in her eyes before she jumped would never leave him—such terror. He shook with rage and fear. What if that had been Mary?

He was no longer hiding from the truth of Carl's presentation as if Carl and his friends were mental cases. He no longer needed to escape the truth, to escape the reality of the times, to escape having to risk his comfortable life. Something had happened to him after his prayer with his kids—an illusion had been washed from his eyes. He knew with a certainty what was coming and that there was only one course: to walk straight into it and conquer for his family. He was no longer afraid. The Restraining One was leaving, but the Holy Spirit had certainly entered his mind. The world was coming to an end, an ugly unimaginable end.

Dave, the whole congregation, just taking off for the desert! Leaving everything behind—work, friends, their futures! Dave was sane, intelligent, even tempered, knew the ramifications of the flight. Dave would be leaving without the Johnson family. It was the right call. Dave had nothing over the word of God. Dave didn't even suspect the world—Satan's reign—was ending. He had a gift that was unnatural, but it was not supernatural. The authorities would not allow Dave's group to remain in isolation unless concessions were made. The future with Dave was fraught with troubles.

Commuters had entered at the last stop; one had sat beside him. He felt the man staring at him. Tim turned; the face was familiar. Where had he seen the face? The man—husky, bulging forearms, tanned, and tattooed—spoke.

"I've caught up with you, my little imposter. Masquerading! I know your kind. I've seen the hesitancy in the walk, the uncertainty of movement, the listening to another voice. Admit it to me, you're an Enslaver, possessed of evil." The man spoke calmly, in whispered, husky voice.

The man of the smirk, the man of the loathing! This was his sickness, his perversity; he had the power to detect enemies of the State. Tim would have laughed if not for the emanations of violence and strength coming from the man; he was rippling with intimidation. Mr. Smirk had evidently been prescribed steroids since their last meeting. Why hadn't someone put this mental slime away? No one knew, no one cared. Why hadn't someone beaten him senseless?

"Ah, you've found me out," Tim said. "I'll sign the documents."

"I'm serious, you goddamned pervert."

"I don't know what an Enslaver is, but I do know what slander is—and assault. You want to go to court?"

The man held his breath, either to explode in violence or to control his rage.

"You want to strike me? Go ahead, if you have the money," Tim said. "You want to beat me senseless, protector of the State? If you can…if you can." He wanted the man to try.

"My apologies. I had you confused with someone else." The man turned away in disgust and frustration. It was apparent he had lost in court before or had done significant jail time. Or did he fear a new psychological exam?

The commuter stopped at Tim's exit. Tim spoke curtly. "I'm leaving. If you're going to do something, do it now. If I ever see you again—if you even smirk at me again—you will be hearing from my lawyer."

Tim rose, walked down the aisle, listening for a word to escape the man's lips, stepped down into Central Station to pick up the next line. Life was becoming absurd, simply absurd. People swarming everywhere, all changing commuters, or hurrying into the station for longer runs. A knot of people had crowded around a man standing on two suitcases. A dark-haired man, one of those South Americans, by the skin color. He must have just begun his begging. In minutes the police would pick him up. The entire plaza was covered by surveillance cameras.

Most of his kind knew to choose the crowded streets, where congestion slowed the police, where crowds were easy to hide within, and money was thrown just to clear the human obstacle from the commuters' path. The man's hands were gesturing wildly now, his face reddening, the veins bulging. Tim moved closer, heard a high, nasal voice; a dark shadow of growth promised a heavy beard. The man's nose was Semitic, the hair curly, the accent not South American. The little man had fire in his eyes. Tim looked at his new watch, the old one taken by a gang; he could spare five minutes.

"I am not ashamed of the Gospel of Christ: it is the power of God for salvation to everyone who has faith, to the Jew and to you. In it, the righteousness of God is revealed through faith from faith; as it is written, 'the just shall live by faith.'

"The wrath of God is revealed from heaven against all ungodliness and wickedness of men, who by their wickedness suppress the truth…"

The small dark eyes, beaded hard with emotion, fixed upon Tim. A Jew, a foreign Jew. He could sense the foreignness in the clothes. From Israel? Impossible with the travel bans. What if he had escaped through North African nations or Europe? What if he carried the plague? He was a Christian, quoting the Bible!

"God gave you up to the lusts of your hearts, to impurity, to the dishonoring of your bodies among yourselves because you exchanged the truth about God for a lie and worshiped and served the creature rather than the Creator, Who is blessed forever."

Tim had to leave. He couldn't stay. The plague was horrible; agonizing pain, and within twenty-four hours, death. The authorities were watching, the cameras recording.

"Since you did not see fit to acknowledge God, God has given you up to a base mind and to improper conduct. You are filled with all manner of wickedness, evil, covetousness, malice. Full of envy, murder, strife, deceit, malignity, you are gossips, slanderers, haters of God, insolent, haughty, boastful, inventors of evil, disobedient to parents…"

Tim noticed a black gang approaching; like a dark thundercloud, they rolled into the mass of spectators. The audience was absorbed in the little man, unaware of the cloud; most in the audience were booing, hissing, cursing the Jew. Many departed quickly when they gained awareness of the gang members. Voodoo Disciples, ten or twelve, mostly men, black leathers, brown faces. The Jew would be trampled to death. He had to leave; he stood transfixed. The gang members stood in the audience and listened.

"Don't you know God's kindness is meant to lead you to repentance? By your hard, impenitent hearts, you are storing up wrath for yourself on the day of wrath, when God's righteous judgment will be revealed. For He will render to every man according to his works…What are your works, you black-leathered men?"

The little Jew pointed at the gang members. The crowd was now quickly dispersing—afraid of the gang members' presence and the violence that seemed inevitable. The gang members appeared stunned at the speaker's audacity.

"Yes, you! Do you obey the truth or wickedness? Wrath and fury are the rewards of wickedness and disobedience, and it is coming now to your nation, your city, your gang, you!"

Nervous laughter sounded from the few remaining spectators. The gang members were smiling at the man's nerve, unsure what to do. They had been insulted but felt no hate.

"Go on!" One member waved with mock encouragement.

"There will be tribulation and distress for every human being who does evil, but glory, honor, and peace for everyone who does good.

"Listen! No one is righteous, no one understands, no one seeks God. You've turned aside; together you've done wrong. Not one of you does good. Your mouths speak death, your tongues deceive, your words sting. Curses, bitterness come out. You're anxious to kill, to spread ruin and misery. You don't know what peace is. You have no fear of God."

The gang members looked at each other dumbly. They didn't appear threatening anymore; they were like little boys dressed in Halloween costumes, hurting inside, empty. Their clothes were ripped, stained with food, snot, and unknown liquids, either too big or too small for the wearers. He could smell sweat, cooking grease, stale urine. They wore poorly crafted designs and emblems of death and fear. Childish. Tim studied the gang members' posture and facial expressions. They slumped, heads hung low, arms wrapped around their bodies, their eyes were downcast, and lips pursed, as sadness and despondency came to their eyes. For a moment they understood themselves. They were just hurting people, never having been loved as children, never having been shown right from wrong, always making the wrong choices from their hate and bitterness. He saw them turn and walk away. The Jewish guy was calling to them. Tim turned to leave; any moment, wrath would come from the gang members. He walked as quickly as he could.

He lost himself in the crowd. He heard nothing from the preacher, was probably whisked away by the authorities, a subversive, an Enslaver. Shouldn't Tim be like this man sharing the gospel? No. His work was to save his family. What was the sign? What was it? The fifth seal? The first four seals were the horsemen—the white horse of world peace, the Antichrist in power; the red horse was war; the black horse, famine; the pale horse, death by plague. The fifth seal was the saints of Israel preaching of God and being slain.

Who knew if this man was from Israel? Perhaps he was South American and not Jewish at all. The sixth seal…earthquakes? The seventh seal, he could not remember; trumpet judgments were just a vague idea in his mind as the seventh seal. No, it didn't fit. Or was it that Tim didn't want it to fit? This was a homegrown, mentally deranged Jewish man. Many of them were wound too tightly. He could have lost his law practice or surgery center and snapped.

Tim turned suddenly. Why was the man quiet? Tim turned and scanned the outline of the crowd—searching for the lone figure standing on his suitcases, breaking the uniformity of the backdrop. To his horror, the little man was directly behind him, smiling, carrying the suitcases, one in each hand.

He wouldn't acknowledge the man. No eye contact—though he felt the man staring at him. What if the authorities were following? He already had a bad name in the Church. A file existed on him. This could be a trap, a setup designed by the Church. Talk to this Jew, and it was prison. Sure, it was prison. What had he prayed Saturday night? For God to help him? Now the help might be here, a prayer actually answered. No, impossible!

I take back the prayer. God, I take it back. Leave, Israelite! Just leave! He didn't want to say *Jew*—the term seemed derogatory. Hatred seemed to cling to these people, and he had no desire to hate. Should he attempt to walk to work, lose the man in the crowds? No, he always took the commuter. It would be suspicious to break the pattern. Maybe the man would give up; maybe he wasn't following. Tim stopped; this was where he picked up the commuter.

"Hello," said the man.

Tim did not respond.

"Hello." The same friendly voice. More charm in this *hello*.

The silence remained.

"Sir, you are to help me."

Tim searched the crowd. No one was watching, no one pursuing the man. What about crowd-control surveillance cameras? A few quick words could safely be ventured.

"Says who? And what of surveillance cameras?"

"Says the Lord, your God. The one camera within range is off—likely broken."

"Where are you from?" Tim ignored the comments, assumed the camera was broken. *Your God.* The words frightened him, yet he did not wish to deny them. God was good, God was all powerful, and God was pretty much all he had to see his family through the coming storm. When he recognized that, indeed, God—the great I Am—was all he had, he humbled his heart and felt the power and majesty of God Who would concern Himself with Tim Johnson and his family. "My God? Yes, my God." Saying the words aloud overwhelmed him with emotion and gratitude.

"Israel. I came from Israel."

"How did you fly through the ban? You get off the plane, come to the central station of Anywhere, USA, and begin to preach?" His voice was terse with cynicism.

"Your city is my assignment. I have no time to be subtle. My time is very short."

The man had not said how he had circumvented the ban. "Time is short, plague carrier." The man saw the visceral fear and answered quickly.

"Martyrdom is my fate—not death by the plague."

"How do you know you're not infected?"

"If I were, you would have already been exposed to a lethal dose."

"No one knows what a lethal dose is or how it is transmitted."

"They know. The plague is in Europe, killing tens of thousands. It is in the United States. Contrary to what you are told."

Was this an honest man before him? A man who knew Christ, and followed Him? A man like Gramps or John? Or was this little man the beginning of the end for Mary, Katie, Matthew, and himself? The man had picked him, which could be considered entrapment under the law, if the State cared to consider the law. Fifty–fifty odds, honest or deceitful.

"Why did you pick me?"

"The Holy Spirit is like a fire over your head. Surely, you know God is with you? I would be a fool not to follow you."

An answer to prayer? Tim doubted. He did remember men in the Bible who had been picked at random. The man who had provided a donkey for Jesus's entry into Jerusalem, the man who provided the room used for the Last Supper. Blinded Paul and his contact, Ananias. As for the Spirit and fire, he had read of this fire phenomenon at the initial outpouring of the Spirit. He had not sensed or felt the presence of the Spirit enter him. No, he had—as recently as his prayer with his kids. This foreigner would have information, might even be able to supply the missing piece of the puzzle. Tim's curiosity had been touched.

"Take the number one commuter to the end of the line. Walk up the road to where the creek runs beside the road. Cross the creek on the small bridge, go up the wooded hill. On the left you will see a playhouse in the woods—just as the woods end and open into a field. Stay there, at the playhouse. You might see a building across the field. This is an unoccupied farmhouse. Don't go near it. Sometime in the night you will be contacted. Take it or leave it."

"I'll take it."

The man's eyes lit in happiness, and his head snapped down and up in an affirmative nod. The little man, barely to Tim's shoulders, walked into the crowd.

***

Tim meticulously scanned all sides of the deserted, dark, country road. The light from the station was behind him. He pulled his night-vision goggles from the recreation bag slung over his shoulder. With the goggles in place, he again carefully searched the road and woods. No human forms, but deer everywhere. The only sounds: tree frogs, crickets, and below these, the unending songs of innumerable unknown insects and bugs. The night was humid, warm, still.

He moved off the road into the trees. He heard no sounds from the deep woods, save for an owl somewhere far away. He opened the recreation bag, pulled out the machine pistol, snapped the fold-out stock into place, inserted the thirty-round clip. He had taken a risk transporting the weapon on the commuter. He had no choice; his car could have been identified and tracked easily by any government agency.

He was about to continue the climb when a weariness overtook him. He sat on a rock. The terror-stricken face of the woman leaping to her death flashed through his consciousness. Then the vengeful stare of Jeremy, at the morning's meeting concerning the paper, who had not taken kindly to only a partial victory. Tim had asked Jeremy if he knew anything about Christ. He had never asked that of anyone before—not of his students during his college-teaching days, not even of people on his Church committees. He asked it just to see Jeremy's reaction. "Are you crazy, Mr. Johnson? Maybe you should be talking to a counselor." That was all Jeremy said as he backed away.

Did Tim really need the risk involved in meeting with this foreigner? The machine pistol was heavy on his knee, promising security.

He had to continue; the world was falling apart, his friends were steeped in radical endeavors, and he was lost. He had thought of inviting Bill or Dave to this rendezvous. He trusted no one. He would talk to this man, learn, see if his views matched those of Gramps and John. Maybe this man had the answer as to what God wanted. He prayed to Jesus that this meeting would go well. He had never been the praying type—life had always been self-evident. His prayer with Katie and Mat had opened his heart. He was at the end of himself, and there was no one he fully trusted—only the Spirit of God, given to him by this image of Jesus melded together by words of the Bible.

He moved up the wooded slope. He saw the form of a deer, then another, move away from him in leaping bounds. Their tails erect, shining white, seemed like wagging fingers, scolding. The deer snorted in alarm. Tim approached the playhouse. The damp hemlock needles were quiet under his feet. He stepped over a broken plastic pail and stealthily, he peered into an open window. The man was huddled in his jacket, sleeping.

Tim tossed an army ration at the man, watching for the possible reach for a weapon in the fear of waking.

"Food." Tim spoke in a normal volume and tone.

The man awoke with a start but quickly calmed. The man's hands felt his jacket as if knowing something had dropped upon him. The hands had not sought a weapon; none existed.

"Eat," Tim said.

"Thanks. My name is Josh." The hands had grasped the food packet as the body straightened into a sitting position—back against the play-house wall.

Tim did not offer his name. Josh understood the fear he must have.

Tim moved inside, handed Josh a canteen as Josh devoured the ration. "Have another." Tim tossed another packet to him.

"Thanks." Josh ate rapidly; he hadn't eaten since noon, had been in the woods since one. Prior to that he had not eaten in forty-eight hours, a stowaway on two flights, trapped in cargo holds during long stopovers.

"Let's move out." Tim rose and Josh rose, dusting cracker crumbs from the jacket and placing the plastic packaging in his pockets. Josh followed Tim to a place deeper in the woods. At some point Tim stopped and turned in a circle, peering into the darkness. Tim sat on his recreation bag; he could see the openness of the ag fields through the trees.

"Make yourself at home. Where is your luggage?" Tim remembered two suitcases in Josh's hands when first they met.

Josh sat on a downed limb, zipped his jacket the last few inches so his collar was fully extended around his neck. The woods were damper and cooler in the new location. A breeze chilled their faces. Josh answered, "Stolen. Just clothes nothing important."

Tim wondered if that was the truth but decided to accept Josh's explanation. The theft of a foreigner's luggage seemed appropriate for this country called the United States. Once a place where integrity was honored and now the bastion of thievery and deception. "What's going on in Israel, and what is it you plan to do here?"

Josh smiled with an inner pleasure. "Two witnesses have arisen; some say from the grave. They are Elijah and Moses, and they preach like the prophets of old—with authority. I heard them and I believed. Many believe. The persecutions have come. One of our own, a false prophet, working for the beast of the European Federation, torments us. Life is not good, hunger, torture, flight, even as our true enemies gather for conflict."

The phrase, "life is not good" struck Tim. "Why do you talk to me as if I know the terms *beast* and *false prophet*, as if I am one of your own? Why are you here?"

"The Lord said to me in the crowded streets to follow the one who has the Holy Spirit. Like I told you, you had the Spirit, brother… like a flame…like a bonfire above your head." Josh began to chuckle. "Such a clear demonstration of God's power, no ambiguity. I am here to tell this city that Christ is the Messiah, the Savior of the world. What's your name?"

"Tim. What does that mean to me?" An uncontrollable curtness was in Tim's tone.

"That you are favored of God! You have time to escape the coming judgment, time to possess eternal life in heaven."

"What must I do?" He hoped to hear the simple key to unlock the unfathomable door.

"Repent of your sins and accept Christ as your Savior."

Resignation, frustration welled from Tim. "I've done that! What else? What else? What else does God want?"

"There is nothing else but to follow Him." Josh was beginning to understand the man named Tim. Likely, he was analytical, methodical, a man who understood works but not relationships, a person who understood giving to get.

Hearing his own anger, Tim became subdued. "I do to the best of my ability."

Josh peered through the darkness at Tim. Tim needed encouragement. "Tim, God doesn't place the Spirit upon a man unless He is certain. And there was no uncertainty in what I saw. Just believe and get out of the way. You have a family, you love them, and they love you. I sense that. Let go of your intellect in this one matter of faith and grab your heart. God is Love. He loves you as passionately as you love your family. He loves you simply because He made you. Just as you made your family. He nurtures you because that is His pleasure and His passion. You and your family are saved. Stop worrying, stop seeking what you already possess and will be revealed to you, and start loving."

Tim stared blankly, his mind twisting from the words it had heard.

"Tim, you've learned of the Lord from someone. You are being drawn to Him. But you are not honest with yourself. You have not repented of your sins or accepted Christ as your Savior."

"Then help me. Help me. I don't see myself as a particularly bad person. I know there is something wrong with me, an avoidance of the truth, a denial of the times. I can't see myself as needing a savior, except from the awful times ahead."

Josh heard the heartfelt anguish in the voice. "You cannot find one sin in your life?"

Tim hesitated, then said, "I turned in my brother to the authorities. I told myself it was for his sake, but it was for my own."

"Just one sin identifies you as a sinner, in need of a savior. And the best of your ability is not good enough—because it is your ability. Your ability is only as strong as your will, and your will is as weak as Adam's. You are his offspring."

"I'm totally corrupt, estranged from God? I can't peel away the bad?" Tim asked.

"No."

Tim smiled. He had found a soul mate of Gramps and his brother.

"I understand what you've said. But I love life. I love being in control, I love my body, my strength, reflexes, my appetite, food, tobacco, wine. I love my thought process, I love my intelligence, I love what I have accomplished, I love interacting with other people. I love my emotions, my feelings, my knowledge. I love what civilization has created. I don't want to hand these things over. I don't want to be a slave of God or of Satan. I'm a success. I'm happy. I am complete…I appreciate God, but I want to live my life."

Josh said nothing. Strange, how Tim knew the cost. He ignored Tim's words; you could not debate a man who loved himself. How would his self-love, his love of the world, the flesh die? Josh sensed the death of self—of the ego—had already begun.

"If Christ is truly in you, you will take me home. I will talk to your family, your circle of friends. This is how it must begin."

"Josh, you're an Enslaver. You've broken the flight ban, the quarantines. You have broken laws. Should I put my life and those of my family and friends in jeopardy for you?"

Josh smiled wryly. What a battle was taking place in this man, such deception.

"You have nothing to lose at all, as you have already lost. You will be dead in less than seven years and spend eternity in hell. You worry about your sorry life? The Kingdom of God is coming, man! Listen to the word of God: 'If any man will come after me, let him deny himself, and take up his cross, and follow me. For whosoever will save his life shall lose it: and whosoever will lose his life for my sake shall find it. For what is a man profited, if he shall gain the whole world and lose his own soul? Or what shall a man give in exchange for his soul? For the Son of man shall come in the glory of his Father with his angels; and then he shall reward every man according to his works.'

"Don't become discouraged or frustrated; the Lord wants you. He will tear down those barriers within. There is nothing you can do. Have faith that He lives, and He cares for you. He is your Father. Do you think Dad isn't watching what you do here, now, this minute? Deny yourself the fantasy of the world's reality. The world's fantasy ends soon. Deny yourself the safety of obeying the State's laws and obey God."

"Denying myself—that *is* doing something," Tim said.

"Just the opposite; it is doing nothing."

"You've lost me."

"Denying is refusing to do, period. Then, and only then, will the Holy Spirit give you wisdom and desire to do what is right."

Tim sighed. "I get it…Come on," he said resignedly.

CHAPTER 12

They sat apart from each other on the commuter. The artificial light shone brightly on the passengers of the almost standing-room-full car. Two women cursed each other over who should have a vacant seat. The electrascreen flashed an urgent news bulletin. The passengers tensed, became attentive, a woman shushed a child. US troops were being sent to Europe as a show of unity for the European Federation. War might break out soon in the Middle East. Could Israel withstand its foes? Would the Federation, not obligated by treaty, become an ally or enemy of Israel? That US troops were being sent to Europe sent a collective gasp from the passengers.

The ensuing message stunned the people into complete silence. The US government had ordered the conscription of all single, able-bodied persons between the ages of eighteen and thirty-five. Tim was no less amazed than the people around him. A drastic measure! Unwarranted by the circumstances! The standing army, professionals, had the capability to handle any crisis. The Muslim countries, riddled by starvation and plague, would be no match for the Federation. What catastrophe was imagined? What escalation was possible?

Tim clamped his teeth in determination and perhaps pleasure. Life had taken on a dramatic excitement. He realized much of his excitement came from those around him. He was locked into a social covenant of shared ideals, emotions, purposes, standards. He belonged to them and they to him; what one felt the other felt. Yes, the world had allures, even in times of possible danger and hardship. The communal sharing of patriotism.

No, they were patriots to a different nation, followers of a different creed. He and they lived in the same geographic location, that is all. The only shared thought was that of resentment—of sharing what little they had with the powerful Federation. But he wanted the shared indignation.

Could he enjoy the moment freely because he was married and over thirty-five and Matthew was only twelve? They were safe. What a blow this would be to the economy—all these potential conscripts had jobs. Who would fill vacancies? All these new soldiers would need food, weapons, clothing, transportation, housing. Who would pay but the taxpayer? He forced down the knowing smile. Finally, he knew for certain: the world was coming apart.

Angry talk filled the commuter as a warning flashed across the electrascreen: Report any strangers, foreign travelers, aliens as a health measure, against the importation of the plague. Any traveler, alien was to report immediately to the nearest hospital to receive a health card. Failure to do so meant imprisonment. Did that mean the southern border would finally be closed? Tim wondered what the penalty was for aiding an alien who was circumventing the law.

At Central Station they exited, stood waiting, still apart, for the next commuter. Tim felt the earth bounce, rumble under his feet. Construction blasting? No additions to the subterranean city were being made. The rumble seemed to move across the earth. His hands went out for balance.

Was the earth opening? The rumble was gone. Earthquake! As a geologist, he had experienced many earthquakes; that time seemed so long ago. Very mild, a magnitude 3 on the Richter scale, he thought.

The subterranean city and the high-rises had been built to withstand much more severe shocks, though they weren't in an earthquake zone. No doubt the architects, engineers, construction workers had cheated on the requirements of the law. Still, at this low level of activity he expected little damage. The earthquake had jarred loose the beginnings of fear. The Bible had foretold earthquakes. Dave, all knowing Dave, had not warned of this quake.

They stepped off the commuter at the nearest station to the warehouse district. The commuter line had not been affected by the quake. The city lights were on, the traffic moving swiftly. He had seen no broken water mains, or gas lines. People were talking of the quake, even to strangers, a phenomenon he had never seen. He supposed people wanted to share the excitement and fear. The occupants of the high-rises were flowing out of the ground-floor doors and collecting like puddles before the buildings. A man urinated against a wall. Young kids tried to sell some homemade uppers. A woman offered her services as an escort; she did not wear the State-designated ID tag showing her name and health status. Two men were kissing in a dark corner.

No taxi was in sight. He chose not to wait for one, but to walk the quarter of a mile to the warehouse district fencing and gate that delineated the hundreds of acres of warehouses, staffed by robotic, wheeled cargo carriers and retrievers. Everyone appeared to be in this unusual friendly mood, caught up in the spirit of a shared wonder. He might be able to make it home without incident. He had always driven this route, never walked. His pace was quick, Josh struggled to remain beside him. He kept his eyes on the brightly lit high-rises to their left, across the wide field. A tag football game was taking place, and basketball under the lights. It was normal to feel safer on the ground; no doubt the tall buildings had swayed. He saw five men come out of the crowd in front of the last high-rise.

"Pick up the pace, Josh. Trouble is approaching."

Tim began a walk faster than a jog. He must pace himself; the warehouse fence and gate were two hundred yards away. Josh was no athlete, already lagging. Tim reached into the recreation bag, fingered the trigger of the machine pistol. Wisely, he had not broken down the pistol after the meeting with Josh. The five men, identified as gang members by the matching gray jackets, were now running in an intersecting course that would meet well before the gate.

"Run, Josh!"

Tim broke into a lope, purposely holding back to see if Josh could maintain the pace. Josh could not keep up. This little man might get them killed, thought Tim in bitterness. By himself he could have made the safety of the gate. Tim slowed, inserted the clip while the pistol was still in the bag.

These men knew where he lived, knew when his family came and went. They could make life miserable for him. If he displayed his weapon, they would back away. But they would want his subservience even more—to steal the pistol, to crush his arrogance. If the weapon was displayed he couldn't call the police, as he had no permit. If he didn't display the weapon, the thieves would rummage his bag and find and take it. He might be beaten severely, perhaps killed.

With a sudden sense of abandon, he thought of killing these five men. There would be no future problems. Even if someone watched from the buildings, it was a long distance, in the night, to see accurately.

But if a surveillance camera had targeted the running men and the lens was clear—the system functioning smoothly—there was no hope for anonymity. He was the only man to live in the warehouse district proper, the only night employee; everyone would know he had been the shooter. He would be wanted by the law or by vengeful relatives or gang members.

"Slow down, man. We won't hurt you. Just want to ask some questions."

The insincere voice was winded, held an unknown accent. Tim stopped; Josh was lagging, they would not reach the safety of the gate. Josh gasped for breath. The five had spread out, encircling. Tim knew for a certainty, from the encirclement, he and Josh would be robbed, perhaps beaten. He couldn't lose the pistol. If they got one pistol from him, they would suspect more weapons. More problems for him. Tim pulled out the machine pistol, swung it in an arc while keeping it close to his body to blur the eyes of detection. The men on the flanks stopped their encirclement.

"Why don't you move back together, make a tight little group," Tim said. They did so, though not quickly and not tightly, with fear and contempt on their faces.

"Nice weapon?" asked Tim.

"Nice," said the leader who had just spoken, a tall thin man in his late twenties.

"You'd like one like this?"

"You know my thoughts." The leader laughed admiringly.

"It could be yours."

"What's the game?

"Safe passage in and out for me, my friends, and my family for life, and this pistol belongs to you." Tim studied the man's height, weight, body movements. Thin, wiry with wide shoulders. He studied the face—flat, white tone to skin, dark straggly mustache. Hispanic leanings with a touch of Asian in the eyes.

"You've got a deal."

"Not so quick. A deal is only as good as a man's honor. I need proof of honor. Two months. No problems with your men. You get the weapon. Every month thereafter, I give you five rounds—till the rounds run out. *If* you're still treating the agreement with respect."

"It's a deal. Two months from now I'll be here." He looked at his watch. "At nine ten in the evening. I see you moving out before then? Well, you know." The leader turned, walked back toward the towers. His men gave mocking glares, turned and followed.

Tim walked slowly to the gate, physically and mentally exhausted. More pressure, more stress, anxiety; but he could handle it. Two months was a considerable time—if the leader didn't attempt to steal the weapon before the deadline or hold a family member hostage for the weapon. Carl was right. People had to fear the law and respect order, even civility. And the fear of death was the only means.

Josh spoke. "Are you going to honor that deal?"

"I don't know. I doubt it. He will not wait two months. I offered two, thinking he would bargain for one. He didn't bargain because he plans to have the weapon in his hands much sooner. Hopefully something will change." Tim thought if he were an assassin on Carl's death squads, those five men would be first on his list. He would have no compunction.

"They will kill with that gun."

"As long as they don't kill me or my family or friends." Tim shrugged his shoulders. He knew such thinking was evil. "Likely, I will not give it to them." He could not give up the weapon.

"You could have given them Christ."

"Ideas, philosophies don't change scum like that."

"The power of God can." Unfortunately, Josh knew, Tim's statement was closer to the truth, given the times.

Tim sneered. "I bought time. No one denied *you* permission to speak."

Josh smiled in defeat; Tim was correct.

***

The family sat on the sofa, facing Josh, who was sitting on an uphol-stered chair. Katie was on Tim's lap, and Mat was tucked between Mom and Dad. The children saw a weary man, roughly the age of their dad, enveloped by a calm presence. Katie was amazed at the dark shadow on Josh's face—it almost looked like dirt or charcoal pencil. His skin was the color of coffee lightened with cream. His cheeks were sucked in like he had eaten raw lemons and a squiggly vein pulsed on either side of his temples. Mat noticed the small book he held with both hands, printed words—not electronic—the Bible. Its plastic, indestructible pages were curved; no doubt Josh had a long-standing habit of grasping the book with both hands. Josh had already finished his coffee.

Tim noticed big hands that knew manual labor. Judging by the muscu-lature, the callouses, the dented and nicked nails, they were the hands of a farmhand. Josh's hair was short, tightly curled, and black. He spoke slowly, a smile forming, as he studied the faces of the Johnson family. The children were eager to hear. Mary, curious but fearful. Tim was stressed and anxious.

Josh spoke. "I am very tired, but I would like to give you some knowledge to think about until we talk again, God willing, in the morning."

Katie and Matthew were in their pajamas, mentally excited, weary in body. The earth tremors, their first experience, had awakened them. Rarely did they have visitors in their apartment and never at night; never were they included in the conversation. When Dad had been a professor, people had come often. Now, hardly ever. They felt like adults, like something of great importance was taking place. Katie whispered to Mat. "It feels like Christmas morning." Mat crossed his fingers in hope.

Josh heard Katie's words and smiled and began again. "This world we live in is soon coming to an end. In less than seven years, I believe. We will see all kinds of terrible things in this time."

"Dad told us that," Katie added, as an afterthought not as an interruption.

"Sh! You're ruining it," Matthew whispered as he pushed his sister.

"No, I'm not." She leaned from her perch to give her brother a punch. Tim brought down the hand and stuck a finger under her armpit. She clamped her arm down, but the finger was gone. She grimaced at the tickle and stifled the laugh.

Josh smiled; he loved children, though he would now never have any of his own. Tim was teaching his children of the Tribulation?

"Good, I'm glad to hear that," he said. "Katie, Mat, I like comments and questions. Now, God will make a new world, but the only people who will get in are those who have a ticket. That ticket is Christ in your hearts."

"Dad told us we missed the first train. But we'll catch the next one," Katie said, clapping and rubbing her hands in anticipation of the ride.

Matthew gave her a dirty look, then added, "We have Christ in our hearts."

Katie gave her throaty chuckle to Mat's words. She ignored his stern face. Tim aimed the disciplinary stare to his children; they knew the look and quieted.

"You know the tickets are free," Josh said, realizing the children knew much and the fire seen above Tim's head in that first encounter truly was the Spirit of God. Josh could not discern Mary's part in her children's knowledge.

"Most people throw them on the ground, thinking the tickets are worthless and Christ is lying. Here is what God says: everyone in the world has sinned and so doesn't equal my perfect grade.

"No one's gotten a hundred." Katie spoke matter-of-factly. Matthew rolled his eyes at his sister's showboating.

Josh understood they had grasped the concept long ago. He would continue, to be certain that nothing in the salvation story was misunderstood or had become twisted. "Since God wants people without sin in His new world—people with one hundreds—He must do something about us. He gives us a ticket that says, 'The blood that my son Jesus shed on the cross will erase all the sins you ever committed or will ever commit. I will pretend your sins don't exist. I'll give you all 100 percent.

"'But I don't just want you to be forgiven and still controlled by human nature, a mind and body that wants to keep on failing. I don't want you to keep failing—or even getting sixties and seventies. I will also get rid of that human nature, that mind and body that wants to sin, and replace it with the Spirit of Jesus.'

"Only death can get rid of that mind and body, and so Christ's death on the cross also killed our nature. As Christ rose from death, we too rise with His perfect nature in us," Josh said. "That's it."

"So why do we do better now?" Matthew asked.

"Because the mind that was lazy or didn't care or just didn't have the ability is replaced with the mind of God, who is none of those things." Matthew thought deeply, said nothing; then Matthew looked at Katie and made a surprised funny face. Katie laughed. She remembered her manners.

"Thanks for telling us, Josh. I've got my ticket now?"

"You're welcome. And you do have your ticket. But Mat brought up a good point. Don't be mistaken…we do better now…but we aren't perfect. We can be deceived into sinning and being stupid. The good news is Jesus's sacrifice still keeps us in God's love. So never be discouraged if you feel you have failed. God doesn't walk away from you. He still loves you. Remember, I like questions, so think about what I said. Don't be afraid to ask hard questions tomorrow."

"Okay; we will," said Matthew.

"Kids, time for bed," said Mary. Neither of them whined, which was unusual. Mary followed the kids into their bedrooms. Tim remained seated, facing Josh.

"That's it?"

"That's it for the trusting heart. Most of us need more convincing. We don't let go of our flesh that easily."

"I suppose that's my problem."

Josh said nothing. Tim found his silence irritating.

"How do you know this is the one and only God talking to mankind? Or that Christ is God? How do you know your interpretation of the Bible is true? Or even that the Bible is true? How do you *know*?"

"He says He is the one and only God. 'Hear oh Israel the Lord your God is one.' And 'No one comes to the Father but through me.' As for the Bible, 'man does not live by bread alone but by every word uttered from the mouth of God.' Every word uttered by God is in the Bible.

"Look, how do you know George Washington was the first president of the United States?"

"People saw him, talked to him; we have his signature; there is a written record so extensive that he must have lived."

"Is it any less with Christ? Thousands saw him, witnessed his miracles, his death, even saw him ascend into heaven. Independent sources verify he lived. You have four witnesses who wrote their accounts, Matthew, Mark, Luke, and John. Did these men become rich through their literary efforts, their possible works of fiction? Did they acquire great wealth, power, even status? They received nothing but a martyr's death. The subtle differences in their texts show they weren't in collusion, formulating a hoax. A hoax of no benefit to them."

"Men are fallible in their efforts," Tim said. "Did Washington cut down the cherry tree?" He referred to a story credited to Washington but which most scholars agreed had not happened.

"If God is all powerful, the maker of man, I believe He could have used men to write the book He wished written, Josh said. "If God isn't all powerful, then He might not have the book He wanted written. You decide if God is all powerful. This belief in God's omnipotence is something that can't be taught but must be within you."

Tim said nothing. Even on this point—the omnipotence of God—he was unsure, even as the book of Revelation was being fulfilled."

Josh spoke. "You can easily make objections for a lifetime, many people do. People try to hide from the truth. You told me yourself that you love your life. You took as much of God as made you comfortable; you and the Church made God to fit your lives. You both retained judgment on what was true and what was not. Your reasoning powers were greater than God's—the God who couldn't even say what He meant.

"God is greater than you; there would be no reason to worship Him if He were not. Yes, He wants voluntary control over you. But you won't be controlled by any force."

"Why should I?" Tim said. "I live a good life. Why would I give control to a voice in my head?"

"You admitted to being a sinner. Are you going to take back that statement? Then how good is your life? Are you going to argue that you don't have a sinning nature, at odds with God?"

"No, I won't argue; not under your standards. Just listen to me." Frustration, anger were within Tim's words.

"Go ahead." Josh spoke patiently and with a kind curiosity.

"Look! Religion, God, have been used in my life to elevate me, to provide comfort, confidence, boldness, to give me an edge in life's battles. The Church assured me I was the good guy, deserving the breaks. God Himself wanted me to succeed with my dreams, aspirations. It was God who wanted me to have the fullness of life's offerings. God was to glorify me, Tim Johnson, so that all could see that belonging to the Church was good. People respond to success, people want success, people give themselves to success. If God's people aren't successful, then why would people be attracted? Who would want God if it led nowhere?"

Josh replied, "To have the truth and live it; that is success. To have eternal life; that is success. I understand. Your life works, works well. Why fix it? Now, I tell you to glorify an unseen, invisible God. His concerns aren't your dreams. His concern is His Kingdom. Your dreams must be His dreams. Christ isn't your helper; you are His slave. You've followed the world's definition of a successful life and therefore a successful God…while you forgot His goals and purpose for life. He has a plan, and you must work for Him. You must totally abandon your plans for His. Obey His will."

"Yes, yes, yes…You've identified the problem. I've got to live for Christ. How do I do that? How do I do that even when I don't want to?"

"By understanding that you are dead in Christ." Josh's eyelids were hanging low, the mental sharpness seen earlier in the eyes gone. "You do really want to die to all your foolishness, your selfish me-centered life, and the world that celebrates your *me* life. You want to be free of yourself more than life itself because you love Mary, Mat, and Katie more than your life. Without your leadership, they will die with the world…on that day fast approaching."

A consciousness, a force, a pang so deep within Tim's soul fluttered like the wings of a dying dove. The presence of desolation swept through him. As suddenly as it came, it left. He loved his kids, his family more than himself, and for them he would willingly embrace death. Tim felt Josh's weariness, and he too was tired. "Go get some rest, Josh. Tomorrow is another day."

Josh rose. "Yes, it is." He moved toward Tim and placed a reassuring hand on his shoulder. "Hang in there, Dad; the Lord is working." He moved to the corner of the room where a bed had been made up. "Good night."

"Good night," said Tim as he thought on the kindness of Josh to place his hand upon him in encouragement.

***

Tim sat alone with his restless spirit. Mary was in the bedroom, sleeping. Dead in Christ? What the hell did that mean? He knew what it meant. The statement dovetailed neatly into what Josh had said about denying yourself, which was a form of death. Then, with that accomplished, God—Christ, who rose from the dead—could work. Josh was an exact doctrinal copy of Gramps and John. Josh could lead Tim to this truth he must experience if he and his family were to live into the next world. He would try, try desperately; yet it seemed he wasn't supposed to try.

All his life, he had loved his God because of what God could do for him. For the first time in his life, that type of devotion and love seemed incredibly selfish. But didn't Matthew and Katie love Dad because he fed, housed, clothed them? He gave them money, allowed them to buy almost anything they wanted. If that was the only reason they loved him, then something was missing.

He gave them things because he loved them, but he wanted them to love him…well…simply because he loved them. They were his creation, his reason for living. He wanted them happy, a happiness deeper than prosperity and momentary gifts. He wished for them contentment and joy.

What was love, when you came down to it? Would his children love him if they weren't fed, housed, clothed? If they couldn't indulge their whims with money? Yes, they would love him.

Why? Because they hoped he would bring them to that place of prosperity? Or was it a psychological need? Or the stability and pleasure that memories, shared moments brought? He supposed that was as pure as love could be—the love of relationship, of delighting in each other for who you were, the way you perceived life and acted within it, and not what possessions you shared, had, or could acquire. If you could not delight in each other, then love would linger for a while and finally disappear. You could stretch love to that point of no advantage, keep it there for a length of time, depending on your faith. No, you could keep it forever, and he must keep it forever; the love of intimacy, creation, and caring. The world, people, circumstances, your own selfishness would always be your enemy.

What if Matthew turned against his dad, became hateful, and could no longer delight in his father's company? How long could he love Matthew? He would love him forever. From his desire to love him, he would have faith forever. Was God any different? For just a brief moment—the blink of an eye—Tim felt the aching soul of God waiting for his children to return to Him, to Daddy. He had never thought of loving God as you would a person. God had always been a force of power to be harnessed. How could you love the invisible? The faceless? Christ had a face; Christ had been visible. He would try to love God, delight in God, for the sake of his children. Purity of motive, Tim had some. Intellectually, he understood that people could delight in concepts or other people simply on their merits, regardless of what material comforts or social status they conveyed.

He had loved God through the natural world that God had created. He had been awed by volcanic eruptions, colorful sunsets, exotic reef fishes, alpine lakes and peaks, deserts. He had been awed by the muscular power of lions, the speed of cheetahs, the flight of hawks. He had taken delight in his children's accomplishments through sports, scholastics. He saw God's work within their thought processes, their awakening logic and abilities to reason through humanity's foibles.

He remembered an African surgery center, where a young girl had come with her mother to have a deformed leg straightened, a debilitating limp removed. He had stopped to resupply with water for his journey to a drilling site. The girl's countenance, at first worried and beset by years of shame and worthlessness, had suddenly turned to beaming joy at the love given by the staff of nurses, doctors, anesthesiologists. The presence of God had been in the center, and he had been blinded but now he saw. For the first time in her life she was being loved by strangers, not treated with contempt or harassed by cruel words. She was basking in the radiance of love. She had worth and goodness and beauty. That memory was etched into Tim's very brain cells. Now it was again before him, and he knew that this was how the holy God, Yahweh, loved.

Yes, Tim Johnson could pat himself on the back for the love he felt for the unfortunate girl in Africa—for all the unfortunates in the world. Wasn't Tim Johnson grand! Yes, his love was corrupt. He was human. But for the first time in his life, that excuse seemed a sham. And for that, he was ashamed.

Tim looked at Tim Johnson, and he knew he wanted to love God with all his heart, soul, mind, and strength. Not for what He could do for Tim Johnson, but for what He had done—shown patience and love to a man who deserved nothing and had suffered nothing. "God help me" were the last words spoken before sleep came.

CHAPTER 13

Josh sat calmly in the passenger seat of the car. Tim noticed the total relaxation of the body. For all Josh knew, Tim could be on his way to a police station and not to a meeting with Dave. Here was a man wanted by the authorities, with a price on his head and the almost impossible task before him of communicating his faith to a hostile city. His work could only lead to torture and death. Nothing but words, ideas on how life should be lived, and yet the world trembled in fear and anger at these mere words. Incredible.

Tim thought of himself and his family. He had placed them in jeopardy. Consorting with a known lawbreaker. How could he explain away the talks he and his family had had with Josh in the past two days? He must rid himself of Josh. He had the information he sought. He had the key. The sooner Josh was gone, the better. No, Josh was a friend, a man who had placed his life at risk for him and his family. He must aid Josh now and in the future, whatever the risk—that is what friends do for friends. That is what Christ would want.

The traffic slowed, then stopped. Before him were three government buses filled with conscripts bound for Europe and the Middle East. The State had moved swiftly, giving the opposition little time to organize resistance. For the first time in the history of the United States, American soldiers had been ordered to war by a foreign power—the Federation. And truly, they were not soldiers but civilians who were to become soldiers. Among the young faces of the men and women, he saw a man in his thirties, looking despondent, old, weary. His mistake was having no children under twelve or valued employment to use as a deferment. The homosexuals, lesbians, transgenders had been hit hard by the conscription—fewer family deferments. They had rioted before the state capitol and in Washington and had frantically sought to adopt children. To his amazement the State had not acquiesced to their considerable political power. The equal treatment they had always claimed they wanted, they were receiving. All the conscripts were bound for basic infantry—cannon fodder; the skilled, relatively safe positions were taken by career soldiers. The traffic unwound, speed increased, the man with the heartbroken visage was passed. Surprising himself, Tim said a prayer for the man.

Josh mused upon the buses of conscripts. Would any see the battle of Armageddon, or would they perish before that final great battle? Would they cross the fields and orchards of his kibbutz? Would they sleep in the tractor barn or in his bed? Would they die on that ground he had walked, plowed? He had talked in depth to Tim, who knew the horrors ahead, the end coming. An earthquake was yet to come, then the seven trumpets, Israel abandoned, then the bowl judgments.

Tim seemed to understand what being in Christ meant. The entire family had been baptized last night. They'd had communion with grape juice and a flat Indian bread. Katie and Matthew had open hearts; the seed had been planted before him. Josh smiled, he thought he would bring water to their souls, but it was they who had soaked him in their knowledge and love. What force would Mary or Tim be to their growth? Mary? Her heart was closed. She had never discouraged his talk, never responded negatively, but her heart was closed, and he could not understand why. Perhaps Katie and Mat needed no human mentor now; the Spirit of God inhabited them.

This Pastor Dave they would meet, what powers did he truly possess? Certainly, Tim's assessments could be believed. Soon he would know if these powers were of Satan or of God. He needed Dave's congregation to expand his base. He did not wish to alienate this man, but the gospel would be presented in purity without compromise. Once he established a firm foothold in Dave's congregation, then he would try the Order. Carl would be tough. The leverage was that Carl was against the present Church; he had values, knew right from wrong. Josh sensed Tim's discomfort—his family was at great risk. They had learned enough now to be labeled Enslavers and imprisoned.

They passed three cars stopped in the emergency lane. The occupants, men and women of assorted ages, were outside their vehicles, fighting, He saw a bloody head, a limp arm, a body on the ground being kicked, then they were gone. Mankind's love was growing very cold as the Restrainer gave people over to themselves. They exited the highway. The night, hazy with humidity, held an end-of-summer coolness. Tim said the fall season was short, and cold would come quickly. On a street of rundown high-rises, bars, porno shops, and drug cellars, they witnessed a white gang roaming the street, destroying signs, fences, commuter platforms, annoying pedestrians. Without fear, loud and brazen, they prowled.

Tim cursed in anger. These people, these half-civilized animals were ruining life. What was their complaint? Carl had been correct in his assessment: there was no complaint; hate came easily, appealed to their nature. Preference, choice, they chose to be destructive. It was the apex of civilization, and these fools were tearing it down. Why weren't they conscripts for the war in the Middle East?

Tim's mind turned to the call he had received from Carl soon after the meeting. Carl had asked him to consider serving on a justice squad. Tim had said yes, without a moment of hesitation. Even Carl had been surprised and said so, thinking a lengthy discussion would be necessary to change Tim's mind. Some semblance of order must be maintained, even if less than seven years of life existed. Fear—that was the only tool left. He wondered what Josh would think of his decision.

They entered the gate of the estate. The access code had been given soon after Tim's initial meeting—a sign of Dave's trust. Dave had been very cautious about this meeting, grilling Tim on Joshua and his beliefs. Questions had been asked about the initial encounter, Josh's clothing, personal belongings, his accent, mannerisms, vocabulary. Dave had suspected he was an inspector assigned to cults, a spy, an informant. Tim knew nothing of Josh's background, which Josh kept hidden purposely and unashamedly—to protect his family, he said. Tim believed Josh. Between Tim's observations and Dave's senses, they had developed a composite sketch of Josh. A kibbutz worker, probably of part-time status, judging by the sun-soaked skin and rough hands, the workman's clothes and fashion. The thin but wiry physique. A teacher also, or someone engaged in a cerebral endeavor involving higher mathematics.

Tim saw lights in the main house. He studied the lit rooms, hoping for a glimpse of the unknown benefactor. He drove slowly to the row of worker's homes. Dave was outside, waiting. This was unusual behavior. Evidently, he wished to keep Josh from entering his home, or even knowing the address. Why? An inspector could easily trace his address and family. Did Dave fear the plague? Tim hopped out, hurrying around the vehicle before Josh had exited.

"Dave, this is Josh."

Josh stood; Dave had remained at a distance. Josh extended his hand. Dave closed the distance between them and shook. Tim sensed a spiritual rebuff between them, even as the men were cordial. Had Dave's powers been rebuffed at some unknown, subconscious level, and Dave had emotionally felt this rejection of himself? Why had Dave shaken hands if he feared the plague? Had Dave already sensed Josh's good health? Or had Dave rebuffed the spirit of Josh?

"Let us walk on the estate and talk as we go. It is a beautiful evening," said Dave.

"Yes, it is a beautiful evening, and I would appreciate a walk," answered Josh.

Tim, attempting to keep the conversation light, interjected, "Is your boss home?"

"Yes. He's having company, a polo match. Five hundred people, plus horses will be here in another two days. This week's meeting will be cancelled."

"I would think so." Tim had been excited about this encounter, but the excitement waned as he listened to Dave's tone, friendly but with a strain of disapproval. The normally placid, handsome face held a wariness when there had always been openness, a tinge of disgust when there had always been acceptance. A dread swept over Tim, as if he had done something terribly wrong by bringing the two together. Tim looked up into the night sky thick with stars. 'Trust the meeting to the Lord,' the heavens said.

Tim listened to the get-to-know-you banter. Josh, through his speech, demeanor, was all that Dave normally was—open, accepting, positive. Perhaps the problem was simply two likeminded personalities, jealous of a perceived imitator. Dave continued the conversation. "You understand I had to meet you first, before introducing you to the congregation. The authorities might wish to label us as a cult. We don't want trouble."

"I understand. I would have done the same," said Josh.

"I will be blunt, Josh…" Dave stopped his forward motion, his musculature tensed, his posture straightened. His eyes had a hard stare. "What do you want?" The tone was skeptical, the eyes rudely penetrating in their unblinking intensity.

"I want to tell you and your people about Christ in a way that possibly they have not heard." Josh's tone was warm, with a friendly boldness. "What they do with this information is between themselves and God. That is all." And that *was* all. You could not convince the heart if the Lord had not chosen and enabled a revelation. That was the mystery of evangelism—that God freely offered all peoples of the world His Son, wisdom, and eternal life, knowing no one could accept their need or the offer without a curiosity, a yearning and divine revelation.

Josh had often meditated upon those he had converted in an attempt to find a formula or a type, some marker in a person's former theology, life understanding, troubles, barriers, or personality that said, "Here is the Lord's servant. Here is the person, man, woman, child who thirsts for the Presence of the Living God." Josh, himself, had come to Jesus hating life, family, and friends; hating his smug Judaism of legalism, of distrusting motives and all human wisdom; and hating himself. He had been forgiven much. For as many who fit his type, he had seen as many who loved life, family, friends, and themselves who had received the new birth.

"Has Tim told you of our beliefs?" Dave spoke coldly.

"Yes, and I must agree with so much of your teaching. Your belief in God's concern and love for us; the knowledge of a bleak future, of love grown cold; your moral standards. All good streams of thought."

"Your flattery is evident. What of our differences?"

This rudeness was uncharacteristic of Dave. With amazement, Tim realized that Dave could not read Josh's thoughts. Was this the rebuff he had sensed at their first introduction? Supernatural forces invisible and battling? He was reminded of a charging fighter locking his opponent in the initial seconds of the fight, throwing and pinning him. The God of Josh had won. With the absence of Dave's sixth sense, the advantage was gone. It was replaced by fear, vulnerability, and the subsequent jealousy, rudeness. The loving, concerned Dave was only a product of his perceived superiority.

"Not flattery, but a commendation, an appreciation." Dave saw Josh as a rival? The awareness startled Josh, yet it settled easily into his thoughts. It had a logic—even though of false content. Josh renewed his conversation. "Differences: that man cannot save himself, through this peeling-away process you preach. Christ saves by His work on the cross. Man has no power in and of himself. Only by Christ's death is sin nullified—before God and within man. As long as we move and have our beings in this corrupt world, as long as our minds retain the remembrance of sin, we may sin again. But that is not from our new nature; it is from the memory of the old."

"Ah, pure Enslaver doctrine." Dave spoke confidently, fearlessly, as if he had the advantage. He could turn Josh in to the authorities any time he wished.

"That is a compliment," Josh stated without a smile but also without rancor.

"To you, I'm certain it is," Dave responded. "You have Christ's purpose and function wrong. He died for our sins, those we have committed and will commit in our fleshly bodies and minds. He died so that the Holy Spirit could come and help us peel away our evil nature. Christ cannot live within us, nor would He want to. Nor do we need to die to our bodies, created in the image of God."

"Christ said we must be born again," Josh said with resolution in his tone. What does that statement mean to you, Dave? he thought silently.

"The Jews of that day had many born-again ceremonies, steps from one life into the next. The most prominent being from boyhood to manhood. The same life rising to a higher level of responsibility," Dave said.

"That which is born of the flesh is flesh, and that which is born of the Spirit is Spirit. I see no levels there—no rising, no evolving. I see a break, a chasm so deep and wide that only Christ can bridge it," Josh speedily replied.

"You have your opinion." Dave's tone was curt.

"No, I have God's facts. Of this image of God you trust so highly in, God said, 'I'm sorry I made them,' speaking of mankind. What else can He do but remake man by rebirth? Make him the man he was when God was pleased, before the fall into sin. We cannot chart our course through life on opinion, Dave."

Little Josh, looking so weak and frail with the skinny arms and legs and inches shorter beside Dave's height and strong musculature, had an authority in his voice that made Dave seem the child, thought Tim. The authority did not come from deepness of voice nor projection of sound, nor from inflection or delivery. The authority came from the Spirit of God within the words of the earthly speaker.

"Yet, there is a place where men disagree, and it is better to call that place *opinion*," said Dave.

"I think we can take frank talk and disagreements, if we respect each other." Josh looked directly into the fullness of Dave's face and eyes and added, "And I do respect you, Dave." He truly did respect Dave—he respected all people, all creations of his God.

"You have said nothing that can sway my beliefs."

"We cannot undervalue, shun, ignore Christ's work on the cross and expect no consequences from God. Christ is to be glorified. You give Him and His Father so little respect for the painfully bought mercy They have given." The soul of Josh ached: God Himself had been mocked, disrespected, belittled on the cross; God Himself, naked and shredded, organs exposed, had endured and become the entertainment for perverse humanity in order to reconcile man to Himself.

Tim listened intently. He visibly saw the pain welling up on Josh's face. For a moment, Tim understood the pain in Josh and the sacrifice of God. This wasn't the time for emotionalism. Both men made good points, but it only seemed a philosophical argument. Did it matter how you became a better person as long as you did? That was the wrong question, becoming a better person. The question was, do you seek a relationship with your God? Even those apart from Christ could become better persons. Do you seek a relationship with your God? Do you want to be His son? Do you want Him to be your Dad, the man you obey? The man who teaches you of life? These statements rising from his mind personally struck Tim's awareness like a blow to the head.

Dave spoke. "Your own philosophy contradicts itself. If Christ gives us a new nature then why is it necessary to forgive present and future sins? If Christ is in you, how can you sin?"

"You are in Christ; in His death, your body of sin is dead," Josh said. "Sin has not disappeared from the world, the carnal flesh, or Satan. You are simply dead to its power when you are in Christ, just as you are dead to weightlessness because of gravity; one force overwhelms another. The world, the flesh, Satan can tempt, trick, deceive you as to your position in Christ. That is where the battle is found. That is a far different man than one who lives out of his rebelling flesh, for the world, for his carnal appetites, believing Satan does not exist even as he serves him, believing he is achieving goodness and righteousness."

"The result is the same," Dave said. "You sin, just as I and my congregation sin. How is your philosophy superior?"

"We sin from Satan's trickery and deceit as to our position in Christ. Our love of the world, the flesh, and ourselves has been broken forever by the cross. You sin, your evolving sin produces an unending stream from the flesh that is your body. You are dependent on the will, on placing yourself in an environment where the opportunity to sin is lessened, or on ignoring the reality of life. Your will, however rightly guided it is, is a work of the flesh. Abiding in Christ is not work; we don't need a sinless environment; we don't need to will ourselves through the thousand and one sins that plague man. For in Christ, we have no desire to sin. Our way is easy; yours difficult and impossible.

"But the issue of sin is not the crux of our difference; rather, it's from whom we draw our lives. We draw our lives, our life force, our motivation, our strength from the God who begot us. His spiritual genetics are ours. He raises us, and we beckon to His voice. He is eternal, and we will be eternal. We know the glory of partaking of Christ's supernatural life. We are God's children through the new birth. All others are illegitimate."

Dave ignored the last statements. "What is your will used for?"

"To keep us abiding in Christ."

"What does that mean, if I may ask, *to be in Christ*?"

"To have our life, our thoughts, our actions aimed toward Him, for Him. To draw our sustenance daily from Him." Josh searched his mind—pleaded for the right words.

"No, you hide from reality. You people are too weak to try to strive, to fight to become better. You are the losers of life, who have given up. You invent a philosophy of surrender. You are people with no life in you, no lust for the good things of life, the lust of struggle. Your bodies aren't only dead to sin, but they're also dead to life. You get neither." Dave's words were spoken harshly with great repulsion.

Josh laughed unaffectedly, without derision. "Your problem is that you're too strong. It seems your will has conquered everything thrown before it. Perhaps your special gift has influenced you in ways you cannot discern."

"Is that bad?"

"Certainly. The word of God, the word from God Himself says, 'You must be born again.' Even Nicodemus, a teacher and student of God's holy word, knew Christ wasn't talking of life changes when he asked if it were possible for a man to reenter the womb. What is of the flesh is flesh. What is of the Spirit is Spirit. Being in Christ, being a child of God, sharing a relationship with Him is life."

Dave glared at Josh, then the eyes softened. "We will see on the other side. God will show us the truth."

"We won't be together, Dave. I will be with Lazarus, and you with the rich man."

Dave laughed. "And why is that?"

"Only that which is born of God will pass to the other side, not that which is born of the flesh, no matter how righteous and spiritual that flesh is. It is who is hid in Christ that is saved, not who hides from Christ."

Dave smirked. "So you want to address my congregation and take people away from me? I should allow this?"

"They have free will, don't they? Besides, you said our differences are only of philosophy. The outcome is the same, you said. It is not like you would be giving your members over to evil."

"What if I have changed my mind and now perceive you as evil?"

"On what grounds?"

"Your denial of the truth has earthly consequences. The State imprisons your kind. I don't want to see any of my flock imprisoned."

"That is for each member of your congregation to decide. Besides, probably in less than seven years, their flesh will be dead, imprisoned for life. Certainly, you allow all people to keep their free will?"

Dave said nothing. He thought it through. He could let Josh address his flock, and he could counter Josh's position in a series of debates; they could decide. Certainly, their free will would be exercised, but at great trouble and cost. He would have to study and prepare for the debates. Valuable time would be wasted when preparations had to be made for the hard times ahead. Besides, Josh was wrong. Why lead his sheep into another pasture when their own was sufficient and superior? He knew better than Josh, and there were times in life when superior minds—or minds knowing a higher level—had to exercise authority. They had arrived at a fishpond. He sat on a bench, Josh and Tim stood. "You debate well. Leave Tim and me for a moment…I have things to discuss with him. I will give my decision before the next service."

Josh extended his hand, shook Dave's reluctant hand. "Thank you." Josh wandered across the vast, flat polo field into the night.

"What do you think of this man's request, Tim?"

"I don't know." Dave was probing him. "Like you said, it's just opinion. Let people make up their own minds."

"What if a significant portion follows this man? We need everyone for the move. We have a cohesive unit, one of interdependence. Break that, and we lose our effectiveness."

"I don't think anyone will be drawn away."

"Not you and your family?"

"No." This answer was hidden from Dave, for it was, *No, we can't be drawn away from what we have never given allegiance to.*

Dave seemed relieved. "We are leaving soon. I feel it. You are coming? I know Mary wants to go."

The last sentence surprised Tim; Mary had never expressed an opinion to him. He had brought maps to Dave to help him avoid computer searches and printings and even gave some of his survival supplies to the congregation. He had helped plan the trip into the dead zone—that area of the western United States long since desiccated by drought. All his efforts had been halfhearted.

"Why leave, Dave?"

"Earthquakes, famine, pestilence, social disorder. You would do well to miss these things. Life here will be savage."

"I don't know that moving to the wilderness is going to make our lives easier. We will surely attract government authorities," Tim said. "Help me to understand."

"There is a realm around us few men see or hear. The course of the world is written in the very earth, the trees, animal life, the sky, even man-made objects, and man."

"You can hear?" Tim asked. Dave's answer was of no help to Tim. He was saying nothing the Bible hadn't said. The question was: How was moving to the desert better than remaining where they were? Josh's arguments should be presented to the people—that was the American way, that was the United States. The truth—its delivery unattached from bribery, coercion, violence—should be presented to everyone. Would the God of Life wish it any other way?

"Yes, and I have developed a discernment," Dave said. "Trust the discernment and live to see the new world."

Dave purposely had not addressed the question. He wanted blind obedience to his discernment, Tim realized. And that wasn't right. A man must follow facts. The facts were: the larger the group effort, the greater the pool of resources. The government wouldn't allow the people to starve; the government had greater power to find and distribute food. If the government failed, there was the Order. If the Order failed, then Tim was on his own—and quite confident he and his family could survive with their food stockpiles. They would live on the margin of government authority, outside its reach but gleaning its food supplies and water, like feral dogs. Even the dogs ate from the earthly master's table.

"Think it over. I'll see you this weekend." Dave walked onto the vast polo fields, into the night.

Josh, watching from the darkness, returned to Tim. Tim and Josh walked back to the car.

"What did you think of Dave? Sense any powers?"

"Yes, he has powers, as did pharaoh's magicians. 'For there shall arise false Christs, and false prophets, and shall shew great signs and wonders; insomuch that, if it were possible, they shall deceive the very elect.'"

"That's a little rough, don't you think?" Tim said.

"The times are rough. I beg you: don't follow him. His evil is of the worst kind—innocence is the icing, and the cake is deceit. He doesn't know he is evil—his innocence is his power, his gift. He will lead many away from Christ."

***

Tim and Josh rode in silence, on the multilane beltway. Tim initiated cruise control, then rubbed his face with his hands, which provided a momentary wakefulness. The quiet, lack of talk, was peaceful to the tired men. Tim and Josh studied the sights outside the windows. Tim had the view of the old riverbed's fishponds, the canal with its loaded barges, the lights and tall buildings of the west shore, the mountain ridge. Josh had the high-rises of Harrisburg, the looping beltways, the commuter rail cars lit from within and crowded with people, the rail lines twisting and straightening into and out of the rail yards and stations.

Tim mused on Josh's handling of Dave and plain Dave stripped of his gift of discernment. Dave had appeared as the very common man he truly was. Josh was genuine, his arguments were sound. In an instant, the interior of the car was filled with inflatable, white pillows of tough fabric; the fabric grasped their bodies. They were airborne, then rolling lengthways over the lanes. A warning buzzer sounded for a few seconds then stopped. Tim's head was rattling, his body being pulled by forces of conflicting direction. In the few separations between airbags, he saw the world tumbling and jumping, cars rolling, bodies being ejected, roadway sections missing, traffic falling, high-rises swaying.

The earthquake had struck quickly and forcefully. He heard nothing from Josh but grunts. They were both grunting, attempting to find the muscular strength to keep their bodies under control. Tim was aware the safety sensors had stopped the engines. The rotor blades beneath had locked. They might be abraded to ooze if they were ejected, but they would not be chopped to a hamburger consistency. He had seen the brake warning light as the brakes locked gently, as if a collision had occurred. The rolling stopped. Then he guessed another rolling vehicle crashed into them. Stunned, they remained inside as the car shook, then heaved. The tall light poles were swaying and snapping; signs, too, were crashing onto the roadway. All traffic was now stopped, shaking, bouncing. Sections of roadway were falling. Tim heard screams of pain and fear. He wondered if the roadway would give way beneath the car. Surely, a broken spine—if not instant death—would be the result. They needed to exit immediately.

The door was jammed. The earth was still shaking. All the windows had either popped out in solid pieces or shattered outward. He was able to pull his hidden dagger from his left forearm sheaf. The dagger had become standard apparel since the run-in with the gang. He began stabbing the safety bags. He exited out the front windshield. Josh's safety bags were deflating, and Josh pulled himself out the front windshield too. Both men held onto the hood of the vehicle. People were leaving their cars, through doors or windows, and attempting to run. Most staggered and fell, then lay on the ground that was beating them senseless. The foolish attempted to rise and continue. Their legs flew out from under them. They fell, bouncing like rag dolls; their arms, legs, heads flailing, bones snapping.

The overpass, only a hundred yards ahead, crashed onto the highway. Bodies and cars bounced into the air from the fallen structure. They heard the distant moans, screams. The highway lights were out. Only the car headlights cut through the humid air now dense with dust. Tim's stomach churned until he involuntarily vomited.

Surely, the shaking would stop! They held onto the inside of the car roof, their legs now inside the car. The cars, which rode on a cushion of air when in movement, had no suspension to soften the blows. To leave the protection of the car was foolishness. They too would suffer broken limbs. The conscious who were upon the road moaned and cursed. The unconscious, their heads on limp bodies were pulverized by the constant banging on the concrete. Tim grasped for his scientific training in his terror; he checked his wristwatch/timer, attempted to mark the time. He saw triple images of the screen, so blurred the face was unreadable.

Suddenly their car and all other cars on the highway were thrown sideways. Tim slipped back inside the car and pulled Josh within. They reharnessed their safety belts. The vehicle began sliding across the lanes. Some cars rolled over and over, over the guardrail, down an embankment. Headlight beams crisscrossed the night, illuminating the roiling dust. Shouting, screaming. The stomach-churning taste of dust. A great roar was in their ears. Buildings collapsing? The earth opening up?

Their car jammed against a toppled truck, which, because of its width, had not rolled. Their car and the truck slid down the slope, carried by an avalanche. Tim watched other vehicles flipping down the moving embankment. Breaking, popping plexiglass; bending, grinding metal; buckling plastics; screaming people. Eyes shaking in their heads—double, triple images. Light poles snapping, clanging on the cement, dust flying. The intensity and duration broke Tim's calm. Minutes must have passed. His body ached from the tension of keeping himself stable.

He was going to die! His head slapped against the door. His neck would be broken against the headrest. He did not call out to God. He could face death alone. He needed no help. His family? Where were Mat and Katie, Mary? Were they dying in agony? He needed to survive—for them. Oh God! Oh God! He pleaded with God for their lives.

The side of his face was numb from an unknown blow. His head ached from having hit the roof repeatedly. He dry heaved—his vertigo was maddening. They heard a deafening grinding. An immense chasm opened above them, swallowing the lanes from which they had come, increasing the velocity of the slide.

Josh was praising God. What was he praising? Tim wondered. The power that might kill them?

The tumbling earth on which they rode crashed into buildings. Debris went flying; the dust was blinding. Then they were still.

CHAPTER 14

They lay motionless. The resting car increased their sense of vertigo. Below them they heard smothered screams, moans, sobs. The headlight beams illuminated the wreckage of vehicles, apartments, high-rises. The roaring became a rumbling that moved to the north and east like surf on a distant shoreline. Tim was dizzy, disoriented, retching. Voices were calling out in fear, panic. Dazed, the commuters sat or stumbled in the wreckage. Bodies lay strewn about. Most of the conscious had broken bones. Complete darkness immediately round them, save for the glow of phones, sparking electrical lines, and the immobile beams of car headlights.

By chance they had come to rest on a natural vantage point atop debris, the vista widened by the downing of surrounding structures. They exited the car through the windshield opening and scrambled to the top of the heap of earth and rubble. The vastness of the city was spread before them. Fires could be seen throughout the jumbled concrete and broken spires of high-rises. Buildings burned, natural gas pipelines spewed balls of flame, the flickering yellow and red light casting shadows on the ruins. Clouds of dust roiled in the air. The explosion of electrical lines within homes and buildings attached to the underground electric river created a popping sound that echoed through the city. The sudden flashes were surrounded in greenish white light.

He smelled a late-summer air with the damp of night holding the dust of cement, crumbled building materials, acrid smoke. The emotions of fear and anxiety had impressed the sensations of dust; the smells of automobiles, trees and grasses, roiled earth; and the flickering light of gas explosions and building fires upon the mind. Even the smell of his own vomit upon the plastic dash of the vehicle stuck in Tim's mind. He saw stars in the sky flickering.

The tremors lessened and then ceased. Tim descended from the mound. He rushed for his trunk and the rucksack of emergency supplies, complete with first aid kit and flashlight. He had to get home. The warehouse apartment that was home surely would have collapsed. The vast warehouse roof was just a shell to protect the contents; it had no strength. The corner might stand, where the apartment was situated. He imagined his family pinned in wreckage, hurting, dying. He slipped his arms into the straps of the pack, shrugged it to his shoulders.

He studied the ground, the slope of the unnatural mound, with the flashlight. Josh was standing beside him—the eyes alert and without fear. Earth covered the top of a crushed two- or three-story apartment building, now compacted to one story. Muffled shouts and moans came from under the rubble. Tim guessed he was five miles from home. He must get home quickly. If his family had survived, they would be visited by looters or the gang looking for the pistol. All his food supplies would be taken.

He reached into his car, tried the ignition. Amazingly, the engine turned over. Josh, ferret like, was penetrating the wreckage adjacent and under the vehicle. Tim examined the rotor blades—one was bent but not severely. Perhaps he could drive the car off the pile of rubble. How many streets were blocked? Likely all of them. Leave the car and walk. What if his family was dead? What then? Don't think about it; think of the journey ahead. Tim carefully determined a safe course down the mound. Josh emerged from the wreckage. "I'm going home, Josh. You're welcome to return to the apartment with me. But if you can't keep up, I'm not waiting."

"I understand. I'll follow to the best of my ability."

Tim slid down the pile; he had no time to be concerned about Josh. No, he was concerned for Josh. Tim understood that he owed Josh a responsibility simply as a guest, friend, and foreigner under his protection. Josh was a good guy, period, and deserved loyalty.

"Josh, are you oriented? Do you know the direction back?" Tim had turned to face Josh directly and studied his eyes as he had spoken.

"Well, maybe a landmark wouldn't hurt."

Tim smiled, turned, and pointed toward the highway looping to the east. "You must cross the highway to the north side—in the direction of the mountain ridge, about a mile to our east. If you see signs for Linglestown, you have not gone far enough. Look for the shopping mall to orient yourself."

"Got it."

"Good luck." Tim patted, shook Josh's shoulder as a parting gesture of goodwill.

***

Tim gazed across the field; he could not see the high-rises through the ground fog and suspended dust. A few beams of light, a few campfires, told him there were survivors. He walked wearily down the road to the warehouse district, straining his eyes to see his building. He was soaked in the sweat of anxiety and exertion.

He had traveled all night to cover the five miles. He had waded lakes formed by broken water mains, pushed floating corpses aside. He had detoured around bodies of water so deep he could not ford them. He had circled raging fires from broken gas mains; the flames feeding on the debris of high-rises and factories. He had stepped over downed power lines, watched a man walk into a wet street and dance the death of electrocution. He had heard the muffled screams and moans from the piles of debris once apartments and high-rises. He had crawled over intact high-rises lying like toppled trees.

Men, women, children had begged him for help, and he had kept moving. He saw broken arms, legs, ghastly compound fractures, burns, abrasions covering—it seemed—entire bodies. He had almost fallen into a chasm; at the bottom, he had seen the remains of buildings swallowed whole. Groups of survivors were gathering. Lone survivors—sitting and dazed or prone, waiting to die—lay strewn about. Police, ambulances, fire apparatus, National Guard were not seen. He had seen no looting. Each individual was in his or her own sphere of shock and bewilderment. He had lost Josh early; Josh had heard a cry within ruins, and he chose to remain to help. Why? Tim didn't know; the cry had been no more or less heart wrenching than all the others.

The fence still stood or, rather, drooped. The entry gate had been popped open by the heaving earth. Tim's eyes searched for the warehouse, the warehouse that had covered acres. He heard a sound; he stopped, listened. The fog moved. What was he seeing? Movement, material. Plastic wrap, protective plastic wrapping, part of the storage process, enveloping all stored goods, blowing listlessly. The warehouse walls had fallen. The acres of contents protruded through the fallen roof.

He ran. He dodged items thrown out from the collapsed walls. The items were from his apartment!

"Stop! Identify yourself!" The familiar voice was firm.

"Mat, it's Dad! Mat, are you alright?"

Matthew stood from his hiding place behind a container. The machine pistol was aimed at the earth. Mat's eyes were hollow, frightened; his happiness bound by some unknown pain.

"What's wrong? Mat!"

Before Mat could answer, Tim heard the cries of Katie.

"Daddy! Daddy! I'm here, Daddy!" Tim ran past Matthew to the sound of his daughter's voice. She lay on her bed, Mary by her side. Mary's face was grave. Mary pulled the cover back, shone a flashlight on Katie's bare leg. A compound fracture!

"I've given her one of the pain pills. To help keep her still. We planned to search for medical help at daybreak, if you weren't back. I've called the emergency number and registered our need for help—there was no interaction with a person." Mary looked imploringly at her husband.

"You did well, Mary." He searched Katie's face—she seemed at peace, with only mild pain. "Katie, we will find you a doctor. You be brave."

"I will, Dad."

The change from Daddy to Dad told him she was aware of her panic and was asserting control. He stroked her forehead, felt a slight fever. The bone looked grisly sticking through the skin, sharp and glistening. One wrong move and an artery could be sliced. With a Clear Scan and a laser infusion, the bone could be set, mended in five minutes. He looked up—to heaven? Or to the breeze picking up in intensity? He realized the apartment had no roof.

He could not assume the light of day would bring help—air platforms with emergency personnel and equipment. The hospital was miles away, the streets blocked. Katie would have to be carried. What if the hospital equipment had been destroyed or the skilled workers killed? Emergency plans would go into effect. No doubt thousands were waiting for help. The Red Cross would be activated, and the medical arm of the National Guard. He knew the medical emergency site of the National Guard, but when would it be operational? He had to take Katie to the city's hospital.

"Are you operational?" he asked Mary.

"Sore muscles, headache, I had a concussion. The walls collapsed in the first minute. We were all in bed. Oddly, the entire roof jumped off and landed beside the apartment. Our beds saved us—we fell straight down to ground level. Katie bounced out of bed. That's when her leg snapped."

The flimsy construction and the beds had saved his family. "We're all going to the hospital. We'll make Katie a stretcher. Let's hide our few belongings."

Matthew began rummaging. "We have a military stretcher, Dad— bought it from the ex-soldier, remember?"

The survival food had been placed in a metal container and hidden in the warehouse; the personal items and his weapons were what he feared losing.

"No, I don't remember. But I'm glad you did. We'll take a few days' food and water—and the weapons."

"I can't believe this has happened. I just can't believe it!" Mary mumbled as she set about her work.

"I told you it would." He couldn't resist the boast.

"You didn't believe it yourself," Mary chastised with her sneering tone.

He said nothing. He'd save his breath for the long trip to downtown Harrisburg.

***

Tim pushed down on the lever of the portable container. The stimulator tea, steaming and brown, filled his insulated cup. His calloused, dust-covered hands were shaking from exertion and lack of food. The sun was at least at the noon hour. He had volunteered to help in the evacuating of the hospital patients and then the removal of debris from the air-platform pad when he first arrived. He anxiously glanced over at the rucksack by Matthew. He had nervously, stealthily transferred the shotgun, which had been sawed off, to Matthew's ruck, without being seen. The anxiety clung to him. What if the ruck was accidently opened, and someone saw the weapons? It had been a mistake to bring them—just added anxiety. People were still in the shock stage and probably would be for days. The frustration stage would be the time of confrontation. He again glanced over at the bag and then at the long columns of patients arrayed on the grass of the riverfront park, between the downed century-old trees, waiting for medical treatment.

His searching eyes returned to Matthew. Beside Mat, Mary sat with Katie. They were waiting for a Clear Scan to be removed from the now-vacant and off-limits hospital, or for the National Guard to fly one in, so that the fracture patients could be mended. He gazed up at the leaning but towering hospital. It had stood. Windows were broken, debris

192

hung from the roof, slabs of cement facing had fallen, floors had been pinched by compression, but it stood. The building codes had planned for survivability of Richter scale 9 earthquakes.

From their journey across the city, down the riverfront park, the hospital had been one of a handful of high-rises that stood intact. He assumed all were so structurally weakened they would have to be demolished—if wind, rain, or another earthquake did not accomplish the task. The majority of tall buildings either had snapped at one-third of their height, leaving stubs in the sky, or had been pulled out by their roots, falling whole, breaking or collapsing only after hitting the earth intact. A few buildings had been supported by their interconnecting walkways and leaned up against each other at precarious angles.

The subterranean city was gone and had entombed whatever souls had been unfortunate enough to be within its depths when the quake struck. Likely tens of thousands of people dead or still trapped and simply waiting for death by fire, electrocution, blood loss, suffocation, thirst. His greatest fear on the journey had been the walk from their apartment. No gang members had been seen. Once through the city, they had walked south along the riverfront park. The riverbed was empty, as was the canal—the boats were sitting on the plasticized bottom. The stately trees of the park had been toppled. The tall buildings along the riverfront had fallen backward, away from the park. All of the river bridges were down, the crushed and mangled wrecks of vehicles within the debris. Water had backed up behind the bridge debris, forming shallow lakes. The vast volume of the river must have been dammed or diverted north of the city—perhaps at the Dauphin Narrows. Was this water an impending disaster, waiting to burst from the debris dam and roll south, picking up the debris of Harrisburg on the journey to the Chesapeake Bay?

The mountains—resembling a wall to the north of the city—running from south-southwest to north-northeast, seemed to have heaved up, perhaps doubling in height. The ridgetop was now crowned with bare, brown, sedimentary rock. The billowy green trees upon the mountain's slope had been shaken loose. Roots, earth, branches, and the soft light-green underside of leaves piled upon each other held the gaze in amazement. The mountain restaurant, on the cliff edge facing the river, a popular meeting place and focal point for the city, was a pile of rubble with an advertising flag still flying on its summit. The tectonic plate that slipped had been north of the city and moved south, jumbling up onto the existing mountains—leaving the southern slope untouched, except for sporadic piles of overspill from the new heights. The city and suburbs, with all of their human structures, remained in place. Curiously, the ancient cut in the mountain made by the river had not been affected by the plate movement from the north. The riverbed, now dry, had not changed location.

For the length of their journey, people had been out, helping the wounded, gathering up belongings, making fires, eating breakfast, cleaning up debris, gathering the dead. Tim guessed that one-third of the city's inhabitants were dead or wounded. No one had spoken to his family; no gangs were evident. Katie never complained. Matthew did a man's work in carrying his end of the stretcher and never asked for a break. Mary picked out their route and removed troublesome debris from their projected path. The family had been focused on the immediate needs of Katie, undeterred by the wreckage and corpses around them. The stress of giving Katie a level and smooth ride had demanded the utmost attention. He was proud of them.

Tim sat down with the work-crew members on the grass before a huge, toppled tree. On the trunk of the tree, at a level spot, an electrascreen had been placed. The men were distracted from the screen by the first air platform of the day, coming in out of the cloudy sky. The tree rustled loudly as the rotors kicked up a wind. The wind, picking up the coolness of the day, sent shivers over Tim's sweaty skin and clothes. National Guard markings on the platform. Too soon after the catastrophe to be flying in equipment—even bureaucracies established for emergencies were still, by nature, slow. Katie had to have her leg set soon. He couldn't allow her to wait indefinitely. If only he was certain that competent, concerned people were working on her need.

Tim spoke to himself. *Matthew, keep those weapons hidden in the ruck. Don't jostle the bag around, don't leave it unattended.* God, he was so tired. When the platform had landed, he gulped down his tea. This would keep him awake for at least four hours—someone had said it was strength four, and he hoped the gossip was accurate. He watched a few high-ranking generals step out of the platform. He'd watch one news report and then take his turn at sitting with Katie.

Heavy smoke blew in from the city, then the dust of crumbled, pulverized cement. The electrascreen showed air platform views of the devastating earthquake. First, around New York City, then Boston, then Philadelphia, and finally Washington, DC. The northeast news division was the only one to report in. The assumption of the newscaster was that the entire nation had been hit. The same scenes Tim had witnessed in Harrisburg, he saw in the other cities. The Washington Monument was down; the Lincoln Memorial, destroyed. The bridges of New York City were gone. Manhattan Island was a five-hundred-foot pile of rubble. The others watching the screen, as worn as Tim, were slack jawed, incredulous.

The local news station took over the reporting duties, showed the devastation through the Susquehanna Valley. North, the river had been dammed by a fallen mountainside. A huge lake was forming in the old riverbed, covering prime farmland, ag towns, and villages. To the south a dam had broken, washing away towns, parts of cities, destroying the production of electrical power. Mountains had gained hundreds of feet in height or been lowered by hundreds of feet. Vast acreage of forest land was down, deer were shown running through ag fields in confusion. Huge chasms ran through prime ag fields. Herds of cattle lay dead in the fields or flopping their heads in agony. Ag buildings housing cattle, pigs, chickens were burning. Fields of wheat and corn ready for harvest were flattened. From storage towers and tanks, chemical spills inundated fields. Broken irrigation systems spewed water and created lakes. Apple orchards—trees heavy with fruit—were flattened.

The city was shown; one brief, high view. Tim searched frantically for details, then the view was gone. A familiar local announcer, disheveled, appeared on the screen, telling people to be patient, to gather food and clothing, to make tents, to sleep away from standing debris and ruins. Tim returned to the huge container of tea. He knew famine was coming. The entire East Coast had been affected by the quake, a quarter of the tillable land in the United States. Crops could be gleaned from the destruction, but not efficiently, not with the big machines that needed ideal conditions of flat land, properly graded. Work crews, people with baskets on their backs and hoes and sickles in their hands, would have to do the work. The dead animals would be useless in a day or two, all that meat wasted. Where would the work crews come from? The healthy male and female population was being conscripted to Europe. Would they be diverted? The US food surplus had been reduced by half to satisfy the Federation. Would that food now come back? He doubted it.

He walked by a line of patients with broken bones, came to his Katie. She was sleeping.

"I'll take over. You and Mat get something to drink, take a nap. Has the doctor been by?"

"No."

"A nurse?"

"Not since we arrived."

"Hold on." Tim saw a tall doctor checking charts at the far end of the columns of patients. He walked over to the thinly built man. "Doctor, my little girl is here with a compound fracture. Why can't she be taken care of?" He realized his words had a tone of confrontation, though he had sought the opposite tone. Tim saw the physician tense with anger.

"Look, you see lots of people here with problems. We only have three doctors for all of them. The electricity isn't on in the building." An irritable arrogance clung to his words.

"We have electricity down here—the portable generator." Tim spoke meekly; he didn't want to ruin Katie's chance at help by having a bad attitude.

"The Clear Scan is up on the twentieth floor, with the laser," the doctor said sarcastically.

"Is it heavy? I'll bring it down. I'd be very grateful. I could send you a case of supplies, for you, personally."

"Sure. Sure." The doctor shook his head in disgust, began scribbling on a small tablet. "Here. Take this to the security guard at the front of the building. Go get the equipment." The doctor turned away quickly, then turned back. "Where's your phone?" Tim held it up. The doctor pressed his phone to Tim's. "Just pressed a picture of the device onto your screen." He wished to be rid of the bothersome man. "Go. And treat the equipment with delicacy—no drops, no hard jolts."

"Thanks." Tim's eyes scanned the groups of loved ones by their injured, searching for strong healthy men. He suddenly turned to the doctor. "But what floor?"

"Damn you. Twentieth floor, room 2015." The doctor tensed again in anger and was seemingly about to strike, then turned abruptly to his duties. Tim stood humbly with a false naivete on his face. Some men were better at pressure than others. Or did this doctor have a family with problems of their own? Tim would have allowed himself to be struck, without retort, for Katie's sake.

Tim walked back up the line of patients, told Mary and Matthew to wait as he introduced himself to the first adult male among the waiting who seemed healthy; a blue-collar type, by the company uniform and musculature, named Anthony. Matthew needed to remain near Katie and the weapons, and Mat was exhausted from the carrying of his sister. Anthony quickly agreed.

He and Anthony entered the building without problems, walked twenty flights of stairs. The elevators had emergency power, but the cant of the building was enough for the elevators to scrape in the shaft. Sweat poured from both men. Anthony had muscle but no cardiovascular endurance but for his younger age. They located the machine, realized it weighed hundreds of pounds. Luckily the machine had portable capabilities, wheels of substance and strength that could be locked into positions.

Tim and Anthony, by trial and error, found the machine's range of motions and capabilities as well as their own. The sweat continued to pour from them in the hot, humid, unventilated stairways, as they pulled, pushed, tugged, lifted. All movements were forced to be done with gentleness. They found towels for cushioning, a metal ramp to span the stairs. After every floor they took a break and wondered if more men needed to be recruited. Anthony left on the fifteenth floor to get help. Tim wondered if Anthony would return. Perhaps Anthony's loved one could wait. Anthony did return with a nephew and the nephew's friend, both teenagers. The newcomers could not understand the importance of gentleness. When Anthony impressed upon them—by curses and a punch to his nephew's shoulder—the delicacy of the machine and its purpose, the new recruits chafed at the time it would take to move it, but grimly obeyed orders. In the foyer, Tim and Anthony left the younger men to guard the machine. The doctor needed to be found to give a final resting place to the device. Tim saw Mary and rushed to her as Anthony trailed.

"Where's that doctor I just talked with?"

"I saw him get on an emergency air platform and fly away."

"Probably giving individual attention to someone with money." Anthony volunteered as he caught up. Lustful eyes undressed Mary.

Tim scanned the area. He saw another doctor, standing, leaning over a tall lectern-type table. Tim dodged through the crowd to stand before the doctor.

"Doctor, your colleague who just left said he would set my little girl's leg if I brought down the Clear Scan. I have the Clear Scan, but he left on an air platform. Do you know when he will return?"

"Days. Some other business." The doctor did not glance up from his laptop computer screen or even glance at the men.

"Could you do it? I'll pay you with a week's worth of emergency supplies."

"I don't need supplies…I've got work…wait your turn." He spoke gruffly.

Tim grabbed the man by the collar, pushed him back and off balance.

"Listen! Bringing down that machine benefits everyone. All I ask is you treat my little girl. And this man's father. First."

"Why are they special? Look at all these people! Who the hell do you think you are?" The doctor, a big man, twisted violently away from Tim's grasp.

Tim's composure snapped instantly. "I know I'm the father of a little girl with a compound fracture. I know I promised this man help for his father. That's who I know I am. They're special because Anthony and I brought down the machine. And all the others are special too." Tim grabbed the collar again, forced the doctor back, swung him over his thigh, pushed the man to the earth. "You're the man who is going to heal my girl, his father, and all the rest. Now."

The doctor weighed the effort of resistance; maybe he could win, but valuable time would be lost, and energy, perhaps the use of his hands for surgery. In five minutes, the leg could be set. "Okay, help me up. We'll take care of them all."

***

Tim and Mary had taken the recuperating Katie to a grassy place, free of debris, on the edge of the second tier of the riverbank. They were at the farthest point from any buildings, knowing that the night would bring scores of people to this open, safe place of rest. Already survivors were setting up camps, laying out blankets. Matthew had been given permission to work with a cleanup crew.

Tim napped. Mary took notice of Katie's every need. She'd be walking in twenty-four hours. Mary had her man back, decisive, resolute. The air traffic had increased. A power plant had been delivered. A field kitchen was feeding hospital patients. Federally issued tents were being erected, filled with the patients and their families. Tim awoke; the tea hadn't been able to keep him awake but brought him out of his sleep much more quickly. The sun, hidden all day, appeared in the sky briefly as a red ball. Dusk was upon them. The air was cold. Mary spoke. "Should I get in line for Katie's meal?"

Tim glanced at the long line of ambulatory wounded or family representatives. "Is it worth the effort? Let's use our own supplies." They saw Matthew running toward them, fright and disgust on his face.

"What's wrong, Mat?" queried Mary.

"Dad, some man tried to kiss me! He tried to get me on the ground and take off my pants. He's a pervert, Dad!"

Tim remained seated. "Did he do anything to you?"

"No, I got away."

"Did his hands or body touch you?"

"He grabbed my shoulders, but I twisted myself free."

Tim's heart was beating wildly, blind rage energized him. His breath came heavily. He rose. It was against the law to use force on children, though a child over sixteen could be solicited. Kids received classes in school on pedophiles and their practices. Still, it was illegal to call them *perverts* or any derogatory name—they were just different, had a different orientation. This one had made a mistake: he grabbed his victim. "Come on; point him out to me."

They walked to the far side of the hospital. The work crew was removing debris from a parking area, throwing it into a pile. "That man, Dad."

Tim followed the pointing finger. The man looked like a pervert—beady, nervous eyes, slight body. "The guy in the green jacket?"

"No, the man with the brown pants."

Tim looked at the true perpetrator; nothing in his appearance gave away his perversity. He was handsome, well built, wearing expensive and handcrafted rugged clothes.

"Where's the boss?"

"There."

They walked over to the man in charge.

"Hey, one of your crew tried to force himself on my son."

The man shrugged his shoulders. "What do you want me to do about it? I got no authority. I don't see any police." His eyes scanned the area.

"Keep your eye on him so he doesn't get someone else's kid. Make sure he works only with adults. When you see a policeman, let him know."

"Sure." The man spoke halfheartedly.

Tim turned away, walked over to the man who had assaulted his son. "Hey, cit. We're in a national emergency, and all you can think about is your lust? How about giving the people of this city a break?" Tim used the common slang for *citizen* hoping to stir a sense of duty.

"You want to tussle over it? I'd kick you into dust." The man rose to his full height, his shoulders thrown back, his fists balled. The anger was gut wrenching; no remorse, no guilt.

"Not particularly," Tim said. "I'm worn. Had you hurt my son, I'd kill you."

"That's against the law. What I did wasn't." The man humphed contemptuously.

"No, you forced yourself on him. You assaulted him."

"His word against mine. Now get lost. Like you said, this is a national emergency, and I have work to do." The man laughed and turned away.

Tim had, with his phone, snapped an image of the man; the man hadn't noticed. Tim whispered to his son. "He's not worth wasting a bullet on. And I'm dead tired. Besides, too many people around. Always chose the time beneficial to you." The knowledge that in this lawless interlude, he could indeed kill the man gave Tim a sense of satisfaction. He had never liked pedophiles and always felt they received more rights, leniency than they deserved. He remembered reading in Gramps's Bible how such behavior had met with death in the ancient Jewish society. Gramps had said the old Jewish law still had validity, though the penalty could be debated now that there were hormonal treatments for sexual predators. Strange that Gramps now made sense. He would come back when the workday was over and find where the man slept—that would give some comfort from the anxiety that came with darkness. Perhaps the man would meet with an accident.

CHAPTER 15

Tim, propped up by pillows, lay beside Katie on her bed. The bed stood in the open air where the apartment had once been. The hazy daylight was reassuring. Behind them, a makeshift shelter with a roof had been erected. They had kept one bed in the open air, facing the view of the destroyed city and their nearest neighbors—and danger, the high-rises to their northwest.

"Isn't this neat, Dad?"

"What, Katie?"

"To be lying in bed with the sun shining on us."

He smiled. "And to be able to smell the grass and see Mr. Woodrow Woodchuck hard at work. There he is. See him?" Tim pointed to the end of the field.

"Yes, I do. But is eating considered work?"

"To a woodchuck it is." He laughed at his answer.

To have his little girl beside him; to delight in her fine features—to clearly see the bloodlines of the English Johnsons and the Irish O'Briens; to breathe in the scent of her shampoo, clothing detergent so familiar to him, and know she was whole of body and health; to know that she knew this Jesus whom he could only pretend to know…It all overwhelmed him with a gratitude so deep and powerful that he thanked God, Jehovah, Yahweh, this infinite God of all power who gave His Son—Jesus—for their redemption and His Holy Ghost—the essence of Himself—for wisdom and knowledge of their salvation. Tim thanked Him and begged for the future to be gentle upon them. Stunned at his sudden thoughts of thankfulness, he laughed to himself. He, Tim Johnson, was praising God, and it felt so right.

The groundhog had become a neighbor ever since he had first been spotted, days after moving into the apartment. Tim tilted his head back, enjoyed the warmth of the sun on his face. There had been no significant rainfall in the two months since the quake in June. Now it was August. The field before them had browned under the hot sun. but the night dews and spotty showers kept the grass alive. Strangely and fortunately, no aftershocks had followed. He was determined to enjoy life. He had no control over events. As security for the warehouse and his own family's safety, he and Mat had propped up the security fence and gate, straightened and strengthened support poles by adding debris to their foundation holes. The day watchman, Doug, never returned to work after the quake nor had the owner or his partner, Carl. The handful of warehouse workers had yet to return.

The earthquake had at last jolted him from hopeful denial into the stark reality of the biblical prophecies. Yes, the world was ending. Life, as he and every other human being had lived it, was coming to an end. John and Gramps had been right. Life was simple now. The game of survival was upon them: they who endured to the end and knew Christ would have eternal lives of joy and contentment. He had the key to eternal life. Christ died for his sins. He was now dead to sin, and Christ lived within him. Period. Just believe it. He had an interest in whether this presence of the Holy Spirit became real in his life. He thought it highly unlikely that he would notice a difference, and yet he had just praised God with a welling and willing thankfulness that he had not thought possible. Josh had never returned, and his worry was balanced by his relief in not being in close proximity to a wanted man. He owed Josh a debt, and he felt as if he was somehow responsible for Josh's well-being.

He thought upon the journey home from the hospital—uneventful. He desired uneventful. That last night, he had found where Mat's would-be molester slept. He had stood over the man as he slept. It would have been easy to drop a nearby chunk of concrete onto his head. Hold the chunk with some nearby clothing debris, and then use the clothing to dissipate his tracks. DNA scanners were common detective apparatus, now capable of picking up the slightest hints of DNA. Why he did not kill the man, he could not fathom. The paranoia that someone was watching? Or had "thou shalt not kill" become so deeply ingrained that his reasoning power—and the validation of self-defense—could not overcome the subliminal?

He humphed quietly at a random memory of his past as a kid, about Mat's age, wading and fishing a stream. He had had to urinate and realized he could relieve himself with his shorts on—one cup of pee wouldn't affect the stream quality, and he was waist high in the water. But his body resisted stubbornly. He had to will himself to physically relax so that a release could take place. *You can pee in your shorts. It will be washed away.*

Perhaps the same force had been in play with murder—no, call it justice. A taboo so rooted in the mind that even the body was in abeyance. He sensed in the days ahead he would need to kill without compunction. Mentally he needed to erase the old laws; eyes and genitals would be fair targets, as would windpipes. Breaking and dislocating bones would be acceptable, as would chokeholds to the death. All confrontations where action was needed had to have death—a stopped heart—as the goal. He was judge and jury now. Circumstances had changed, and behavior needed to change.

These thoughts frightened him. He had no wish to be a callous murderer no different from a gang member. He had no wish to become an unthinking animal, no wish to gloat over the death of another. He must put a check, a rein on his actions. Within his mind he would simply say, "Lord." He would call upon the Spirit within him to show him the way. Whether he was contemplating someone's death or actively engaged in the act, he would give the Lord that opportunity to check his thoughts or actions.

Since returning from the hospital, no one from the high-rises had challenged them or approached them. Where was the man who wanted the pistol? Where were the loungers? Dead? Wounded? He watched air platforms dart across the sky, their flight so much like that of bees. He counted only three, hovering over the city. More were visiting the hospitals, the police headquarters downtown. Those over the city, he thought, were dropping off supplies, picking up wounded. Thank God Katie's leg had already been mended.

An air platform flew toward the stubbled high-rises before him. This had never happened before. The craft darted, hovered around each building, then landed by the nearest building. Bodies in fluorescent jumpsuits stepped from the platform, moved around, surveying the site. Supplies were carried from the platform, stacked before the entrance of the building. Figures clustered around the supplies. The supplies might keep the gang members satisfied—and without the desire to harass him. Maybe the gang members who knew he had a weapon were dead. In his heart, he knew he was due for a visit.

A few fires still burned in the city; the smoke drifted lazily through the ruins. Recovery was going badly—two months and few bodies had been collected. The stink coming from the city, when the wind was from the south, was nauseating. Electrical power had only been restored to key buildings. No streetlights. Few machines were clearing away debris. The highways, roads, streets were passable only for short distances. The ag fields were desolate—no dust trails from tractors, no planting, plowing; just shimmering waves of heat. He had been contacted by no one, not the Academy, not Carl, not Pastor Dave, not the warehouse owner, not Doug the day security, not the authorities.

The electrascreen would pulse to life three times a day, morning, noon, late afternoon for brief news broadcasts or public service announcements. Tim's analysis of the news reports confirmed to him that the federal government had insufficient resources and was using what they had piecemeal, trying to satisfy the voters of every district and helping no one. The State was as muddled as the federal government. He had learned the Academy was closed, and through the conscription lists posted on the public service announcement screens, that Jeremy Lines had been drafted. He felt neither elation nor pity but hoped the best for Jeremy.

The ag companies recruited for workers. Tim knew the solicitations had gone unanswered, the vacant fields said as much. Surely, crews could have been organized for the ag fields immediately after the quake.

The crops must have dried to dust where they lay, and the dead livestock rotted where they died. He thought it did not matter, as likely one half to three quarters of the human population of the metro area was dead.

The thought of food brought his mind back to the robbery, the one simmering anger in the quake aftermath. He had been visited by someone. Someone who knew the emergency supplies had been hidden in the metal container in the warehouse. Half his supplies had been taken, probably within the week immediately after the quake. He had buried the remaining supplies.

Only Dave and his people, most notably Bill Smith, knew of the supplies. Only Dave could have read his mind as to where they had been hidden. He had told no one. Only Dave would have the warped decency to leave half, a year's supply. Dave had stolen the supplies for his trip into the dead zone. This was the only logical conclusion. Why had there been no time to leave a note of the taking or to invite the Johnsons on the trip? Pious, honest Pastor Dave.

There were a few minor irritants, setbacks in the two months. He had freed his car, gotten it halfway home. He returned to it the next day to find it stripped and worthless. He had done some preliminary salvaging through the warehouse but found nothing of value. No relevant equipment, no machinery, no food. He heard coyotes at night in the city, saw them rooting through the debris, seeking human remains. The coyotes might become dangerous to the living, once the corpses were gone.

"Look, Dad!"

Katie pointed to the air platform headed their way. She had recently gone from using *Daddy* to *Dad* about evenly. What had caused the change? When would *Dad* be the unquestioned title? He wanted to hear *Dad*. This told him she was maturing, and that time was moving to its end. He rose from the bed. The craft was overhead. He saw the men looking down upon him. A voice sounded.

"Your food-distribution point is by the buildings to your north. Go there to register. A disaster coordinator is presently at the site. Receive your work assignments immediately. Thank you and good luck."

Tim waved in appreciation, though his mind was filled with unease. The platform sped off toward the city. Would everyone work? Who would ensure that everyone did? He didn't want his property stolen while he was working. Who would ensure order in the work groups or fairness in the distribution of supplies? One disaster coordinator? He'd better be carrying a laser.

"Come on, Katie. Let's go see the disaster coordinator."

Matthew and Mary had come out at the approach of the air platform and had heard the directions given. It had been decided to always travel in pairs, Tim and Katie, Mat and Mary. The two men would always be armed, always with a military-grade knife. The pistol and shotgun would be carried on any lengthy trip outside their perimeter. Mary and Katie carried large shoulder handbags to conceal the weapons. Both carried small knives. Tim looked back as he walked. "We won't be long. Leave your bag with Mom; they might check bags."

A line had formed. Most of the people were unwashed, though water still flowed from broken mains. The odor of rotting flesh was still trapped in the ruins. Most people were living in makeshift tents made from bedspreads, sheets. Someone had salvaged plastic wrapping from the warehouse district for their tent. This was possible proof people had been wandering through his area. The disaster coordinator was scanning foreheads and ID cards, then a box of supplies was handed to each individual. He saw people coming from the ruins of the other buildings. The word had traveled quickly.

As he neared the scanner and the boxes of supplies, he realized the coordinator was a woman. She was in her mid to late twenties, braided blond ponytail, tanned, attractive features. He guessed her to be a body builder, from the wide shoulders and heavy thighs hidden in the baggy jumpsuit. Still, a feminine body, wiry, not blocklike. She carried no weapon. He shook his head at the idiocy of such a policy.

"Let's move, people!" Her voice was husky, carrying a manly, authoritarian tone. She had power and knew how to use it unashamedly. With steroid supplements, she could hold her own against a normal man. Probably a State-school product. He had noticed that unisex quality in others of her type. Raised without sexual role models, the women gravitated to coldness, authoritarianism. She moved to the supplies, threw boxes at the people. Tough woman, not a trace of femininity in her movements. Definitely steroids. She would need the steroid edge for the work she faced.

He watched the computer screen, bringing up information on each number entered—home address, age, occupation. She evidently had access to the tax rolls for the buildings. By the end of the day, she would know just how many had survived. He wondered if she would make the figure known. He could draw an estimate from this number as to the current population of the city. Katie was scanned, a box handed to her. He was scanned.

"Johnson, you're a crew chief. Report here tomorrow, 5:00 a.m."

"Yes, ma'am."

"And tell the rest of your family to report."

"Yes, ma'am." The air platform had probably done a facial recognition.

He was given his box. He asked no questions. Probably picking crew chiefs from educational level, work history.

"Read the screen at the end of the line." She glanced at him—he appeared physically fit. Wife and two kids—that was odd. No other spouses or former spouses, she remembered from the dossier. Johnson…that name, Timothy Johnson…a remembrance she couldn't place. Tonight, in her free time, she would study his file more deeply. Tonight! Shit! It was only a year and a half or two years ago, if that. Timothy Johnson was the name of the brother of John Johnson, the deserter from the Eastern European war.

She was part of the security force that had been rushed to Captain Van Ord's murder site. A reconnaissance patrol had refused orders to follow its captain into the city. A shootout between Van Ord's men and the patrol broke out, and only John Johnson had escaped. Johnson and a man they called Animal, a white racist. It happened in the last weeks of her second four-year army hitch, and it wasn't a cut-and-dried action. Talk had lingered for weeks, as this John Johnson had made it to the States. They thought his destination was to a brother's home in New York. A professor named…Timothy Johnson? She glanced at Johnson and his daughter, filled her lungs to call him back.

Then she quietly exhaled. These were times when knowledge needed to be guarded. What were the odds? She would get her confirmation from the web—in the quiet of her tent.

People, boxes in hands, were reading the message that repeated on an announcement screen. He and Katie moved over to the screen. The message said supplies would come weekly. A tent city was to be erected. They belonged to zone twenty-one. The entire county was divided into zones. Their IDs had automatically been stamped with the number twenty-one. A patient list would be made. Doctors would come to the site. Everyone would be expected to work for food. Children under thirteen would be cared for, provided with schooling. Everyone over thirteen and not medically disqualified would work. Not working meant imprisonment.

"Hey, man; how ya doing?"

Tim turned suddenly. The leader of the gang stood beside him, so close he could smell his breath. Only one other member stood beside him, a shorter, stockier man.

"Great. Glad to see you survived." Tim could not remember a name… had one been given?

The leader laughed. "Sure. I haven't forgotten our deal. It's still on?"

"I don't break my word."

"That's good, because neither do I. Two more weeks, man. Maybe we should speed the transaction up, with the troubles and all?"

"No, all the more reason to keep it as it is." Tim didn't reveal that the deadline had passed weeks ago.

The gang member turned his eyes to Katie. "A beautiful young lady. When she flowers, she'll attract the bees. Bzzzz." He laughed easily, with no thought of being rude or threatening. You liked a woman, you took her. The hell with Daddy. He'd take her when the juices flowed.

"My name is Tim, and yours is…?" Tim extended his hand, hiding his loathing had become automatic and perfect. The man grasped the hand.

"I knew your name…Timothy Johnson. My name is George, remember?"

Tim's last name could have easily been gotten. That gave George no edge, did not frighten. "No, I don't remember. We'll be seeing much of each other in the next three weeks. Maybe even be on some of the same work crews. Your part of the bargain must be maintained; free passage isn't the issue but being free of harassment is."

"Oh, I understand…Your wife and children are safe. But if my part of the bargain has changed because of the new circumstances, I think you should give a little too."

"Like what?"

"Give me the pistol early."

"No…"

"You can't blame me for trying." George showed his teeth in goodwill and happiness, turned and walked away.

"Let's go back home, Katie. And don't let his talk upset you."

"About flowering? I heard worse than that every day at school. Gee, Dad."

He had never known this about her life at school. She probably knew more about sex than he did. All the information likely crude and smeared in brutality, violence, dominance, and subjugation. He thought upon George. George had not threatened harm to the family if the weapon was not given up early. Did George sense his own powerlessness? Certainly, most of his gang were dead. Did George understand that Tim Johnson might be hard-hearted and bold enough to shoot George dead? Or did George have a certain amount of honor? Thinking there was honor in anyone was likely a thought that would lead to your death. Honor should be forgotten; it was just a tool of subterfuge.

***

Their campfire was fed from wood gleaned from the wreckage of their apartment and the crates and pallets of the warehouse. The night was windy, cool, the sky clear, the Milky Way thick. Tim counted a dozen light sources in the entire city. The electrascreen promised that solar panels were being distributed in great numbers. The solar-panel farms once existing on high-rises had all been shattered in the earthquake. It would be easy to verify that future promise in the evenings' dark. The gray ruins shown dully in the starlight. He could see across the river—or where the river had been—now that the high-rises had been leveled. Every direction you turned, the views were more expansive and open.

Katie wrapped the blanket more tightly around herself as she sat on the chair cushion placed by the fire. The chair, a wooden antique, of which the cushion was an accessory, had completely splintered in the quake and had been burned days ago. She listened to the wind play on the warehouse debris behind her. That sound—as if metal roofing was being trampled—could be a man prowling.

"Dad. Are we safe?"

Tim prodded the fire with a stick. He planned to cook stew over the fire once a bed of coals was established. "Yes, we have electronic eyes all around us. Plus, Mat put out a string of metal pieces that will clang if it's tripped."

The electronic eyes had been part of the military gear bought from the ex-soldier. A laser beam connected the devices; once it was broken by a passing object, an alarm would sound.

Katie wondered if the sound she heard was the homemade trip wire. She would remain quiet, see if the electronic eyes made a sound. She didn't want Matthew to make fun of her for being afraid. Tim, using his stick, collected the scattered coals, then placed the grill over the coals.

"Besides, we can see the last building across the field. I've got my eye on anyone leaving the tent city. The perimeter fence Mat and I fixed only has three new gaps. Easy enough to see anyone coming in."

"Feel safe now?" asked Mary.

"Yes. Though there are sounds back there."

"Just the wind, dear; just the wind," Mary said softly, kindly. Mary remembered back to her childhood—at the age of ten. Katie was really ten? Two years since this strangeness had begun? The memory, a camping trip with mother and father; she was the only child. Like Tim's, her family was an oddity with two parents. Dad liked to fish. The fishing became the bond with Tim and her father until he died only years after her marriage.

"Dad." Tim heard a quavering in Mat's voice.

"Yes, Mat?"

"I did some exploring around back of the warehouse area, as far down as the walls to the highway. And I found water coming out of a pipe in that wall. It's real clear. There's a pool there. Birds come and drink. And coyotes."

"You think we should take our water test kit down there?"

"Yes."

"See anything else?" Tim could tell by the undulation in Mat's voice that an emotion had been touched—something shocking.

"If you follow the highway wall in the opposite direction from the water, it runs next to the high-rises. Down in a ditch I found fresh bodies."

"Not old, decayed bodies? Any bullet holes, stab wounds?"

"No old bodies. Dad, one man had his throat cut ear to ear. Mostly all knife stabbings or machete slashings." Mat shuddered. Katie hid her face in her blanket. Mary rubbed Katie's back through the blanket. How civilization had fallen—hard. Why? she asked herself; and how did this fall intertwine with God?

"Well, the gangs are still busy then. A power struggle going on? Or common thievery? Stay away from that area." He said it matter-of-factly. They had to see this as just a part of life. Adapt, downplay, but have plans for action and reaction.

The family listened to the popping of the wood. Mary continued her musings; she had once thought the world was entering a dark age—perhaps hundreds of years would be needed to recover. Immediately after the quake, she had entertained the idea that the world had just worn out and then wondered if civilizations could wear out. In a sense, it didn't matter—her children had obstacles placed in their paths. Their quality of life, their aspirations had been altered. Life was about survival now. Still, God must be reached for and understood.

Tim knew of the water flow from the pipe and the pool. His first day as a security guard, he had walked around and behind the warehouse district. Though his work was only to monitor cameras, he had wanted a feel for the surroundings. The pipe had evidently been a shunt to drain a spring that he believed had its source on the other side of the highway, where offices stood.

The highway, twelve lanes with two commuter tracks and one freight track in between, was an effective barrier to the surrounding city. The highway was elevated, as the mountain ridges sloped gradually, thus the necessity for a wall of solid concrete over fifty feet high. The quake had not visibly disturbed the massive wall. In the mile-and-a-half length of wall behind the warehouse district, there was only one maintenance ladder scaling the wall.

He hoped he had downplayed the seriousness of the corpses. He wished to know when the bodies had been killed by their state of decomposition but hadn't wished to dwell on the subject. Weapons would be impossible to conceal while working, leaving his family defenseless. The weapons must remain hidden, but where? George would come looking. He had to keep track of George. He worried about kidnapping: Katie held hostage till the machine pistol was given.

He knew one way out of the anxiety, the worry. Kill George soon.

George wouldn't have shared knowledge of the weapon—afraid of competition. Only the original four gang members with him knew. They probably had been sworn to secrecy. Tim had seen none of them at the distribution point. Maybe they were all dead, by the quake or murdered. In principle, he had no qualms about killing George. George had no right to the pistol in the first place. Tim had made the deal under duress with a man who was about to assault or kill him. Tim feared being seen, which would lead to blackmail or revenge. He feared the authorities—one manly woman in a fluorescent jumpsuit, without a weapon? He didn't like to think such thoughts. Mary handed him the kettle of stew. He placed it upon the grill. Matthew was standing, alert, peering into the field.

"Dad, it looks like coyotes coming. They're chasing something."

Tim flicked on the beam of his flashlight. A dog was running toward them, running for its life. Someone's pet, the owner now dead, the dog fending for itself. Eight or nine in the pack, spreading out, hoping for the dog to turn to the right or the left, then they would have the angle on their prey.

"Should I get the pistol?"

"No. We can't waste bullets or tell the world we have weapons. He must do it on his own. If the coyotes come into the campfire light and threaten, us then we might shoot—if our baseball bats don't send them fleeing. Katie! Put more wood on the fire."

That would keep her attention away from what he knew was coming. The dog was winded, fear of death in the movements, the eyes. The dog knew where the break in the fences were located and made a beeline. Tim's beam of light went into the eyes of the coyotes, hoping to blind them. They did not slow. The dog was nipped on the back legs—it faltered.

The pack was upon it. Matthew ran out. Tim followed, shouting and waving, shining the light in their eyes. The coyotes backed off only after Matthew came to within feet of them. Tim rushed to the dog— blood was pumping out holes in the neck. The back was shredded along the backbone.

"A lesson to you and to me, Mat. We've got to stick together to survive." Tim rose, grabbed the now-dead dog by the tail, walked farther into the field. The dog was surprisingly heavy. The coyotes watched. Tim wanted the sounds of fighting and eating to be distant from his campfire.

Mat had tears in his eyes as they returned to the fire. He didn't mind the corpses of the murdered people as much as the dog dying. The men probably got what they deserved; this dog had done no one any harm. Childish. This was Satan's kingdom, and the weak died. He and his family would not die—their citizenship belonged to the kingdom of heaven.

As Tim and Mat entered the glow of the fire, the shrill alarm of the electric eye sounded. The rear perimeter, the only one not in view, in the ruins of the warehouse, had been breached. Tim grabbed his machine pistol.

"Mat! Stay with the women. Kick the fire out."

Tim clenched his pistol tightly, began running across the open field to round the corner of the warehouse debris. The intruders would flee after having been discovered. He rounded the corner, faced the long side perimeter of the warehouse, directly across from the tent city. He saw two figures in the debris, about to come out. Seeing him, they returned to the safety of the debris.

He moved into the debris, not knowing if they were armed. He moved silently, having walked the ground before. He heard the two men whispering, saw them rise, run for the field. The starlight cast shadows. He could plainly see them. One tripped. He rushed toward the man. The little man, George's sidekick from the morning. The tall form of George, running across the field, was unmistakable—the wide shoulders and long, skinny legs gave him away. George had a butcher knife his hand. The little man was now on his feet running. Tim steadied his pistol, the extended stock pressed to his shoulder. The laser sight flickered on his target, George.

The sound might bring people from the tent city. If he missed—a wasted round. He let them escape. He went into the debris, examined where they had hidden. He found rope, handcuffs, rags for stuffing in mouths? A tube of sex lubricant.

What was the significance? George hadn't intended to hold a hostage; what was the need? George was going to tie them up, torture them for the location of their supplies or the weapon, and kill them, after he had raped whomever he wished. Could anything else be deduced? Yes, the dog had been a diversion created by George. Why did he still believe men were good? Why? Why couldn't it sink into his head that evil, perverse evil, had been so close to his family, just like the well-dressed child molester after the quake. George and his friend must die, quietly, quickly, very soon. Not tonight; they would be sleepless, alert, on guard. Not tonight.

He returned to the smoldering fire and with his boot, dragged the dispersed embers into a pile. "One more piece of wood and then bedtime. Just a coyote." He wished a few moments of family time before the fire, to calm nerves and elicit any comments that needed to be spoken. He sat and looked up at the thickness of stars. Somewhere out there, the heavenly hosts were gathered, waiting for the end. "What the…" His eyes were glued to movement, pricks of light—white, yellow, red, and a mixture of all three, and even blues, indigos, oranges. The entire realm of heaven seemed moving, roiling, moving toward the earth. He heard gasps from his family, excited exclamations. Awe, wonder, fear. "Down into the pit! Quickly! Tim gathered up Katie, at the same time pulling up Mary by the arm. Matthew had popped up first and had his mother's other arm.

Tim caught a hurried glance of the eastern horizon, the length lit up like a thousand sunrises. He saw agitation upon the earth, exploding objects, fires. They were in their pit. He grabbed the metallic sheets of steel that operated as their door. He heard explosions, deafening, coming toward them; the light was intense. He closed the door, and within seconds, they heard the earth all around them explode. Mat and Katie hugged, Mary hugged both, and Tim grasped the entirety of his family and waited for death.

CHAPTER 16

Tim awoke in the predawn gray light within the pit. His family slept, still embraced. He disentangled himself from them and assorted clothing, tools, rations, and slid the metal door slowly over whatever debris was upon the floor of their above-ground living space. He smelled smoke, hot metal and saw small piles of ice upon the ground and what appeared to be meteor fragments. He examined a fragment more closely and concluded it was a fragment of lava. He had been deceived by an optical illusion when he had first glanced at the night sky. Not meteors coming from deep space but burning lava of such great quantity that it filled the stratosphere. Where had this volcanic eruption occurred? Certainly, a great distance away, as there had been no earth shaking and no sound. The hail? Had the density of the lava and its heat literally cooked the moisture in the air and then dropped it into the cold atmosphere?

Tim studied the eastern horizon. The desolation of the hills and fields, the drought-parched grasses and trees consumed to blackness. The ruins of buildings had small fires burning in their wreckage. The hail must have fallen after the lava fires. The fields around his warehouse apartment were black. The tent city that had been rising and growing was flattened, save for a few tent poles that had remained upright. He saw the disaster coordinator's tent poles had been purposely rearranged after the storm into a flat roof with a lean-to wall on one side. He saw the glow of a computer screen within.

Tim pulled the door over his sleeping family, walked down into the tent city, approached the lone tent of the disaster coordinator. The tent camp was quiet, wrapped in the cool of predawn. He saw a few bodies lying in the open. George was not among the bodies. Where had the people gone? The quiet was eerie, no breakfast rattlings, no fires started, no mess tent or voices of the cooks. No delivery vehicles, no air platforms in the distance. Nothing but birds on the damp, black field; the birds searching for toasted insects, grubs or worms. A husky voice came from the tent. "That's far enough."

He guessed she had a silent force-field alarm encircling her tent. Was a weapon within pointed at him?

"What do you want, Johnson? I said 5:00 a.m. That's twenty minutes away." The tone was irritated, gruff.

"I wanted to talk to you in private."

"About what?"

"Law enforcement, making certain everyone is on a work detail."

"Come in." She sighed in exasperation. Odd that he had no need to talk of the event of last night—it was as though he had expected it. She wouldn't mention it. She would see where the trail of silence led.

He walked into her tent. She sat on the edge of her cot, her hair down, her jumpsuit pulled up to her waist. Her bare chest hung before him, firm, protruding, the nipples erect. Her shoulder and arm muscles were thick, as was her chest under the ample feminine softness.

"You like these?" She held her hands under her breasts, offering them on the flat of her hands. No sense of desire or need was in her tone.

"Very much so. Quite stimulating." He laughed from surprise but thought her crude and realized it was best if she thought he found her attractive. "But I'd like to talk business."

"Talk." She said in a monotone. He couldn't tell from her tone if she had been serious in her offer.

"My son has found freshly murdered corpses behind the buildings to the rear of the apartments." He threw his head slightly to the rear. She deftly slipped a weapons shield over her torso, all the while her eyes bored into his. She arranged her breasts within the semisolid shield.

"I am the disaster coordinator, not the police. I prefer to be known as and addressed as the 'DC.' A police officer will be assigned as soon as one is available. I don't know when. I do have the right to imprison, with exploding cuffs, anyone disobeying my rules or engaged in criminal activity. I don't have time to become an investigator, nor is that my job. But what is your particular need?"

"I believe you have answered my question."

She searched his eyes with a hard look. He saw not an ounce of mercy or kindness or partiality. She suspected he would murder someone. Hell, what was another body? Timothy Johnson wouldn't kill unless it was necessary—she had read his file. She knew that John Johnson had been his brother. He had been a capable killer and an Enslaver who had escaped into the Enslaver system of intrigue. She wondered if Tim Johnson now knew where his brother was hiding. Odd, that she would have contact with both brothers—but life was turning odder by the day. Luckily, she had not been grabbed by the army for conscription—a DC was considered a vital job.

He spoke. "For your sake, I hope you carry a weapon."

"Have you heard something?" He had no need to know what, if any, weapons she had authorization to carry.

"No, I just know these people," Tim said. "If they find they can't do business with you, they'll kill you."

"Tell me something I don't know. Besides, why should that worry you?"

"You're the only link we have with the government and aid. I like your chest."

A slight smirk caught in the corner of her mouth and quickly disappeared. He was about to ask for George to be placed on his work detail, then thought it was better that she was unaware of any connection. He sensed she didn't want to know anything. For this one day, he would have to chance George staying busy on a work detail, away from his home. By tomorrow, George would be dead.

"Get out of here, Johnson."

He began to turn. She spoke quickly. "Were you expecting a night of lava fire and hail?" She honed her eyes upon his to see what would flush.

"Sure, why not?" He laughed into her eyes in an inclusive mirth.

What a piece of work, she thought, not displeased.

***

Tim glanced up at the vultures circling the apartments. Behind the high plateau the apartments had been built upon was the mountain ridge heaved high by the earthquake. The brown earth, boulders, and sedimentary layers shimmered in the reflecting heat of the sun. Between the newly scorched and exposed earth and the apartments was the tangle of downed forest on the old mountain ridge, tinged black from the fires, drying in the heat of the rainless summer. He wondered if the keen eyes of the vultures had picked every carcass clean. The sky was cloudless, the air windless. Not an air platform was seen. An unnatural summer's heat had come to torment the work crews.

Tim's eyes came back to shirtless, tattooed George, digging a latrine. George had not been killed the day after the lava storm—that was two months ago; now it was October. The majority of people had taken refuge in an abandoned high-rise when the firestorm had come. Life droned on like the buzz of flies over a carcass. The rest of the crew members were erecting tents or digging drainage ditches. Everyone seemed eager, almost joyous that a plan had taken shape—something positive was now being done. School had been organized near the tent city, as were a temporary hospital and logistics center, where supplies and records were kept. Mary had been assigned to the school. He need not worry about Katie, with her mother so close. Mat was in his work crew, and he kept a close eye upon him. He always partnered Mat with the less volatile and nonperverse men.

The disaster coordinator, or DC, as she liked to be called, was moving between the various work crews, talking to the leaders of the work crews. He watched her stride toward him. She walked like a man even as her chest told of her womanhood. She had a sexual appeal, though he had never envisioned himself being attracted to a woman of her type. She would need male companionship soon. He wondered if he was on her short list. He was attractive, well built, had a good mind. He needed inside information. Mary didn't need to know. His thoughts aggravated him; he loved Mary.

"Johnson. I got word from headquarters. We are assigned a policeman—ex-storm trooper. He'll arrive tomorrow."

"Great. Wonderful. Thanks for the news."

"No one is to sleep in the buildings or rubble. Everyone in neat tidy rows. We're not going to have enough tents. Find some suitable material."

She had turned and was walking away before he had thought of a response.

His mind focused on George. Should he allow George to live? Would the ex-storm trooper put fear into the criminal element? He remembered the meeting of the Order, the reports of police officers being killed. That was prior to the quake. Certainly, the power of the gangs had been broken by casualties. They would regroup. It was wise to kill George tonight, before the arrival of the law. George had not pressed his demand when the two weeks expired. Why?

He studied George as he shoveled. Tall, lean, George had the reach in a physical confrontation. George was not particularly strong, and he was tiring quickly from the hard physical labor. George's lone friend was in another work detail. None of the original gang members had been seen since before the quake.

He would tire George out with hard work, then toward the end of the day, when George was exhausted, he would kill him. He felt confident he could do it with his bare hands. He had a length of wire in his pocket—a garrote. A pang of conscience stole over him. It seemed corrupt to use his position to weaken George for the slaughter. To kill him in cold blood, no differently than the coyotes had killed the dog. He remembered the tape, rope, the lubricant; he thought of his wife and children, especially Katie. He was not an animal; George was the animal. Justice demanded that George die. Perhaps the word was not justice but prudence; George was a killer/rapist waiting to kill and rape. Do to him what he wished to do to you, or the old truism that the best defense is a good offense. He must be killed in the easiest, safest way, without words or reasons given. The farce of chivalry and fair play or the presumption of innocence had long been dead.

To shoot George would be humane. The weapons were buried; a shot would alert people to the presence of a weapon. The police officer might be inclined to investigate, fearing for his own safety with a gun in circulation. A gun could not be used; a knife, a garrote, a chokehold were in play. At the end of the workday, George would be united with his friend. Then, it would be too late; he couldn't risk a witness escaping.

Material for tents? The warehouse might provide something. Even the roof could be dismantled, the rectangular pieces propped together. George would come along, and George would not return. This spur-of-the-moment plan left him uneasy; he needed to think things through. There could be no loose ends. Circumstances didn't allow planning; he had to react to the moment, the opportunity.

Near the end of the workday Tim approached George, who had been purposely left by himself to finish the latrines. He appeared exhausted; his pants were soaked through with sweat. Conveniently, it had been decided to run a water pipe to the tent camp from the water main in the last building. Tim had moved the remaining members of his crew, including Mat, to this project. Digging had been necessary—not to bury the pipe, but to ensure a sufficient grade for gravity to maintain a flow. The crew was exhausted; their thoughts were focused inward. They had forgotten George, who was a stranger to them anyway.

"George, the DC wants us to find some tent material, or shelter material. I thought the warehouse district might have what we need. At the same time, I'd like to make the transfer of the pistol."

"Why, man? What changed your mind?" Suspicion narrowed George's eyes.

"The law is coming tomorrow. What if he makes a weapons search? I don't want to jeopardize my family. Besides, we won't need weapons with a law man here."

"You're going to give me the weapon then turn me in…is that it?" Anger flashed across George's face. Tim noticed the body had not tensed. The emotion wasn't energizing the flesh.

"No. We'll bury the weapon. Only you and I will know. After that, you can do what you want." George's own suspicions blinded him to the real reason for the trip. Did he think he wasn't recognized that night prior to the firestorm?

George dropped his shovel, deciding he needed the weapon. Besides, this boss, Tim Johnson, was expendable. Perhaps it was time for him to die. The gun and easy access to the little girl and the wife.

The two men walked side by side across the blackened grass stubs, the hard earth. George had no weapon; the butcher knife he once carried could not be hidden. Even sheaved and strapped to a calf, the knife would have shown through George's soaked, tight-fitting pants. George became nervous as they neared the acres of debris of the warehouse district. His eyes darted repeatedly toward Tim; his body movements seemed tensed.

"Let's bring someone else," George stated.

Was he doubting his own strength for the hauling or for a life-and-death struggle? "And chance them discovering the hiding place?"

"I don't want the pistol anymore." George spoke angrily and stopped in midstride.

"What if this law man is crooked? Or another gang kills him?" Tim said. "You'll need a weapon." Unconsciously, a desperation had entered his voice. He knew his tone had spooked George by the widening of George's eyes.

"You're trying hard to get rid of this weapon," George said.

"I want you off my back. For my family's sake."

"I'm not interested. The deal's off." George crossed his flattened hands in a slicing motion. The display had been quick, the fear had brough strength and quickness into George's tired body. The killing would be much tougher now. "Yeah, but now you can blackmail me. You know I have an illegal weapon. What if later you decide you want it? We're both trapped by this pistol."

"That's your bad luck," George said, sneering. George turned away, took a step back across the field, his eyes slyly keeping Tim in view.

"Wait." Tim grabbed his arm. "I have a solution. We'll destroy the pistol. No, better yet, you take half and I'll keep half. No one can use it without the other giving permission. Or we can secretly destroy our pieces if we think there will be blackmail."

George turned back, shaking loose of the arm, giving no decision. His eyes studied Tim. He took a step toward the debris, indicating agreement. He would kill this boss—today, in minutes. He waited for Tim to proceed. Tim was forced to lead the way. Now, he was tense; George had the advantage behind him. George had everything to gain by killing him now that he didn't want the weapon. No, George still wanted the weapon.

Tim moved deep into the fallen warehouse. He couldn't trust George. Couldn't take the chance with his family.

"Back off," Tim warned George as he stood before the pistol's location. George complied. Tim unearthed the machine pistol; the shotgun had been hidden at another location.

"Step away from it," George ordered.

Tim backed away from the weapon. He steeled his resolution—for Mary, Mat, and little Katie, whom he would not allow to be raped and killed. He had never given premeditation to such a crime. The times were demanding that he become a killer. *Lord*, he said to his conscience. He would succeed; George would most certainly die, and God would be praised.

A thought passed through Tim. Did George fear a loaded weapon? Or did he hope for a loaded weapon? Suddenly, George lunged for the pistol. With two long strides, Tim kicked him in the head. George rolled over. Tim kicked again. George pulled the trigger. The weapon held an empty clip. Tim kicked again. George moaned, temporarily unconscious. Tim kicked and kicked with his heavy work boots. Then, with George lying helpless, he slammed a nearby metal bar into his head. He felt for a pulse. George was dead. He placed some debris over the corpse. He carried the metal bar deep into the debris of the warehouse. Tonight, he would dismember George; the coyotes or vultures would feed upon him. Tim thanked God for the victory, felt no guilt, and knew God had approved.

He walked back to the tent city, scanning the figures in the work crews. He must appear relaxed, calm. No one watched him. His work crew were still erecting tents. He came up to them just as the end-of-the-workday horn sounded. Now, they were to fall into formation before being dismissed. This was the ritual every day.

He lined up his people in columns. Their steps stuttered, they milled, bumping into each other as they found their places, alphabetical order. Fatigued and worn, they had lost their zeal for the rebuilding process. No one seemed to know that George was missing. Tim's stomach was churning. His people were at the head of the long line of work crews.

"Johnson?"

"Yes, DC."

"Status of your men."

"One absent; all others accounted for."

"Where's your missing person?"

"In the warehouse district, searching for tent material."

"Alright. Stay in formation till I'm done with the others. Same time tomorrow."

A palpable surge of relief passed through his body. He faintly heard the DC going down the line. The first obstacle had been met. His people stood wearily. One or two might have seen George and Tim go to the warehouse district. Maybe none. No one had any interest in George. Only George's friend in another work crew might raise questions. What would this lawman do if he arrived tomorrow, and George was reported murdered? Did he need to kill George's friend? The friend was a follower, without the will to pursue vengeance or the pistol—if he even knew of the pistol.

He saw the other crews disbanding before he heard the DC's order to disband. He walked through the crowds to the school tent. Mat was beside him. He would tell none of his family members of the murder. George's friend approached suddenly; Tim snapped into a fighting posture. Hatred flooded the man's eyes.

"Where's George? I know he was in your crew."

"He should be around somewhere. Maybe still in the warehouse district."

"He wasn't in formation."

How did this man know that—an informant in the crew? He had been four squads away at least. How could he have visually seen George was missing?

"You're gonna get yours, Johnson."

"Come with me. Let's find him and put your mind to rest."

The man turned away in rage. Mat said nothing. Tim kept his eyes on the man as Mary and Katie joined them. The DC approached them from out of the crowd. Tim shuddered.

"Johnson. Tomorrow you and your family move down with everyone else. Everyone will live in the city; a curfew will be enforced, electric eyes placed around the camp. Those orders came in from the police."

"Yes, DC."

He was enraged. Now he must kill the friend of George. Perhaps the DC would need to be killed in time. Now his freedom was gone. Now he had to become a part of this savage mess. Maybe this police officer coming tomorrow would need to be killed.

***

"Wait here." Tim spoke to his family as they placed their bundles, packs on the ground. What wasn't essential to everyday use had been buried. They were half awake. The sun had yet to appear, the day was already hot. The DC pulled open a flap angrily, then closed it as suddenly when she saw Johnson.

"Come in, Johnson."

He entered her tent.

"See you brought the wife and kiddies. I like a man who obeys orders. By the way, a man came to me even earlier this morning than you. Said he found his friend in little pieces in the warehouse debris. Would you know anything about that?"

She watched his throat tighten even as his eyes momentarily glazed. He would lie.

"No."

"It's nothing to me. I know you're the good guy; this George character had the arrest record. Besides, the police declare an amnesty their first day in a new zone. They don't want to deal with all the crime that happened previously. Relax." She then added dryly, "Why are you here?"

"To ask to be allowed to remain at our site by the warehouse."

"Afraid of revenge?"

"Yes. And I don't want my wife or daughter or son raped and

murdered." He didn't want the tension of living in a crowded place with rapists and killers.

"Ah, go out and kill the little tick now. He came alone—probably has no one behind him." She thought back on her own rape; before the pain could well up, she quashed the memory.

"You're callous with life," he said.

"I've smelled enough rotting flesh to know life is cheap. What do you think I did before this job? Teach school? Johnson, I've killed more people than you've screwed in your lifetime. Military police—on the front lines; deserters and criminals. The majority of those people didn't deserve life." She ran her hand across her throat. "Look, I like you. Like every part of you. The more I see of you, the better it will be for you. You're not dumb, right? Read between the lines. Now…"

They heard the rapid approach of an air platform. By the time they had exited the tent, the platform had landed. A uniformed police officer jumped off the platform, duffel bags of gear strapped over his broad shoulders. He dumped his bags and quickly unloaded large crates from the platform, which pulled up and away in seconds. He wore dark blue; his body armor shone; his helmet visor was down, hiding his face. A laser stun stick hung on his belt, as did a laser pistol. They saw rifle cases with his gear.

He lifted the visor as the dust settled. Ferocious eyes—mocking, cynical and perverse. Five hundred pounds of muscle. Caucasian features. The platform was gone, the trooper strode toward the DC.

"Get lost Johnson. I'll work on your case." He saw fright run through the DC. A sexual fright and desire. Tim walked back to his family as the DC and the police officer moved into her tent.

His family said nothing, simply stared with expectant faces.

"Make yourselves at home. We may have to stay awhile. The DC says she'll do what she can."

Tim watched Mary's strength, resolve visibly deflate and leave her body—her shoulders sagged and back hunched, her countenance fell as she sat on the rolled bedding she had carried along. She looked so thin—and she was. She hated her fellow citizens—hated their children and them. She hated the constant sexual advances of men and women, the filthy talk. Their apartness in the evening at their apartment had given her a time to recoup and relax. Katie's gaze went directly to Matthew's face to read his demeanor. She felt as if this was all a big con, but she wasn't certain. She hated her classmates and the constant anxiety she felt around them—they were always grabbing, fighting, arguing, and the adults always wanted to touch her. She didn't want to live in their neighborhood. She wanted them far away.

Matthew spoke. "We wait in hope for the Lord; He is our help and our shield. In Him our hearts rejoice, for we trust in His holy name. 'May your unfailing love rest upon us, O Lord, even as we put our hope in you.' That's from Psalm 33. Cheer up, Mom, Katie."

"Well done, Mat! What a memory." Tim's eyes were lit with pride.

"Yeah, good job," Katie said positively, but without the overflowing strength to impart emotion.

"Yes, an apt quote, Mat," Mary said decidedly. She knew she was wearing down in determination and hope. She praised Mat because he was her son and she loved him, but inwardly her heart was in agitation toward the God concept, and this God of the Judeo-Christian world, even this Christ sent to mankind. Her personal philosophy that setbacks were just opportunities had fallen over the cliff of nonfulfillment. The setbacks were daily, and they led to no opportunities—just more setbacks. Like her father always said, "Nothing succeeds like success." This Jesus was bringing very little success. She got it that this time on Earth—this seven years—was punishment directed at mankind, and that had she been paying attention to what He had wanted from her, she would have been spared the seven years. The anger wasn't at herself but at Him, if He really existed. Could she really say that after all that had occurred? Damn it. He existed, and the damn Bible existed, and fuck them all. Suck it up, Mary. Don't show it to the kids; love them, Mary.

Tim scanned the warehouse district from where they had come. "I'll make another trip, with a wheelbarrow this time. Mat, keep the family together—stay at this spot so I can keep my eyes on you." A wheelbarrow, ancient technology, was the motorless version of the rotor cart.

Mary was rubbing Katie's shoulders. Mat sat beside them. "Will do, Dad."

CHAPTER 17

Tim stood wearily at the head of his stinking, sweat-stained work platoon. Where was the DC? Everyone was anxious to break formation, rush to the food lines. Peters, the law officer—the former storm trooper—was probably getting a quickie from her. It was common knowledge throughout the camp that he had her under his control. The rumors were that Peters had not been satisfied with just the DC; other women were his, sometimes in pairs. Occasionally Peters would sodomize men to make his power known.

Food lines, communal meals in the mess tent twice a day, breakfast and dinner. People had to rush, push, shove, even fight for a place in line. Sometimes the back of the line received no food. The individual food packets had run out a week after Peters arrived. The weak, the sick, the orphans, the aged always were at the line's end. An understanding of sorts had been reached between the healthy as to a place in line. The DC said not enough food was coming in, though she requested it. The food was coming in; it was feeding that hog of a man, Peters, and his handpicked deputies, sex partners, and sodomites. What they couldn't eat, they hoarded.

The DC rushed to the front of the formation. The number of people had doubled over the preceding months. Evidently, many had initially refused to enter the tent camp while their own supplies had held out. Most of the holdouts had been able-bodied gang members, who now had established their gangs in the camp.

Tim hated his life. He had responsibility for his work detail and so had rank and some power over those under him. His power and decisions brought no adulation—he was an authority figure to hate. He had taken readily to the military format of the new life. His people—male, female, adults, young adults—were contentious, petty, lazy, threatening him or his family daily with harm. They cursed each other, argued, fought, sniveled, whined, imagined favoritism and privilege where none existed. They sought out the wounded places, both emotional and physical, of those around them. Skin, hair color or distribution, or thickness or thinness, foot size, head size, hand size, private parts, breasts, musculature, voice quality and inflection—all were the focus of ridicule and contempt. They were seeking that evil sweet spot where a man or woman winced, turned the head away or shed a tear or raised an angry voice. A limp in the gait, a weakness in the hand, a scar, skin rash—nothing was left unexploited. Many times, Tim's feet or hands or shovel handle struck at the perpetrator—simply to give a crew member respite, peace from the ever flowing filth, belittlement, and degradation.

Work was done with antiquated hand tools, shovels, picks, wrecking bars, and wheelbarrows. With insufficient food, work had become a lethargic ordeal, a constant fight to make the body give up its deposits of stored energy. Three months of this hell, and nothing had been accomplished but to remove a fraction of the rubble. A machine could have accomplished the same work in three days.

"All present and accounted for, DC."

He spoke automatically when the DC had turned his way. He hadn't heard what she said, just assumed, as he assumed every night that she had asked for a report. She had lost her desire for him after the arrival of Peters, told him as much. Said he wouldn't compare with Peters. The bi…witch. His mind was now thinking in curses, negative thoughts, which he attempted to immediately correct. Why did he care if she rejected him? He had halfheartedly tempted her for the inside information he may have received. He chose to honor his wife and remain outside of foolish entanglements. He didn't enjoy lying and sneaking. He enjoyed teaching, by example, Katie and Mat a true bond of marriage. Even though marriage would soon be coming to an end? He couldn't give up on integrity—too much a habit.

Curses, crude, perverse curses all day long, from every mouth—old women and men, even children. No institution or teaching, no virtue— nothing and no one—was sacred in the foul utterings. He had heard his mother's, his wife's genitalia described and cursed; his father's penis, his own were mocked and belittled. Even Mat and Katie were viciously cursed, threatened with sexual harm. He had flattened a man with a shovel—the wound took some stitches—to silence the spewings of filth aimed at his kids. Such talk had stopped from all mouths for a week. But the golden rule—do onto others—was decidedly dead.

His mind slipped back into thought. Mat was by his side. The formation had broken up, the dash to the mess line had begun. Mat ran ahead, he held their place. For the first three days he was pushed, punched, thrown back. Each day, Tim came and soundly beat the men. Now Mat's place in line was secure. To see your son come up to you bruised, bloody, holding back the tears. Each day going back for more. He knew Mat had hurt deep inside. All adults male and female were potential enemies, and at any time fists or legs could strike out in hate. The stress was taking a toll.

He looked out across the field to the road that led to the destroyed warehouse district, the road he had so often traveled in his car. Thirty or forty coyotes in three or four bands lounged. The young ones played, all the while keeping their eyes on the tent camp, their noses to the smell of food. They hadn't dispersed back to the countryside once the rotting bodies had turned to leathery skin and rock-hard viscera. Poison had been requisitioned but had yet to arrive. In the evenings, the coyotes had entered the camp, been beaten with sticks. Peters liked to come out and shoot them for sport, unconcerned with stray laser bursts tearing through the camp.

Tim watched one of Peters's deputies patrolling with a long, weighted baton swinging in his hand. A criminal—all the deputies were criminals. George's friend, whom he now knew as Plug, had been deputized. Strangely, Plug had made no attempts to harass Tim or avenge George's death. Perhaps, Plug feared the killer of his friend? Did Plug know of the pistol? Or is that why Plug did nothing, hoping Tim would lead him to the weapon. If that were the case, Plug didn't want to share the weapon with anyone, or he would have enlisted aid for the purpose of forcing Tim to talk.

Tim walked down the length of the line. Near the front, he stepped in with his family. No need to be first; that only put a target on his family's back. He had no sympathy for those at the end—not from a hardness of heart, but from the distraction of the constant vigilance to maintain his family's position. Mary and Katie had their arms tight around each other's waists. Mat's eyes were constantly searching the movements and the gestures of those around him. He saw the stiff-lipped whispers that communicated the hate. Mat's fists. drawn up, were loose but ready. Tim relaxed for just a second under the shadow of his son's vigilance. Inside the tent, two of the cooks were arguing, cursing with a vehemence he knew was the prelude to violence. Tim took a step toward the kitchen. The fight would destroy, ruin food and must be stopped. The man in front of him turned sharply, punched him in the chest. Tim recoiled back from the blow.

"You ass. If they fight, we'll lose our supper."

The man glared evilly, breathing heavily. Too stupid to process the truth of the words. It was too late. In the kitchen, a knife arced downward. Boiling water was heaved from a huge pot. Screams of agony carried over the gathered people. Blinded, the scalded man crashed into the serving counter, knocking the contents to the floor. The agitated line broke, men rushed to the kitchen, grabbing food. Women and children screamed as they were knocked to the ground. Tim pulled his family out of the mad scramble. When the man who had punched him turned toward the spilled food, Tim punched him on the back of the neck and the skull. The man fell and did not rise. Tim looked quickly around, no one had noticed in the scramble to grab food.

"The hell with it! The hell with it!" Tim yelled angrily. He whispered to Mat, "We'll eat the rations we have left in the tent." They walked away from the noise and frantic body movements of the melee, down the empty dirt streets to their home, two rectangular pieces of warehouse roofing leaning against each other in the shape of a pyramid. At the center, they had room to stand. As Katie pulled away the sheet that acted as a door, she said, "Someone's been here."

The bedding was in disarray, trunks ransacked, duffel bags sliced open. The family entered; Tim dropped the sheet. He pulled up his bed, removed a mat; the cache of food, hidden in a spacious hole in the ground, had not been disturbed.

He pulled out four meals, then closed the hole, returned the bedding.

"It won't be long before they discover the hole." He passed the meals around. They sat wearily, began eating. He didn't have the energy to address the ransacking.

"Matthew, you're getting crumbs on my bed," Katie whined.

"Keep quiet," Mary hissed angrily.

They heard footsteps outside; their sheet was pulled away.

"Any trouble here?" Plug, with the heavy baton in his hands, smiled.

"Get out of here." Tim was incensed at the pulling away of the sheet, the exposing of his home. Plug, who had probably ransacked the home, now knew, by the presence of the meals, of a hiding place as yet undiscovered.

"Sorry." Plug let the sheet fall, began laughing hysterically.

"I'm sorry, Mom," Katie said through her tears.

"See what you did?" Matthew sought the shame and guilt that would torment his sister. Katie slapped her brother. He balled his fist to punch her; Tim clamped his hand upon Mat's fist. Matthew tried to rise to leave the shelter. Tim grabbed his arm, gently pulled downward as he said, "There's nothing out there but trouble. Let's finish our meal. We'll take a little nap then walk up to our apartment, watch the sun set." Katie, already finished with her meal, brushed out her bedding, cuddled up with her blanket. Matthew threw down his packet in anger, buried himself in his blanket and began a whining argument with himself over the unfairness of life, the evil of his father and sister.

Tim dreaded this time of the daily routine. Supper pulled weary bodies into sleep, yet it was too early to sleep. There was no electrascreen to watch, no books to read, no sporting events, no classes to attend; just dead time with weary minds and bodies. He had gotten them into the habit of a brief nap, then an early evening walk—away from people, usually to their old apartment site where some good memories remained. The family's weariness overcame their emotions; soon they were asleep.

Tim awoke to the covers moving. Rats! They had become numerous in camp. He jumped up, nerves on edge, brushing wildly at the covers. No rats. Katie was gone, her bedding dragged out beyond the sheeting that was the rear door.

He bolted through the sheeting. Saw a man carrying a bundle in his arms, walking peacefully. He ran to the tall, frail, older man.

"Katie!"

She awoke as he grabbed her out of the arms of the man.

"I didn't mean no harm, Mr. Johnson. She's such a cute girl. I've admired her every day." The man reeked of sweat, urine, defecation. His wild beard held hair matted with hardened food stains.

Tim placed Katie on her feet; she stood, fully awake. "Mr. Bensen. What are you doing here?"

Tim asked, "You know this man, Katie?"

"I see him every day at lunch. He works in the school kitchen."

"That is over. No more saying hello to Mr. Bensen. He will pretend you don't exist. Isn't that right, Mr. Bensen?"

"That's right, Katie."

"And if Mr. Bensen ever comes near you, you scream. Daddy will come and kill Mr. Bensen. Isn't that right, Mr. Bensen?"

"That's right."

Tim gently grasped Katie's hand and began walking back to the tent. Another threat to catalog in the list of threats to his family. The streets were becoming crowded as people returned from the mess tents. Everyone lived half in a tent or shelter and half on the street. Fire circles were everywhere, most not lit. As evening's darkness came, fires would be lit, scavenged food items cooked, or teas and coffees made. A gang of youths was at one tent, evil mischief in their eyes. The eyes frightened Tim till he saw the spread legs of a women protruding from under a prostrate form. The sounds of sex filled that area of the street.

He looked up at the rubble of the last high-rise. The vultures were returning to their roosts. Drawing in the huge wings, they settled on the concrete, turned, appeared to hunch their shoulders and stare down at the affairs of the two-legged beasts. They looked so black against the pale concrete. At the base of the building, the Satan worshipers had already gathered, heaping wood in preparation for their nightly bonfire and service. They would dance naked, men, women, children; they would drink, take hallucinogens, sacrifice any animal unlucky enough to be caught. Then the orgy would begin and continue until the last member was satiated. The world Church, or Harlot Church, had yet to send a priest or priestess, though some people had begun meeting on Sundays.

The gangs were reforming and recombining, meeting at the high-rises in the evenings before curfew. He had heard of only two; in time, they would do battle and there would be one. One which in turn would seek conflict with other zones. Strange the other zones were unknown worlds to him. What was life like in those other places? Oddly, the gangs had not reformed along racial lines, but by age. The teenage gang, the old men gang. He knew that racial tension still existed on a personal level from the insults spewed from his platoon during the course of the day. Age was the commodity. Youth was power, resiliency. Age had no wisdom any longer—the old order of convention was gone, and resources, wisdom accrued with age had been destroyed or obsolete.

Mat and Mary were standing outside, their frenetic eyes searching the camp, when he returned with Katie.

"Katie was kidnapped by a Mr. Bensen. Know him?"

"The man at school!" Mary answered in surprise.

"Mat, if Mr. Bensen ever comes around, find me. He knows he will die."

Mat's eyes became soft. He loved his sister; she was his only friend in the world. Why did he hate her so often, why did he try to hurt her? He had heard it called sibling rivalry, a fighting for affection from parents. But it was something deeper. He wanted to love her, protect her, but he wanted to make her tough. No, that was camouflage for his evil. A quiet thought entered his head that "tough" as he knew the word wasn't the answer.

"Let's walk up to the apartment, remember happier times." Tim turned to his neighbor, only fifteen feet away, sitting with his partner and lover at their fire pit. Had they seen Mr. Bensen walk by with Katie in his arms? Tim suspected them of stealing firewood from his pile. Tim looked at the pile, counted the pieces—fifteen large, ten small, a handful of twig-size pieces. It was pointless to ask them to watch his home for other uninvited guests, it was pointless to threaten. Yet, if the pieces were gone when he returned, he would search for them, threaten for their return, fight if his wood was not given up. Life was a living hell.

***

They sat on the bed, not yet damaged by rain, and looked down on the tent city, the rubbled high-rises, the view of the destroyed city. The heat was intense—January seemed to be a summer month now. The electric eyes were watching their rear, they saw no one in their immediate vicinity. Here they felt safe, the stress melted away.

"Dad?" asked Mat.

"Yes?" Tim felt the expenditure of energy used to say that simple word.

"How long is this going to go on?"

"What?"

"Living with these crazy people," said Katie, answering for her brother. The two had discussed the situation. "Why doesn't the DC give people numbers in the food line, so we don't have to fight?" asked Mat.

"I intend to ask her tonight."

"Why can't we live here?" asked Katie.

"I'm going to ask Peters that tonight. I have had enough of living with the crazy people. Perhaps it is time to leave."

"Look, Dad!" Matthew pointed in alarm, excitement, amazement. A band of coyotes was running from the meeting place of the Satan worshipers. A bundle of stolen material was being moved along, sometimes in the mouths of two or three, sometimes by one. The object was heavy, unwieldy; animals joined the effort and fell away. The bundle dropped, was rolled with snouts, nipped with teeth.

The bundle attempted to stand. They heard crying echoing across the field, saw arms, feet. A child had been snatched. People came running from the meeting place. The coyotes nipped, lunged, stood on hind legs, knocked the child to the earth. The men closed in, the coyotes ran off, stopped, watched the bleeding prize that had almost been theirs.

Katie hid her eyes. Through her tears, she asked, "Why are the animals acting like that?"

"Because once they ate mice and rabbits, which are now scarce in the drought. They find people easy to kill." Tim spoke like a teacher. His sympathy for others, even a child, had been emptied long ago. The child was nothing to him; only his children mattered. He knew the thought was wrong. The golden rule of civilization: do unto others as you would have them do unto you. That rule began when you could love others as much as you loved your own.

Mat spoke. "Josh said the animals would start eating people because people are losing the spirit that makes them human. We are just becoming flesh like any other animal. Our spirit and intelligence were once our shield."

Tim thought the explanation plausible. He continued his thoughts aloud. "I wonder if Josh is alive and what he is doing." An echoing, all-encompassing boom resounded in the sky and shuddered through the earth. They had no time to cover their ears. They felt their flesh quiver as the object came from space, lightening the sky to daylight as it streamed toward the earth. Burning red hot, white hot; shock waves pounded onto the earth. The object seemed larger than the earth itself. "Cover your eyes and hug the ground!" Tim yelled. The family instinctually turned onto their stomachs, burying their heads in their arms. The light was gone; the object gone. They rose.

"What was that?" Katie said in awe.

Tim held up his hand, "Wait. It came from the east. Certainly, it would have landed in the Atlantic Ocean." The faces watched each other, expectant and fearful. Mary spoke. "It could have broken up just before striking, dispersing the impact and shock."

"That's the meteor that kills the oceans and seas," Mat said. "I remember reading about it."

"God made it happen; right, Mat?" asked Katie.

"Yeah. He's trying to get people's attention." Mat's eyes showed the adrenaline, as did his body tension.

Katie answered flatly, "He's got mine."

"Dad, are you sure we're saved?" asked Matthew. He knew he was saved as well as Katie. He asked in the plural because he knew Dad and Mom were not—diplomacy.

"No one is ever sure."

"I think we should be," said Katie

"Why?" inquired Mary.

"Because we should be sure. We should know." Matthew reached into his inside jacket pocket, pulled out a paper. "I found this sticking to a wall at the front of the last high-rise."

Tim took the paper; the edges were peeled. He read: "Prepare yourselves for the coming of the Lord, Jesus Christ. He will judge all mankind. Repent of your sins."

"Dad, He'll be here in a few years, if we survive."

"I've told you He is coming," Tim said defensively.

"But do we belong to Him, Dad? I don't think you and Mom do. Have you given Jesus everything? Dad? Mom? I'm scared, Dad. Scared for you and Mom. Without you two, Katie and I don't have a chance. This is a mess, Dad." Matthew began to whimper and then to cry. "I don't want anything bad to happen to Katie, you, or Mom."

"Don't cry, Matthew," Katie said, comforting her brother. She hugged him; she felt her brother's pain; they cried together. Tim grasped Mat's shoulder with his hand, even as he scanned the field.

"We are saved by faith, Mat. Take God at His word," Mary said softly. She spoke the words but felt no concern. God would do what He would do. She had nothing to give Him; she moved and thought on instinct. If He wanted something more, then He would need to give more understanding to her. She was done with herself, done with her perky philosophical code of thought and action, done with her broad-brush stroke of the God force; she was done thinking of the Bible as writings of an ancient people. She was a walking skeleton with an emptiness in her stomach that hurt. The emptiness in her heart was for her superior intellect and pluck, which had been destroyed. Let God fill the hole. She had lived a lie, and it appeared she would die in that lie.

When the tears had run their course, Tim left his family to check on the hiding place of the weapons and supplies. No tracks, no disturbance. He saw a movement in the debris, not furtive. He sought an angle, peered through the debris. Something black and big. A bear! A bear, damn it!

Must have moved down from the flattened mountain forests. Weren't there enough grubs, dead cattle and deer in the country? The bear raised his nose, smelled Tim and ran into the debris at incredible speed. The bear's fear gave Tim boldness and curiosity. What had the bear found? He walked deeper into the debris, past the electric eyes.

He came to a nude corpse, a man, twenties, his pants rolled down around his ankles. The smell of feces came from the pants. The hands and ankles were tied. The bear had dragged the corpse by the neck for twenty feet. The neck bore the marks of the bear's teeth: the body had not been eaten. The corpse was partially rigid and beginning to bloat. Tim guessed the man had died that day. Used prophylactics were strewn about the blood-dampened earth where the man had died. Tim rolled the man over with his foot. A stranger to him. Stab wounds to the chest and torso. Two of the blades had broken off, still protruded. Why hadn't this man been in a work crew the entire day? Why had the killers been given permission to leave their crews? Order, discipline was nonexistent in the camp. Peters was more interested in his own appetites than in his job.

Tim had seen enough. He would demand that the DC live up to her responsibilities. He would demand order from Peters. If they gave no satisfactory solutions, did not act, then he and his family would leave. Go to the next zone. If the next zone was in chaos, then he would seek the whereabouts of Pastor Dave or Carl Stasic. If none of these possibilities was a solution, then his family would live in the ruins as outcastes.

Anything was better than what they had.

***

"Johnson! What brings you here? In the night, I might add. Was it the big light show? Did you pee pee in your little-man pants?" The DC spoke flatly. The mocking was all in the words. Before he could speak, the low rumble came, then a shaking, then a wind of force. She waited for the wind to die, but it did not. Deep down she was frightened—but truly, she didn't give a rat's ass. Everybody dies at some point—she had no goals, no dreams; she had lived it all, and it wasn't worth holding onto. She had had more sex than twenty normal women—what more was there? She had had the adrenaline rush of combat many times. She had had the satisfaction that comes with killing men. She had caught and killed the man who had raped her as a child years ago. Life held no promise and no allure. "Come on, Johnson; speak. I'm a very busy woman. Just hold your crotch, and the words will come." The DC's tone never changed; it was confrontational, challenging.

He looked over the spacious tent. She had received a much larger, more luxurious model than the original—thicker fabric, a floor, a heating and air-conditioning unit. Perhaps the wind would knock it down; he would like that. She now had a large desk, topped with a computer. He saw another box on the desk, probably her security system. The cot had been replaced by a bed. He sat on a solidly built metal chair, well cushioned. She was in her undergarments, the jumpsuit laying across her bed. Was she attempting to entice, or had she been so long in male company that her undress was natural?

"First. We need an orderly system in the mess lines," Tim said.

"I'm well aware of that. Tomorrow begins a new system. People will be called in rotating shifts, grouped by the last digit of your new ID number. What's your next complaint?"

"Found a tied corpse in the warehouse debris, multiple stab wounds, six prophylactics around the sodomized body. That means at least seven men were free to cause mischief today. How did they get out of their work details?"

"That, you have to take up with Peters. I'll buzz him."

"Did you ever mention my request to move back to the apartment?"

"No. Don't be a fool. Coyotes snatching children, murderers running around. You've got to meet your work obligations here. Why sleep up there?"

"So I don't have to worry about dying in my sleep, or having my son or daughter kidnapped and raped or murdered. I've got some electronic eyes, my own, for my security." He had no intention of remaining in the zone. Permission to sleep outside the camp would give him at least a twelve-hour head start for an escape.

"I know Peters; he won't go for it."

"I could keep watch over the camp from there."

"You gonna stay up all night? Please…" she shook her head in disgust, pressed the buzzer for Peters. His deep voice sounded almost immediately.

"Yes?"

Tim noticed the DC had the call on speaker.

"Got a report of a murdered man in the warehouse area, at least six perpetrators, the crime done today. You gonna do something about it?" By law, she should have warned Peters she wasn't alone. The hell with him—his wasn't the only cock in the camp.

"I know about it. An internal affair. Why? Who's raising a stink?"

"Peters, you got to bury bodies. What if someone sees it, begins worrying about the safety of themselves or others?"

"Bury bodies. Right." He spoke as if taking notes for future use. "That it?" With the tone of *why are you bothering me?*

"No. The boss of the first work crew came to me a couple days ago, asked about moving outside the perimeter to his old place."

"He's got that nice-looking wife? Works in the school? I'd like to know her. Yeah, maybe we can swing a deal." Peters's voice held interest and motivation.

"I'll pass it on. You mean you want a piece of her?" DC rolled her eyes at Tim. Tim sat tensed. The DC had covered his presence, protected his identity. But she could just as easily call Peters back once her guest had left.

"You got it. Is that it?" Peters said with an impatient, inquiring tone.

"No. Do we have a cover story for the meteor in the sky? Are we going to drag it out of the ocean and worship it?"

"Someone cornered that idea. It is what it was—a meteor. Period."

"Yes, that's it. Over and out." She turned off the speaker.

"You heard. That's it, Johnson. Get out of here, unless you got something for me." She smiled at him. He stared at her, exited without saying a word. She had lost her appeal long ago. Yeah, he would get out of here. Permanently.

The DC sighed deeply till her lungs were emptied. She ran her hands through her thick, long hair. The way Johnson had looked at her disturbed her. He was the only normal man in the camp—perhaps in zone twenty-one. Peters and his crew weren't worthy of authority over a pack of rats. His was the only normal family. He and his family were her measuring stick as to what was real. When she made judgments, pronouncements, or fed the masses the State's lies and foolishness, she watched the Johnsons react, watched their responses. She watched their appearance—clothes clean, holes sewn. She watched their weight and skin coloring—healthy on the rations, she knew no drugs or alcohol were in their systems. Did their behavior ring true to the unending challenges to sanity? Before the troubles, they would have been normal with many others like them—not two parents living together, but two parents who cared about their kids; now they were above the norm and really useless in measuring the people she had charge of. Tim's family and each individual within still had integrity, purpose. No one else did; not even her.

He had looked at her with the slightest trace of contempt. Had she become a caricature of herself—the tough girl persona? Why hadn't he mentioned the meteor? Because he had foreknowledge of it. It was not a surprise. She knew the Enslavers had an end-of-world theory and meteors were part of it. She'd learned much about Enslavers since her study of John Johnson, Tim's brother. The long evenings had to be filled somehow, and if she could find John Johnson, that would be a game-changer for her career. And there was someone in the city posting old-fashioned paper bulletins containing Bible verses claiming the end was near. Oddly enough, she gave these bulletins credence. Had Tim Johnson become an Enslaver? Stupid question. Of course.

She had even taken a daring chance and visited the black web, searching for this Enslaver crap. They were blamed for a thousand and one conspiracies; they were labeled as a force of evil, blamed for every tragedy. But in this jumble of accusations, she had found their Bible—a printing from hundreds of years ago. She read of this Christ talking of the end. She had found commentaries. As strange as it seemed, the bad guys were making sense.

***

Tim stood in front of his work crew, finished his verbal report to the DC. He listened as the neatly lined platoons to his left reported to the DC. The morning was still, the sky clear, the air hot; the sun had risen as an orange ball, as it had for the two months since the meteor and his meeting with the DC. His platoon smelled of stale sweat. It was March and as hot as July.

Washing facilities were overcrowded, the same pushing, shoving, fighting as prevalent as it had once been in the mess line. As for the mess line, the DC had been good to her word and implemented a more orderly procedure. Personal bathing brought its own dangers at the one communal shower head. Leering men sat there; making the pretense of seeking cleanliness, they were lusting over the naked flesh. The possibility of gang rape was real. Wise bathers wore boxer shorts with a homemade blade fitted to the waistband. Tim was always reminded of the Bible story of Sodom and Gomorra, where the men of the city sought to gang-rape any newcomers to their town. He still intended to leave; each night he had pulled out supplies and loaded rucksacks; a minimum of gear could be taken, as their strength was waning daily. They would have a big feast the night before they left—eating what they couldn't carry. He sought information on the other zones—nothing. He waited for the right moment.

As he waited this morning, worn and tired, sweat already rising on his brow, he heard a sound; the sound was familiar, but he could not remember what made the sound or when he had last heard the sound, a whirring noise. He saw the formations to his left break, swing forward as individuals sought to see around the bodies to their left. The people gazed, stared at something. The whirring grew louder. He saw dust in the air, over the heads of the formation.

Vehicles! Military vehicles, huge wheels, cross-country scout cars, four of them. Armed men in body armor and camo. They stopped before the DC in a cloud of dust, dirt, pulverized grass. He could smell metal, lubricants, hot engines. Fear overcame him. Conscriptions squads? What if he and Mat were now eligible under new standards? He watched an older man with white hair under his soft cap dismount, talk to the DC. Something familiar about the man. Peters was before the man, armed with his rifle, wary. Peters went up and down the line, ordering the people back to their ranks. The ranks reformed. The DC came toward Tim's platoon.

"Johnson. This man…" she swung her head back to the man at the vehicles, "wants to see you."

For the first time, he saw worry and anxiety on her face. She cared nothing for him; her anxiety was for herself. This man must have good news for him. He stepped out hesitantly, walked slowly, studying the man. The thin man had a broad grin on his tanned face. The thinness, the white hair had hidden his old friend.

"Stasic! I'll be damned. Carl!" Tim extended his hand, Carl grabbed the hand, pulled Tim into himself, patted him on the back. A sudden surge of superiority and worth overwhelmed Tim. A man of power knew him, cared for him, and all watching were envious. Carl's uniform smelled of cleanness, not a rip or stain. Carl was shaved, his hair groomed, aftershave clung to him. Carl's grip was strong, and the body moved in strength, not the lethargic movements of the common man. Tim Johnson was somebody again in the presence of Carl.

"Thought we had forgotten about you?"

Tim's elation was so great he could not speak.

"How are you making out?"

Tim shrugged his shoulders. Tim looked at the helmeted, visored men in the vehicles, familiar faces—men of the Order. Carl took Tim by the arm, led him around the side of the vehicle, out of hearing of the DC, who had nervously joined Peters. Peters was calling his deputies, who were slowly coming forward.

"Ready to join us?" Carl asked.

"Yes. But what does that mean?"

"The European Federation president owns the United States. See the DC and the police officer? See these tents? The food you eat, the medical care you receive is not coming from the federal government—the US government is bankrupt. The money is coming from the Church, and the Church is led by the president of the Federation. He is rebuilding the United States. He has the plague antidote."

"I don't understand about the plague."

"It's here in the US, spreading rapidly; that's how he coerces people to join him. Some say he spreads the plague purposely. It hasn't hit here yet, but soon. The good news is we have the serum too, stole it from them."

Carl stopped. He had told this story to so many men, so many times that it had become stale. What he was about to say next always caught in his throat, always gave him a chilling electricity.

"We're going to take our country back, give it back to our heritage, our history, our children, the true citizens. Do you want to be a part of the struggle?"

"I've seen enough of this life, this system, Carl. Yes, we'll come."

"Good. We're gathering our people at the Camp. We've got stores of food, weapons. We're irrigating farmland. We have the remainder of the National Guard on our side. Those not sent to Europe or who didn't join the gangs and the Church are with us. We have heavy weapons, air platforms. We're going to break the hold of the Church, the power of the gangs. We're going to reestablish law and order, without favoritism."

"Do you want us to come now?"

"Yes. We'll provide everything."

Tim thought of the hidden supplies. He would not mention them; maybe later he would need them.

Carl walked around the backside of the vehicle, strode over to the DC and Peters. Carl's voice came with authority, demanding, desiring confrontation.

"I want this man's family brought here. And the family of Jennings, ID 200340056."

"Only Jennings's daughter has survived," volunteered the DC.

"Bring her and the printout that verifies the death of her family."

The DC double-timed to her tent. Carl stared into Peters's eyes.

"You have any problems with this?"

"No, sir," Peters said firmly, then in a submissive tone added, "But I'd like to know under whose authority you're acting. It is against the law to take people out of their zones."

Peters glanced up at the laser rifles aimed at his head. A rage welled within him. If given the opportunity, he would fire, would destroy them all. He had been bred for conflict. He was a god among men, superior. He could very well destroy these four vehicles and their occupants.

"By the authority of the Constitution of the United States of America. If you don't recognize that authority, then by the authority you do recognize—the lasers pointed at your head."

Peters breathed hard; hatred steeled the eyes, piercing Stasic. Stasic, unflinching, met the stare with eyes harder than Peters's. He hated such men, superior bodies and inferior souls. Men who could not be moved by ideals or truth.

Tim's family and the little Jennings girl appeared, wide eyed, shocked, wary. Till the Johnsons saw Carl. Peters turned away, took a few steps from Carl. Never had his rage been so difficult to tame. He didn't fear death or failure. He had seen this Stasic character before—in the presence of high-ranking people and politicians. How much power did he possess? Carl turned to the lead vehicle, called up, "Weapon."

A laser rifle was tossed down. Carl handed the weapon to Tim and spoke. "Is there anyone else we should take along?"

Tim thought for only a second on his platoon. None was worthy. He looked at the DC. She would fight; she had the skills, abilities. She had protected him from Peters, done her job reasonably well. Personally, she disgusted him. "I'm thinking of the DC."

"As a group they can't be trusted; they took oaths, have stock in the prosperity of the Church. She's into this deep—into incentives, benefits, even a retirement plan. We can't risk an informant."

"That's it then. I'm ready."

Carl smiled. "Get on board."

As the towering vehicle pulled away, Tim looked down on the DC, gave her a gentle salute that trailed to an open handed, unmoving wave. He had no desire to be bitter; sheer joy was his emotion. God had come through! Just when he needed Him most, He had come through! The vehicles picked up speed as they turned away from the formation; still the men kept their rifles aimed at Peters. The weapon in Tim's hand gave him such a sense of power. Now all things were possible. Power in his hands, power under his feet. Like-minded men beside him. Life was good again.

CHAPTER 18

At the end of zone twenty-one, past the last partially intact high-rise, before the unbroken pattern of destroyed buildings, Tim saw armed men at a homemade barrier of wrecked vehicles. They did not raise their weapons. Tim leaned into Carl's ear. "Carl, who are they?"

"Peters's men; didn't you know?"

Tim only shook his head in the negative. Carl continued. "Peters has a cadre of soldiers, a small army at his command. Where he and his men fit into our enemy's battle scheme is only conjecture."

Katie and Mat were eagerly looking out the side of the vehicle. Katie smiled, her hair blowing; she freed the sweat-soaked hair from her temples with a comb of her hands, a toss of her head. She liked the speed. It had been so long since something other than their legs had carried them. Her prayer had been answered—escape from the tent city. She sensed this momentary freedom, the lifting of mental strain, might only be temporary. Hardships lay ahead. She could face the hardships; Jesus was her friend and constant companion. Or was her friend the Holy Spirit? She laughed—they were one and the same, no formality and no fright at some religious doctrine crossed. She was loved by God; her story played on their electrascreen. They talked about her around the kitchen table—the angels, Jesus, the Holy Spirit, God were watching her and talking sympathetically about her trials on Earth and her heavenly homecoming. Who was she that they loved her so? Tears came to her eyes; to have friends was everything. Her worries weren't for herself but for Mathew, whom she needed while on Earth. If he went to heaven before her, it would be tough. Mom and Dad were her concerns—they were utterly lost.

The scenes of destruction streamed by; the vehicles dodging debris, bumping over rubble, tilting against mounds or earthquake-slanted earth. Narrow pedestrian pathways had been cleared through many high piles of rubble. Concrete, the earth, wreckage all bore the black smudge of burning. They saw a commuter moving on a shortened run. Some highways were clear, a few dented cars moved. A pack of coyotes bolted across a street in front of their convoy. At some places, the stink of corpses was strong, as if the rotting juices had been absorbed into the concrete.

They moved south along Front Street, stopped at a barricade, where the tension was thick between Carl and the leader of the barricade's guard detail. Weapons were pointed, the man backed down. They came to a tent city located on Riverfront Park, talked to the local DC. Another family, named Smith, joined the caravan. Two kids their age, and Smith had a wife. Along Market Street, open-air markets, businesses in booths were open and attracted customers. Canned foods, dried, freeze-dried foods, fresh foods for sale, a barber shop, hairstylists, a launderer, clothing, shoe stores, furniture stores all offered products for barter. US currency was worthless, as was the Federation's script. Three commuter cars were running. The street was crowded.

They reversed their direction, traveled back up Front Street. The plastic-hulled barges sat on the plasticized cement canal bed of caked mud, puddles, litter, and bird carcasses. The heavy barges had kept the canal bed from washing away. The huge rectangular fishponds were nearly empty, a thick, muddy soup of catfish and tilapia bodies. Most were dead, some still squirmed seeking oxygen. No bridges had been rebuilt; what was the need? Traffic, an occasional car or truck, pedestrians, bicyclists had worn a road beside one collapsed bridge. On the remaining riverbed, dust devils swirled. The dust had the smell of the once-potent river, bird dung, rotted fish, river mud. They barreled through the same checkpoint; the men on guard gave obscene gestures. Some of the men in the vehicles returned the gestures.

They veered west, still remaining on the east side of the riverbed, and came to a vast chasm in the riverbed, running east to west. A military bridge had been erected to cross north and south. By the chasm they saw crushed vehicles being stripped, broken down for recycling; the unusable parts thrown into the chasm. Debris of no value, cleaned up from the city streets, cascaded into the chasm in a haze of dust. Farther up the chasm, a dozer pushed more wreckage into the depths. Tim looked up the riverbed at the mountains to their north, raised perhaps a thousand feet higher; the new ridgeline, a mass of sedimentary layers, looked like a serrated blade. The downed trees had lost all their leaves. The forest was a tangle of heaved up trees, roots, and branches intertwined. When would the forest fires restart? he wondered. The fire and hail of months ago was a surface burn compared with the depth of deadness waiting. Atop the mountain restaurant ruins, a black skull-and-crossbones flag flew. What evil was there, where once he had spent such pleasurable evenings dining with his family?

Mat, stiff backed in his seat, wind upon his face, viewed the odd sights before him. Nothing was as it had been. How strange it all was. Where once buildings had blocked your view, there was sky. Where once buildings cast shadows, there was intense sunlight. All was changed. All was wild and fantastic. The rubbled buildings of the city were like a granitic mountain range. The river chasm was like a miniature Grand Canyon of the Susquehanna River. The mountains now twice their height had barren jumbles of rock outcrops high in the sky where vultures swirled in the clear air. Where the river had cut the mountain in millennia past, leaving cliff-like ends, the new upheaval honored the riverbed but had spewed giant boulders at its edges. He liked the sensations, liked the excitement of this new but fleeting time.

Thank God for Carl, who had taken him from slavery. He knew this ride, this new future with the Order could only be temporary. The end of this present age and world was coming. His Dad and Mom didn't truly believe it was coming. They had suggested this was only a dark chapter in world history, like the plague that ravaged Europe in the Middle Ages.

Humanity would persevere, and life would continue. No return of Jesus, no judgment. How could he awaken them? How could he make Christ real? How could he create a need within them? How could he change their allegiance from self to Jesus?

They hit open highway going east. The flanking buildings to the north were now behind them. The formerly lush ag fields lay black and barren, littered with the white bones of individual carcasses of deer and cattle, broken ag machinery. The hot breeze streamed through their clothing. Mat looked over his family's faces, studied their expressions. Katie was solid in Christ. She was happy at the moment, squinting into the sun and wind but knew the temporary nature of the gift. Dad was lost in his ego. He now deemed himself important. A man of power and wealth had snatched him from hell. The correlation burst upon Mat and made him almost reveal a smile, laugh. Jesus was the man of power and importance who would ultimately snatch them from hell.

Jesus was the man Dad should have been clinging to. He had unsurpassed power and wealth, but Dad didn't believe it—and it was meant to be that way, for the world. That is why Jesus came to Earth as a nobody, born of nobody parents, born in a nobody town, at a time in history when his nation was a nobody nation. All Jesus had going for him was the truth about people's relationship with God, and people, who they truly were. Jesus tore apart who you thought you were, what you thought you needed from life and others. Jesus was just the opposite of what humanity wanted from God—their own private magic genie or a political leader or a general built like a storm trooper. Jesus could only promise a new awareness and reality and suffering. Jesus saw so far and so deep within that people couldn't begin to understand. Soon the world would understand.

Mat laughed. How clever was God? Who could match His wisdom? The Spirit of God rushed upon him like a scented spring breeze. His body sighed; his mind knew deep peace. All that man mocked about Jesus showed the true heartlessness, the false intelligence of mankind. Who would follow a man who told them they were wrong and who hated the mess they had made of themselves, everyone else, and the earth? Mat knew the presence of the Spirit was upon him, giving him peace. He needed to share that wonder, that feeling that was worth more than anything else in life. The Holiest God knew Mat Johnson existed, and He cared for him. Mary was smiling at Mat, noticing his peace. Mat rose in a crouch and touched his mother on the forehead. He stayed in his crouch and touched his father upon his heart. He touched Katie, and she laughed peacefully and closed her eyes. Mat touched little Emily Jennings, who rested her head upon Katie's shoulder. He looked briefly into his father's eyes before returning to his seat.

How like the wind the Spirit was. Mat closed his eyes and entered into deep and wondrous prayer for his family. His mother—he could not fathom her heart; surely it was good, surely God would reveal Himself to her.

Tim studied his son. He was in some deep and good place. What had the touch meant? Katie squinted into the wind and sun, at peace. Emily slept. Mary seemed to have a peace. His family, they could survive without him. He wanted to believe this, for it lifted a burden from him. Mary was an attractive woman, men noticed her—Peters did. The kids were now street smart, savvy; Mary could watch over them. They could watch over themselves.

He had no cares when the burden of his family was dismissed. He did not regret rebuffing a relationship with the DC; he regretted not putting a laser burst into Peters's brain. He regretted not sticking a knife into Plug. He regretted leaving Mr. Bensen alive. Scores to settle. He would not be so kind in the future; he would not allow opportunities to pass. He was at peace at having killed George. Tim sensed, felt his leanness, his taut body. He had power. He was a survivor.

Mary wondered why Mat had touched her. He had been feeling something—definitely peace. Had he wanted to share a thought? How had she raised such good kids? Sharp retentive minds, health, and athletic ability—enough to give confidence. Never sidetracked by the temptations of belonging to their generation's drug and sexual rampages or weird gangs. Not stuck on themselves, not cruel or callous to those around them. They believed their newfound religion. She had seen them praying at night or reading their Bibles. Their questions and comments had been sharper than hers at the Bible study. She had been inculcated through the faith of the Church; they had not. This made her wonder all the more.

They saw smoke billowing from the south and passed scorched fields, black and dry. A large patch on the mountainside had burned—was burning. From the volcanic activity? There had been no lightning storms since that time. They saw more unburned mountain as they came into the holdings of the Order. The unburned mountain plots of downed trees appeared to have been saved purposely. Wind turbines were turning high on the new mountain ridge, the great blades finding a gentle breeze. Men of the Order must have moved the turbines a thousand feet higher—quite an accomplishment. Green fields radiating from long irrigation pipes sloping down from the mountain ridge were passed. Active, bellowing, grunting, cows, pigs inhabited spacious pens. They turned into the mountain, to the Camp, which had once seemed like their weekend home. Bunkers, watch towers had been erected; trenches, dug. A killing zone was cleared from the highway to the border of standing trees, trees that once shaded the Order's Camp. Solar panels were everywhere. As they entered the site, they saw most of the trees had fallen, the roots in the stony soil having no grip on the earth. Saws were buzzing on the mountainside; the figures of men seen climbing over, around the downed trees.

On one athletic field a new wooden building had been erected, a saw mill; boards, studs were stacked in great piles. A development of single-family homes had been erected up the mountain. The vehicles containing the families continued up to this development. The vehicle stopped before a home at the end of the development. The homes were simple, rustic. New tree plantings were evident along the street, with buried irrigation tubes aimed at the roots. Carl was out of the vehicle before the families could rise from their seats.

Carl beamed. "Here are your homes. Tim, your family is on this end. Smith, you are beside him. Furniture, bedding all stocked. A woodstove for heat or even to cook. Electricity will come soon. Settle in. You men— including your sons—come down to headquarters when you're ready, and I'll show you what is ahead."

"We'll come now, if that's alright," volunteered Tim. Mary and Katie could inspect the home. Smith studied his wife's face, received a nod, and nodded his head. "We're ready too."

Carl looked at the Jennings girl, standing forlornly; Katie holding her hand. "Would anyone like to take Emily in, till we can find her a new family?"

Katie began tugging insistently on her mother's hand.

"Mom! Take her! Take her! Please…" Katie implored.

"Sure. We'll take Emily." Mary extended her hand to Emily; Emily's little hand grasped her hand shyly. Mary noticed the gratitude but also the deep vacant sadness behind the glimmer of life. Something was deeply wrong with Emily. She wanted to love the child but felt something inside her that couldn't; Emily was another responsibility, Emily depressed her. Emily wasn't her responsibility. She didn't want to invest the time to untangle the mangled soul. Mary felt an anger at her own hardness of heart. She would love this child, and that was the end of it.

"Good! Good!" Carl turned away with the men following closely, trailed by the sons. He began talking. "I don't want you two to think you were the last on our list to be picked up. You two were in the roughest locations, with the most stubborn authorities. We had to pay for the right to enter your zones."

Tim's mind perked. Peters and the DC seemed to know nothing of the surprise visit. If Carl was telling the truth, which he always did, there was a higher authority that had been bribed.

"We're just glad to be here, Carl," Tim answered gratefully.

Smith nodded in affirmation. "That's right, Carl."

Tim heard Mat talking to Smith's son, introducing himself. Smith's son was named Daniel. They entered the large meeting hall. The cool air of the air-conditioned room sent chills through Tim. It seemed like he had been born in heat, couldn't remember when he had last been cool. He had lost so much weight he was cold. Offices had been added to the hall, desks spaced around the periphery of the room.

Older men sat at the desks, worked before computers, communications screens. Young preteen boys acted as runners and secretaries.

"Were we hit hard by conscription, Carl?" asked Smith.

"We hid most of our men; they're out working at this moment. Some of the good ones were shipped to Europe and are now in the Middle East. It's shaping up to be a hell of a war."

Carl moved to the center of the room, where a huge three-dimensional map of the city and surrounding countryside had been built. The map had been made after the quake. Fault lines, chasms, dried water courses, newly created ponds, destroyed buildings were all shown in graphic detail. Tim's trained eye could see the underlying rock strata, the movement of plates. The newly organized twenty-one zones had been marked, as had the old gang territories. Small flags marked police substations, headquarters, government buildings, aid stations, operating warehouses, commuter lines, electrical stations.

"Here is our city, our county, and surrounding areas of importance," said Carl. "If you want hard data, numbers, press Z plus the zone number on this computer." Carl pressed Z 21 on the adjacent computer. A screen came up showing population data—names, ID numbers, genders, ages.

"We know as much as our adversary does. Very soon we will sweep into the city, destroy anyone who raises a weapon against us. The DCs, police, any of this new regime will be killed or captured, brought to trial, put to death if found guilty. We will take over the administration of the city and the rebuilding. New laws will be enforced. Rape, death. Child molestation, death. Thievery, death. Murder, torture then death. If those laws don't bring order, then torture before death will be added to the other crimes."

Tim understood the need for extreme measures. "What outside opposition can we expect from the Church or the Federation?"

"They're stretched thin. These uprisings will occur simultaneously across the nation. Once we destroy them here, they will have nothing to throw against us. Though we might have to send aid to some other part of the state or the nation."

Tim noticed Gramps's farmhouse near the northern edge of the greater metro area of the map. How strange that he had once thought Gramps's house the key to survival. Though it yet might prove helpful. He still had a significant cache there, known only to him, if not already looted or stolen.

He noticed the flag atop the mountain restaurant. "Who is here, Carl?" Tim pointed.

"A gang of between forty and fifty men with their sex partners. They've been raiding what little north-south traffic comes through this area."

Tim moved down to the south edge of the board, to the mansion where Dave lived as a caretaker. A small flag had been inserted.

"What's this?"

"A man with money, some global power has a following—sixty to twice that. We haven't been able to ascertain whose side they're on. They profess neutrality, seem to have a religion all their own, but have weapons. You know them?"

"No, just scanning the edges of our known world…studying the south edge of the board." Pastor Dave hadn't departed yet, or had departed and returned? Carl's information could be wrong. Was he wrong about the owner of the mansion being more than a disinterested party as Dave had also suggested? Weapons? Dave had never professed to be a pacifist but never claimed to have weapons.

"What is the new policy to be on religions?"

"What it was before the Church. Believe what you want, as long as it doesn't involve criminal activity. You want to worship the blood of a chicken, go ahead. Just don't sexually molest a child in the process, or rape anyone. We have a Jew from Israel out here somewhere, putting up flyers about the second coming of Christ. When was the last time this world saw a sheet of paper? We've got no problem with that. We'd enlist his aid if we could locate him. The authorities are out to crucify him— he's really got them angry; talks trash about the Church." Carl laughed gleefully at the Church's misfortune. "You haven't seen him or any of his flyers, have you?"

"No," said Tim.

Smith shook his head and answered, "No," at Carl's gaze.

"He'll turn up—probably too late for us to use him."

Mat didn't even cast a glance toward his father; he wore the same poker face he had displayed when Carl had mentioned Dave and his group.

"We'll assign you two to the area where you lived. Go in there and clean house."

The image was appealing to Tim—returning with a weapon in his hands. He already had his list of the men he would kill. "Sounds good to me."

"Good. Go to the armorer and draw a weapon for your son, Tim. And Dan, draw weapons for you and your son. Then go out to the firing range, get in some practice. No more than twenty shots. There's an instructor at the range every day assigned to help you and others. I'll tell your group leader to visit, fill you in, give you a role. You two have the most up-to-date information. Actively participate. We need you."

Smith smiled. "Thank you kindly."

"The time is short. I don't know the hour, but the time is short. Go, gentlemen; I need to remain here."

Tim and Mat walked into the oven-like air. Mat remembered when this area had been covered by shady trees. He smelled the hot sawdust piles. The Smiths were allowed to gain distance.

"Should we tell Mom and Katie to keep quiet about Dave and Josh?"

"Yes. We don't know where Josh is, so we can't help. Best to say we never met him. Pastor Dave? I have to think on that one. Maybe I could be a contact between Carl and Dave. I'm curious to see if any of my supplies are in his possession."

"That would be interesting to know," said Mat. He began to walk toward their new home. His father stopped. "Let's check out the old lodge building. Maybe we can pick up some intel on the city or world events." Tim moved toward the buildings of the old Camp.

Mat followed, remembering the good times of the past. He saw the outdoor swimming pool with people actually relaxing, lying in the sun, and children with enough energy to play, diving, swimming, playing keep-away with a ball in the pool. Strange how a few good-sized meals a day was the difference between sadness and no future and happiness and hope. He saw some girls his age, knew he had no time to marry, no time to raise a child. Smith's kid, Dan Jr., was already at the pool. Mat trusted God with his broken dreams.

Tim paused suddenly in his walk, and Mat stopped abruptly, almost walking into his dad. Mat followed his father's eyes to a younger man of great natural size striding across the dirt before the buildings. He had an athletic walk. "Know him?" Mat could not read his dad's emotions.

"Yes. That's Jeremy Lines—he went to the Academy. He wanted to go to a military academy. I saw on the newscasts that he had been conscripted. Wonder how he got here."

"Ask him."

Tim smiled; a sadness was in his eyes. "Our last meeting was uncomfortable." Mat did not press his dad for an explanation. Tim wondered if Jeremy was a security risk. Was Jeremy a patriot to the ideals of his nation or to the ideals of the world? The riches and glory would come from the Federation. His reemerging nation could only offer sacrifice. Yes, Jeremy was a security risk, and Carl would need to know.

They stepped inside the old lodge of blinds and muted light. The walls were still hung with ibex and antelope, moose, buffalo, grizzly heads. A stuffed polar bear stood on hind legs. The lodge had a bar, empty and unused, except for the antique water cooler that remained working, even stocked with waxed-paper cups. Tim was certain there were no companies left to produce paper cups. Tim scanned the tables that collected sitting men; most tables were empty. The men congregated near the oversized electrascreen. Tim chuckled; he called out, "Smith, how'd you get here so quickly?"

"Just not ready to go back to the family. My son made a beeline to the pool. Come sit."

Tim and Mat pulled up old table chairs, as Tim glanced at armies moving on the electrascreen. "What's that about?"

"That's the Federation's army massed in Italy waiting for the call to enter Israel. My younger brothers are there. Islamic terrorists hit their bases daily. Every Muslim country of the Middle East is readying for the war. Russia is massing. China is massing. Every country in the area. India is massing to protect her borders. All politics. None of these countries are worth having—plagues, famines, earthquakes have ruined them like they've ruined us. That queer president of the Federation, the head of the Church, took our best men away from us. Took our food, our weapons. Then took our country."

"Do men think the world will recover from these natural disasters? Is that why they still covet the land?" Tim hoped the reasoning was true.

"You think this is gonna get *better*?" Smith's demeanor flipped in a second from placid to accusatory rage. Mat glanced at his father; Smith was correct, but Smith was showing an anger that didn't fit the circumstances. They sensed physical violence was held back by the flimsiest barrier.

"I don't know. Help me understand," Tim pleaded.

Dad, the diplomat. But with his right hand under the table—no doubt gripping his little stabbing knife. Smith's reddened face began to drain of blood, and he took a deep breath. Mat watched the tensed-up muscles relax.

"I got my problems as you can see." An embarrassment marked the tone.

"It's okay; we all do," Mat said, responding to the embarrassment. Smith would be okay; the apology told him so.

"Really want to hear your opinion," added Tim.

"Thanks for the understanding—that's rare these days." He continued quickly. "It's worse than they're telling us. We have hundreds of thousands of troops on our southern borders. Our air force strafes and bombs twenty-four seven. Warlords from as far away as Chile, Argentina come to penetrate our country. We slaughter them. The survivors head south and then get picked up by another army coming north. One army penetrated to Las Vegas, Nevada, before being annihilated. Central and South America are wastelands, no rain, no jungles, no forests, the savannas have turned to dust. The mighty Amazon is a trickle—doesn't even reach the ocean. The water, originally taken for irrigation, has evaporated completely. Australia is gone except for a fringe of survivors on the northern coast. China has already taken Myanmar, Vietnam, Laos, Thailand, Cambodia, Indonesia. Japan. The oceans are dying."

"How do you know these things?" Tim was in disbelief. He envisioned these countries, which he once knew intimately in his geology days, superimposed upon them the descriptions given by Smith, and imagined the horror and hardships.

"I was in the Air National Guard for twenty-five years. Flew every kind of weather mission, humanitarian aid mission, rescue mission. Have contacts everywhere, friends I kept in touch with by short wave radio.

"The earth is dying." Smith choked as he spoke his prognosis.

"Can we do anything to stop it?" Mat asked, wondering if Smith was a candidate for the gospel.

"No, just play it out like men. Guard our families, live for hope, and kill the mother-fuckin' scum of society and the bastards that stole our country."

Mat, gathering his thoughts and words, said, "Did you hear about the Jewish guy saying what you're saying? Only he adds that Jesus Christ is returning for his people?"

"Yeah. Josh. Even met him, listened to him speak. He was in our zone many times. They think he had his printing press there. I had been instructed by Carl to keep the authorities and punks off his trail." Smith smiled wryly. "Some died by my hand."

"Do you believe him?" asked Tim

"Fuck no. Well, I'll believe him when Jesus Christ is standing before my eyes." Smith laughed. "Anything is possible."

"Have you heard your ticket has to be in your hand before He comes to collect?" asked Mat.

"Sure; I heard the whole story. I even gave my life to Him publicly before Josh. Haven't seen any changes, but like I said, anything is possible."

Tim realized Smith had indicated to Carl just moments earlier that he knew nothing of Joshua. The response had been preplanned by Carl and Smith. Did they know Tim Johnson and family knew Joshua? Or was it just the protocol, to keep info compartmentalized? Smith had forgotten his audience and had exposed Carl's secrecy. Tim saw no awareness upon Smith's face or eyes that he had spoken what should have remained hidden.

Mat had both forearms on the table and had been hunched over, facing Smith, but now he reflexively pulled back. Mat remembered Carl inquiring about Josh and Smith's answer. A layer of intrigue existed. It was also apparent Smith did not know Christ as his savior. Mat realized doubt crowded Smith's mind. There was no peace, no assurance, no confidence. Smith. seemed like a copy of his father—intentions expressed, faith given, and nothing occurring in their hearts.

As if Tim had listened to his son's thoughts, he said, "You're where I'm at, Smith." Tim seemed buoyed by Smith's sharing. It was good to know he was not alone in his questionings and doubts. Mat wanted to ask if Smith had communicated Josh's message of Jesus to his family but thought this might be personal to Smith and would give away more about the Johnsons than the Smiths. Tim stood. Mat followed his lead. "Back to the family. Thanks for sharing." Tim and Mat shook Smith's hand.

CHAPTER 19

Tim and Mat circled their new home, studying its position on the ground, discussing the defensive pluses and minuses. It was evident to Tim that Mat had a solid foundation in soldiering from the countless classes he had received at the Camp. Mat probably knew more about soldiering than he did. No sprinkler system was beneath the rock-hard earth; lawns a waste of water, time. Two narrow basement windows, too narrow for men to enter. As the stone foundation was high, entry into the first windows would take a ladder or a man with a boost from another. Ten steps led up to the porch and door. These would slow an assault. The doors were solid boards of oak, the window narrow with thick, wooden sashes. They wondered what could be seen from the second-story windows. Probably a good view but would leave you open to far-reaching laserfire. As they walked up the steps to their front porch, Tim spoke. "Let's ask for landscaping stone in these yards; they're noisy when walked upon—no sneaking enemy."

Mat opened the door while answering. "Good idea." Suddenly Emily was running toward Mat and leaped at him with her arms open. He grabbed her, lifted her up, hugged her, then squeezed her. "What a greeting!" He was overwhelmed at the six-year-old's response to his entrance. Mary and Katie came out of the kitchen. "A home. We're in a home!

Rustic but well built, and with bedrooms." Mary's face beamed. She went to Tim and embraced him, resting her head upon his chest. Tim saw the couch before and facing the fireplace and flopped down with Mary in his arms. She was so thin. Mat, with Emily in his arms, sat on a cushioned easy chair. Katie sat on the matching chair. "Does anyone know why I am so loved?" asked Mat.

Katie responded. "Your gift of touch on the ride in."

Mat felt a deep contentment for the honor of bestowing the presence of the Spirit. Studying Katie's face, he wondered what his sister had experienced. He asked, "Where you aware—"

She did not allow him to finish. "Yes, and I told Emily."

Mat snuggled his head into Emily's neck and whispered, "You know Jesus now, or soon will." Emily laughed as Mat's words tickled her neck. She gave a quick kissing peck at Mat's cheek.

Tim was asleep. Mary gazed at the far wall, lost in thought, resting in the heat of Tim's body. She had heard the conversation—Katie's words, Mat's comment to Emily. Emily had felt something. Mat and Katie had felt something. The touch of the Spirit? Isn't that what Mat whispered to Emily? Why hadn't she? They had talked about the Holy Spirit when discussing the Gospel of John. She let it drop. The professor's home, the home when they were in the Church's custody, the farmhouse, the warehouse apartment, the tent city, the rustic cabin. So much change, and none of it good. But this new home offered promise—if the battle for their nation was won. At best, you could say the immediate past had been a test of character.

What was character? The beliefs that took you through the hard times without scarring your soul so that when the trials were over, you could enjoy the return to prosperity and work fulfillment. Was there an end? She still found it difficult to believe in a heaven, or that the God force— no, God—wanted the world to end. What had she or the people of her culture done to God that He or She or It would be so enraged? Perhaps other peoples and cultures deserved wrath, those who spent their days in debauchery and indolence, accomplishing nothing.

From her birth, Mary had remained positive, and the cultural norms of please, thank you, good morning, good night, may I help you, after you—kind words used to buoy others, lift them—were her spirit and vocabulary. She liked people, liked being liked, liked achieving. The tent city experience had opened her eyes. Now, all her goodness had no earthly reward. The old way was gone; no politeness, no hopeful thoughts from others, just silence or curses, or words that tore you down and elevated them—crude sexual words, violent words. Mary's only commodity now was that she was "a cunt." She had heard that word whispered behind her back or spoken softly within her hearing. Sometimes as a curse word and sometimes with a brutal sexual desire. She could not become part of this world; she was laughed at for the world she came from. Only with her family and the few good people, such as Carl's group or Pastor Dave's group, did she see a glimmer of the past.

The only purpose now was to stay alive. Funny, this end-of-living scenario wasn't new to her. In high school, she had become fascinated with historical life-ending tragedies. Shipwrecked men eaten by cannibals—or by each other; ships sinking and not enough lifeboats; populations captive in wartime, starving and humiliated; soldiers in last heroic stands, well aware of their fate. Astronauts in space, then the mechanical failure; hurtling through space, knowing they would not return. Astronauts marooned on planets with limited air, food. Plague or virus or radiation victims counting days or hours till the end. Not the usual girlie fare, but the boys had loved it. Ironic that she was now, supposedly, within the greatest tragedy of history—the end of the world.

As a girl reading the stories, she was intrigued by and thought only of the emotional trauma and the life decisions the participants were forced to make. Now she was forced to think of God, His nature, His purpose. If there was no God and these were the random acts of nature, a planet simply at the end of its lifespan, then it was over. No one would read of her noble thoughts and actions; no heavenly beings would be recording. Or would they? What of the book of life? she wondered. Would space explorers from a future civilization, from another planet, find her bones and analyze and suppose this and that, reconstruct her face and gawk at her?

She was what she was, and she had been trained in the way of a God, a supreme being. She could not think outside this construct and didn't wish to, for it led nowhere. She had always thought she knew what He or It or She wanted and tried to live it. Now, people—her own family—were telling her she had missed something essential, maybe even had lived a lie her entire life. Now, her life experiences said the Bible as originally written was true, and that God was God and Jesus was His son. God was male, and what was considered feminine was within His maleness. Mary Johnson was now ready again to entertain that thought, and it pissed her off, or in her old wording, she was angry. Mary fell asleep upon the sleeping form of her husband.

Mat looked at Katie, who looked at sleeping Emily in Mat's arms. "I was hoping we'd end with a family prayer," he whispered.

"Jesus knows…," said Katie. "Let's go out. Barb, Dan's sister, said they would have a fire down at the picnic pavilion."

"Okay." Mat opened the door, and Katie followed. They stood on the porch that smelled of fresh wood and glanced to the east. The star-filled sky always offered hope. Christ would come from the heavens with His angels, and then it would be done.

"How much do you think is lef—" Katie's question was interrupted by a blazing meteor—like a burning torch—streaking across the sky in its descent. They heard the hissing of its burning, saw the land lighten into day. The tail was long, thick. The comet was swallowed by the eastern horizon, and darkness returned.

Mat spoke. "That was the third trumpet judgment. One third of the freshwater in the world will be unusable. Hopefully, the Lord will be gentle to our country for the few saints who remain."

Katie sighed. "I'm turning in. Meeting people doesn't sound as good as sleeping in a real bed and not worrying about being molested." She hadn't given a thought to Mat's explanation of the meteorite and the consequences.

"I agree. But what about supper?" Mat followed Katie back into the house, locked the door.

"I can sleep without eating. I've been doing that for quite a while," said Katie.

Mom was gone from the living room; Emily either had followed or had been carried. Dad was snoring. Mat threw the afghan on the back of the couch over his father. As he followed Katie upstairs, Katie looked in on her mother. There was Emily, snuggled beside her. Mat passed her and was already in his room, sleeping. Katie turned into her new bedroom—smelled the fresh-cut pine of the walls; smelled the clean mattress, clean sheets and comforter—and sighed. Her shoes were off, and she was sound asleep.

Mary awoke an hour into her sleep. Her clothes were twisted and binding, and her shoes were not off her feet. She groggily stripped off her outer garments, shoes, and socks. She pulled Emily's shoes and socks from her feet. She saw underpants sticking out at the waistband of the heavy fabric of the pants. She gently pulled the pants off Emily's narrow hips. She saw welts along the legs. Mary pulled the sweatshirt over Emily's head, and the T-shirt came up with the sweatshirt. The tiny back was covered with welts—some still crusted with fresh scabs. Mary covered the little girl, went downstairs, knelt before the cushioned chair, her hands on the seat.

She tried to pray for Emily; she tried to ask God for the wisdom to help this little girl. She cried in shame at the woman named Mary who had wished to reject this little girl. She cried in shame at the Mary who had never had to cry to God before because life had been so good. It just had challenges—challenges the fool named Mary could handle, could conquer, and wear her pride like a halo. She could not think cogently enough to pray. She could only cry and beg God to help the little girl named Emily. Who but God could put the little mind and body back together again?

When the last tear had been shed, the last mucous mess expelled from her nose, the saliva wiped from her lips and chin; Mary went back to her bed, placed her arm around Emily, kissed the little girl's soft hair, her tiny head, and said, "You're mine."

Had God cried for little Emily? She knew Jesus had wept. If Jesus wept, then there was no impersonal God force—this creator being of all power that made man in His image, yet had no emotion, needed no emotion, and could not weep? If Mary wept and God could not, then her love was greater than God's love. She was the superior being and should have created the world.

No, God *was* emotion, rightly apportioned, rightly displayed. God's emotion had created life, the world; God showed anger and love, delight, kindness, mercy. These were not byproducts of God; these *were* God; his character displayed for His children to see and imitate. That's why Jesus came to creation—to show mankind God was not just logic and mathematics and science—the giant computer in the sky. God, before all things, was emotion. He was Spirit. He was passion. He was love. God had sent Mary to love Emily because Emily's hurt had touched Him, grieved Him.

All her life, she had thought of God as an impersonal force—maybe even an *it* and Jesus as a ticked-off semihuman teacher belonging to God yet separate, maybe even a creation of God. She had thought of Jesus as an example, a prototype of mankind, not the very likeness of God. All her life she had thought of mankind as better than God. Mankind had emotion, and mankind, in its dressing up of the mannequin, *God*, had arrayed Him with its emotions. Just as humans anthropomorphized animals, so had they the God force. He *was* emotion. It was emotion that stirred the very cosmos into being.

How could she have been so deceived? The logic and theology of the world had lied to her. Her very self—her flesh—had lied to her, because the lie made *her* god, the decider of her emotion and will. Only now, when she was confronting a dying world and God's truth written in an ancient book; only now, when she was in her dying flesh, could God's spirit burst into her consciousness.

In that instant the Spirit of God grabbed her heart, soul, mind, and strength, and she felt her troubled spirit leave and peace came, and she knew He would never leave. She yearned for the morning to tell Tim she was saved. Mary rubbed the little arm of Emily and whispered, "Wait till you hear, Emily…it is glorious."

***

Archbishop Gilroy sat second from the window; he allowed Father Winkler to sit at the window for the transatlantic flight to Rome and the Vatican. Winkler had never been to the Vatican or to Europe. Archbishop Gilroy had been many times in his fifty-year career serving his god. He turned and looked down the massive aisle of the supersonic jetliner.

Every seat filled with the men of the priesthood; the colors of red, black, white; the vestments, the hats, the collars; the trousered men and robed men, the uniforms of the new order. On the lower deck, the same sight. In total, a thousand servants of the Lord. Everyone would meet the new pope—the first to be the leader of the secular and the spiritual.

Winkler had gained attendance status for his role in crushing the scandal of the satanic bible and calming the consternation ensuing from the intrigue of the Johnson family. Winkler and he were to receive accolades for their handling of this affair. Gilroy smiled, for he knew the true and highest accolades were for his effort in "realigning" the true church with the new order. Winkler's role had been contrary and halfhearted, but it looked good in the press to have a young, handsome, virile priest attached to the story. The press wasn't interested in an old homosexual, boy-loving archbishop. Winkler was not pleased to be attending and had not wanted any honor.

Gilroy had read Winkler's private diary and his emails to trusted friends, and for this, Winkie hated Gilroy. Gilroy had made him a Judas. The wrecking of Johnson's teaching career by Gilroy's official decree—that Timothy Johnson was an enemy of the Church—had destroyed any hope of meaningful work and left only employment of the lowest menial form. His dearest friend, the most precious family, would suffer undeservedly. Winkie's guilt, shame, and consternation at having been used had settled into a seething rage. He had kept tabs on his friend Timothy Johnson and his family up until a month ago, when he had been ordered to stop. All communications attempted by Father Winkler had been intercepted and stopped.

Gilroy mused on the ascendancy of Babylon—the world church was whole, in the control of human hands, directed by the true god, the god of the flesh and man's aspirations. The fallen angel was now the risen king of creation. The bliss, the fulfillment, the happiness that would reign upon the earth would be overwhelming in pleasure and delight. There went one of the delights now—the effeminate priest from the Midwest, what was his name?—walking down the aisle.

He knew there was more upheaval to come—death, realignments within the Church. Realignments with governments, war—the final battles with heavenly forces. But the victory had been won; the death hold was in place; only the writhing of the doomed remained. He was handed a sherry by a passing hostess. He sipped; the sweetness and lingering taste and scent on his tongue was good. He was tired. He tilted the glass empty, placed his glass in the holder and fell asleep.

***

Tim awoke to a quiet home. The afghan was upon him. He felt peace. He inventoried his business of the day. Of first importance was a meeting with Carl to discuss whether Jeremy had been fully vetted, if there was such a process. Jeremy was no patriot; Jeremy should have been accepted at a military academy. Jeremy would have never ended up on a conscription list, not with his family's money, his father's connections, and his own athletic and scholastic record. Was Jeremy a spy? The old way, the manners of another time, would have been to talk to Jeremy personally and present those thoughts directly to Jeremy. The times were perilous, especially with an insurrection planned soon. He knew Carl started his day early and was probably already at the command center. Tim rose, quietly walked upstairs. Mary and Emily were together, sleeping. Mat and Katie were both in their rooms, sound asleep. The family was safe from harm.

He walked down to the kitchen and found a protein bar in a basket of treats left by the welcoming committee. There was a time when such baskets held fresh fruits and baked goods. He put on his work boots and a long-sleeve cotton shirt. By habit, he rolled up his left sleeve and slid on his dagger sheave and dagger. He was rolling down his sleeve as he opened the door. Hot already, and the sun not officially risen. He smelled a hint more moisture in the air than in the tent city. The earth was moist around the newly planted saplings along the street.

He noticed a movement in the dead-standing trees in a remnant of the forest beside the trail. He stopped and waited, hoping the object, person or animal, would show itself, when to his front, seeming to step out from behind a tree trunk, Jeremy stood. "Mr. Johnson! What a surprise. I thought I had seen you yesterday at a distance." Jeremy approached rapidly as he talked, as if excited to see his former teacher.

Too much coincidence. Tim snapped into a fighting posture. Jeremy had been on his way to ambush his former teacher; kill him dead before he could inform others of Jeremy's past. The creature in the woods, by coincidence, had slowed Tim's walk and exposed the secrecy of the ambush ahead of him.

Jeremy suddenly slackened his pace and stopped. "Too much paranoia, Mr. Johnson."

"Perhaps." Keep the kid talking till, hopefully, others were in the vicinity. Jeremy was a first-class wrestler with twice Tim's strength and agility. "Why no military academy?"

"It takes bribe money, Mr. Johnson, and we didn't offer enough. So many inflated records that everyone applying is equal. So how do you break the tie? Bribes."

"You could have gone to related departments—law enforcement; certainly it was not necessary to be conscripted."

"Law enforcement and others take applications globally and have a preference for international candidates because of our international population. Besides, I always wanted the military. I was going to join the military and go the officer-candidate route."

"What branch?" His answer was plausible.

"The army—thought I'd shine more." Jeremy took a step forward. "Satisfied?"

"You don't mind me talking to Carl?"

"No. Shake, Mr. Johnson." Jeremy took another step closer as he extended his hand. "I thought about what you said about God, Mr. Johnson." This topic would lower the old stooge's defensiveness, prior to his neck snapping. The FBI training said this topic was the way to an Enslaver's heart and mind.

"No." Tim put up his hands. Jeremy was playing him now. "Stay a—"

Before Tim could finish the word, Jeremy rushed him. Tim, attempting to move to his side, readied himself for the shock of Jeremy's half-crouch dive at his feet. Tim heard a swoosh of air, saw a column of blood exiting Jeremy's skull. He heard the final exhalation of Jeremy's lungs as he lay at Tim's feet. A man came out of the stand of dead trees, a laser rifle in his hand, a chameleon suit on his frame. He was talking into his throat mike. He finished his conversation and approached, taking off his mask.

"Sorry it was so close. He took me by surprise—I thought he knew his element of surprise was gone. My name is Mike. I was guarding your home last night. We knew you had an unpleasant connection with Jeremy. He's been under surveillance since he came to us. Carl is coming. In fact, here he is."

Tim turned.

Carl was striding down the dirt path. "Well, well, well. Did you have a suspicion?" Carl was taking a listening device from his ear.

"Yes, I caught a glimpse of him yesterday and sensed from prior contact that he was no patriot. I was coming to you this morning when he waylaid me."

"What was your incident with him?" Carl asked.

"When I taught at the Academy, he tried to manhandle me for a higher grade."

"I knew of this. Just wanted to make sure we hadn't missed any other event. He sent an angry email to his girlfriend about the incident. I heard your conversation with him this morning from the office. We have sound sensors everywhere—outside and in public buildings. Not in homes. He had been accepted by the FBI and was working for them undercover here. If anybody comes snooping, or even members of the Order ask, just tell them you got a glimpse of him here but never made contact and never saw him again."

Carl wondered about Jeremy's God remark—evidently a ploy. Jeremy had ranted to his girlfriend in an email about Tim's mentioning of God. Was Tim an Enslaver? It didn't matter; Tim was a good man. Carl remembered his days as a young man, when his business had been destroyed by the Church and he had cried out to Jesus. He supposed Jesus heard, for he came back and rebuilt his business. He had vowed never to discourage anyone from calling on that name.

"Okay, boss."

"We'll take care of the body." Carl paused then spoke again. "You know, he thought he was quite the man, based on his genitals. Quite a collection of male genital shots, over a thousand, on his phone. I guess it was his confidence builder even though he had lots of women. Strange kid."

Tim turned toward home. "Who would have thought?" He raised a hand in the air and gave one wave as he chuckled at Carl's knowledge and thoroughness. If you believed the Bible, Jeremy was already in a place of darkness—it seemed fitting and at the same time tragic.

CHAPTER 20

The night was cool; meteors streaked incessantly across the heavens—the Milky Way was thick above the Camp. Yet this night sky was not that known from the ancient days of man's beginning. Some strange realignment had occurred that astronomers could not fathom. Some areas of space had thinned, and others had grown in density. In one area, no stars were seen. The sun, too, was affected. One third of daylight had been lost due to sunspots.

The ag lands to the south and east were nearly void of man-made light with only the batteries within a few individual homes providing weak, solar-powered light. To the west and south, the scattered, scarce city lights could not create a glow on the horizon. The bare mountain slope behind the Camp was lit with starlight. Tim's eyes could follow the slope west and east for some distance. The craggy heights were delineated by the stars. The wind turbine blades were turning on the crest of the mountain.

Tim squirmed; twenty men, sitting and standing, were packed tightly into the rotor-propelled personnel carrier. Eight more men than the recommended capacity. The carrier sat with a collection of vehicles, wheeled and rotor driven, that hid as groups within stands of naked trees.

Soon the vehicles would coalesce as a serpentine coil on the fields and roads through the Camp. This was the force that would liberate the city.

The date was July 4, 2245. History would be made again. A second revolution. In history it should be known as the day the United States of America threw off the shackles of the European Federation oppressor. It should be known as the day of the Second American Revolution, when people born in America but not Americans of the founding fathers' spirit and creed had their chokehold broken. Tim, looking through the packed bodies, could see the dim lights of the driver's control panel. The heaters had not been turned on; the hatch doors were open. He heard engines turn over, then the engine of his own vehicle whirred to life. Once the engines were on, the convoy needed to move quickly. The fear of heat-seeking drones and satellites motivated speed. The great blades lifted them. He smelled the fabric of clothing, the rough materials from fibrous plants and vines, and the wicking inner-clothing materials made from oil-based products. The convoy began to move; Tim's stomach tightened in anticipation. The standing men swayed, stepped on the feet of the sitting men. He repositioned his body; the movement had pushed him into his son, sitting beside him.

The machines hummed over the dirt road. The smell of damp, burnt fields entered the carrier. When the macadam highway was reached, the engines were given full throttle. West to the city they moved, carrying the hope of history. Though having a nervous anticipation, Tim felt strong, confident. His body was in the best of health after the year and five months in the Camp. From November 2244 to July 2245, they had trained as soldiers as they worked as field hands, farmers, carpenters. He had regained weight—food had been plentiful. They had been given steroid supplements, lifted weights, ran obstacle courses; their bodies became resilient, hard and lean; they trained with weapons and in tactics.

The laser rifle enveloped by his body, butt end resting on a foot, grasped with his strong, gloved hands, had become an extension of his eyes. What he could see, he could kill. He leaned back against his rucksack crammed with clothing, sleeping gear, electronic eyes, first aid supplies, rations. His helmet slipped forward; a head movement lifted the visor up, and he shifted the helmet to a more comfortable location using his rifle's flash suppressor as a prod. Up, through the standing men, he watched the stars stream by. He kept track of his location by the contour of the road, the position of the mountain.

With difficulty he turned his head to study the face of his son; determined, with a heightened lucidness. A seeming presence hovered over and within Mat. Where had Tim noticed this phenomenon before? His brother? Yes! His brother, John, had had this presence. Who would have thought in this day and age, in the United States of America, a man would be riding into civil war with his son at his side? Tim Johnson, once a well-known and respected geology professor and respected member of the Church, was now a soldier seeking to reclaim civilization from barbarism, to tear the nation from the grip of a global tyrant and sycophant citizens. Mat was fourteen. Just a boy, but in many ways—in character, emotions, knowledge of the Lord—an old soul. Smith's boy, Dan Jr., same age as Mat, sat beside him. Neither had his driver's license. In their hands were laser rifles. Dan Sr. was in another carrier—a policy attempting to prevent two of the same family from dying in the same incident. Tim had broken the rules with a bribe, a Hershey's candy bar. The company had stopped production two years in the past.

He was confident of the mission's success. His side had the overwhelming firepower, supplies, equipment. His side was disciplined, had detailed intelligence, a strategy, goals. His side had the element of surprise. His side was righteous. They might not have the numbers, but they had the determination. He knew the mentality of the bulk of the men he would fight against. An overwhelming force before them, and they would rush to surrender. Only the police and DCs would fight to the end.

The chances of being killed were almost nonexistent, in his mind. One of these men beside him might receive a violent wound from a ricochet, or a knife. One or two might receive incidental wounds—a laceration, a broken bone, a sprain—from moving quickly over rugged ground or through quake debris. This understanding of the conflict ahead gave him a clear-headedness, a casualness that allowed him to enjoy the moment. His past of karate matches and public presentations had taught him how to deal with the stress of waiting before performing.

The others were edgy, aggressive, impatient. One talked in anticipation and joy of killing. Graphically the man described his victim's deaths.

Another talked of sex, rape. He was told to shut his mouth, and he did. Why were these men so tight, so frightened? They were no different from him: none had seen combat, all were fit, well trained. They had an anger he did not share, a desire to inflict pain and suffering, physical and mental, on their enemies. Kill or be killed was their attitude; everyone was their enemy.

The truth was that the majority of the people were not the enemy but the objects of liberation. Most were not good people morally, but they were needed to make the city run. They could perform work, and they provided work by their needs. Even as criminals, they created jobs for police, prison guards, judges, lawyers, counselors. Many professional people were trapped in the city, in the new system—educated, productive citizens who needed to be set free from the fear of their fellow citizens. These distinctions seemed to have been lost by the men in the carrier.

Three-thirty a.m., the rotor commander yelled through the intercom, "Yellow! Yellow! Yellow!" Tim forced himself to his feet, as did all the sitting men. They were packed tight against the standing men. The convoy, still at high speed, passed a staging area; vehicles were gathered, rocket launchers and artillery pieces were positioned, ready to fire. Impressive weapons, probably would see little use, except to frighten the barricaded enemy into surrendering. Guards crouched on a perimeter, sound-detection-unit dishes pointed west; men were gathered in small groups. The staging area was passed.

Tim knew only a handful of soldiers would remain at that site to hold the road junction, block any flight from the city. The majority of the gathered forces in the staging area would be used to cut the city in half, hold key positions, capture or kill whatever human debris was swept toward them.

The convoy entered the interstate beltway. Scout units had marked the course with portable beacons. Chasms, downed overpasses, light poles, wrecked vehicles were passed swiftly. The looping highway was absent of civilian traffic or enemy forces. Surprise was essential. The men in the convoy began to hear sporadic fire from antiquated powder guns, then explosions from grenades and homemade bombs. The sounds had a hollowness, bouncing from the concrete rubble of high-rises, and seemed pathetic. Still, it was hostile fire; someone was resisting. Tim smiled in delight; this was living. He glanced at his son excitedly. He wanted his son to catch his excitement and not to fear. Mat grinned at his dad's enthusiasm, worried about his casualness.

Dad didn't understand the fighting would be fierce. He underestimated the enemy, the thousands of steroid police troopers who were convinced they were gods—the American troops of the European Federation, of the federal government; they'd be high on drugs, of superhuman strength and stamina, and of heightened awareness and rage. They would have had their steroid soup of supplements for weeks, as well as abundant and excessive food rations. There had been an underground market for supplements in his dad's work crews at the tent city. Mat watched men and women transform from the ingestion of the drugs. He had never told his dad. Dad would have been killed if he had interfered. Mat knew the intimate thoughts of these men and women; their motivations were to debase, to mentally and spiritually degrade their foes. They wanted to possess objects, collect trophies of their sexual prowess, and eat till they could eat no more. They were human animals who laughed at death under the spell of the deinhibitor drugs.

Dad was not the man he thought he was. He only had the memory; the body had moved on and aged. His agility and suppleness were gone. He was half a second short in his reflexes, in his awareness of a situations and the course to be taken. The older men like his dad had a command presence and experience, but it was the younger generation that had the strength, skills, cognitive speed. The younger generation had gone to the Federation forces. The Order had the older men.

He was thankful for the nine months of plentiful food, training, the afterhours at the pool, the secret worship sessions with Katie and little Emily at their hiding place called "The Rock." They had included Smith's kids, Dan and Barb, in the group—Dan had a crush on Katie, and he had a crush on Barb. Dan was respectful and found the Lord filling his life. Barb, too, embraced her new faith with eagerness. He and Barb had kissed few times, and he wondered about marriage. He had read in an old book that Dan found that after the cleansing of the earth that was coming, there would be a thousand-year reign of Christ upon the new earth. People who had survived the end in their earthly bodies would be lifted from the earth while it was cleansed and then returned to the earth. These people would be able to marry, as they would not have received their resurrection bodies.

They had found a cache of old music drives of Christian songs and a player one day while exploring the dead forests. They found the foundation of a building, steps leading to a basement, a closet with a locked metal locker. Probably an old church. Dan was a whiz with batteries and wires. The drives were so old that songs of the real Christ, the real God, the real Spirit of God were sung. Songs from before God had become a *thing*, a *force*; before Christ had become just a good man meaning well; before sin was just not having proper knowledge. The songs were sung by people who truly knew Him in a personal way. Mat snapped his mind from his reverie. He needed his head in the game to survive.

The attack force entered the city, and the convoy traveled a narrow street bordered by ruined, rubble-strewn high-rises. The column was to attack west, then stop at the riverbank and turn north all the way to the mountain's heights. Tim and Mat would pass through their old environs of the warehouse district. That was the plan. The column came to a jarring halt. The standing men were cast forward with great speed and violence. Tim heard equipment and flesh smacking into the metal hull.

"Damn it! God damn it!" someone cursed hatefully.

"Fuck! Fuck!" came from another. "His fuckin' jaw's broken!"

"Close the hatch! Close the hatch!" yelled the driver in insane panic. The hatch doors came slamming down, knocking one man unconscious. A ringing in the ears, the body quivering, everything black, vibrations, curses. A grenade or a small mortar round had been dropped on the just-closed hatches. The vehicle sped in reverse; people were thrown forward then backward; equipment, weapons, the sides of the carrier raked the flesh. The carrier crashed into the vehicle behind. The soldiers went sprawling again; equipment slammed into Tim's face. His nose was bleeding. The vehicle shot ahead, swerved, tilted crazily; people were thrown atop each other. Tim heard someone's bone snap. Tim's feet touched the hatches. The vehicle straightened; the soldiers fell to the opposite side of the carrier. Nonstop curses, moans, insane screams.

Muffled explosions from outside. The speeding carrier stopped suddenly; everyone was thrown forward.

"Out, motherfuckers! Out! Get the fuck out!" the driver yelled. The rear ramp popped open. Troops were stumbling, falling, crawling, sprawling out. Matthew, out of the vehicle, pulled his father toward the first high concrete in sight. Tim was on his knees, Mat pulled him to his feet. Tim regained his senses. Dan Jr. was gone, probably to link up with his dad.

"Where are we?" Tim spoke aloud to himself.

"A distance from where we ought to be." Mat spoke aloud to himself. Mat scanned the street, the buildings.

"Move out! Move out!" someone up the street was yelling, up the long lines of stopped vehicles. One vehicle burned. Mat and Tim ran in a crouch, past their opened vehicle. They looked in; the unconscious man was laid out on the floor, the man with the snapped ankle streamed curses in a hoarse and weakening voice. Other carriers were just opening; these men mixed with the men moving to the head of the column. Tim laughed at the dazed, angry, frightened faces of the men. What scenes of destruction and chaos are they running to? Tim wondered. He tasted his own blood coming from his nose. Mat was looking at him, inserting a wad of gauze up the bleeding nostril. Explosions echoed down the street.

Suddenly, a great orange light illuminated the men, the canyon-like walls. All heads turn to the north. The earth rumbled, debris from the surrounding high-rise ruins fell on the men and vehicles. The restaurant on the mountain ridge, visible to the breadth of the city, was engulfed in a man-made rising sun. Downed trees on the surrounding slope were ignited, incinerated. This was to be the signal for the beginning of the offensive, a visible sign to the attackers, a symbol of the end to those in power. One bandit gang was destroyed. Unknown to the onlookers, the bandit gang had left hours before to take up their fighting positions.

Tim's mouth grimaced in such uncontrollable delight that his face hurt. The bright light, the rumbling earth, concussions shaking the earth—artillery hitting a position; the sight of the armed, uniformed men moving; the smell of explosives and concrete structures in ruin heightened his wild excitement. They leaped across the bodies of two dead men dressed as construction workers, both with canisters of homemade bombs strapped to their waists. Ahead, men were crouching, bunched behind concrete retaining walls or building foundations or the scattered internal contents of rooms, some looking forward, some gazing upward. The high walls of the buildings hid the men in half-light, gave them a smallness.

An explosion ripped into the group directly before Tim and Mat. Mat saw a wisp of smoke from the top of a distant high-rise. A chunk of concrete whistled past them. Dad was down as a wall of dust rolled over them. Mat examined his father from head to foot. The helmet was dented. A concrete fragment had knocked him down. Tim quickly regained consciousness. They crawled to a protecting wall. Mat squirted water into his father's mouth, then over his face.

"Enough! Enough!" Tim said angrily. The anger not directed at his son but at the enemy. Tim's body shook. Mat looked into the eyes—slightly dazed, but fearful, angry. His dad was now, finally, in reality.

"What was it?"

"An old rocket-propelled missile. From that high-rise." Mat pointed, making certain his finger did not extend beyond the height of the concealing concrete.

"Where?"

"See where the east wall has fallen against the support beam? Where the metal communication tower points to?"

Tim poked his head up for a second, saw a narrow crevice, appearing dark; shadows hid in the recess. The communication tower, hanging at an angle, did, by chance, point directly to the recess. "I don't see anyone."

"They pulled back in. They could have shot once and left," said Mat. Just then they saw heads bobbing, rolling out a launcher. Mat and Tim both steadied their weapons on the edge of the concrete. The laser sights burned fluorescent into the dark recess. They fired. The silent death exploded the heads of the men. One, wounded, was lost from sight. Mat aimed, fired at the concrete ceiling above the man, hoped for a ricochet or a concrete chunk to fall. The entire crevice erupted in yellow-white light as the remaining missile rounds exploded. Mat saw many men in the crevice light up as torches, feeding the flames. He felt accomplishment and satisfaction. Burning men fell through space to the earth.

They moved out immediately; men had bunched behind them, fearful of the danger ahead. Too many men in one place. They stepped through the body parts and blood puddles of their fellow soldiers and the enemy. So many men dead, and they had yet to reach the jump-off point. Squads were entering the inhabitable floors of the buildings lining the street. A man had been captured; they saw men savagely striking the captive, cursing him. They came across more bodies, some civilians; emaciated old women, men. He guessed them to be holdouts from the tent cities. He was beginning to believe the enemy had known the route of advance or the day of attack. Why so many armed men on this one street?

***

The morning fighting never waned, slow progress was made. The opposition were fighting like demons—drug-possessed men, who only sought to die at a high price and outdo each other in bravado. No ground was conceded, none given, all with a price. Tim realized his enemy had no concern for death. The enemy's job was to punish him and his side. The combat drugs had conquered the fears of death and mutilation. The enemy seemed giddy, joyous in their fighting. The men around him seemed worried and tentative in their movements.

Platoons and squads were forming at the commuter station at the entrance to zone twenty-one. The sun was high in the cloudless, blue sky. The gathering men were fatigued, stained in sweat. The men sat, squatted, lay, drank from canteens, ate rations beside the cover of a long, four-foot-high retaining wall. They looked ahead at the wide expanse of athletic fields they needed to cross to the four scarred and pockmarked high-rises sitting in close proximity; the fifth was a distance away from the others. Beyond this last building, Tim and Mat could see the rubble of the warehouse district and their old apartment. The expansive tent city had been hit by mortars; shreds of tent fabric, clothing, and body parts lay in the heat of the day.

The commuter station had been designated the jump-off point. The convoy should have arrived a half hour before the presunspot sunrise time. All the buildings, the tent city should have been taken hours ago, the combatants separated from the civilians. The day's work should have been over. It had yet to begin. Now, the enemy combatants were fully warned, hiding in the treacherous rubble, the maze of apartments, rooms.

Tim listened to the explosions periodically resounding through the city. He heard the staccato popping of powder weapons. The lasers, you could not hear so much as feel, as the power packs of the generators hummed and hung in the air, gaining strength through the vast and incessant discharges. The enemy was well armed, determined. The element of surprise had eroded. The men watched as artillery units moved into position behind and further down the retaining wall, to an unobstructed position within range of all five buildings. High in the air, appearing as a tiny speck, an air platform hovered. Mat thought the artillery placement premature. His training courses at the Camp flowed through his mind easily, readily—weapons and terrain, defensive fire, suppressive fire, fields of fire, camouflaging gun emplacements. Who knew what weapons capabilities the enemy had hidden in the buildings? The captain joined the platoon, hunkered quietly, glanced at the buildings, and then shouted, "Johnson! Johnsons, come here! Explain a few things!"

The captain had been handed an air photograph map, recently transmitted from the air platform, by his commo man. This was the Johnsons' turf. The captain held up the twelve-inch by twelve-inch flat computer screen and studied the scene.

Tim and Mat responded immediately to the request, noticing the air platform dropping from the heights, circling the high-rises, coming to a hovering position before the first building. Tim knelt on the pulverized concrete earth beside the captain and the screen. Mat seemed in a panic—

he pulled at his father, literally dragging him toward the thick trunk of a barren, fallen shade tree. The captain looked at the two and then was pulverized by a blast that shot out blood and gore in a fifteen-yard radius. Red goo stuck to father and son. Tim pulled a handkerchief from a pocket and wiped his face. His son's strength had been incredible—his situational awareness, acute. Tim thankfully realized his son's worth and sadly acknowledged his own lack.

The waiting platoons heard a loudspeaker from the air platform call for the inhabitants to surrender. No concern was given the vaporized captain and the handful of men once around him. In fact, few had seen him vaporized, and those who did had not registered the thought in the category of reality, and so to them, they had seen nothing. The men watched the buildings with interest. Within minutes a few people came out under a white flag. Simultaneously, the air platform was a ball of flame, dropping to the earth like a rock. A heaviness entered the men as the platform hit the ground. They saw a burning human form bounce out from the flames. He writhed on the ground for a few seconds then burned like a candle.

The handful of civilians under the white flag came running across the field. The black remains of powder-like grass and man-made litter caught fire. Soon the entire field erupted, burned, engulfing the civilians and tent city remains. A napalm canister exploded—a flamethrower in operation? No one knew. Smoke entered the nostrils of the waiting platoons. The artillery opened up in full automatic, shredding the buildings from bottom to top. Behind the waiting men, Mat heard an explosion and then another—enemy fire. He knew the enemy would walk its artillery fire up through the Order's forces. Smoke, pulverized cement covered the view of the high-rise as cement chunks skittered along the field.

At the commencement of the enemy artillery fire, Mat ran over the open ground toward the first apartment building. Tim followed, not knowing why Mat moved but knowing he belonged with his son. Mat ran toward the building, realizing his side's artillery barrage upon the buildings would cover him and the enemy's artillery barrage behind was the real danger. Safety lay in the building. He heard explosions increasing behind him, men yelling. He heard the rain of body parts upon the living. The platoons would follow him, thinking they followed their captain. Behind them, an artillery piece blew apart, along with the crew. The enemy had rockets; what of artillery? How many foot soldiers of the enemy militia possessed lasers? The forces of the Order had seen only two air platforms the entire day. One was destroyed. Where was the other? Destroyed? Without the skies, the advantage had lessened even further.

They had trained for clearing the high-rises as secondary to the taking of the tent city. No one had taken the training seriously; everyone assumed the high-rises would be empty. What was the sequence? Break down doors, barriers. Attack; don't hesitate. Kill anyone with a weapon in hand. A quick body search, tie hands—who had the wrist cuffs? Send the people out. Search the rooms for hiding occupants. Empty out all the inhabitants, keep them moving to the prisoner zone, an electric field that should be going up this very minute but was not. That was all. The detective squads could then investigate apartments, search for weapons, drugs, horded supplies.

Mat and Tim halted in a debris field of large concrete boulders before the building. Dust was rolling like fog over the men. The platoons halted at the extreme range of flying debris, just as the last round slammed into the building. A lieutenant ran to Mat and Tim. "Where's the captain?"

"Dead, blown up," answered Mat. The lieutenant's jaw hung as he searched inward through the list of dead, wounded, living officers. "Then I'm in charge." The dust began to fall to the earth. The lieutenant motioned the platoons into the building as he remained in place. Tim began to follow the platoon. Mat restrained his dad by a grasp of his sleeve and was about to ask the lieutenant if a squad should secure the far side of the building. Before Mat could call to the lieutenant, the platoons entered the building. An expectancy gripped Mat, waiting for the first commands to echo from within, or screams, or hostile shots. To Mat and Tim's horror, they saw two blasts at the corners of the building, heard a total of four blasts. Momentarily confused, hesitant, they then bolted as the building began collapsing.

"Goddamn! Goddamn! Peters! Peters did this!" the lieutenant screamed hoarsely as he ran for his life. Tim ran as the roar and dust engulfed him, the next building looming in the corner of his eyes. He felt Mat's presence beside him. Were charges set in this building, or were armed men waiting in ambush for the attack to balk, stall, at the fear of more set charges? Tim dove into, behind, the shelter of a concrete retaining wall. Mat and the lieutenant fell in beside him. The looie raged. "Set charges! A fuckin' trap! Done visually, he's watching us now. Where's he at, Johnson? Where's Peters at?"

Tim looked back; the dust was still spreading over the field, running like a tidal wave. Through the thinning haze he saw the prisoners, gathered by their white flag, being bayoneted even as the remaining platoons and squads ran forward. Tim gazed at the warehouse district, the old apartment. He could see the bed, still out in the open. The bed had been moved nearer to the lip of the high ground. Anyone wishing to use the bed for sexual purposes would have moved it back into the debris, where the act would have been hidden. Peters was under the bed, in a foxhole with a view of the entire battle site; Tim was certain of it. The artillery had raced to the ruins of the first building and was now pouring fire into the second. Tim spoke.

"There's no one in that building. Peters has them wasting ammunition."

The looie stared into Johnson's eyes. "A shell game?"

"Exactly. Let me see the recent photograph," Tim said calmly.

"Let me see the screen! Now!" yelled Mat. There was no time to speculate, ponder. Or to drop just the right amount of ordnance. Like his dad, the lieutenant was moving at a slower speed. He could see with his eyes the mattress had been moved. Rounds falling now were needed. The warehouse debris was the place to hide Peters's forces. Here they could rally out and sweep behind the dying advance.

The looie handed the computer tablet to Mat. Mat was close to the looie's face, pointing at the screen, marking the sites with the pointer. "Rounds at these sites, shrapnel, high explosives, phosphorous. Now! Now! Now!" Mat's voice was urgent but not frenzied. The looie remained calm, deftly screened in the area, sent the dispatch under his password, to the artillery batteries. A pause in the firing, then the warehouse district erupted as if a volcano.

Just then, an explosion ripped into a squad of men by the door of the second building. Flesh, blood, bone fragments, uniforms, weapons, gear splattered against the overhanging ceiling, walls, and blew out toward Tim and his group. Mat remained calm; he knew that was the last round from the enemy as he watched body parts, artillery barrels, rockets heaved up in the churning concrete clouds of gray from the volcano of the warehouse district.

"Sorry for my rudeness, Lieutenant. I knew we needed to rush." All sets of eyes watched the carnage of billowing dust. Debris was spewing out and across the field—metal sheeting, wheels, body parts, concrete. They saw men streaming from out of the dust in terror, sometimes whole squads or platoons of enemy soldiers. Storm troopers in their camo armor looking like armored cars, federal units clothed in gray, national guard in camo, and militia in rags or work overalls. They were sliced by flying metal sheeting and knocked down by the projectiles from the blasts and laser fire from the Order. Finally, some sense of fleeting victory and payback.

The barrage stopped; the gunners reloaded. The billowing smoke began to fall and thin. Peters's forces, understanding the quiet might be a prelude to assault, withdrew. The survivors hidden in bunkers streamed out of the debris, looking like so many rats in a garbage pile. Tim watched, wondering if Peters or the DC had survived. Suddenly, the looie, Tim, and Mat saw forty or fifty armed men running from the rear of the nearest high-rise. Peters had kept a surprise in one building to divert attention from the hillside. The artillery began firing again on the relatively few enemy in the warehouse debris. Tim aimed, fired as his bead touched a man. The man fell like a wet towel from head to feet. He was aware of his son firing. The lieutenant had his face close to his screen, readying a barrage strike.

The looie cursed. The artillery barrage on the hill lessened in intensity, became balky, then stopped. The men listening knew the last rounds had been fired. Almost simultaneously with the cessation of the artillery barrage, shock waves and a deafening roar preceded the fall of the three remaining apartment towers. Mat grabbed the looie's arm to grab his attention. "Forget the warehouses. We're being flanked on the left." Mat pulled to raise the lieutenant as Tim, in confusion, rose to follow. Mat pointed at the personnel carriers behind them. "Get them moving to the left!"

The looie was on his screen. He understood the private's assessments were correct. They were being outflanked on the left.

The personnel carriers, in the rear, were already moving across the blackened field, through the debris of the burned tent city, to the warehouse district on the right. Tim gritted his teeth in apprehension. The artillery rounds gone; they would receive no more; the air platforms gone; so many casualties; so many dead. So far behind schedule. The number of men streaming out of the debris had been far greater than their own numbers. Now enemy soldiers moved from the apartment buildings, the dust hiding their movements. Where had all this manpower come from?

Tim and Mat spread apart as they moved, half running and half slow walking, picking out targets through the dust; a sudden appearance, a laser bolt sent. The looie was behind, collecting stragglers, while communicating on his screen, attempting to coordinate an attack. Grenades burst, shrapnel sang, old cartridge rounds popped and clattered, self-propelled rockets whizzed and exploded. The smell of the explosives tingled in the nostrils; a faint gray smoke wafted in the air.

Tim's throat was so dry it seemed to tear when he attempted to swallow. He bent to a knee and pulled his canteen. Tim saw the looie grab an arm, then the other arm dropped away, fell off onto the ground. The men around him were shredded by laser fire. Tim fell to his back; his canteen, still in his hand, extended above him, exploded. A group of men behind a concrete debris pile made a determined stand. Somewhere out beyond them, his son moved through the dust and haze alone.

A desolation came to his soul—his son would die alone. No one to protect him, no one watching his flanks and rear. They would shoot him down when he was helpless, laugh at him, desecrate him. Mat, his beautiful boy, his joy from birth, a good kid who always tried to do things right, always sought to be good, a sharing kid—never a trouble, always a joy. They had no right to hurt his son. He would not allow it. He had a laser rifle, a bayonet, a combat knife. He had his fists and his feet, and he would kill and enjoy the killing of those who would hurt his son.

Tim affixed his bayonet. He burst from the ground, ran, weapon extended. He would not let his son die. He would not let his son die alone. They would not gloat over his body; they would not mutilate him. Jesus! Jesus! Come to my son! Holy angels of God, surround him with your power. Don't let the goodness of my son be defiled. Oh God, hear the cry of one fool for the life of his son!

"Here I am, motherfuckers! Kill me, you sons of hell! Kill me! Kill me!" Under his breath he spoke. Each explosion pounded in Tim's heart. Rage was upon him. His laser cut the haze, enemy bodies crumpled around his periphery. He crisscrossed the space before him, vaguely aware of his surroundings. "Mat! Mat! Mat! Speak, Mat!" Tim stopped, he listened; he had hit a pocket of quiet, he heard only distant sounds. The enemy dead were incredibly numerous as if platoons had been cut down as they moved. He knew no prisoners would be taken. Move back into the debris, hide. Then Mat would not find him. Tim bellowed a long, drawn out "MAAAAT!"

He heard a voice. A taunt from the enemy? His son? He had to go before his location was targeted. He ran into the billowing haze sweeping toward him—grit and debris fragments pattered against his clothing and stung. He saw a man jump up encased in armor the size of a compact car. A storm trooper! An arm missing, the good arm dragging a heavy-barreled machine gun. He fired at the good arm, and the man and the arm fell separately. Jesus, where was his Mat? He heard a noise on the ground, saw a dark cluster of rounded objects. The clanking of metal, the pulling back of a bolt. He rolled a grenade to that place, underhanded as if bowling. He heard the shrapnel slicing into bodies. His laser swept the sight. Forward, forward. Do not stop till Mat is found. "Maaaat!" he yelled again.

"Here, Dad!" The voice was to the right, the land sloped. He saw a pile of concrete rubble. A form was behind the rubble. Ahead, over the rubble, enemy dead were on the ground. "Keep your voice down," Mat scolded, then saw the utter helplessness and crazed joy in his father's eyes as he ran to him. His dad loved him! He had always known but had never seen how deep and wide, how overwhelming that love was till now. Tim was examining Mat's body, then touching, seeking laser shot or broken bone. "Calm yourself, Dad, I'm alright. Looks like you've seen a ghost. Your face is as white as a ghost. Get those eyes out in front—I feel them coming." Mat spoke in kindness.

Tim spoke in a whisper. "It's the dust…the dust."

Tim moved to the left end of the rubble pile and searched the dust haze for movement. He worried about their own forces stumbling on them from behind and firing. They waited. The dust settled. They saw no one behind, no one before them. Tim implored, "Let's leave. The dust is settled, and the day is closing. We are alone. None of our people are following. Let's retrace our steps. If we find no one, we'll sleep in our old haunts, maybe in our corner apartment."

"Wonder where everyone is? We're no good by ourselves. Yeah, let's go back." Mat faced toward the uphill slope that would lead to the apartment buildings.

"Some suppressing fire before we go?" asked Tim.

Their lasers reached out, and they were gone.

***

Tim bobbed, dodged through the containers, roofing debris, and body fragments of the enemy within the warehouse district. Mat trailed behind him, searching for hidden enemy soldiers and booby traps. Tim knew of a place, had often thought of its potential in a scenario such as they found themselves, when he had walked to the site of the buried shotgun. One corner of a rectangular container with a broken seam. The break was long, the container material flexible, allowing bodily access into the container. The container had not been destroyed by the artillery barrage. He glanced behind, saw no one. He pried; Mat squirmed through. Handing Mat his weapon, he forced himself in. Wisely, the bulky and weighty rucksacks had been left by the carrier. The corner snapped back into place. He wedged a small piece of wood into the crack, for air, light, and access to the sounds of the warehouse. They waited and rested.

They had seen no one while retracing their steps, nothing but dead and dying bodies and pieces of bodies. No walking wounded. Dead calm. They heard no sounds of fighting anywhere. They had come across the body of Plug near the first apartment complex. Face up, missing his legs. They had backtracked to their drop-off point. Smith and his son, Dan Jr., were feet apart. Never made it into the battle. Smith's hip socket and pelvic area had been hit by something big and was missing. Young Dan had caught a round in the eye. Mat appeared greatly saddened at his death. They had been good friends. Many of the tracked and rotor vehicles had been hit at the drop-off point. Where were the work crews, the mechanics to service the vehicles back into the fight? Valuable vehicles, weapons, ordnance just sitting on the battlefield. Was it over already? No second wind? No counterattack? They had taken rations from their previously discarded rucks and heat blankets for the night—stuffed their cargo pockets.

From the vehicles they had crossed the field to their old apartment. The mattress they had slept and sat upon had been shredded but was recognizable. An extensive foxhole was underneath, littered with human body parts, blood. Upon their refrigerator in blue paint the words "Gone to the desert" were printed with a date that was two months ago. Pastor Dave had at least tried to gather them back into the flock. Tim and Mat had smiled. They were esteemed enough to be wanted; they wondered if they had been wrong about Pastor Dave's earlier departure.

Within their place of refuge, within the container, they heard outside men grunting, panting. Moving quickly, tripping, stumbling in their desire for speed. This wave of enemy combatants passed by. In time they heard slower footsteps—cautious, stealthy—passing through. Explosions began, sounding in the depression behind the warehouse district. Renewed fighting or an ordnance drop on reorganizing combatants? Tim and Mat remained in their own thoughts, resting as best they could, keeping movements to a minimum. Tim thought briefly of leaving the container, firing from the rear on the enemy forces. Such an action could only lead to death and have no impact on the battle. He pondered upon the numerical size of Peters's forces. How had the Federation known of the attack? He wondered why Peters's men had not attempted to escape but had begun a flanking movement. Someone had been watching the battle, someone had known the flanking movement would meet with no real resistance. An air platform high overhead, a satellite feed, a drone— or a command post on a distant high-rise within the city, overlooking the entire assault on the city? What would the penalty be for fighting on the losing side?

CHAPTER 21

Darkness came. They drank and ate their rations. They were side by side, within the container. They lay among the legs of a heavy, rectangular piece of unknown machinery above them. Tim turned on his side toward Mat. He gazed at the face of his son. Mat's eyes were closed. That fear that his son was alone on the battlefield—that excruciating anxiety had come to pierce his soul. He needed to just gaze at his son. Tim's soul was fluttering like the wings of a dying bird. He thought of that day Mary had told him of Emily's scars and of the commitment to love Emily as her own—as her family's own. Mary had mentioned an awareness, an understanding of the character of God and that all God did, He did through His emotion of love. He whispered, "Mat."

"Yes?" Mat whispered.

"I love you and I am proud of you. I'm not worthy to be your father."

"I love you too, Dad…and you are worthy." Mat heard a sigh, a stifled crying. He would not open his eyes—the emotion would be too much for his composure.

Tim remembered back to when Mat was seven; they had watched scary movies, so scary that Mat was afraid to sleep alone, afraid to the point of tears and pleas. Tim had slept beside him, placed his arm around him, and held his ever-so-tiny hand until he fell asleep. He thought it had been the greatest moment of parenting. A brief moment where Mat learned that his daddy was beside him to protect and comfort. "Do you remember the—"

"Scary movies." Mat completed the sentence.

"Now, you've paid it back. I survived combat because you were at my side," said Tim.

Mat didn't answer; by the sound of his breathing, he was asleep. Tim gently placed his arm over the arm of his son. Tim's thoughts raced over the afternoon's combat when his son had disappeared into the billowing dust. That was a moment of hell that seemed to last an eternity—helplessness, visions of his son in torment. Who could love a God who could put a man through that? Where had God been? If he were God, he would never leave his son in that hell. Perplexingly, he realized that God *had* left His Son in that hell. Watched Him degraded and tormented by the enemy, watched as a mocking thorny crown was embedded into His flesh, watched as his Son's back and ribs were shredded to transparency, watched as his Son's hands and feet were nailed to a cross.

Tortured and tormented by the powerful of Jewish and Roman society in cold, stone-walled rooms where no friend was seen, no kindness given. Walked through the throngs of the city, jeered by the ignorant and hateful. Nailed to the cross on a hill. The spectators had their show—entertainment that probably satiated them for weeks. Had God loved Jesus as he, Tim Johnson, a man, loved his son, Mat? What a hard God He was to watch His Son suffer for the scum called mankind. Tim just didn't get it. He needed to get it, he wanted to be with his son in that place called heaven. He wanted to watch Mat grow and learn and become a good man. Smith had never had that chance with Dan.

But if He hadn't allowed his Son to suffer for the sins of the world, the gates of heaven would never open for Mat and Katie or even himself and Mary. Couldn't God have designed a better way? He gave a piece of

Himself to show mankind how much He loved them. He had given His Son. The Maker of the universe hurt for mankind. He had proven His love for humanity. He had proven His love for Tim Johnson and Mary, Mat, and Katie. He had done it voluntarily—just to prove to hardened hearts His great love. He had proven the validity of life's great struggle between good and evil, between reality and deceit. The love of God was unfathomable, wide, deep for His children. As Tim gasped at the implications and sobbed, the veil of coldness left his heart. He begged forgiveness of God till his tears and sobs were worn from his body. God, the Father, and Tim, the father, were one in their anguish and hope. Tim understood God! Tim's shame and stupidity coalesced into tears and were wrung from his mind and body. Mary was right—God possessed emotion, God was the author of emotion, and that emotion was love. God loved Tim Johnson and his family. Sleep came.

***

In the darkness, after a few hours of sleep, they crawled from the container. Slowly, quietly they crept through the debris to their vehicle, their former convoy, seeking survivors, hoping to pick up their rucks. Now, the wheeled and roto carriers were gone, except for the one hit by a rocket. That carrier had been stripped for replacement parts. The bodies were gone too, dragged away to a central location on the edge of the warehouse debris. All useful equipment had been taken from the bodies and surroundings —including their rucks. Whose forces had stripped the battlefield?

They saw no living person, no guards at the bodies, no one scavenging through the remains of the tent city, no campfires on the field or by the high-rises. Where had the civilians gone? Granted, the night was dark; clouds pressed against the tops of the high-rises. They could almost smell moisture in the air. In the city an occasional flash would light up concrete walls, travel up the walls, reflect back to the streets from the clouds. Then an explosion would sound hollowly. A few fires burned where debris or military vehicles had been ignited by ordnance. This flickering light seemed as feeble as civilization.

They turned back into the debris after checking their food cache and the burial sites of the machine pistol and shotgun. All were secure, though an artillery round had uncovered a corner of the food cache. Some quick scooping of loose dirt with hands, a few well-placed pieces of debris, and the site was secure. A fear had stolen over them, a nagging suspicion that the war was being lost. Where was the remainder of their force? Why was this zone quiet? What had happened in the city?

They smelled woodsmoke as they neared the end of the warehouse debris. Looking down into the once-scrubby depression bordered by the warehouse and the concrete beltway, they saw the fires. Emaciated civilians huddled by the fires. The smoke flattened out only feet above their heads, pressed down by the cool air of the damp depression. Tim and Mat walked into the tent city, not a word was spoken to them. Mat studied the faces of the people. He read of the brutality done to them—rape, sodomy, torture. Hopelessness, emptiness, and bitterness were all that remained. On the faces of others he saw callousness, a denial of humanness, of feeling and emotion. Their flesh was all that remained—their flesh with the desperate instinct for survival. Those traits of a higher nature, of what was best in humanity, were nearly extinct.

Outside of the makeshift camp, along the looming retaining wall of the highway, bodies had been collected, thrown into a loose pile. Civilians and soldiers, stabbed, shot, hacked apart, raped, sodomized. Throats cut, breasts, penises hacked off, eyes gouged out. Grenades had been placed up orifices and detonated. Women, children, the old, the young. They saw soldiers of both sides. Only the men of the Order had been tortured. Peters's men had won the day. Mat and Tim followed the signs on the earth and quietly vowed to die fighting if surrounded. Dropped equipment, blood trails, bandages, burned earth, and scarred concrete walls splattered with grenade detonations and blood. Past the pool of water, past the sound of water falling from the pipe in the side of the high concrete. Mat kept his eyes on the massive rim of the wall, a perfect place for a sentry. Tim focused ahead on the trail.

A mist rose from the moist ground. Here, weeds and grass still grew, green and pliant. Their footsteps were soft, slow. They heard a scream— muffled, distant, hideous, unrelenting, panicked, desperate—the man's soul begging for release. They saw reflected firelight coming off the backside of a high-rise ahead, spreading onto the narrowing depression behind the building. Elongated, ominous shadows were cast onto the concrete retaining wall of the highway. Then they heard the mocking laughter, jeers, taunts of men.

Father and son moved out of the depression, up toward the rubble walls of a destroyed building. Behind a fallen concrete wall that had peeled away from the fallen building they saw the bonfire, the tortured man. Thirty men of the Order, gagged and bound, waited against the wall, waiting for their time in hell. Adjacent to the men, a pile of corpses had been thrown against the wall. Only fifteen of the enemy guarded the prisoners, inflicted the torture. Tim crouched, transfixed at the scene of unspeakable cruelty, unaware Mat had left his side.

The man was on his knees, begging. His eyelids had been cut away; his ears, his lips, gone. Raking, bleeding wounds covered his naked flesh. He was tied to a leash that was tied to a stake. He scrambled madly on his knees and elbows from his pursuers. Tim turned suddenly; Mat was beside him. Mat whispered.

"No patrols, no reaction force waiting, only these worn guards. We can take them, Dad."

"No! No!" he whispered in panic.

Mat heard the fear and understood. What was done to the prisoners could be done to them. He did not value life the way in which his father did. Heaven waited on the other side of death. He had seen enough of life, of people. He didn't want to die; he had Katie to protect and Mom. But Katie wouldn't want him to do nothing. They had promised each other to never let their love grow cold—for each other, for their family, for humanity. Jesus had said men's love would grow cold; they had read it on the flyers and in the Bible. They had willfully, consciously determined to love. Would not Jesus Himself free those men? Was it not written in Isaiah "proclaim liberty to the captives and freedom to the prisoners"? That was the intent, the goal, the Spirit of the Lord God. Mat fixed his bayonet, moved into the concrete debris on the hillside, nearer to the fire. Tim fell to his knees and begged God for Mat to give up his foolish plan. But Mat moved into position, and Tim could only do the same. They would die as a family—he would shoot Mat if he were captured and then blow himself apart with a grenade.

Mat steadied his laser on huge chunk of concrete. He had thought this out carefully. A force within pushed him through his fear, the fear that death lurked for him and Dad—and failure. He would dare much and win much for his Lord. Think calmly, coolly. Why be a fool? To succeed, that was love; not blind, thoughtless emotion leading to failure. He chose the order of fire; his first targets would be the enemy who could not be seen by the others; he would shoot from farthest to the nearest man to the gathering.

They were all guilty, whether they tortured, guarded, or watched. Silently his laser bursts found flesh, the bodies slumped. Seven men dead, and no one knew—except, perhaps, the prisoners nearest Mat's victims. Now he had to be fast, line the targets up, put the bead on, fire, move on—like a machine. The enemy would clearly see these comrades killed. He took a deep breath, exhaled slowly. Just as the exhalation was almost spent, he fired his laser eight times quickly; there was barely a movement in his barrel.

Then he sat quietly. The prisoners arose dumbfounded. Gathering courage, they went to the tortured man. Mat, watching the hillside, saw someone rise, move quickly. He fired, heard the man fall. A hidden sentry, dead. He stood, waved his arm at the prisoners, spoke. "Gather your weapons and come."

***

Father Winkler gazed at the serene, blue sky over Saint Peter's Square. The Vatican, July, a few wispy clouds unable to cover the brightness of the sun. A comfortable day to wear his priestly robe, though he would have preferred his businessman suit of the modern working priest; men who lectured to classes, held meetings with parishioners, gave guidance to individuals and families, men who tore down stages, carried stacks of books, erected stages—the men of the real church. He wished the day were over; he wondered how many of the five thousand sitting cardinals, archbishops, bishops, priests, and deacons thought the same. Perhaps even the pope, standing beside his close confidant and political partner, the European Federation president, wished to be somewhere else. Perhaps even the Federation president didn't want to be at this gathering on this beautiful day.

Thank providence, all five thousand at least had seats, as convening such a gathering never went smoothly and on the prescribed schedule. Well, the pageantry was impressive; it would make good material for the electrascreen news cycle. The red of cardinals, the purple of archbishops and bishops, the blacks, browns, greens of priests. The multicolored uniform of the Swiss Guard. Head coverings and hats of all shapes and colors, stoles of the same. Flowing robes, capes, narrow tunics, gold and silver crosses or wood. Monks and nuns on the periphery, necessary for the day's event of recognition. All these from the country known as the United States—the poor cousin of the European Federation. It made him sick, the politics of globalism that had destroyed his church and his nation. But what did he know? He was just a foot soldier, an order taker.

He looked at Archbishop Gilroy, three rows ahead and not seated on a folding chair but seated upon a substantial oak chair—almost a throne in size—with thick cushioning. His dainty little tush needed the padding. God forgive those cynical and hurtful thoughts. Winkler had disdained the man ever since Gilroy had forced him to turn on Tim Johnson and Tim's brother, John, and Gramps, their grandfather. That mystery had set the Church on fire with double dealing, intrigue, slander, and, some say, death. Humorous in hindsight that an element of the Church worshiped man and not God, worshiped Satan and not Christ. Gilroy was the extinguisher of it all, and now he sat like a conquering general upon his throne.

The Swiss Guard ringed the event, the entire square. Their fourteenth-century uniforms were colorful and their laser rifles, pragmatic—now that Muslims were engaged in hatred after hatred of anything not of their particular brand of Islam.

Gilroy glanced over his shoulder and spied Father Winkler.

The man was uncanny, thought Winkler; it was as if Gilroy knew he was being thought about.

Gilroy smiled. They were probably laughing at his imperious chair—the chair that would preserve his life. He turned to face the distant podium, heard the heralds blow their trumpets. The speeches came at first indistinct, and then, as corrections were made to the sound system, speech became clear. By the time his holiness took center stage, all could hear clearly. His opening words were off mic—caused by the frailty of his holiness, who was facing the Federation president as he talked.

Someone turned the sensors' volume higher. "And so, I bestow the papacy to my esteemed colleague." With the last line, the papal hat was lifted from his head and seated on the head of the kneeling president. The five thousand were shocked. People looked at each quizzically; others began to speak powerfully, angrily. Many rose to their feet yelling, others dashed off on urgent errands. Many began to move toward the stage. Gilroy watched, hiding his amusement—the Church would change hands before their very eyes. The cameras were now dead, the Swiss Guard blocking exits. Gilroy was safe on his wooden chair with the high back and the sides reinforced with laser-blocking material. This was his reward for destroying the last remnant of the old church—the church that bound mankind to that maggoty Christ and that feeble Yahweh.

Father Winkler became aware of the advancing Swiss Guard, could see their faces—no smiles, no sympathy. They appeared to be Middle Eastern by facial features—thick eyebrows, dark hair. Perhaps they were even Mongolian or Eastern men of the steppes and deserts.

An order was given, and en masse, their laser rifles fell from their shoulders, and stocks met shoulders as eyes aimed through sights. Flashes were penetrating the crowds. The men of holiness were running, tripping over chairs; bodies were falling, yelling, screaming; the blood streaming between the bricks was gathering volume. The great obelisk seemed to shine in the sunlight. The roar of the dying, panicked crowd reached toward the heavens. Where to run? A gate was packed with a crowd pressing into the Swiss Guard. Winkler would pretend to be dead; hope someone wouldn't check his pulse or place an assurance round into his flesh. He should pray! No, the time for prayer had passed.

"Just die like a man, Winkie." Tim was speaking to him from one of their many personal talks, when Katie and Mat were sleeping and Mary had retired to her room to read. What had they been conversing about? The end times? Tim's brother, John, and Gramps? "Just die like a man, Winkie." Tim was relating an incident with Chinese thugs on some forgotten atoll in the South Seas, where he'd been searching for a rare-earth element. "I determined to die like a man," had said Tim. Now it was time to die like a man, thought Winkie.

He would run to the enemy, and he would fight. He crouched, made himself low, saw the wall of Swiss Guard moving toward him. He used jumbles of men praying or giving aid to wounded friends or just to those in need; he used fleeing groups of people as cover. He saw the group before him riddled with laser fire. He fell as if he, too, had been wounded. His head faced toward the advancing executioners. He saw the glee on the faces of the Swiss soldiers; saw the killer before him searching the crowd beyond him. Winkie sprang, caught the guard with a right cross that was driven by the weight of his body. The man was falling backward. Winkie grabbed the laser from the man's hands, turned the barrel to the head, blasted the face of the man. Winkie gained his feet, fired at a guard to his left. The guard's face held shock as the laser cut into him. How good it was to stand! A blast hit Winkie's back. He saw a fellow priest stooping, looking at him. He handed his weapon to the priest as another round went into his spine. The priest dropped the rifle and raised his hands to surrender as laser fire cut him down.

Gilroy sat tightly in his chair. All such chairs were not to be fired upon. The Swiss Guard belonged to him. He was one of them. He could see the line of troops to his right and left pushing the crowd toward the speaker's podium. A Swiss Guard to his right turned to look at him. He smiled. Gilroy smiled.

"Gilroy?" asked the guard.

"Why, ye—"

The guard savagely thrust the barrel deep into the mouth of Gilroy as blood and tooth implants flew. As Gilroy gagged, the trigger was pulled. The contents of the head splattered against the high-backed chair. The guard laughed at the mess that had been an infidel.

The president of the European Federation, the pope of the new World Church, surrounded by his body guards and aides, smiled triumphantly at the spectacle of death before him. He turned 180 degrees to align himself with the corridor that would lead to his luxury vehicle. He studied the faces of his aides with a soberness of palpable weight. "On to Jerusalem," he said solemnly.

CHAPTER 22

Tim arched his back after heaving the last corpse of the day, a young woman, onto the back of the truck. She couldn't have weighed more than eighty pounds. Starvation, illicit drug use, respiratory disease, heart failure filled the truck daily. He guessed her to be a starvation case—likely someone or a group had stolen her food rations on a routine basis. Stolen? No, just taken. Brazen robbery was prevalent, and if you had no raw, overwhelming power on your side, you acquiesced. What did the thieves think as they watched her grow weaker each passing day? Likely they abused her during her decline and made promises they would soon stop stealing from her. Her hair had been combed, her clothes were neat and relatively clean. She was not a drug user.

Miraculously, in North America the plague had been contained in the international port cities—those over five million and usually with ocean access. Tim's partner, a tall, thin, black man, moved stiffly after the heave through the ash haze to the driver's seat of the open-bed truck. It was the man's first day of work; he was sore and sullen, only wanted to sit, thought Tim. The man seemed an apparition. There was a familiarity to the man, named Burnell. Tim could not place him within the context of his life.

A vehicle appeared out of the ash haze. One vehicle sighting a day was the usual, and this was it, as their day was almost done. A police vehicle, slowly cruising, passed them. Elected police—that was one of few good outcomes from the insurrection. He was sad that his side had not won, but at least they had not lost. Sad? When he realized victory would not be theirs, he cried like a baby. The United States of America was as dead as the corpses he heaved daily. Compromise, a cessation of hostilities. Complete amnesty—given because his side had managed to wipe the new census information from the computers. No record existed of him leaving the tent city and joining the Order. Visual identification by witnesses or members of the opposing army were inadmissible in court. Besides, Tim didn't think there was a person alive who had seen him fight that day.

An anxiety within Tim welled up, grew as Burnell moved into the cab. Three cans of food sat on the floor of the cab of the truck. Found on the body of a stray corpse, one not at a collection site. A man who had simply fallen over on the street and died. He had promised one can to Burnell, not because he had a right to it but to avoid the possibility of thievery. Burnell could be putting the cans in his coat pockets at this very moment. Two federally provided meals a day, people were hungry. You would think a physical job such as this would merit a higher calorie rating. Fortunately, he and his family still had the food cache, which they drew from on weekends, and the food he was able to find on his job. The plentiful tea and coffee rations, spiked with appetite suppressants and mental stimulants, carried most people through the day. Tim breathed deeply, felt his ribs press against his skin as if wishing to be set free.

He thought back to that time of new beginnings, almost three months ago. It could have been twenty years ago if measured by the monotony and emptiness of living. The president of the Federation, and now of the World Church, had brokered the peace; he had needed the return of the forces he had lent to the United States to fight the rebellion.

Those forces had gone to North Africa and the Middle East. The news was that Israel was safe for the time being; the current war won. Another war was on the horizon. The common man gave no concern to Israel's living or dying as a nation. The Federation president was seen daily striding upon the newly rebuilt temple and temple mount, uttering proclamations. It had been said the food stores of the defeated countries would soon be pouring into the United States. Tim had seen none of it, except for a bottle of olive oil from Morocco.

Tim wondered why the loss of his country—the United States—had been such a temporary hurt. Did the immediate pain and necessity of surviving, the fear of retribution, blunt his sense of loss, or was it simply helplessness? Hundreds of years of existence, traditions, culture, and achievements in all fields—technology, science, biology, an endless list—were now for history books, if anyone was writing. The history of humanity's rebellion would soon be complete. Perhaps Tim's pain was transitory because the United States had died hundreds of years ago when people turned away from the wisdom of God. That was Gramps's and John's belief, and now Tim understood and believed.

He had understood even more deeply the wisdom of his brother and grandfather the night he was watching the electrascreen news and there, among a vast host of the Church hierarchy in Saint Peter's Square at the Vatican, he saw a black-robed man—Winkie, Father Winkler—his closet friend and confidant from his New York professor days. Yes, Winkie and Archbishop Gilroy from the days of his brother, John's, trouble. The camera did a panoramic sweep of a riot, the Swiss Guard attempting to keep order. Within that confusing scene, Tim had seen a small drama unfold. He had isolated the event and slowed the motion. Wink moving to the point of conflict, punching a Swiss soldier, killing him, and turning his weapon on another soldier and killing *him* before he, too, was shot. Wink's facial expression began with anger, went to rage, then to resolution and finally peace, even as his body collapsed in death.

Tim knew then the history of man's rebellion was soon to end—had ended for the world. The World Church of the Beast had eaten its mother, the church born and corrupted since the death of Christ. Three and a half years were left—or thereabouts, depending on when the count was started. Wink had been on the wrong side of God's story. Tim prayed for God's grace upon the man who had been his friend and had turned his back upon him. No doubt on orders from Archbishop Gilroy. Wink had married Tim and Mary. Wink had baptized Mat and Katie. He and Wink had spent hours talking, discussing politics, world events, their local church—back in that time when a younger man named Tim, full of energy and desire, moved across the stage of life. How foolish the man named Tim Johnson had been—full of the pride of life. The display of death within the Vatican had broken the moral precepts, the order that had once created civilization. Evil—Satan—now sat upon the throne. The facial features of the Swiss Guard were not lost upon Tim; they were hired killers from a region outside the borders of Western civilization.

A fine, gray-white volcanic ash began to waft downward from the black sky. Late afternoon, and the sky was black. For months now, the ash had been falling intermittently, sometimes mimicking snowstorms, sometimes like a gentle rain. All through the summer, the ash had fallen. All through the summer, earthquakes had resounded, though none equaling the intensity of the first quake. It was fall now, he had to remind himself; simply a name with no bearing to climate. The land produced nothing; the soil was rock hard, buried in drifts of ash. No rain. Tim took off his protective mask, folded it neatly into the carrying case on his belt; he would soon be inside the cab. These people whose corpses he was collecting weren't dying from the plague, but from violence and from other airborne diseases caused by the dust. Lungs full of ash killed.

His eyes, unconsciously and almost within a stupor, gazed down the street. The collapsed buildings, softly muted by ash, seemed surreal. The ash piled like snow along the street took him to reveries of his professorship in Upstate New York. He saw a wolf cross the street far, far down, obscured by the falling ash. The wolves ate bodies. The wolves had eaten the coyotes, the stray dogs and cats. What a sad scene to look upon…a city in ruins.

He moved suddenly to the cab, realizing Burnell could be pilfering the cans. If not, he was holding up Burnell and didn't want to antagonize a possible long-term partner. Partners had come and gone – many not lasting half a day. The job was brutally physically taxing without a partner. He didn't need any confrontations, any clashes of personalities. He sat; Burnell had his mask off, for the first time since they had begun. The cans were still on the floor. Thank God Burnell had not taken them. Burnell was of the black race, had a light-brown skin, a hooked nose, Semitic features—like a Bedouin of the desert. He would talk to Burnell. Burnell might be his partner for a while, though most came and went, unequal to the grisly work, not comprehending the benefits of unrestricted access to the city. He had failed to procure extra food for his family only two times within the span of his work history. Burnell began the slow drive through the white-gray ash.

Tim spoke. "They say someone is cheating on the food distribution. The rumor is justice will soon prevail." He had given Burnell an opening for conversation, for friendship. He wondered where along the distribution chain the pilfering took place. Probably everywhere. He recognized his weariness, anticipated the workday's end. To the incinerator, then home. To hold his Katie, to sit close to Mat, to watch Emily draw, and to help Mary prepare a meal—these were his pleasures. It didn't seem Burnell intended to answer. Tim glanced over, hoping to read Burnell's mood. The eyes stared ahead at the road. Maybe Burnell was not so much sullen as hurt? Maybe his hearing had been lost? Burnell had never driven before; was he taking undue caution? Where had he seen the face?

Ahead, five corpses hung from gallows. He had passed the bodies for the last seven days. The labels, under the corpses, read in order, *thief, pedophile, rapist, shirker, Enslaver*. The man labeled *shirker* had been the fattest of the five. He had found some scheme outside the state-mandated food rationing to bring in the food. The Enslaver was harder to read—a woman in her fifties. Enslaver was now the term for any non-church member. Atheists only had to believe in personal honor—truth telling—to remain citizens. Enslavers were the only people who couldn't find a philosophical compromise in the new World Church.

The DCs were now elected, as were the police—a concession to the insurgents, as was the strict penalty of death for all crimes. The United States was just a name on maps. The European Federation bankrolled the US government, kept control of all programs, disaster relief, and rebuilding, and government panels kept watch over the DCs and police. The Federation's Church had gained everything, It was now free to reeducate any of a different religion, even atheists. There was no United States of America, a nation free intellectually and spiritually; sovereignty had been lost. A great nation was now a poor cousin to the European Federation.

Enslavers. The word worried him. He and his family were Enslavers. He read the old Bible, sat for an hour every night reading. He meditated on what he had read. A half hour was spent on the news on the electras-creen. Best not to think. Had Josh died? Immediately after the cessation of hostilities, prior to the falling ash, he had seen a group of people in the dry riverbed, by a spring of water. One had looked like Josh, could have been. Water baptism? How strange they had looked, so furtive and yet free in the ash-filled canal.

A tension, an anger, a dread came over Tim. Soon he would be forced to choose between the Church and the title of Enslaver. No. He would just say he was a member of the Church. The Church was taking a census, giving a microchip identification to its members. Although the quake census information had been lost, the past census was still in the data banks—listing him as a member of the Church. He just had to say he and his family were still members.

What of his part in the uncovering of the microdots and the shake-up in the Church hierarchy? The census people carried lie detectors that were 99 percent infallible. Drug injections were 100 percent infallible. He could plead innocence in the case; it had all been documented. What of the Bible study at home and his knowing Josh—who now had a reward on his head? Or his relationship with Pastor Dave? What would his kids say under questioning? His kids were full-blown Enslavers. Mary might have some wiggle room.

He knew the microchip implantation was being interpreted as the "mark of the beast," that phrase found in Revelations, and a mark that no follower of Christ should acquire. Strange that on his quest for Christ within him, he always sought that definitive something that would prove he possessed Christ and therefore was bound for heaven. Now, his ad-versary sought the same thing—that definitive something—refusal of the implantation, an act of noncompliance that would prove disloyalty. State aid was coming to an end; the Church would resume aid—if you be-longed and obeyed. The chip would mean steady food. The Church had its own food bank. The chip would mean a better job—the Church had its own works projects. It would mean safety—the Church had security people who watched over the flock. Without the chip, Tim and his family would have to live as outcasts, scavengers in the ruins of the city. They would have the truth, Christ, and nothing else. He had his hidden food, his hidden weapons. A tough life, but he and his family would belong to

Christ. They might survive. What was a microchip worth when the world was ending soon?

The world, the flesh and the devil—he had read these were the enemies. The world system, the collective attitudes, philosophies, actions that ruled popular culture, that told people what to want, what to aspire to, what to wear, what to eat, what pet to have, what tattoo for one's body, what sexual attitude for one's lust, what drugs for one's self-medication. What physical objects to possess, what mental processes to espouse. All of it tainted and corrupt. He had lived within it, gloried in it, had great success—for a while—in it. He had cultivated the idea of its goodness within his children and aimed their lives toward it. And now the Great It, self-hypnosis completed, demanded his soul and his family's souls.

His mind snapped into the present, Burnell was staring at him. He had said something. A look of recognition was on his face. Burnell knew him from some other time.

"What?" he dementedly barked at Burnell.

Burnell seemed nervous. "Do we take the bodies down?"

"Yes," Tim said abruptly.

Burnell slowed the truck, anticipating a stop.

"No, not now. Not till they fall of their own accord. Then we dispose of them." Tim realized he had lost himself in his thoughts. It was increasingly more difficult to come back to reality—he wondered if it was starvation or stress or an underlying neurological problem aggravated by stress.

No anger flashed on Burnell's face at the wasted movement and time caused by slowing down. Usually there was the flash of anger; all men were irritable, explosive. Burnell's seeming calm reminded Tim of the past times when humanity had an equilibrium. The sky had blackened completely. The days were shorter now, not simply because of the ash blocking the sun but because of sunspots that had blackened the sun, the reflected light of the moon, planets, and some stars. These spots and corresponding darkness had increased since their appearance somewhere in the time frame of the insurrection. Burnell put on the headlights. Lightning flashed, deep thunder rumbled, no rain would come. Black forms passed over their heads. The thunder had sent roosting vultures into the sky. Thirty or forty, seeking a rainproof overhang on a higher building for a rain that would not come.

The city was the home of hundreds if not thousands of vultures. They had flown hundreds of miles to congregate in the city. Here in the city was the only source of food. It was an impressive sight, in the morning, when the sun spilled onto their craggy perches high overhead. The sun dried their dewy, outstretched wings; gave lift to their bodies; sent them into the sky. He had killed one once, as it refused to leave a corpse, and he had thought of eating the bird. But the scrawny, mite-infested body with the naked head had been repugnant. What diseases were carried in the flesh?

He wondered of Pastor Dave. Was life any better in the desert? Had the volcanic ash descended on the colony, destroyed their crops? Had the deep wells dried? Had the authorities forced them to move into a city? Perhaps they had never completed the cross-country trip through a quake-ravaged land. Perhaps their skeletons lay in the dunes of drifting ash.

A commuter passed slowly by on an adjacent track, crammed with people going home. A work crew trudged along the street, army surplus helmets on their heads, masks on, iron wrecking bars and sledges over their shoulders. The second-to-last man carried a spool of detonating wire, and the last man, explosive charges in a metal pack. Tim thought of Stasic, the man who had made his fortune in demolitions. Where was he? All the ruins were to be brought down, hauled away to fill chasms or to eventually be recycled.

That seemed to be all men did now—tear apart rubble, carry away the litter of a civilization. No stores, no factories, restaurants, health clubs, theaters, farms, businesses, no insurance agents, salesmen, no work but to tear apart the rubble. Leisure meant to sit at home with your feet up, watching the electrascreen. Pleasure was to drink a containered beverage salvaged from the rubble of a home or supermarket. Money was worthless; prestige was worthless; material possessions were just junk, even the most priceless painting, the most exquisite jewelry, the largest yacht, the rarest car or antique, the finest mansion. All worthless.

The windshield wipers swept the ash away, the engine hummed, the rotors kicked up the dust, the ash ticked against the fiberglass body. The outside seemed silent. Burnell inhaled, filled his lungs, blurted out, "I know you." Then turned and stared.

Tim tried to read the face—anger, hatred? He studied the face, tried to fathom the intonation of the words. They passed through the fenced gate to the incinerator plant. One other truck was before the opened orange mouth of the furnace. Burnell pulled behind the truck.

Tim tensed, as he finally matched the face to the time. The fight aboard the commuter, the man who pushed him, the man who had fought him, finally to be subdued by the storm trooper. Vengeance was coming. He had already scrutinized Burnell for a weapon; he did this to every man who came into his sight. Tim angrily grasped the door handle. Never peace. Never. Only calm before the next storm. "Well, let's get it on. Why waste time, shithead?"

He burst out of the cab, circling the truck. Never give your opponent time to react; always do the unexpected. Violence was coming. Why shrink from it? He could take Burnell, so much more worn than years ago. So much weaker by the way he tossed the corpses. Burnell was skeletal in weight—perhaps the reason Tim had not recognized him. Tim was before the door. Burnell had not attempted to leave the cab. Tim grabbed the handle, pulled, shook. Locked.

Burnell put down the window a few inches. "I don't want to fight. I don't." His voice was pleading. He liked this job—he could support his wife and kids. Violence would ruin the new life he envisioned.

"Bullshit! That's the way of this world. I got over on you, and now you want to get over on me."

"I'da knocked you out while your back was turned. I'm done with violence." Burnell's tone was adamant.

Maybe, if his back had been turned, Burnell would have struck. Tim never turned his back on any man no matter how seemingly peaceful the moment. The first truck had pulled away. The orange light was cast onto the ash before the cab. Tim felt the heat. The surge of adrenaline was already subsiding. "Pull forward. Let's do our job." Tim's tone was begrudgingly sincere.

Burnell pulled the truck ahead. Tim moved to the rear, uncertain of Burnell. Burnell faced him across the width of the bed and the stacked bodies. "I want to apologize for my behavior that day on the commuter. Is there any way in which I can make it up to you?"

"No. Let's get to work." Burnell had sounded honest, but everyone was an actor. The times demanded it. Tim pulled out his air-purification mask. Burnell's body posture, facial expressions seemed to indicate sincerity. Maybe Burnell didn't have the energy, the will, or the motivation to seek vengeance. The gangs, though trying to rebuild, had been severely crippled by deaths, the upheaval of neighborhoods, the iron discipline of the State. Burnell, with no men behind him, could simply be a coward.

Burnell pulled his mask out. "I'm truly sorry."

Tim said nothing; talk was difficult through the mask. Besides, only time could prove Burnell's heart. He supposed God knew Burnell's heart, but God wasn't talking to Tim Johnson. The heat of the furnace had penetrated his clothing. He looked in to the orange glow that made ashes of men. Yes, that was it; now Burnell was an ash man. They heaved the bodies into the glow in silence; only near the end of the stack did the grunts come from their tired bodies.

The two men moved back into the cab. The truck had to be parked, mileage taken, the corpse count entered into the computer, protective suits washed, hung to dry. The blackness had left the sky; a gray haze hung, not of humidity but of finely suspended dust. You could look at the sun, a red ball setting, without damage to your eyes. Tim spoke as Burnell moved the truck out.

"Are you coming back tomorrow?" The problem had to be resolved. He didn't need a night of anxiety. Kill Burnell now, throw him into the furnace, no one would know. The lot was empty; they were the last truck of the day. Either kill Burnell or make peace. It was easier, more expedient to kill him. Who would know? Someone was always watching. But a steady, intelligent partner would make work easier.

Burnell spoke. "I know you must still carry bad feelings for me, and I deserve those feelings. I can only say I'm sorry and forgive me."

Burnell was attempting to lull him into a false security before striking. No one was ever sorry. To admit to failure was to admit weakness. "Why are you sorry, Burnell? I held the three of you back. The officer subdued you. How much time did you get?"

"One year."

"What are you sorry for?"

"I pushed you. I insulted you. I cut in front of you. I struck you, and you never gave me any provocation. God doesn't want people acting like that."

"God?" Tim laughed. "What do you know of God, Burnell?"

"I know He walked into my heart and changed me. I plan on working this job till I die or He comes. Give me a chance to show I've been changed."

"Who is coming?"

"God." Some could tolerate the name *God*. The name *Jesus* always infuriated.

"Or do you mean Christ—Jesus?"

"Yes; Christ. Christ is coming. My Jesus is coming. Now you can turn me in, neat and tidy. I'm an Enslaver. Jesus is coming soon for His people." The truth was out. A great relief visibly sighed within Burnell's body; He had spoken for his Lord.

Tim smiled. Burnell had purposely made himself vulnerable. Simple faith. Tim remembered his panic when he had lost sight of his son in the concrete haze of combat. Powerful and precious, hope promised, and hope fulfilled. The name of Jesus resounded on that day. So many desperate people depending upon, clinging to that name. Only fools did not.

"Don't sweat it, Burnell. Let the past…pass. I hold nothing against you. Nothing." Tim was shocked at his own largesse. But he had said it—and he had a deep, welling peace for saying it. God the Father giving His Son over to the scum of His creation, mankind, to be tortured, humiliated upon a cross for the world to see. That was love. God had forgiven him of his countless evil acts; could Tim do anything else but forgive Burnell? Burnell had paid his earthly sentence, done his time in prison. Whether Burnell was sincere or a liar didn't matter; that was an all-knowing God's department. Tim's forgiveness seemed to bring a peace to Burnell. The truck had been parked. Burnell turned off the ignition. Tim handed a can to Burnell.

"No, man, I can't. I didn't find it; it's yours."

"I might expect the same from you in the future. We can talk about that tomorrow. This one is free; no strings attached."

Burnell took the can. "Thanks, man."

Tim noted the deep and honest sincerity in the voice and in the sighing exhalation of his lungs. The feeling of doing good for another—other than his family—could not be found in his recent memory. The majority of humanity could not feel or express thankfulness. Burnell knew Christ. Burnell could experience the emotion of thankfulness. A sense of worthiness was the reward for the act of kindness towards Burnell, and this was pleasant to Tim's soul.

They walked to the office building, entered their work day end time onto their computerized time chart, returned the keys. Burnell still had the peace, he spoke. "The Spirit is here for you…to change you."

"Couldn't be. He left the earth." Best to keep distant with the appearance of ignorance at this stage of their meeting.

"He's here, man. The world is crazy, but He's still here."

"How is He here, Burnell?"

Burnell looked down at the floor, searching his heart for words—scripture, noble-sounding phrases. He had none. He only had his story. "I…I…I don't know where to start. I was an evil man from my childhood…I stole. I lied. I mocked. I taunted all that was good. I hurt people…really bad. No Daddy to show me the way. Physical pain and emotional pain. Nothin' but drugs…and sex was to hurt other people. Didn't have one friend. I was existing…big member of the Voodoos, people feared me…but I wouldn't have minded an overdose or a knife thrust or a garrote to end it all."

Burnell looked deeply into Tim's eyes as the tears streamed. "But my real Daddy had a plan. He had been waiting through it all…waiting for that time when I would be sick of myself…so sick I could see through myself. On the day you and I had our confrontation, that was the day He chose. Facing the time sobered my thinking, and Daddy put me in a cell with an Enslaver, and I learned what it was to be free. The year flew by. I was out and I met Tisha—now my wife—and her daughters—now my daughters."

Tim sensed Burnell's joy and his physical weariness. Tim moved into the locker area, knowing Burnell would follow. Tim unzipped the jumpsuit, pulled off the heavy boots. Burnell spoke, a happiness on his countenance. He enjoyed talking about his Lord. "A man isn't a man unless he feels, unless his emotions are touched." Burnell had his boots off.

"Tears never changed anything. Have your cry, have your wallowing in self-pity, or joy, or whatever, and life is the same when it is over." Tim would hide from Burnell a little while longer. He remembered his tears when he told Mat that he loved him; when he understood how God had loved them both. He remembered Mary's telling of her experience with Emily—that God was love, and all other emotions and logic flowed through that.

Burnell shook his head as he hung up his jumpsuit, began the rinsing with a hose. "Life may be the same after the tears, but the man isn't. I think you're lying to yourself. No facts ever convince you God is alive, the maker and ruler of the universe." Burnell stopped; he was done. Yet, he spoke again without thought. "Why can't you love your daddy?"

Tim hung his suit. Just words, always more words. "What did you say?"

Burnell was shaken, thinking he had crossed a line. He uttered the same words again. "Why can't you love your daddy. God is your daddy. You have a son?"

"Yes."

"Do you love him?"

"Yes."

"And he loves you?"

"Yes."

"Then love your father God just as you would want your son to love you. You are the apple of His eye, the reason He gets up in the morning and starts the world again. He thinks of you all the time. Without you, He is empty. He would die for you if He were not eternal God. That is why He could only send a part of himself—His Son—to die and rescue you. His Son, He loves as much as He loves you."

Tim's heart was breaking again. He would and could not show this to Burnell. Burnell shouldn't have mentioned his son. Be stoic; emotions pass. A valid point had been made by Burnell that Tim had discovered on that day of combat—the end of the story that had begun with his arm around Mat. The eternal God could not die. That was a contradiction in terms. The best He could do was send the nearest being to His heart—Jesus, His Son. God really wanted to die for His creation—for Tim Johnson—the poser, the world lover, the flesh lover, the rebellion lover. The man who always wanted to impress, always wanted to be on top, wanted every woman to love him, wanted every convenience and every status symbol. The man with a pipe in his mouth, the big-time professor surrounded by adoring students. He had become a teacher to be adored, a professor to be intellectually admired, a field geologist for prestige. He had a beautiful wife and perfect children to reflect his glory. All this, accomplished with the gifts God had given to him but which he claimed as his own. He hadn't done anything that hadn't been easy to do—or he wouldn't have done it. Never did he need to will a thing—not hours-long cram sessions, not attracting women, not athletic prowess. There was no repetition, no strain, no shyness. There were no flaws to hide.

God Himself wanted to die to prove His love, a proof that brought freedom, a proof that brought release. God wanted to die for Tim Johnson—the phoniest, most self-satisfied creature to walk the earth. God wanted to save Tim Johnson from eternal death.

"I hear you, Burnell. I truly do. Tomorrow, I'll tell you my story. See you tomorrow, Burnell?"

"God willing."

Tim smiled to himself and answered, "Yes, God willing."

Tim continued his walk out the door. He had kept it together emotionally. Burnell really seemed to have changed—amazing. But why amazing? Tim Johnson was changing; Mat and Katie had changed. Mary was changing. He felt the ash enter the broken seam in his go-to-work boots. The setting sun had given no heat through the haze. He was always cold. The two cans hung heavily in his pockets as he trudged home. God really loved Tim Johnson? Should He not? Yes, He should not. *That* was the miracle.

Burnell walked out the door of the incinerator's equipment room. Within his pocket he held onto the can of found food. Canning food had become a necessity as world conditions had deteriorated and sophisticated methods of preservation could no longer be supported by technology. Beef stew, his favorite. He put his face mask on. He was weary; he thought he might be dying. No energy. His chest felt tight. His legs were moving now—not on their own, but because he willed each step. The body just wouldn't do it on its own. He remembered that as a kid, a teenager, he ran without weariness. He was due for some testing, but the appointments were months in the future—the healthcare system had been strained by the earthquake and then was strained again and again by each new disaster.

Tisha and the kids were waiting for him, so they could eat together; that was her rule: wait for Dad. He hoped the kids would turn up their noses at beef stew or he could bribe them with his portion of the regular meal that Tish had cooking on the stove. He laughed to himself, knowing the shock that might dance across their faces if he claimed it all for himself. Being found by the Lord, being saved from himself was the best thing that ever happened to him. In his right mind, he'd found Tish. No, the Lord had brought them together. In his right mind, Tish could love him. In his right mind, he was a good daddy. It didn't matter they weren't his kids by passion and blood.

Johnson had been the beginning of the change – the transformation. He had been used by the Lord even though he was unaware of it. Burnell remembered his drug-addled mind, his fat, lazy body, the years accumulating the curses of drug use, poor nutrition, a mind of hate, no objectives, no future, no way out. He had been so evil that even his gang had done nothing to free him from his charge – no intimidation of witnesses or stealing of surveillance evidence. Funny how the Lord worked in the life of a man or woman. Truly all things worked together for good for those predestined to be in Christ—even the bad years. What were the bad years compared to eternity in the presence of his Lord? Nothing. That was what the bad years amounted to. He had great sadness and hope for those who had not known this new life and who would not hear, "Father, forgive them for they know not what they do." He could forgive them, but he could not change their destination.

He stepped up to the door of his apartment, entered the code, and entered. There in the living room, gathered at the table, was his family. No fuss; they were hungry and waiting to devour the meal. He loved them immensely and intensely. He was a blessed man. They watched him take off his coat as he retrieved an object from a pocket. He held it up, showcasing it with his free hand.

"The greatest foods ever produced by man, vegetables and beast. Beef stew!" All the little countenances—ages seven to three—fell. "Aw, Daddy, that ain't no good," Tanya, the seven-year-old, scolded. She still carried the southernisms in her speech from her early years.

"Daddy, that isn't anything special." Anya, the five-and-a-half-year-old, spoke precisely, reflecting the diction of her preschool teachers of an urban, northeastern area.

Little Flo, three years old, said nothing. She was just observing, debating whether she should enter the possible fray.

"Then your mother and I will eat it."

"Go ahead, then," Tanya chided.

Tish was beaming. She saw the sudden change in attitudes when Daddy entered the home. Little hearts leaped with joy—she saw it in their smiles, the lifting of their postures, the movements of their hands and feet. Finally, a man of love and goodness in their lives. She had waited for his presence for so long. Her husband winked at her as he sat and folded his hands in prayer.

"Heads bowed, minds on God, our Savior."

"Thank you, Lord, for our family and our happiness. Thank you for straightening every crooked path in these times of trial. Bless this food for the use of our bodies and us in your service," Burnell prayed.

"And Lord, bless the heart of Mr. Johnson—the donor of this can of food. Let him see you clearly in all your holiness and goodness. Amen."

"Amen, Daddy," Tanya said solemnly.

"Daddy, who is Mr. Johnson?" Anya asked softly and with great curiosity. She liked to hear about Daddy's day and the strange people he met and the strange sights he saw.

"He's my new partner at my new job, picking up the dead people so the living people won't get sick."

Tish spoke. "That's important work girls. Nobody likes getting sick."

"Amen," Flo said loudly.

Laughter filled the house. When there was silence and forkfuls of food had disappeared into tiny mouths, Anya spoke. "Does Mr. Johnson know Jesus, Daddy?" She worried about people outside their home because she had been told by Mommy and Daddy to be careful about speaking of Jesus. In fact, it was better not to talk. She worried for Daddy.

"Yes, I believe he does. He wants to talk tomorrow about Him, I believe. Pray for him tonight that he would have peace and understanding." He would tell Tish the full story tonight in the privacy of the bedroom.

"Okay," said Anya. And the sounds of eating continued into dessert.

CHAPTER 23

Matthew rose from his unpadded metal chair in the sentry bunker, his eyes never leaving the firing ports of the bunker. Dad would be coming soon. How smooth and muted the ruined city appeared under the coat of ash. A dizziness overcame him. He steadied himself by a hand on the concrete wall. Oddly, he liked the tingling sensation overcoming his body. Hard labor and not enough food. He was better off than most; his family had the hidden rations. Twelve hours of shoveling, hauling rubble, six hours of guard duty.

He wished they had been allowed to remain at the Order's Camp after the insurrection and not returned to the area around their tent city and old warehouse apartment. The government had wanted everyone in the city. He supposed it was all the same. The Camp's irrigated fields were under ash, the lumber operations had ceased, and there was no other work at the Camp. Shoveling rubble was better than no work. The ash and old concrete were converted to concrete block of various sizes to be used in building construction or landscaping. Two of the high-rises had been completely demolished and hauled away. With clarity, he remembered the fighting, the deaths that had occurred around and within the high-rises. The past, the present, the future were all in the hands of God. He trusted and knew peace. The depression along the highway wall had been filled almost to where the pool of water had been.

The water pipe from the highway retaining wall had been tapped by the city. The ducks, geese that had once visited the pool never returned. Only the starlings, sparrows remained as steady visitors, drinking from the dripping pipe. Occasionally, one or two crows would stop, a pause in their cross-country wanderings. In the mornings, the paw prints of wolves could sometimes be seen.

He remembered the day soon after the first ash fall when deer had come to the depression, pawing through the ash for the last bit of green vegetation. He had taken his laser, assigned to all sentries on guard, and shot all eight. He had only escaped punishment—every blast was monitored—because he had given half the carcasses to the captain of the guard. The deer meat had been lean and tough, but his family had slept with full stomachs.

The animals were almost gone. The wolves had eaten the coyotes. The bears had died of starvation or had been shot for food, as had the deer. Any animal that ate vegetation was gone. In the rubble of high-rises, rats still clung to life. Their population explosion, caused by the plentitude of human corpses, had ended with the dissipation of the flesh. Human bones made up much of their diet now. He remembered the owls, seemingly everywhere, swooping down on the seething masses of rats. The wolves had burrowed into the debris, bodies tense and jaws snapping, for tasty mouthfuls of rat.

He knew the Church census men soon would be coming to his zone. This was his anxiety. He and Katie belonged to Jesus; they could not receive the chip implantation. And yet the Bible said to honor your father and mother. Mom and Dad had to say no to the chip. They could lie, they could run away, they could tell the census men their beliefs. If only death would come quickly. What did the Church do to children who would not accept authority? Reeducate them?

He wished to die and go to heaven, but he had his sister to watch over. He carried a very small-bladed knife, easily hidden, and a larger dagger strapped to his forearm. He had a wire—his garrote—in a pocket. He knew choke holds and hand holds that could leave men wincing in pain. He carried himself with a confidence that kept troublemakers away. He never saw a soul from the old work platoon from before the uprising, never saw anyone from the tent city. The people of the Order were never seen. He never saw the faces of the thirty men he had rescued from death. He often thought of Dan Jr. Dan had professed his faith—his bond with the Lord had been real. Dan was in a better place, happy. What had happened to Dan's sister, Barb?

Mat had been spit upon, called filthy names, shoved, hit, attacked by a gang only once since returning. He had fought well, made them all hurt. He sought them out singly after the altercation, when they were alone. He killed two with his dagger and beat the rest with his fists. No one ever suspected him of the stabbings. Or if people did, they said nothing.

A man had called Katie a dirty name, grabbed her. He had gone to his sister's rescue and warded off blows as Katie escaped. They decided not to tell Dad—he had enough stress. Mat had studied the attacker's habits, schedule, acquaintances. Days passed. He gave great thought to killing the man. Finally, in absolute quiet and stealth, he had dropped a piece of concrete from a height onto the man. That was the type of world it was. He didn't mind always being hungry or that he had no future on Earth. If it was ordained his sister was to die before Christ's return, he wanted her to die peacefully, not by violence or disease; just peacefully. That is why he lived.

A figure came trudging out of the ruins to where the commuter station had once been. A path had been plowed weeks ago, making walking easier. The figure was Dad. Always the last worker home.

"Everything okay here?" A faint smile creased Tim's face just from the joy of seeing his son's face, to know he had a partner, someone he could trust with any task given. Matthew's handsome face was gaunt, the cheekbones prominent. He still had sound wind, but his muscular strength was waning with the absence of calories. Tim was proud of his son for his poise, his unending determination. There was no quit in the kid. Where was the future for his boy? Not in this world. No wife, no kids, but a profession, possibly? Surely, God had work for His people on the other side of this Tribulation. How much worse could this punishment become? It was true the Lord took care of Tim's family—mentally and with physical health and more calories than the masses got. He was depressed that he could not envision his son's future, that his son probably would not know the life of husband, father. Mat had mentioned a thousand-year reign of perfect life on Earth, but it seemed just a dream. The future was God's business, not his. He had no choice but to trust the Lord.

"It's okay here," Mat responded.

"Everything's okay—but it isn't?" Tim challenged his son for the truth; he had detected an anxiety in his son's voice.

"Dad, what are we going to do when the census people come?"

"When I get everyone together, we'll go over that. They're still in zone nineteen. We're just going to answer truthfully, but not volunteer anything."

"Dad, we can't get that chip. That's the mark of the beast in the Bible. We can't belong to Christ if we have that mark. God wants to see Christ's blood, Dad, not the mark of the beast."

"Where did you get all that? Show me the verses." The Bible had become Tim's book of truth.

"It's true. I can prove it and will. It's in Josh's flyers. We've got to run, Dad." There was a frantic quality to Mat's voice.

"Where to?"

"Anywhere. The desert with Dave. Or into the uninhabited ruins of the city, or the country. We've got the food cache."

Tim sighed deeply. "The food cache won't last forever. I'll think about it. Got your keycard?" He had no strength to run, nor did Mary, Katie, or Emily. Unknown to his family, he had a cache at Gramps's home.

"Yes."

"Love you every moment."

"Love you more." Mat grinned as he gave his standard comeback.

Mat would be coming home late at night when the family was asleep. Tim wouldn't see his son awake till this same time tomorrow. He gazed ahead as he walked. He had to tell Mary and Katie and Emily of his love for them. Life was short and precarious—he wanted them to know his heart. It was good to see that two more of the piles of the high-rise ruins were totally gone. A prefab village had been erected on the recreation areas before the former site of the high-rises. Two-story buildings, constructed of a molded-paper product—the downed trees had been put to use.

Quake proof, the buildings twisted and turned but did not collapse, though the plumbing sometimes popped loose. The truly paper-thin walls of the apartments afforded no privacy; that was the only drawback. Luckier than most, Tim's family had an end unit. Even the top floor was a blessing; it was much more difficult to break into and enter. The ground floors could be entered by slashing the walls with a strong-bladed knife. Water and electric were in every apartment but rationed by an automated system. Only enough water to drink—personal cleansing was by chemical means. The sky was darkening again from the night, from another storm of volcanic ash. Many of the apartments were already lit, the light shining through the walls. A breeze picked up, cold as winter.

He walked up the steps, gave the secret knock. Mary opened the door. She had been working with the elderly till they had all died, the last only a week ago. She said nothing to him, turned sleepily back to her cushioned mat, used as a bed. He would wait to say I love you. No furniture taller than two-and-a-half feet was allowed in the apartments. Katie lay on a rug, drawing, the paper on the hard floor. Beside her was Emily, studying Katie's drawings. Katie looked up and smiled. "Hi, Daddy!"

She had reverted back to calling him Daddy and not Dad. He had worried about this, perceiving a return to childhood. But why shouldn't she return if she wished? She rose, hugged him. Why was she always so happy to see him? Her simple loved amazed him. Strange, how she and Matthew had become happier as life worsened. Was it that they couldn't understand the historical context of the sufferings? Didn't they understand the bleakness of the future? Didn't they understand what they had lost? Did they see this as one big camping trip? No. They had seen bodies in all states of putrefaction. They had seen ugly sicknesses, beatings, rapes, animals attacking men. Mat had killed men with rock, knife, choke holds; he had watched them blown into vapor. His children knew reality, the evil of the human heart.

"I love you, girlie girl." He picked her up as she hugged him. He hugged her. "Why are you so happy all the time, Katie?" he asked in a soft, inquisitive voice. She shrugged her shoulders and looked at the wall to her right, her eyes holding an untroubled blankness, and then returned to his gaze.

"I don't know. I like being with you and Mom and Matthew and Emily. We get enough to eat and drink, though I am hungry most of the time. I have plenty of time to play...or I should say to roam free within my imagination." A term coined by her mother. She became lost in thought. Her eyes suddenly sparkled. "Jesus is coming soon. I want to hug Him. Then it will be better. No more hunger, no more killing, no people acting crazy and mean."

"I hope," he said as he gently lowered her and embraced the waiting Emily, giving Emily a hug and a kiss on her temple. Katie inserted her hand into her father's free hand, smiled, and spoke.

"Dad. You go back and forth. It makes us dizzy. One moment you trust Jesus...the next minute, you don't. We've got the Bible. We've got Josh's newsletters. We have those old drives with music and sermons we found at the Camp. On top of and besides all that, we have the Holy Spirit as our guide. We are living in momentous times, Daddy, and Jesus will bring us through."

"Yes, He will." His confidence had returned. "Could I see the newsletters?" Possessing these might endanger them. The old drives were dangerous too.

"Sure." She slipped from his grasp. With one hand, she unzipped the mattress covering, reached inside. The hand came out with a thick stack of papers. She seemed to calm as she handled the papers, taking time to straighten them. He sensed they had great value to her. She sat up and handed the papers to him. "Matthew and I read them at night with the flashlight. He gets them off of a wall on the edge of the city. No one sees him take them."

Tim took the papers. Definitely Josh's work. He thumbed through the stack, saw one entitled, "The New World Coming." He read, and yes, hope and a good future were in the words.

"Why don't you share these with Mom and me?"

"Mother expresses no interest; she is ambivalent to God. We read them to Emily." Mom had become Mother.

"And me?" He was still digesting *ambivalent.*

"You're too interested in surviving."

Tim sat cross-legged on the rug. The revelation of the truth stunned him. Mary had stopped communicating since the revolution had failed and they lost their home. He had thought it a temporary depression. They had simply lost touch with each other's thoughts. Did Mary hate God? She still gave love and attention to Emily. She still functioned as mother and wife. Was he so indifferent that his children felt they could not trust him? Did they think he would be hostile or uncaring, uninterested?

"Why don't you hate God for all this misery?" he asked.

"He loves us, Dad. He sent Jesus to make us clean, and Jesus sent the Holy Spirit to help us. People didn't leave Him any other choice. Everyone wanted to live the wrong way." She added, "I haven't always been good."

Tim pulled Katie into his arms. His hands went completely around her upper arms. After the failed revolution, the growth spurt that had started during life at the Camp ended. Weight was again leaving. How frail yet full of life she was. He hugged her gently, he felt her soul melt into his with complete trust and peace. She was the best his life had produced. Pure, kind, loving, giving, vivacious Katie. He was dirt compared with her. God had given her to him. God was good, God was kind, even in the midst of this horror called life.

"Oh, my little girl. How wise you are."

He would not cry. She was a burden; she wasn't always good, kind, pure. The words of Burnell came to him. He begged Jesus to let him cry. He hugged his little girl, drew her deeply into himself. His soul cried to Jesus for help becoming a good father. He cried to Jesus to give him the strength to go on, to nourish the lives of his children. He cried to Jesus from thankfulness. "Come here, Emily; let me hug you again. I can't get enough of you two."

Emily stood and rushed at Tim. He caught her and held her tightly. He'd loved her as his own since that day he had seen her wounds. He had prayed to God that day for a love for Emily that would wash away the pain she had received.

Mary rose from her bed, having watched the emotional displays with envy. Love was nothing anymore. Mary turned in disgust, just as they heard muffled feet running in the ash.

"Dad! Dad!" Matthew was bounding up the steps with panic in his voice. Tim, his body tensed for action, jumped to the door. Mat was not one to overreact; something real had produced the panic. Tim pulled open the door just as Mat leaned into it. Mat slid to a stop in the middle of the room, the laser rifle in his hands. "They're here already. Two armed storm troopers and two men and a woman in black, carrying black boxes."

"Who?"

"The census people. We've got to get out of here. They're no good. They're trouble. I know it!"

"Calm down. We can handle it. They might not get to us today. Did the troopers have body armor on?"

"Yes."

As had become his habit, Tim had previously formulated an ambush scenario. A part of his mind ran through the strengths and weaknesses of the plan and the actions that would need to happen. At the forefront was how to disable a storm trooper. The greater part of his thinking analyzed the *why* question. On his travels, he had not seen armored storm troopers accompanying the census people. A new policy? For protection of the census people, or to take away the dissenters? Had zone twenty been skipped? Or had zone twenty-one, containing his family, been targeted? Why had the woman in the ground-floor apartment been skipped?

"Everyone sit." Tim obeyed his own command. Katie, wide-eyed and anxious, sat cross-legged beside him. Emily sat by Katie. Matthew knelt facing the door. Mary rose up on her mat but did not join the group.

"They're asking everyone questions about the Church. Tell them we love the Church. Don't volunteer information. Don't become upset if your mind drifts into other areas. Don't try to build a wall in your head to any area. Don't be nervous if they ask questions about things other than the Church," Tim said. "Just answer honestly."

Katie was completely lost, her eyes blank. He probably should have said nothing; innocence had its own defense. Matthew's jaw clenched in determination. Tim wondered if Mary would turn upon her own family. He was about to suggest lying down, relaxing until the census people came, when he heard people coming up the steps. Matthew should return to his guard post. One less family member to worry about.

A rough, businesslike voice came through the door, devoid of friendliness or warmth. "Mr. Johnson. This is Inspector Simmons, a representative of the Most Holy Church, wishing to talk to you and your family."

Simmons? The name had a familiar ring. Tim opened the door, offered his hand, then quickly remembered the custom had ended with the plague. He withdrew his hand as the man said, "I am Simmons. We are coming in."

The hulking forms of the storm troopers at the bottom of the stairs blocked light from the stairway. A man and woman stood behind Simmons. Simmons's face spoke of boredom; his body's tension exuded aggression, or at the least, profound wariness. Simmons studied the faces of those in the room. His gaze lingered on Emily. Tim kept the smile on his face as his body's strength rose to match Simmons's state of readiness. No one could be assumed to be civil in this time. Where had he heard that name?

"Certainly. Come in. You're all welcomed. Would it be possible for my son to return to guard duty?"

Simmons had already grasped the laser, watching the boy's eyes for resistance as he took it away. Mat smiled submissively. Tim knew his son was extremely agitated; Simmons did not.

"No. I'll send one of my men back with the weapon. He remains until we're done with the interviews." Simmons turned to the man and woman. "Jones, take this and hand it off to a trooper. Tell him to stand guard in his place, if necessary, till the boy returns." The woman took the laser. The woman was Jones. Tim's eyes enlarged, and his soul leapt in fear. Their former DC stood before him. Hair tied back, light makeup on the lips and eyes, a fuller face. She exuded professionalism and health. Mat's eyes and demeanor had not reacted. Katie smiled at the group. Mary recognized the DC and Simmons. Simmons seemed alerted, decided to prolong a Jones-Johnson meeting. "Jones is our new department coordinator for zone twenty-one." Simmons studied Tim's reaction.

"Good! DC Jones was a wonderful disaster coordinator for the zone," Tim said. Simmons? Simmons had been at Gramps's house! Before the Tribulation began! Simmons had seen the open Bible, questioned Matthew. Simmons had attempted to start a conflict. It was Bill Smith of Pastor Dave's group who told him later that Simmons had had a stun stick ready to use. At that time, Simmons had worked for the State; now he worked for the Church. With a foreboding that shivered his soul, Tim knew his family was doomed. Yet Simmons seemed unaware they had met before. Emaciated bodies were hiding the Johnson family.

Jones moved between Tim and Simmons, placing her hand on Tim's chest for a moment, a gesture of friendship and familiarity. Her clothes carried the scent of perfume. "Mr. Johnson was a work platoon leader. Conscientious and hard working. In fact, the entire family was an asset." Her voice had lost the mannish roughness. That ought to crush Simmons's probings—she hoped. She remembered the departure of the family from the tent camp—taken by Stasic. She had seen him return over a year later, on the day of battle, with his son, Mat. No one else knew; all the riffraff had died somewhere within the intervening time frame. Peters still lived but had never engaged Tim in conversation. Peters only knew of the good-looking wife. Peters had caught rounds in the battle, lost some of his mobility and most of his memory. Peters was on the decline, a worthless ward of the State. She was the only link to the past.

"Haven't we met before? You look familiar." Simmons's initial surge of aggression had calmed; Jones had vouched for this man.

"I can't recall, but it is possible. Have a seat." Tim motioned toward a thick mattress.

"I brought my own." Simmons reached out to the man who had yet to be introduced. The man's hand rested on a metal bundle. On his shoulders was a single strap, attached to a black box. The kids looked on attentively, nervously, but within the bounds of normalcy for having uniformed strangers walking into their home. Simmons took the metal bundle, and a stool unfolded. "Hoagland, do your search and set up shop. Jones, hand the laser to a trooper, as I requested, and get back on track."

Tim noticed Mat's anxiety was increasing as the two made a cursory search of the apartment. Or was it because the laser was not within reach? Had Mat hidden a weapon in the apartment and was afraid it would be found? Or was it the Enslaver teachings? Tim studied Mary; she seemed to like the company, pretended not to understand the threat. She seemed to be the Mary of old, wishing to welcome guests into her home.

"Clear," said Hoagland matter-of-factly.

"Clear," announced Jones seconds later.

"Mr. Johnson, before we go further, send the neighbor child back to her home." Simmons was looking at Emily as he sat on his stool.

"Emily Jennings lives with us. Certainly, you know; we reported her presence when we applied for this apartment. We were told her presence would be reported to the national database. Her parents are deceased. We intend to adopt her."

"Perhaps so. A thorough search for living blood relatives must be initiated, Mr. Johnson." Simmons's voice had dropped to a whisper with the first word uttered. "She may remain here until we check further into her history and possible relatives still alive." Simmons knew Emily was bound for an orphanage. Adoptions had been banned. It was practical and expedient for the State to produce loyal citizens by placing them in State-run orphanages where 24/7 indoctrination gave the best results. Such revelations of the new law would disturb the emotional state of the household and clog the lie-detector data. Not even blood relatives had rights to children if the parents were deceased. "Now, back to your family."

"Certainly." Tim hid his panic—little Emily couldn't be taken from them. No one would be able to cope with that loss. Simmons wasn't eating just two containered meals a day, nor were Jones and Hoagland. The three had a surplus of food; they had vigor, health. Their energy was evident in every movement. Till this moment of comparison, Tim had not realized how weak he truly was. Simmons's eyes smiled, even as they coldly searched Tim's soul. Tim understood the reasoning behind the no-adoption law; the State would find it easier to shape the child's mind.

"You're a man after my own heart. The Church is taking a census. Recent upheavals have fluctuated the rolls—deaths, moves, people wishing to join. To better serve the congregation, the Church must know who and how many are in the congregation. That is the first order of our business.

"The second order of business is to determine the spiritual needs of the congregation. The material needs are evident, and the Church is involved in those issues. Everything your government provides is coming through loans from the Church. There are big plans—polar ice caps, the Great Lakes are already being exploited for human consumption and soon for irrigation. Deep wells are being drilled. There is a plan to scour the air of all harmful substances—most notably, volcanic ash. The greatest minds in the world are working.

"Your spiritual condition is our concern at the moment. We need unity of thought for unity of action. In conjunction with our questions on your spiritual state, we ask questions about friends, religious teachings received other than through the Church, organizations you might belong to. We reeducate, we offer religious training. We are not out to get anyone because we need everyone.

"When everything is in order, we implant an identification chip. You belong totally to the Church, and the Church takes care of its own."

Simmons voice trailed off as if the last subject had no real importance and was a minor part of the process. The voice trailed off from a speech given ad nauseum. He looked at each member of the family sharply. Where did he know these people from? His eyes bored into Tim's eyes. "You have no problem with this process, do you?"

"No. Good idea. Let's get started."

Simmons rose. "We'll use two separate rooms, have two interviews going. Saves time. We'll start with you and your wife."

"Fine."

CHAPTER 24

Tim stood; the dizziness came as he gave a supporting hand to Mary and pulled her up from her position on the floor. He followed Hoagland into a bedroom. His children would be alone with Jones and Simmons. Could he trust Jones? He had in the past. Why did she help him then and why now? Was he supposed to believe she had a heart? What was her angle? He trusted no one, especially not Simmons. He stopped, turned to Simmons. "I'd like to be in sight of my children."

"Certainly, as long as no communication takes place." Few were as cautious as this Johnson. The Church needed vigilant men.

Simmons didn't seem disturbed by the request. Tim was seated on the bedroom floor, facing the living room, where his kids had been placed together.

"Good?" asked Simmons, looking at Tim.

"Fine," spoke Tim. Everything was fine—his mind answered sarcastically. Hoagland already had the wires placed on hands, neck, temple. The machine was activated. The questions began—at first, general in nature: name, age, marital status, children, identity number, work history.

Simmons came in, scanned Tim's forehead for the invisible identification number, the old-tech version of the chip.

"Still in possession of your identity card?" asked Simmons.

"Yes." Tim reached into his innermost pocket, pulled out the slender card in its protective case. Simmons took the card, then went into the living room to scan the children.

"Have you, Timothy Johnson, ever met, had an association with, me, Ronald Hoagland, the test administrator?"

"No."

Hoagland saw a jump in the meter—Johnson was stressed but telling the truth. Hoagland knew his work—Johnson knew one of the interviewing party: Jones.

"Have you ever met or had an association with any member of the interview team?"

"Jones, as you know." Tim wished to stop, but simply wishing would register. "I recall Mr. Simmons, when he was a State inspector." Simmons was no longer in the living room, where he might have overheard the reply. The black box beside Hoagland was recording every word.

"What was the nature of that meeting?"

"He served notice that the State wished us to leave the home we were residing in at the time."

"You told Simmons earlier you had never met."

"I had forgotten his name and even that I knew him. It was at least three and a half years ago. I have identified him within the few moments we have conversed."

Hoagland's face gave him no clue to the machine's interpretation. "Now we shall proceed to your spiritual state." Ronald Hoagland, whose eyes had been on the meter for the entire interview, now shifted his gaze directly to Tim. Hoagland had developed a stare that turned men into whimpering boys. Hoagland and his machine could send people to re-education camps, to prison, to death. Hoagland had seen so many facial expressions, nuances, body postures, heard so many words and intonations revealed by the machine as truth or lies that he no longer needed the machine. He loved his power.

"State your feelings toward God and the Church."

"Why is God doing this to us?" Tim said. "I'm angry but resigned. I suppose He knows. I must endure, but I'd rather have life back again. The Church is doing all it can; you are proof of how much the Church cares. I have faith." Tim studied Hoagland's face; he must have heard that story many thousands of times. The question had nothing to do with anything, except to make people believe the Church cared. A chance to talk to a sympathetic person, to vent frustration. Tim ventured a question, not expecting an answer. "Sound familiar?"

Hoagland, expressionless, spoke. "The standard line. People are pissed at God. They don't want to hurt their chances of more aid, so they praise the Church."

Tim laughed nervously at Hoagland's honesty. Hoagland did not laugh; he was not even pleased that his words had been taken humorously.

"The final questions. Have you ever personally known or met anyone who professed Enslaver doctrine?"

Hoagland watched the meter jump to the highest reading. Tim understood all the other questions were just camouflage for these final questions.

"Yes, my grandfather, Henry Johnson; my brother, John Johnson; his girlfriend, Diana Rochembeau. All deceased, five or six years now, I think."

Hoagland said nothing. The meter didn't go down; Johnson was withholding.

"Anyone else?"

"Yes. A Jewish man, Joshua…I don't know his last name. When I eventually realized what he was about, I broke off contact."

"How long ago was this?"

"The night of the big quake, we parted company."

"And you haven't seen him since?"

"No."

"For what period of time were you in contact with him?"

"A week, maybe."

"Did he mention any friends? Did he state his business?"

"He was supposed to announce something, was trying to sell something, wanted to establish an infrastructure, but never mentioned anyone."

Johnson was lying or withholding information. What decision was to be made on the future course of action must be made by Simmons. Interviewers were expressly ordered not to press liars to the point of panic in the first interview. Most liars led the team to more subversives willingly, if handled with gentleness.

"What groups have you belonged to in the last seven years? Under the agreement of amnesty, you are under no obligation to mention the Order or any subgroup that fought with that national organization against the State." Hoagland saw the sudden decrease in tension and judged that Johnson probably had been a member of the Order.

"Just organized groups?" Tim asked.

"Any group, Mr. Johnson." Hoagland spoke the name firmly, with impatience and authority. The meter said Johnson was holding back. Putting *Mr.* or *Ms.* before a holdout's name and using an angry tone and a stern expression usually scared the information from them.

"None."

Hoagland's eyebrows raised calculatingly. He knew that Johnson was unsure of his answer and fearful of the truth. He was going to push Johnson a bit; the man could handle a push, wouldn't panic. These damn interviews lasted forever.

"There is a group you're afraid to mention. Come clean, so we don't have to use the serum. It takes time, has some uncomfortable side effects."

"Okay. They're more a group of friends than an organization; that's why I hesitated," Tim said. "The group was led by a man named Dave. Average size, long hair, well built, charismatic. We attended a few social gatherings. He never said anything against the Church. Haven't seen him or his group since the big quake."

Hoagland's expression remained blank; he was smiling within. Johnson was holding back and lying. Contact with two subversive groups was the reality—and personal contact with two of the most wanted men in the Northeast. This could mean a bonus. Johnson and his family were definitely getting the truth serum, unless pressure on the children made Johnson open up. He hoped to administer it to the boy, alone. Young boys who were mentally helpless and physically powerless; Hoagland nurtured an anticipation of debauchery and evil.

"Do you know the names of any members of this group?"

"Yes."

"Do you know the whereabouts of this group?"

"No."

Hoagland's face remained blank.

"Mr. Johnson, your interview is complete for now. We may ask more questions today, or we might return." Hoagland had added these final words, words not in his careful script, to add greater pressure. He wanted clarity, a resolution, and he wanted to watch the unraveling of Johnson.

Mental breakdowns were a perk to his profession. "Representative Simmons will review the data in a few minutes."

Hoagland pressed a key on his machine. "Katherine Elizabeth Johnson is next."

Katie walked stiffly in from the living room to stand before Hoagland. Her eyes were semiblank, frightened, partially glazed.

"Just be honest, Katie. It's fun," Tim said as he moved past her to the position on the living room floor, where she had been sitting. He noticed as he folded his legs that he was covered in sweat. He hoped all interviewees finished in a sweat.

An annoying thought pressed against his mind. Something was not adding up. Hoagland had not asked for any names. He should have asked for the names, but he'd gone directly to another question: Do you know the whereabouts of this group? Then he had not followed up on that false response. Was Hoagland hoping he would lead them to the group? Hoagland could be weary, his mind drifting through the innumerable interviews he'd conducted. No, Dave's group was wanted. Hoagland had backed off purposely.

Through his thoughts, he heard his daughter's voice—so precise, so willing to give the truth. She had no idea what the term *Enslaver* meant, even as she believed as they believed. He prayed that Hoagland didn't describe an Enslaver's beliefs. He felt confident Katie could not betray anything. Whatever information she gave about Josh or Dave would be general. Only the flyers worried him, and these could be explained as the curiosity of children.

Hoagland had said Simmons would review the interviews. Would Simmons remember serving the eviction papers? What impact might that have? A deeper scrutiny, more questions? Simmons would remember the Church's hatred of Tim Johnson. He was already under suspicion. Would Simmons act immediately? Would the family be broken up today? They probably knew he had been a member of the Order. All this crap—possible reeducation, more questions, truth serum—to belong to a Church he loathed. Gramps said it would be Satan's church. Mat reminded him it was the church of the beast. Why was he willing to enter?

Was it policy to march away suspects immediately, before they could escape? Why else would two storm troopers be accompanying the interviewers? One would be enough for security. Had Simmons known of Emily beforehand and planned to take her after the interviews? Why wasn't Emily being interviewed? They had come here ahead of schedule for Tim Johnson, brother of John Johnson. Simmons had seen the name Tim Johnson and verified it was the same Tim Johnson of the old farmhouse. The Church had been contacted. Yes, Simmons knew and was selling out the Johnson family to advance his career.

No! Had Simmons sold them out, he would have come under no guise, carrying test equipment. He would have come at night with special units of the police. Simmons had no clue who Tim Johnson was.

When were these chips issued? He saw no evidence of chips. Would this process take days weeks, months? Tim felt trapped, a physical pressure closed in upon his mind. Everyone was paranoid these days, himself included. He had to fight against this fear, this paranoia.

Mat had yet to enter the bedroom; Mary was still being interviewed. Why was her interview taking so long? His once brilliant mate was possibly the most naïve, if not stupid, woman of their time. She could easily send them all to prison. Tim noticed Mat's eyes were closed; he was preparing himself for the interview.

Matthew prayed for his father, prayed he would act decisively. If his father did not, he would be forced to act. These men and woman were evil, beyond the black uniforms with the red emblem, beyond the weapons, beyond the well-fed, vigorous bodies. When would his dad wake up? These people would take the family away, divide it. He would never see his sister or Emily again. If it appeared the family or Emily would be taken that very day, he would act. Acting without his father's prior knowledge, without his approval, frightened Mat. What if he had missed some crucial detail, some fact that would be catastrophic later in its implications? He needed a mind greater than his with more experience to give him the order to act. Oh, Lord, please open the eyes of my father; please.

The storm trooper by the door had lowered himself to a sitting position, his eyes were half closed in sleep. Tim heard Hoagland's questioning turn to the subject of Josh. Katie responded that Josh loved Jesus. Hoagland began quizzing her on this Jesus. Certainly, they wouldn't imprison a little girl; the Church needed youth. Did the Church need her father? Why would he willingly give his children to these people and the evils of their church?

Who were these well-fed, arrogant men? Why did they think they were so morally superior, when they were the direct antithesis of morality? They were evil men. Fat Simmons probably liked his women young. Hoagland was a child molester, no doubt. Or a pansexual. These men were going to take his children into captivity and tell them what to think. He saw his family's fate; prison, starvation, separation, perversion, torture, death. He sat there, dumbly allowing it all to unfold. All this because he had sought the truth for himself and his kids. And because it wasn't the truth of the Church, he was a subversive, a menace to society.

Hoagland was asking her about the flyers she had mentioned. An anger, a ferocious sanity overtook Tim, a ferocity directed at his own stupidity and at the insanity of these people. He must calm his mind. This welling compulsion within couldn't be good. Rational thought must prevail. These men wanted nothing but good for his family. These men, the Church, needed this family and families like it.

No! Evil was in his home. Evil that would undo the good in his life, his only worthwhile accomplishment—his children. Why couldn't he associate with Josh or Dave? Why couldn't Katie and Matthew read the flyers? Why did it even matter if the flyers were the truth? Why couldn't they believe in a God Who loved them? Why couldn't they believe that Jesus was God, was their friend? Just to believe was their right, their right before any government, any church, any group of people. The Creator of the universe had given them that right—to seek Him. For the first time in his life, he knew God did truly exist. Everything prophesied in the Bible was coming to life, playing out perfectly. *That* was reality. Damn his rational thought, his cute mind so in love with its worldly logic. Damn society, perverse people held together only by the fear of the law. Damn himself for his gutlessness, his desire to live, to play their game.

He had followed society's idea of life—a good job, prestige, power, money that brought food, good clothes, material benefits. Here is where society's life had brought him: to one worn set of clothes upon their backs, a paper home, ten gallons of water a week, two containered meals a day. He lived on a dead Earth with people whose souls were dead. Oh, how glorious it was! What was left of a man when he was stripped of the distractions, the superfluous, with only his soul for company? He was a sinner from birth, and if all the bad could be revealed and peeled away from his soul, only a rebellious, self-centered hater of God would be exposed. His only hope was the mercy of God, an indwelling God, to wipe his soul clean. He only had a destiny outside this world. He had only his conduct, his thoughts, his God. *Love God with all your heart and with all your soul and all your mind.*

He realized the extent of his illusion. A lifetime of illusion, self-generating, feeding upon the illusions of others, the world. He had followed, found great comfort in the game, in the pursuit with society. It had all been a sham. What he once held as precious was trash. If he had been offered the finest clothes, the most prestigious job, the greatest riches, he wouldn't go back. The Church wanted to prolong this lie, this deception, rally men around the falsehood, make them believe the lie was returning in all its glory. He'd rather see his family torn apart by a pack of wolves than to reenter the world's foolishness.

The Lord God had given him his children. Not the State, not the Federation, not society, not the people around him. He alone was responsible for Mary, Mat, Katie, and little Emily. He alone decided, planned their future, nurtured them. He knew he had no wisdom to do so—he knew his children belonged to God, not to Tim Johnson. They belonged to God and would return to God.

Like a pneumatic sleeve, Tim popped to life, every muscle tensed and bursting with power; he moved toward Hoagland with incredible speed. A rage was upon him. This smug Hoagland questioning his little girl. This girl, given to him by God, to be raised to know God. Smug Hoagland dissecting his family with words, so he could dissect their souls. Hoagland looked up in shock, about to utter a word. The head of Hoagland was between Tim's hands, the hair greasy, the flesh cool. Tim felt Hoagland's perverseness. Hoagland's massive head was snapped on the weak neck.

Matthew was up, rummaging through something in the corner of the room. The storm trooper still slept. Simmons was walking out of the bedroom; the wife had given the information that would destroy Tim Johnson. Tim's fist blasted through Simmons's head; he fell back into the bedroom, on top of Mary and Jones.

The storm trooper awoke, began to rise slowly, drawing his weapon from the holster. Mary screamed. Simmons was attempting to rise. Jones pulled the stun stick from Simmons's belt and pressed it against Simmons's head. A lethal burst spasmed Simmons's brain.

Mat was crouched against the wall next to the door. The storm trooper went toward Tim, in the far room, passing Mat, deeming a boy no threat. Matthew came up behind the trooper. The trooper was focused on Tim. Matthew stuffed a stolen grenade up the body armor of the trooper. The explosion was instantaneous, muffled, contained by the body armor. The trooper fell to his knees as his lungs, bowels turned to liquid within the shell. The liquid flesh, blood, bone, organs flowed to the floor. Mat grabbed the armor shell at the shoulders and pulled the body to the head of the stairs. The body slipped easily on the wet floor. Mat heaved the body down the stairs, into the trooper ascending.

"Oh my God, Matthew! Oh my God!" Katie whispered deeply as she stood in the bedroom doorway watching. She watched the pool of thick gore and blood spreading. Matthew tried to release the laser pistol from the trooper's wrist. Thank God it had not been in the combat attachment, designed to blow up with the death of the storm trooper. The weapon would not release. Matthew had another grenade in his hand and threw it with all his speed and strength at the trooper ascending, hitting him over the eye of his face shield. The grenade stuck in the orb of the face shield surrounding the eyes and exploded, blowing the face, then the head away.

Tim, speechless, stared at Jones as she rose. She spoke. "Hell! I'm one of the redeemed of the Lamb, Johnson! Took you a long time to figure out where you and your family were going."

"Where?" asked Tim.

"Druggings, torture, sexual molestation just to wear a chip in your body for some chintzy rations." Jones smiled through her laugh. "The wisdom of the Lord is mighty to save." She laughed again. "Something close to that."

Tim studied her demeanor; Jones was elated, Jones was euphoric. Jones wasn't the old Jones. Silence came. No footsteps in the volcanic ash, no doors slamming, no one running up the stairs. "Grab the water jugs, the packs, the blankets; dress warmly." He spoke to the kids as he grabbed a sobbing Mary. "You coming with us, Jones?"

"No, I can lie my way out of this one. These two clowns taught me all the secrets—how the tests could be beaten. They were bursting with pride, bursting with lust to sell themselves to me. Not realizing I was adding up the data. Besides, I've got killer backup pills if things get too rough." She spoke of poison.

"Why are you doing this for us?" Tim wondered if she was sincere; she could turn them in as soon as they wandered out into the darkness.

"Johnson, you're a stupid sh…guy." The kids were listening. "Told you I was ex-military, worked the battlefronts. I was on the Polish frontier when your brother bugged out. I was at the mutiny site where Van Ord died. Probably passed by your brother. I followed his flight through the computer trail, though I wasn't assigned to it. I revisited that site. When I met you, I saw some of his features in yours, and the notes said he was running, possibly to his geology professor brother in New York. I found the connection. I feel like I've been reading a book about you and your family. Then I got into that old-time religion of your Gramps, and Jesus hooked me with His shepherd's staff. Jesus is my Lord and Savior; could I do anything else but help you?"

Tim, bewildered, searched her face. How? Jones was the least likely candidate for being born again. Her face beamed like John's friend Diana's had; her face had shone with the glory of God.

"So what's the secret to the testing?" Tim said.

"Empty your mind. Think of Christ, of the eternal love of God, of the immensity of life before you. Does something to your brain waves, your biological readings. The tests can't read a heart at peace—filled with confidence and joy. It just can't. No one on their side has picked up on it yet."

He searched her eyes. She was telling her truth. Matthew stepped out from behind his father and spoke. "Dad, we've got to move."

"Okay; let's go." He saw his ragtag family behind him expectantly waiting—waiting for him. He was the power, the authority; he loved them and they, him. Jones saw Tim's eyes misting. Her eyes softened, and she wondered who she would have been with a dad like him in her life. So frail they were, the little family, and the night so cold.

"You're the man, Johnson. The Lord's man. He will not fail nor forsake you." Jones patted Tim on his shoulder. "Go…and conquer. The cross conquers, Johnson." Her words were charged with the electricity of life, emotion, the soul.

In the back bedroom he slipped into his coat, ruck, face mask; he thrust a knife into the wall, and with all his strength, opened a slit in the wall. Blackness and ash blew in on a cold wind. The ash had been piled high below. The woman in the first-floor apartment had used it as insulation and to thwart thieves.

"Come on. Time's wasting," said Tim.

First went Matthew, Katie, Emily; then he gave a gentle lift to Mary as she stepped out and fell into the pile of ash. He quickly made one last check of the rooms. Jones sat and watched his last check. They would all be sentenced to death for killing government officials and the storm troopers. He took his knife, plunged it into the heart of Simmons and Hoagland so that no ghosts would haunt him. Two fewer men to do Satan's work. She understood his actions. "See you on the other side, Johnson?"

"For sure. The cross does conquer." He jumped into the black night of hissing ash. He was sure for the first time in his life.

Jones remained sitting. She just wished to rest and think. Her fingerprints and DNA were on the stun gun. She could say Johnson grabbed her hand and forced it into Simmons's skull or just wipe it clean and place Simmons's prints on it. Or perhaps no autopsy would be done, and the heart stab, evidently done by Johnson, would be considered the cause of death. She'd been stunned—knocked out—early and when she awoke, they were gone. Period.

She was weary of mind. She'd had no forewarning that Johnson was in the apartment complex. Simmons always kept the itinerary secret. But reflection was wasted time. She should erase the Johnson family interrogation data from the files before too much time had elapsed between erasure and time of death. Too much time might lead to questions, like how did Johnson know how to erase? The system wasn't intuitive like a normal computer. Time of death could be calculated to within five minutes now with the new formula and software. So, Johnson had erased the data before she regained consciousness. Or Simmons or Hoagland had by accident or threat erased the data. Even then it could be found in the cloud. Or should she claim that no interrogation had taken place? Whatever. Wipe it out now.

She thought of suicide as she went about the deletion. One pill; a stain would be left on her tongue. The investigating officer would think she had been forced to take it or had taken it willingly. It didn't matter. She would have peace and heaven awaited. Her continued life would be of value to the Lord; there were more of His people to help and save. Strange, God had chosen her, of all people. A heart as cold as ice, foul mouthed and aggressive physically and emotionally, a promiscuous lover of men and women. She had lived life without kindness or gentleness and with cynicism and mockery for all that was good.

She loved Jesus much for she had sinned much. She must acquiesce to His love. He was Lord, and He made no mistakes. She must fill her remaining days with love for others. *Love thy neighbor as thyself.* She prayed the Johnsons would remain true to each other and to their Lord. She had bought them some time—the deletions complete. She felt no need to rise; she was warm and comfortable. One last chore: the body cams of the storm troopers must be destroyed.

CHAPTER 25

Tim led his family, breathing filters and vision-protection masks upon their faces, to the hidden cache in the former warehouse district by their old corner apartment; a half-mile walk at most from their paper apartment. There they stuffed their rucksacks with dehydrated food, vacuumed-packed food, dried food. They had clear bags of factory-packed water. Everyone carried a ruck, even little Emily. Mat carried an extra prepacked ruck. Tim, too, shouldered an extra bag. He could share the load with Katie. Tim had a thankfulness to the Lord for the foresight to bury what appeared at the time an extravagance of food. The buried weapons and the ammunition were retrieved. Tim kept the sawed-off shotgun, the machine pistol went to Mat, and both were hidden under their trench coats. They did not speak—could not, through the ash storm. They held the trailing pack straps of the person ahead and followed Tim into the night.

The falling black ash created a density to the power of darkness that encased them. The ash whipped against their plastic environmental masks. The beam of Tim's flashlight barely penetrated to the ground. The ash hissed, the cold numbed the near skeletal bodies; lightning flashed and thunder rumbled, the sound so muffled, so brief that the mind absorbed the sensation without notice. He knew where he would lead them—to Gramps's home, to the hidden cache of supplies no one knew of but him.

Only essential lights shone in the city, appearing as fuzzy splotches in the dense blackness. No commuters, no traffic, no pedestrians. Even the guards stationed at the borders of zones were huddled in their shelters, masks on, bundled against the cold and grating ash; they did not peer into the black wall of darkness. The city's survivors were in their apartments, watching the one hour of electrascreen reruns of happier times or gnawing upon a found delicacy, taken from the ruins or stolen from another. If they had alcohol, they were drinking; if they had prescription drugs or over-the-counter narcotics, they were swallowing; needles went into bodies. Sexual perversions were being satiated. Some drew or painted, some wrote, some read books, some searched the radio waves for someone to tell them the truth, some played games alone or with others.

From this fallen humanity, some secretly uncovered their hidden, unlawful books and attempted to find answers from philosophers, intellectuals, poets, writers, holy men of the great religions or cults of the world. Some opened a book called the Bible, searching for answers, searching for God even as He sat in the room with them and searched their souls. The wind whistled through the newly constructed wood-framed apartments; the ash hissed against the compressed-wood walls. The walls shone dully in the night from the meager light within.

The family passed through the outskirts of the city, floundered down the steep, ash-ladened riverbank, waded through the ash drifts of the old riverbed, where the flat, empty fishponds lay. On the west shore, on hands and knees, they crawled up the old riverbank to the commuter tracks. His intent was to hide for a day outside of zone twenty-one, where a search might be conducted. Crossing the riverbed had placed them in another county with different jurisdictional authority and, he hoped, would foster the confusion of cooperation in any search efforts. His second goal was also accomplished: to *not* cross the heaved-up first mountain, a hard climb through ash drifts and no doubt rigged with sensors or under satellite surveillance. He also did not wish to pass through the narrow river defile around the mountain, which was most certainly controlled by thugs and strewn with entrapments. Tomorrow they would recross the riverbed farther north and simply follow the valley to Gramps's home. They stumbled, they rested, they began again, they slept in the ruins of a commuter station.

A dull light came, with no visible sun. The wind and the ash fall had stopped. The ash was inches thick upon ruined buildings, roads, hills, flats, distant mountains. The landscape was smooth, as if melted; no jagged, ragged edges. In the east, the ruined high-rises of their city, a third of their original height, appeared as soft mounds. It seemed a winter scene of snow, except there was no whiteness, no frigid cold. To the west, the roiled clouds were the deepest black, piling higher than the family thought sky existed. The air was cold and still. In the old days, the sun would have appeared in the east with light. Now a scabby sun splotched at either pole with brown spots sat like a rock in the sky.

Something spattered upon Tim's face. He looked up at the missing roof panels. It happened again. He looked at his huddled family. Matthew's brown, ash-ladened coat was splotched, then the splotches joined, then the coat was dark with rain. Rain? It was raining! He couldn't remember when raindrops had last appeared with volume and duration. The drops increased, created a sound on the fabric of coats. A hollow sound.

They thought it would soon end, a few splatters, nothing more. The rain increased in intensity, became steady. The drops were heavy, carrying ash. A wind blew from the west, the storm clouds, unnatural, frightening were upon them. The wind whistled through downed trees, through the ruins of buildings and their clothes. The ash stung. A dread came upon them. They staggered to their feet, moved into the deeper ruins of the commuter station. Here, the intact roof had collapsed; one side was raised a few feet from the ground, high enough to allow their entry.

Night came to the day. Hurricane winds howled. The rain came horizontally. They heard nothing but a roar in the distance. They heard the rain pounding the metal roof till it became an unbroken, unyielding pounding upon the mind; cartwheeling pieces of debris clattered against the roof and other obstructions. The rain was not a blessing. It was just another curse upon the earth. The rain was absorbed into the heavy ash accumulation of months. When the ash could hold no more moisture, the rain carried the ash, creating a sludge. The sludge moved, crept over the flat land, rolled off the mountains and hills. Unable to be absorbed by the rock-hard earth, meeting little resistance, the ash-ladened flood gained momentum.

The sludge moved through the Johnsons' shelter only inches deep. Between the rain squalls, they could see the hill across the tracks stripped bare of all forest debris, the downed and rotting logs, and even the stones and soil. The man-made riverbed to the east, past the fishponds, had already filled. They knew this by the sound, an abrading roar, and by the sight of tree trunks within the river of sludge cartwheeling above the banks. The fishponds between the river channel and commuter tracks had completely filled, the sludge moving slowly south. Soon the commuter tracks and the station would be a part of the movement.

They waded into the slow-moving sludge, holding hands, moving toward the now bare hill across the tracks and road. Branches, logs, man-made debris knocked into them. Below the sludge, huge rocks rolled into feet, ankles, calves. Tim broke the force of the current, Mary and the children attempted to stay within his lee. The density of the sludge caused Tim's thighs to burn with exertion. The hill consisted of sharp edges of shale, in a few places the base soil still had form. Only one piece of debris remained—near the summit, a large tree trunk whose stubbled roots had wedged between protruding sedimentary layers. Up the hill they crawled, free from the sludge that had already been swept away by gravity, only to slide back on the slick earth. The wind and rain buffeted them.

Slowly they gained ground till they sat near the summit, on the east side of the massive tree trunk. The heavy wood could pose a life-threatening situation if it moved and they were within its range. They kept their distance. As if on a toboggan, they sat together. Katie between Tim's legs, Emily between Katie's legs, Mary between Matthew's. Tim's and Mat's coats were used as windbreaks and plastic ponchos, as rain shields. They shivered uncontrollably. Rations were broken open and eaten. Within an hour, the land around them was completely inundated. The tracks and road were covered. The old, natural riverbank first formed by glaciers in a time before men, delineated the surging flow. The river had reclaimed its old bed. The river was grinding, cracking with tree trunks, buildings, vehicles, bodies, wires. Huge dead trees, long ago denuded, would catch on the riverbed, stand upright, and cartwheel, thrashing and flinging any object caught in the protruding spikes of roots and limbs. Unrecognizable debris of all shapes and sizes could be seen in the heavy sludge. They saw a living body clinging desperately to a roof. Male or female, they did not know. They knew this person would die. Where had this lone figure come from? Hundreds of miles to the north? From the fringes of the city? The imminence of death was an aura on the forlorn soul. Mary reflected on the survival stories she'd read as a teenager.

What persistence humanity had to cling to life so desperately. The living body in the river would suffocate on wet ash or be flung into a rock or a tree, and the body broken. Who would know it had lived but God? Who knew what it suffered now but God—and a handful of onlookers like her family? If the body was lucky, it would snag somewhere, and when the raging river subsided, it would be found by humans who would cremate or bury it, Mary thought. Probably wolves or vultures would make a meal and scatter the bones. If unobstructed, the body would be cast into the Chesapeake Bay—that desert of ash and receding water. Maybe the body would even be compressed and fossilized to be found by alien scientists two thousand years in the future. No alien scientists; the world was ending! Just God and His angels to take the soul to its appointed place, and soon the body would follow.

God offered eternal life. Mary could live above the depressing vision of earthly life. She could be with her family into eternity, if she liked. If she lived life His way, by His rules. His way had goodness and truth within. She now believed He was a God of emotion—those qualities that animated life and made humanity more than animals. Yet this life He cast them within was so cruel, so painful that it was easy to see Him with negative emotions, perverted emotions. But He couldn't be the deceiver; that was Satan's name.

The question now was could she believe in Satan? Could she believe that he existed apart from God? What a weird question; no one thinks like that—a being who was *not* God trying to screw it all up. Why weren't the people of the Church, the theologians, giving an account of Satan? Why had he been placed in the back room of consciousness and forgotten? Why had the focus become the primitive natures of humans, to be slowly abraded away with knowledge and logical actions?

Why was it so damned muddled? Because the deceiver wanted it muddled. Or did God want to hide the fact that He was Satan? Such was the charge of the religious leaders against Jesus. This was a big battle while on His earthly walk; the men of renown just wouldn't accept His goodness as pure. Why couldn't Mary accept His purity of goodness and love? How determinedly Satan clung to God.

In time, they guessed it was late afternoon, the rain and dark clouds disappeared and were replaced by a ceiling of solid-gray clouds. Beneath the ceiling the air was clear, cool. They could see for miles. The mountains to their north had been scoured to bare rock, jumbled rocks, boulder fields, ridged layers of sedimentary rock. Only a few dead trees had managed to remain, pinned in the rock or jumbled in piles at the bottom of ravines. They wrapped their sleeping bags around themselves and pushed the heat pumps interwoven into the bags to the ON position. The heat revived them, stopped the bodily tremors.

The city could be seen across the expanse of floodwater. The remaining high-rises seemed to have lost half their height. Vultures circled in the clear air. Around the family, the floodwaters had created a vast inland sea, dotted with islands, dotted with the forms of survivors both animal and human. Tim was reminded of the arctic islands splotched with seabirds and seals. The air smelled fresh, not of life, but of soil, rock, like the smell of fresh cement. If he had chosen to ascend the mountain ridge and remain in zone twenty-one, he wondered, would they have perished on the mountaintop when the rains came?

Now he wondered if the river would ever fall so that they could cross and access the supplies at Gramps's home. Were the supplies still in existence? The cache was on relatively high ground within the valley floor. But the entire valley floor was narrow and the possible runoff from the vastness of the mountains would be formidable. The entire valley had probably flooded and been scoured. That the supplies were wrapped in waterproof materials seemed little consolation.

Only eating seemed to revive their awareness and thought processses. They ate their food oblivious of rationing; people dead from hypothermia had no need of rations. They ate till warmth returned. They wrung out their clothes, then rewrapped themselves in their bags. Though they had just eaten, they would need to eat again soon. They were like shrews or hummingbirds, now that their fat reserves were gone. Ingested food was only for the moment. They wondered at the destruction of the raging river. Wondered at what would become of the Chesapeake Bay, the ocean when the semisolid mass of floodwaters hit? Tim studied the terrain to the north. The naked mountain ridges astounded him. He could not judge distance on their slopes; all familiar markers were gone.

The return to Gramps's home would be fraught with danger. The flooded river needed to be crossed, the valley traversed, likely through log and debris jams. He tried to remember the lay of the land, the high spots, the low, hidden by the sludgy water. He must counter his pessimism. He began thinking hopeful thoughts of the future. The rain might produce plant life, the rain might be the beginning of seasons, of planting and harvesting, a return to normalcy. He smiled a cynical smile. This world was passing away. The only good in the future was the embrace of Christ.

The hail storm came without warning from the northwest. Its approach was hidden by the western mountains; it came quickly, descended upon them. The pebble-sized hail stung them through their sleeping bags. The hail grew in circumference, pounded them so severely they sought shelter under the massive tree trunk wedged on the hill. They wedged themselves between the trunk and the knife-edged sedimentary rocks, praying the tree trunk would not slide from its seemingly precarious hold. They placed their clothing and rucksacks against the sides of the tree. Water came underneath the tree from the height of the hill, a fabric penetrating trickle following gravity, flowing on the wet rock. They shivered on the rock, despite their sleeping bags, wondered if they could survive the night.

***

His face was burning. He opened his eyes. The sun was directly above him in a cloudless sky. He and his is family were beside the tree trunk. He turned his head to avoid the burning rays. The blueness of the sky delighted him. For so long the world had been gray haze. Mary was in the dry, hot sleeping bag beside him, the kids in their own bags directly beside her, a plastic covering over them. Their wet clothes had been again strewn on the tree trunk. He could not remember the move to outside the shelter of the trunk, or the spreading of the plastic sheeting. The wind was from the west, warm and buffeting. He stood and studied the river. There was barely a current, but the depth appeared greater than his height. The water had dropped twenty or thirty feet in the night. The rain had only been a local storm. He thought their sleeping bags would make sails; just a simple log for each could float them across the river. He began shaking his family awake. "Up. Up. A sailing we will go."

***

Tim stared and studied the surreal and foreboding river. It was easily a mile to the far shore, where the mountain ridge's edge, bare and steep, dropped huge boulders into the river and upon the shore. Single avalanches occurred sporadically. For the first time, he saw the great upthrust that had added at least a thousand feet of height to the existing mountain ridge. This plate movement on the day of the great quake had pushed up the northern slope of the mountain, adding to its height. The valley he had once known was gone. The way to Gramps's house was a trip into uncertainty. Did Gramps's home even exist? Yes, foggily, he remembered the map in the headquarters of the Order's Camp. Gramps's house existed. He sighed with relief even as he worried that his memory was degrading.

The sludge was thick in the river and created a sound of grating, rushing far above the decibel level comfortable to human ears. The river had looked benign and passable from the encampment on the hill. Now, ten feet above the water, fear entered everyone as the inexorable mass rolled on to the Chesapeake Bay. Mary held Emily's hand tightly—no stepping to the edge of the bank would be allowed; the next footstep might lead to drowning or a frenetic ride on a current, carrying them to death.

"Let's make a boat," Tim said. "Maybe we'll camp here tonight and see what tomorrow brings."

"Too wet and open. We can spend the night at the tree trunk…don't you think?" said Mary.

"Good advice. Let's stick with make a boat," said Tim. He was heartened that Mary had volunteered advice, that she saw herself as still belonging to a family.

Matthew was already searching through the debris scattered on the second level of the bank. In time, they found a piece of a dock made of plastic wood with supporting pontoons still attached. Two long, slim, plastic pipes were used as masts. A rudder came together when a long pipe and a nondescript rectangle of heavy plastic were combined. Two intact shovels were found for paddles, and a plastic pallet was relieved of two of its slats, making two more paddles. A flag pole was found for poling the craft, if necessary. Plastic crate packing became a sail. Rope was found to strengthen the dock through intertwining and weaving.

At the end of their boat building, Tim, exhausted, made use of a tree trunk for a seat. He studied the river. His assessment, his judgment may very well decide the death of a family member or the entire family. How many fathers through the span of ages had sat down to read the waters—from the Cree father on some northern lakeshore to the Eskimo father on an Arctic bay, or the African daddy by his dugout on a river filled with hippos and crocs or the South Seas islander contemplating the open ocean or the Norseman, the fjord. How many of them failed? God knew. Tim had seen the bodies of a family floating on the Amazon's waters on a geologic expedition many years ago. He had seen waves smash an outrigger outside an atoll in the Pacific, killing a young fisherman. What abode did these people inhabit now?

He thought the current might be five miles per hour. He believed the west wind was steady at ten, maybe fifteen. He looked up at the massive mountain end on the far side, at least two thousand feet above them. Rocks, soil, avalanches from the recent rains were still sending debris into the river below. He chose a shoreline landmark—a knoll with a large rock on top, straight across the river—as his reference point. He picked a large, projecting rock—a single boulder, long and flat—on the far shore as his target, their place of probable landing, hundreds of yards down from the knoll. He would paddle for the knoll and hope to make it but would feel secure if they made the shore prior to the flat boulder. Aiming at the knoll would give their craft the proper angle to the current.

Mat sat beside him and was shown the plan of attack. Mat agreed, then stood, searched and found a rotten branch, and broke it into a foot-long piece. "Get your timer ready." Tim understood and cleared his solar wrist computer to zero. Mat heaved the branch to a projecting rock ledge in the river and watched the branch float toward a jumbled pile of tree limbs breaking the water's surface. He knew more than one tree was beneath the sludge water and hoped the limbs would be at the same position tomorrow. He marked his spot on the bank with a part of the rotten tree branch not used. When the floating branch touched the tree limbs, he raised his hand. "Mark."

"Mark," said Tim loudly. "Twenty-three seconds. Okay, family, to the tree trunk we go and pray for better conditions tomorrow." It was not too long ago that a man had no need to pray about going from point A to point B.

***

The new day began in the muted light of sunspots. The heat was humid as the sky pulled up the moisture from the earth and river. The wind was steady from the west and would help their little boat across the river. They ate the last of their rations. Tim told his family of the rations he had hidden on the farmhouse grounds and warned the cache could have been found and pilfered. Tim and Mat reevaluated the river current with the test established the day before. The current and the water level were substantially reduced—forty seconds for the branch to cover the same distance. Their eyes could see the water carried less sludge. Ten feet of bank was exposed from the day before. The volume had dropped by a rough estimate of half.

They boarded their boat. Tim controlled the rudder. Mat had the shovel paddle on the southern side of the craft, so as to pull upriver. Katie controlled the sail from a sitting position, by a rope attached to the spar, with Mary sitting directly behind. Emily sat, held onto a rope tied to Mary.

They had time to adjust themselves in the current-free water near shore; the current was pushed out into the river by a curve in the shore upriver. Within seconds of entering the river current, they realized their sail was negated by the drag of their craft in the thick water. Mat struggled against the viscosity of the water. Tim pulled up the rudder and grabbed the second shovel paddle. He crawled to Mat's side of the boat even as he requested the women shift to the upriver side of the craft. Paddling had an urgency, a pace. The boat began to spin. Katie crawled to the rudder as Mary took the sail.

Emily, with small corrections to her position, stayed centered in the boat. Tim noticed her patience and lack of fear as she correctly chose her positions, as the crew crawled to their new positions. "Good job, Emily." She smiled as she looked into Tim's eyes. He knew she had found a family she trusted and loved. He saw her utter delight in belonging—in being loved and cherished. It was that same overwhelming emotion he had seen in the little girl in the African surgery center when she realized she was loved and had worth. It was the same quality of worth and warmth that washed over him when he shared his canned goods with Burnell.

Mat matched Tim stroke for stroke, even as Tim's arms ached and he wished to stop. But he would not stop until they were safely on shore. The body had to do what it was told, whatever the cost in pain. "You're the man, Mat." Tim grunted the words through his pain. He thought of DC Jones's words to him and how the encouragement had lifted his spirits. Mat was a man and was *the* man; no longer could Tim perceive him as a child.

Providence came and rescued them, for in the eastern channel of the old riverbed another river—of clear water—flowed; beneath this clear river they saw the sludge river. But in the clear water, devoid of the sludge drag, the sail propelled the craft and brought them to shore, closer to the knoll than the rock. Tim laughed a quiet thankful humph as the pontoons struck scattered rocks and the bow dug into the river shore of sludge.

He stepped into the sludge, searched the bank quickly, then turned and pulled the boat up. Yes, the Lord had brought them through again. The Lord had always brought them through, all their lives, but he had not been able to see. Now in this starkness, this emptiness, with the thrills of the world stripped away and the desires of the flesh gone, he saw. During his life, he had only accomplished what God had put into him to accomplish. But the pride of life had told Tim Johnson to take ownership, to boast of himself and his accomplishments. He dropped to his knees and spoke quietly. "Thank you. Thank you, God of the universe. Thank you. Thank you for this family and for life."

Shouldering their rucks, the party watched Tim and Mat heave the boat halfway out of the water. The sail was taken down, no camouflaging was attempted, and they left the boat behind. They wished to hurry from the bare riverbank, where drones or patrols or brigands might wander. He was thankful that a drone had not sent a distress call to authorities when the flimsy craft had been spotted in the river. No air platform to their rescue or even to inquire after them. He had believed for some time that the vast hinterlands between the few large cities were basically wilderness and without government oversight or concern.

At the edge of the boulder fields, in the loom of the mountain, he sensed a premonition of danger. Or was it tragedy? Who, Lord? The Lord simply gave peace. Maybe the two-thousand-foot mountain above them created a false premonition of danger? Maybe he should have hidden the boat? He decided to attempt a hiding of the boat. He took Mat with him to the shore, they let the boat drift down into some semisubmerged trees that had jumbled together in a cove. He tied the craft to a branch, and then they threw debris upon it. Rock and soil slides were tumbling from the cliff face of the mountain. He spoke to Mat. "Something is going to happen." Mat studied his father's face and said nothing. As they trudged back to the family, Mat sensed that the happening would give no appearance of being good.

They needed to hide in the valley of trees before taking a rest break. He reminded himself the food was gone; the trip up the valley would be tough without nourishment. They moved in a single line in the scramble around the mountainside cliff of falling debris. The order of march was Tim, Katie, Mary, Emily, Mat. Emily needed to be near Mary, for Mary's peace; but Emily would not be able to hold the pace, and only Mat now had the strength to carry her. The climb through the debris fields demanded much—patience in choosing a foothold and balance for contrasting surfaces and the movement of the eye from earth to rock, to the boulder field. The sound of landslides near and far played in their ears.

The climb demanded much from muscle with no strength, lungs with no breath; the cold sweat of exertion was carried away by a humid, hot breeze. Rubbery legs carried them up slopes, wobbly legs took them down slopes. They had half falls supported by weak arms. They tripped and stubbed toes and feet. They slipped on wet rocks and with contortionist moves stretched muscles to aching to keep themselves upright. Sometimes they fell on the hard rock—attempting to roll to minimize damage.

Then it happened. Happened so quietly, so matter-of-factly, that it seemed it did not happen. Just a passing dream. Emily saw a collection of mushrooms and had bent to run her hand over their tops before moving on and holding her place in line. Mat watched Emily and smiled at childhood. He was last in line but farther back from Emily, as he had studied the boulder field for a traveling path of least resistance, for enemies, for dangerous loose soils and rocks. Mat yelled as he saw it coming. Tim turned to see a car-sized boulder moving at speed with quietness.

Emily was crushed beneath the rock. The rock rolled over her. Mat and Tim knew she was dead.

Mat was first at her side. The boulder had come from his right, its immense size hidden by the jumbled rocks of greater size upon the slope. The quietness had come from the roundness of the rock and the wet forest debris and soil it had rolled upon. None of these facts dispelled his sense of failed responsibility. His mother was at his side; she sat and gathered up her Emily into her bosom. She wailed in anguish. Emily had been her duty, her charge, her hope. Upon Emily she had poured her love, a love that kept her humanness alive, a love that reminded her of God's love.

"Lord Jesus, raise this girl from the dead. Raise her as you raised so many others. I know you are able, Lord!" Mary called out to the heavens. Katie joined the prayer and then Mat as they implored their God to give heed to their supplications. Tim joined the group when hands had been lifted to the heavens. He knew it was not to be and yet he joined in deep, heartfelt prayers beseeching God—not for Emily, who was resting upon His bosom, but for Mary, who could not live without her.

Tim was first to cease when his throat was raw and no sounds came, then Katie became silent, then Mat silently prayed till his mind went blank. They knew Emily was at peace. They knew she would only have had hardship if she had remained. Mary was wailing breathless prayers, her beseechings unintelligible and desperate. Now the family silently prayed for their mother, who believed she could not live without her little girl.

Katie was beside her mother, consoling her with gentle words. "You loved her, Mom; and she knew your love and had confidence in it. She basked in it like the heat of a gentle sun. She died so quickly, without a fear in her mind. She had a family. She *has* a family. We will see her again, Mom. Death is just a short parting."

Tim looked upon his family and sat. He took Mary's face into his hands and looked into her eyes. "Mary, look at me. We will see Emily soon. She knew her Maker, and she knew her Savior—Mat and Katie made certain of this. We must hold together in our faith and not doubt." Tim picked Mary off the ground as Katie separated Emily's body from her grasp. Tim held his wife; he hugged her to the core of her being, and he wept with her.

As Tim and Mary cried, Mat and Katie wrapped Emily in ponchos. She would come along to Gramps's home to be buried. They knew her spirit was gone and was with the Lord. They knew her body would be gathered up by the Lord on that last day very quickly approaching. They wanted her body to be buried near Gramps's home, just to know her body was safe.

***

Tim awoke in the predawn gray light of the sunspotted orb. The dead forest had absorbed the rain, and now branches were breaking off, trees toppling; the woody scent, resuscitated by water, added a pungency to the already moist and humid air. They had arrived in the night, knowing the old farmhouse was close. They had flopped to the earth and slept where they collapsed. He knew they were near, for the small creek adjacent to the farmhouse sent cascading sounds of water over the quiet, dead forest. The flow from mountain runoff would last for days. The road to their farmhouse had not been crossed by them…they were near. He must scout; make certain no one lived in the farmhouse. Then he must find the buried cache and fresh, untainted, wholesome water. Death's beginning was only as distant as the next meal. Death was close all the time, it seemed. He determined they would eat from this cache till they were full—no rationing, no thought for the future. He just wanted to feel healthy, full, energized just once. Then they would go back to the city and the final cache in the warehouse district.

Eventually they would be caught. They would enjoy their freedom now. Tim rose. He studied the naked woods, looked up at the high mountain ridge rising beside him, the ridge top still in the haze. He listened and smelled and his eyes scanned. He caught whiteness through the dead and thinning trees, high in the trees; The farmhouse. The sun was hot now. Recently, the sun seemed to have grown hotter than he remembered from his youth, or even from months ago. The breeze was hot. He walked slowly, barefooted toward the old farmhouse, the machine pistol strapped to his side. He stopped again. He listened to the limbs falling in the valley and upon the mountain slopes. On the mountains, entire tree trunks were falling. His stomach hurt from its emptiness, and his worn body ached. He had a peace; he knew God was with him, standing here at this very place. Memories of little Emily walked and paused through his memory. He would hold her again in heaven.

He had much to be thankful for—his family was still functioning, striving to know the Lord. Mat and Katie knew Him intimately. He was close to knowing all. It was Mary who was his concern. He thought of the book of Genesis and how God had walked with Adam in the stillness of the first mornings of humanity's creation. Was the Lord nostalgic? Was He reviewing and tasting the moments of the past, knowing that what *was* was being swallowed by what would come? The tangled journey of mankind's rebellion would become straight. Adam's love of self would die, and the deceits of the fallen angel would be exposed. All that was happening was bearable and good, for it led to a new plane of existence, a new relationship with the Creator, Father God. Could he call Him Daddy? He wished he could. His earthly dad hadn't been much of a father—too absorbed in his wife and his own life of pleasures. "Thank you for walking with me, my Lord, my God."

He would have fallen to his knees and cried to God if not for the Holy Spirit touching his shoulders and reminding him that a hungry family was depending upon him for food and water. An expectation came to Tim. He walked toward the whiteness he had seen through the trees. As he neared the farmhouse, he realized people had occupied the house since his family had called it home. By the litter, food wrappers, containers, torn and worn clothing, he guessed a succession of people had come and gone.

Various pieces of furniture had been brought inside, the wood stove had been stolen, probably early in the troubles. The furniture brought to the home was lightweight, extremely portable—chairs, a stool, a spindly legged table, cots.

The fireplaces had been used heavily; dirty pots, pans, empty aluminum-foil trays still within the charcoal remains. He saw a fresh spatter of food near the hearth, probably not more than weeks old. He smelled some butt ends of unburnt wood in the fireplace—fresh. Now that he thought of it, the table had no coating of dust.

He went outside and circled the house once, then widened his circles. No footprints, but then the flood had scoured everything. He found a well that he had not known existed. It made sense that a farmhouse built before indoor plumbing would have a well. For how many hundreds of years had the well been covered? The shrinking, moistureless dirt and the fires denuding the undergrowth had made the well site visible. Still, three feet of earth had been removed by someone before the stone lip had been reached. A heavy metal plate, the original lid, covered the opening, put back in place to prevent evaporation—or ash and stray animals from falling in. He slid the plate to the side; the water was inches from the top, swelled from the rains. He tasted. The water was sweet. Not trusting the purity of the water by taste, he sampled with his water purifier—the reading, excellent. No dead animal or human at the bottom of the well.

He continued his outward circle. On the edge of the wood line where an ag field began, he found a hole, man-made. He dug and found feces. He guessed this to be a latrine. He could not tell the age of the contents, which had been affected by the rains.

He continued into the woods, searching for a lone tombstone. He had buried the supplies nearby. He found a long shallow trench on the hillside that had washed out. He saw bright rags, wet and compressed, caught on tree trunks. Human bones, femurs, skulls, fingers, a pelvis were scattered farther down the hill. A grave, washed out by the flood. Four or five people, he guessed. The bones had no teeth marks. He surmised they had been killed recently, for in the beginning the predators—coyotes and wolves—had been thick and surely would have disturbed the grave. The clothing appeared to be of modern materials. He had seen so many skel-etons that their presence did not disturb his calm. Probably the recent visitors had made the farmhouse home and then were killed by thieves.

He found several tombstones, lying facedown. These were new to him but very close to his tombstone marker, which now, too, lay on the earth. Life and death had started in years numbered *1 7*…then the num-bers were gone; indecipherable numbers and letters; rain, water, snow, lichens, moss had eaten the clarity away. How short was the time of the European migration into this new world of North America. How short the time of native peoples' migration upon the continent. He took twenty paces north from his marker, examined the spot, found a slight depression in the earth in a rectangular pattern. He pulled out his small collapsible shovel, snapped it into place, and began to dig.

***

As he walked toward his campsite, he saw his family stirring, twisting, yawning in their sleeping bags. He scanned the dead woods. Nothing moved. The utter stillness, the utter quiet save for the moving creek, held him. Once he would have heard traffic on the road, the commuter trains on the line to the east, air traffic above. Sometimes the ag machines could be heard in the surrounding fields. Once, you could hear insects—crickets, grasshoppers, flies, cicadas—and tree frogs, birds singing. Once, you could look at the earth and see ants. Once, deer were numerous; raccoons, opossums, foxes, turkey were seen. Not even a vulture was overheard, not even the shadowy glimpse of the passing of a starving wolf.

The sun was incredibly hot, his skin already turning red. The heat grabbed his attention; nature had changed again, to a new degree of suffering. Just as he took a step forward, he heard a sound. A bird? A robin? Yes, definitely a robin singing. He scanned the woods, saw movement. A robin perched on a stubby branch, looking down on his family.

How many years? Only sparrows and starlings in the city now. The robin flew down to the earth before the sleeping family. Warily, head turning, it proceeded to pick up invisible bits of something. Tim guessed the small crumbs from the crackers eaten at their last meal on the west bank of the river. Probably shaken from the sleeping bag the night before. Tim grinned madly. The robin was a gift, an incredibly rare gift. The robin did not symbolize hope for a returning Earth. The robin was a promise of a new Earth scoured clean of the wickedness of man. Thank you, Lord God! Thank you! A stream of endless, sincere gratitude washed over Tim's mind. Yes, he wanted the earth to return to what it was. He wanted to live again.

Now was the scouring time, the harvest time, and the cleaning of the fields, this was the time of anger at the rebellious. People had purposely forgotten God, gave Him no praise for His goodness, gave Him no authority over this incredible world. They had hated themselves and their fellow man, while they kept silent about their Creator, who was to be their guide and their help. God was sorry He had made man. He had given them His Son to remind, to lead, to restore, and His thanks was a bloody, beaten, tortured body; His son killed.

Tim wanted an end to the earth. He wanted judgment to come. Not before a harsh, demanding God. But before a grieving Father God whose kids had left his side, raised themselves in their gang, decided right and wrong without him. When they listened to anyone outside their gang, it was only to their God-jealous relative—the deceiver, who had no decency, no respect for His creation. God's children would rather turn to the chemical potions of the mind than to His word. He called them home, and they would not come. He called out his love, and they mocked him. "Go home, old man; leave us alone." They flaunted their evil and called it good. They molested their children, they degraded His gift of sex, they loved their own bodies, they stole, murdered, and spoke hateful, destroying words.

Tim had been a part of it all simply by birth and was ashamed. Tim had not committed big crimes of filth, of hurting and degrading others, but rather, the worst crime of all—disrespect for his Father, apathy toward the words from His mouth. The love due his Father was given to the world created by men just as rebellious as himself. He had lived within the lie. He was guilty. He only wanted to obey. He only wanted to love his Father now.

Tim came into his wakening family and tossed water, juice, energy bars, trail mix.

"Eat and drink slowly; you know the drill. We have an abundance of fresh water, so once you've eaten, we'll wash up." Tim dropped to his knees before Mary and handed her rations. Her face still captivated him, and her scent, trapped in the sleeping bag, beckoned him. He kissed her on the cheek; imperceptibly, she moved away. "I still love you as much as the day we married," he whispered.

She only took a glance at his eyes and then turned away. Maybe she just wanted to grieve alone. He would show affection in little ways until she chose to talk or to return his love. "I'm going out a ways to monitor what seems to be a trail. Always stay alert." His kids responded in the affirmative. Mary said nothing.

When his family was out of sight, he stopped. His eyes caught movement through the dead trees, figures moving through the woods. Slowly they moved, as much from stealth and wariness as weakness. Thirteen people, he counted. Some carried walking sticks, all had packs on their backs. All had an article of military clothing upon their bodies—most people did; military clothes were abundant and rugged. No one carried weapons. His machine pistol could cut them all down with a single trigger pull. He had no fear of these strangers.

They seemed to have a purpose, knew where they were; they were not refugees passing through. They had been the users of the house! He was certain they would circle the farmhouse. He crept close to his family, using a large tree trunk as cover. He would wait for the travelers to come upon him. He settled his body for comfort, rested the machine pistol on a downed limb, then sat as if a stone.

They walked right up to his position, their eyes searching the woods, looking to the tree trunk but not past it. He burst out laughing; they scattered to the right and left, falling to the ground. The lead man, small, with a dark beard and eyes, merely knelt. The eyes focused on Tim as Tim rose. Tim's family jumped from their sleeping bags at Tim's laughter.

"Josh, is that you?" Tim bellowed with surprise and elation still in his voice.

The kneeling man rose.

"Yes, it is Josh." The eyes narrowed in scrutiny, stared at Tim, studied the people behind, then opened wide in joyous recognition. "Tim and his family?"

"Yes."

CHAPTER 26

Tim was upon Josh and grasping his hand, shaking it vigorously and repeatedly. The travelers gathered around the two figures, their tired faces lit with wild joy, feeding from the emotion of Josh and Tim. Tim hadn't realized how much he had missed the company of a friend, of a person who could be trusted. Matthew and Katie were beside their father. Katie bounced up and down- more a flex of the knees. She was too worn to jump. She yelled excitedly.

"It's Josh, Matthew! It's Josh!"

Josh smiled at Katie's delight, her love for him. She had grown much taller since last seen but was so thin. Mat had grown too. You could see his muscular strength through his thinness. His voice had deepened. A scraggly beard had formed. He was fully a man. He mussed her hair with a free hand. Matthew grinned, taking Josh's hand from his father's, and shook it.

"Sit your people over here." Tim spread his hand to the fallen trunk in their camp, covered in plastic sheeting, a piece of plastic that once covered the newly recovered breakfast supplies. The travelers slipped the rucksacks from shoulders and sat on the earth, resting their backs against the trunk. Tim's joy suddenly vanished. They would see his food, want some; he and his family would have less. Anger came suddenly and broke as quickly. Give it all away, let them eat till they could eat no more. At least they would have the memory of a good time, a full stomach in the company of friends. He would trust the Lord, not life, to feed his family. Christ had fed the multitudes. The Spirit of Christ was here. Christ would feed his family.

"We have food. Eat with us."

Tim watched the faces brighten at his words; for a moment, he hated the eagerness in their eyes. As if he saw the glimmer of superiority, a laughter at his foolishness. No, it was simply delight, appreciation at an unexpected gift. Katie and Matthew had already begun rearranging their guests for optimal comfort on blankets and on sleeping bags. Mary remained aloof, although Tim noticed a crooked smile. That was her cynical smile, and he feared an outburst.

"Josh, come along to the cache with Mat and me—and bring one more person." Mat heard his name, and knowing the food must be retrieved, went over to his dad. Josh called the name Tom, and Tom, a tall lanky man in his forties, was quick to respond. Mary was standing now—so that she could better serve her guests, Tim hoped. She had always been a kind and selfless hostess. He thought back to their last guests in their professor's home—Gilroy and Winkie. She was by him. "We're going to throw a party for our hungry guests," Tim said in a whisper.

She whispered into his ear, "Taking food out of the mouths of your family for strangers?"

Josh overheard the bitter words and looked into Mary's eyes for the shortest of times, searching for some vestige of goodness. She had been beautiful at one time; traces remained, even through the loss of weight and the stress of worry. The furrowed brow that had once spoken of a keen mind now portrayed selfishness, a stinginess. A body posture once of calm and peace had tightened, lurched with an anger. The calm eyes held a hardness.

Tim studied Josh's eyes, knowing he had overheard the remark. Tim took Josh by the arm, gently and moved toward the cache of food. As they distanced themselves from the crowd, Tim spoke. "Josh, we had added a member to our family—seven-and-a-half-year-old Emily, who came to us when she was six. She died two days ago. Hit by a falling rock. We were to bury her today."

"Mary loved her?" asked Josh. Josh looked into Tim's eyes and saw Tim's hurt. Josh sensed the girl had been loved by the family and had been the prop in Mary's life. Her reason for living and for service. Now she would feel betrayed by God, and with the promise broken, hatred would follow. "Let us help bury the child. Let us be a part of your mourning."

"Yes, that would be good."

Josh hoped that through words or actions, he could turn Mary back to the Lord. She was being swallowed by the flesh and by Satan. The deceiver was shouting into her conscience and her soul to abandon Christ. She was very close to the precipice and the fall that would never end. The pain that awaited her in hell caused him to wince; he could hear Mary crying in shame as God showed her life to her through the conscience she had killed. Josh broke his mind from Mary, as he felt his own soul emptying. The visible fire he had seen upon Tim at their first meeting was not upon him anymore, but it was stronger than ever; the Spirit of God had been absorbed within Tim. Katie and Matthew? They were children of the King.

***

Tim passed out crackers, peanut butter, dried fruit, apple juice fortified with vitamins. One of the women in Josh's party combed Katie's hair. A man was cutting Mat's hair. Matthew had the collection of posters in his hands produced by Josh's ministry and was reading them to a group of interested people. That his children instinctively trusted these people amazed Tim. For years they had trusted no one. Even he felt at ease. He knew this was the presence of God's Spirit—he was with the deepest kind of family. No evil thoughts were percolating through the minds present, only praise for the mind of Christ; no interest in their needs but only the needs of the others. Mary sat surrounded by women from the group who engaged her in conversation.

375

He unpacked the one-burner stove, pushed a button; it hissed to life. He placed a huge pot of water on the burner. They would have beef stew for the main course. He was enjoying being the host and doing something good for people. People who could appreciate God's goodness.

He sat, listened to the hiss of the burner, the munching sounds, the quiet laughter, the words of Matthew seeming to keep rhythm with the snip of the barber's scissors. Katie's face spoke of complete calm, happiness. When Matthew had finished reading a flyer, Katie solemnly spoke. "The Holy Spirit is here, Matthew!"

"I know, Katie." He did hear a showboating Katie, but he felt appreciation for a little girl who had been through much. He loved her.

Tim also sensed the presence of God's Spirit. He had sensed Him upon his first waking that morning. He understood the presence as he stood in the naked woods. He had communed with the Spirit, and the Spirit had not left him. Now the Comforter was upon them all—even one who resisted the presence.

"Tell me your story, Josh, since last we parted," Tim implored. Tim bit into a cracker smeared with peanut butter. His salivary glands exploded with moisture. Still, he had to gulp down his juice as the glob of peanut butter stuck in his throat.

"Not much to tell. I helped save a man that night of the quake, both physically and spiritually. To God be the glory. He owned a business, severely damaged. The building became my headquarters. A computer business. That is how I first spread the message. Then the Lord placed an old copier in my hands. I used the plastic scrolls till they ran out and my power tap was discovered. My patron, a Hebrew man, was captured, tortured. He never gave up my location or our friends. He is in heaven now.

"I went back further into history—to the printing press. The State museum had no need of it. Probably the bureaucrats still don't know it's missing. I hauled it away into the country. My first paper was from an arts and craft store. When this type of store were all scavenged, I made paper from the dead trees. The Lord's people plastered the city with the flyers."

Matthew held his pile up to Josh. Tim saw Mat's smile and was thankful for the happiness his son was feeling.

"Yes, Matthew. The same ones." Josh paused, thinking of the men and women who had died to send those flyers. "The printing press eventually broke and was unusable for quite a time—but we had reams of flyers already printed but not yet circulated."

"What of the airwaves?"

"Too dangerous. Though I did interrupt the electrascreen for a brief message—and also the radio bands."

"Have you heard anything from the outside? Washington, Europe?" Tim asked.

"Just what everyone hears. My connections with Israel were severed long ago. Because of the information I…we…have, we can see the true story behind the electrascreen propaganda.

"The Antichrist—the beast, the leader of the European Federation—is now the head of the Church; the authority given to him by the last and final pope. He is collecting his kingdom through the microchip. Do not allow these to be implanted."

"We didn't! We didn't!" Katie gushed her words quickly as if still in competition with her brother. She realized her competitiveness and refrained from the gushing. She added, "Matthew and Daddy killed the men!"

"Good, good. It is good your dad and brother had the wisdom. Soon Christ will come to us. In much less than two years, I believe."

Shivers of fear and apprehension went through Tim. Josh continued speaking.

"Be vigilant in these last days. The beast will do all he can to confuse you. His prophet predicted this rainfall and says the droughts have ended. Many believe." Josh's eyes saddened. "These are the Lord's disciples," he said of the people around him. "We have been using your grandfather's house as a refuge for the last month—we come and go. We are organizing a public meeting, a revival service, to be held north, along the river, when the floodwaters subside. Then, we will go back into the city and openly preach the gospel one last time."

"Why, Josh? You won't utter two sentences before your people are taken away to be tortured or killed. God isn't asking you to commit suicide." A desolating sadness overcame Tim as he realized the finality and the brutality of the forces against the Lord's people.

"No, He doesn't ask, but we are compelled. Besides, suicide is not an accurate word. We've bribed gang members, leaders of zones. They might hold true to their agreements."

Tim said nothing. Josh was still a fool. Yet, it was this fool and his flyers that had given Katie and Matthew hope, accurate information for their souls; had given them the strength to not just survive but to remain good and loving through this hell on Earth. Whatever had been good in man was still to be found in Josh and his people and nowhere else. Tim knew God had made the difference; that was the only conclusion that could be reached. Knowing Christ, abiding in Him was life and truth.

The water was boiling. He threw the contents of six packages into the water. The aroma of beef stew was immediate—eliciting sounds of approval from the gathered. The robin looked down on the proceedings from a nearby branch.

Why wasn't God insignificant to these people gathered? For the same reason the Lord was in Tim's life. He had called them out of the confusion of the deceiver's lies, called them out of the world of men, called them out of their flesh. Once called out, you could only look upward, embrace the promises of the One, the Great I Am, who called you. They who were so convinced of eternal life, of a heaven, that they would follow a lifestyle that could only lead to misery, torture, death. Love? Did they love their fellow man that much? Tim wondered if he could die a martyr, be tortured for another man, woman, child. Only his own, only his seed, part of his being, could elicit sacrifice. That people would die for ideas…ideas were merely words, sounds made with tongue and mouth, sounds that blew away in the wind. Words were merely scratches on a surface. No; from the beginning of man's creation, men had died for ideas. "In the beginning was the Word, and the Word was with God, and the Word was God."

The scent of the beef, potatoes, carrots, peas rising from the stew brought back memories of happier times, camping trips with the family, geology field camps. No mosquitoes, no annoying bugs of any kind on this camping trip. He wanted to make this known and then remained silent. In a way, it was sad that so much of creation was dying or dead. He stirred the stew, turned down the burner flame.

"Tell us the future, Josh."

"As it is written in God's word. The power of the heavens will be shaken; the moon will turn blood red; the sun, black. We are in the time of the final judgments—the bowl judgments of Revelation. Boils upon the skin, some kind of plague that will not affect us. The oceans are nearly dead. Perhaps the volcanic ash is responsible. Even the spring waters are contaminated—because of the chemicals the Antichrist used to create rain? The sun will become ever hotter upon the earth. They say complete darkness will come, but I take that as symbolism for spiritual darkness. Fiery hail will come, more meteors upon the earth. The sun will return with a heat that will scorch the earth. The heavens will roll up like a scroll.

"The battle of Armageddon is near, the armies moving toward their appointed place and time. I believe the Antichrist will scour the earth for more men for his army. Christ with his angels will descend from heaven. Then it is finished." Josh searched Tim's eyes. "Are you ready?"

Tim looked Josh in the eyes. "I am almost there."

"No, you are there. Believe." Josh looked deeply into Tim's eyes. "Hurry, brother. Hurry, brothers and sisters; strengthen your hearts with God's word." Josh ran his eyes among the gathered, his cognizance rested on Mary, he could not discern her path—her course of action.

Tim rose quickly, stirred the stew again. He rummaged in his cache for eating bowls, utensils; Katie began handing out the disposable bowls and spoons. Words of thanks came from each of the partakers as Tim ladled out the stew. "God is good" filled the quiet. Silence descended as the last bowl was filled. Tim popped open a vacuum-packed loaf of whole wheat bread. Enough for each person to receive two thick slices. The bread smelled as if it had just come from the oven; in the sterile air, the scent was overwhelming. He sat back against the massive tree trunk, broke his bread into the stew. All the faces beamed with delight, thanksgiving; even Mary's face seemed to possess a joy.

Amid the slurps, the sound of plastic on plastic, the long draws on the apple juice, the beating wings of the robin were heard. He alighted before them, filling on the cracker crumbs, the dropped peanut butter.

Matthew and Katie were the first to receive seconds, then Mary, then the others. The pot was sopped clean with bread. The bowls were licked. The bodies sank back, the eyes dreamy. No one could remember when their stomachs had last been full. No one desired more.

Josh lay back on the earth, his head propped by his pack, and spoke. "Come to the meeting, Tim. Follow the river north; at the town once known as Dauphin, go to the next mountain; by the river's edge, you will see the gathering. Two days from now. We will feed all present."

"We may come." Josh saw the debate within Tim's thoughts.

"Please, Dad," begged Matthew.

"Yeah, please," said Katie.

"We will see." Tim wondered if Mary would agree to attending.

The conversations died; the bodies became lethargic as the full stomachs tugged at the minds for sleep; eyes closed, sleep came. Silence surrounded them, silence for miles. Even the robin slept. The sun beat down; in half sleep bandannas, sweaters, shirts were pulled over faces. By midafternoon the heat had awakened everyone. A grave must be dug, a eulogy given for the memory of Emily and for the body waiting for that time to once again support Emily in her eternal life.

***

The heat pulled sweat from the bodies of the men and women digging the grave. The work spread among so many was not taxing to their strength. Tim and Mat found the headstone with the legible numbers and carried it back to the gravesite of Emily. Laid facedown and flush with the surrounding earth, it would provide a barrier, along with gathered rocks, to any wolves passing through.

The sun darkened over the earth even as its arc across the sky was not yet completed. The heat did not lessen. The people collected around the burial site as Tim carried the frail and undersized body of the tightly wrapped Emily from her place of waiting. He had preserved her, in the wait for this moment, under the earth in an eroded alcove along the creek bed's banks. With solemnity, Mat, standing within the grave, reached up and took the body of Emily from his kneeling father and placed it at the bottom of the pit. His father pulled him easily from the pit. Josh had his plastic-paged Bible open. He looked upon the crowd and at Mary, surrounded by women but distant and aloof. All gathered had approached her and given their words of encouragement and condolence, and she had accepted gracefully.

"Listen to the words of Job, a man acquainted with grief and trials. A man who lived before Moses, in the time of the patriarchs—perhaps four thousand years ago. The book of Job, chapter nineteen, verses twenty-three to twenty-seven."

Josh read:

"Oh, that my words were recorded, that they were written on a scroll,

that they were inscribed with an iron tool on lead, or engraved in rock forever!

I know my Redeemer lives, and that in the end he will stand upon the earth:

And after my skin has been destroyed, yet in my flesh shall I see God:

I myself, will see him, with my own eyes—I, and not another.

How my heart yearns within me!

"Job has seen our Lord. Emily sees our Lord. And soon…very soon, they and we will see Him stand upon the earth the King of His rightful kingdom. So let us not lose heart. And when we stand with the redeemed, let us seek Emily Jennings, though she will be complete in her happiness, and say, 'Well done, good and faithful servant.' Now, Mary, come and tell us about Emily."

Mary came to the front of the gathering and stood beside Josh. "When the request came for us—our family—to parent Emily. I wanted to say no. I saw so much hurt…could feel her contorted and twisting emotions. Perhaps, I feared mental illness within her. I was worn from keeping myself and our family whole in body and mind. I didn't want her.

"Then I saw the wounds, scarred and scabby, on her back and legs, when she fell asleep and I was preparing her for bed…She had a mother and father and was an only child when the troubles came. Her father was killed in a robbery attempt a year after the day of the quake. A year later, her mother was raped to death before Emily's eyes by a gang of thugs. Emily really didn't understand the act; she only saw brutality. She was not raped, thank God. But she fell into the hands of an abusive caretaker who whipped her for the slightest reason, who took half of Emily's food ration for herself. Then, Carl Stasic saved her and offered her to us. I loved her with all I had within me, as did my family. She was my joy and my purpose, and I knew God had given her to me."

The narrative had been forthright, and the voice matter-of-fact and calm.

"Where is God in all this, in the story of Emily? Can anyone tell me?" Mary asked as she scanned the assembled. It was a plea and an accusation. "You, Joshua, savior—you have all the answers. Answer me! Why was she punished for the sins of the world? A six-year-old child, who then suffered for two more years?"

Joshua heard and was not angered. Emily had been Mary's purpose in life in a world gone mad. Satan's scheme was to blame God for Satan's

actions, to separate man from God and gather man into the Satanic kingdom. He raised his hand to show that he would answer. He held his hand
high as he waited for God to give him wisdom and words.

"God our Father is the only source of love in this world. Humanity
has turned its back on God's love, and chaos and hate flourish. We are
not *of* the world, but we are *in* the world, and so too we suffer. Emily
suffered because of humanity's evil. God will not force His creation to
love Him. We must willingly come to Him. Emily went to Him. Emily
knows the Lord Jesus. Emily has a new life in a world where Christ
reigns and there is no evil. Her mind is healed from the past—as if it
never happened. She has an eternal future. She learned of Christ from
your family and you, Mary. Do you think that had no worth then and
to Emily now?

"All our pain on this earth is momentary, though it appears enormous
and consuming. Each day of eternal life makes the moment of earthly
pain a small, transitory event."

Josh was attempting to take away the reality of her pain. Mary wanted to hate that which caused the pain. And God, ultimately, caused her
pain—not humanity. Humanity merely followed the script; it was not
the author. He could have written it some other way. She didn't like
His script or Him. "There is no eternal life, Joshua. There is this life of
hell now, and then there is death. Nothingness. This Bible myth is just a
subterfuge of a godlike power to keep the little human figures busy—it
is an amusement of God, the longest-running series on His electrascreen.
How bored He would be without us!"

A woman Mary's age spoke. "My family is dead, Mary. My husband,
murdered by thieves. My son, killed by a missile fired by an Islamic
terrorist group. My son had been conscripted by a false government for
an evil world leader. My daughter died from a drug addiction—the only
way she knew to cope after a gang rape. You blame a pure and loving
God for the actions of man and Satan."

"Satan is a creation of God," Mary retorted.

"As is mankind," the woman said.

Mary understood the implications—created beings had choices. "Why did God set it up this way? Why did He force us to choose? Why does He play with our hearts?"

The woman spoke. "He's not playing. The very pain we feel is proof this is no game. God knows the pain of losing a Son. He is sharing this life with us, fully committed in emotion, heart, soul. This is the way it has to be."

Josh saw his disciple, Sandra, falter. He would carry the burden. "Mary, the scoffers of Jesus's day used this very argument. That He casts out demons by Beelzebub—the demon, himself. They could not comprehend that you don't need to be evil to have authority over evil. A house divided cannot stand."

"Of course it can stand—forever, if a liar wishes. And no side gains ascendency. One could make the argument it is collapsing now and again will be rebuilt. A continuing horror; round about, we go," Mary said. "You are all going to die—permanently die—and it all means nothing. And even if this God can keep your lives going a little while longer, He will tire of you. He used you for His amusement, and He will destroy you from His boredom. I've had enough."

Sandra had regained her strength and took up the challenge. "You have made yourself of purer motive than God. We in our sufferings do not amuse Him; He loves us. He suffered and died on the cross to show His love. He has endued within us all His strength of motive, character, and love—we are made in His image, and that is tangible, everlasting. God's substance is pure and good. You are momentarily stunned by the pain you feel and believe a lie. Let us pray for you."

"No. I am tired and want to rest. Good luck to you all. I have no anger toward you." Mary turned and calmly walked back to her sleeping area, a rain fly stretched between two tree trunks with her bedding beneath; a downed tree acted as a partial wall.

Tim brought Josh back to the task of burial. "Let's cover the grave and conclude the service. Mat, help me shovel." The dirt was cast into the grave, first hitting the covered body and slapping the plasticized material in which Emily was wrapped. Katie began to weep for her mother. Josh opened his Bible to John 11: 25 and read. "Jesus said to her, 'I am the resurrection and the life. He who believes in me will live, even though he dies; and whoever lives and believes in me will never die.' Do you believe this?"

"We believe," answered the people in unison.

"I believe," Tim spoke aloud, trailing behind the others. His heart was in agony at Mary's denial of faith. He had neglected her in his goal to keep Mat, Katie, and Emily alive and learning of Christ. He had seen her only as a partner in this endeavor—not as a woman who was hurting and lost. How could he bring her back? His eyes looked into Josh's eyes, which stared into his.

Josh answered the anguish on Tim's face. "Pray unceasingly. Remind her of her worth, the journey you two took when first you met and married. Tell her of your need for her. Every mind born has its reason not to Love God and accept His Kingship. Every mind born fights His authority. Emily was never Mary's child, but God's. She must believe in His goodness, His purpose, His love. Bring her to that love."

Tim's eyes left Josh's gaze, the chin fell, he went into himself. He had been torn in two, and the half that was Mary was writhing in desolation.

***

The people of God gathered up their packs, filled their water containers and canteens from the well, quietly thanked Tim and his family for their generosity, silently filed into the dead woods, headed west toward the river.

CHAPTER 27

Tim watched his company as they quietly assumed their hiking order, quietly cinched straps, buttoned pockets, adjusted belts. A few members made last-minute adjustments to shoe tightness or looseness and then resumed their positions. A handful of whispered words were spoken. Smiles lit faces in an aura of goodness. They praised God, and the name of Mary Johnson was on their lips. She would not be lost to Satan's lies! She would know peace! She was of the redeemed! They spoke these words to Tim, Mat, Katie, and Mary as they walked by in their traveling order. They grasped the hands of the Johnsons in solidarity to the Truth that was coming. Then they began to sing a melody with words of strength, hope, assuredness.

He watched the column, hands raised in praise, meander through the standing dead trees; saw the living line curve around the large, tangled trunks of blown-down trees; saw the line rise ever so slightly at the gentle ridge and saw each individual sink over the crest. And then they were gone. Yet, the sound of their song continued, carried to heaven by the angel bands.

The silence around his family was a living thing, so palpable that it squeezed their bodies, encased them in an embrace. He knew this was the presence of their God. Father was right here with them, had always been, and always would be. The time of rebellious man was coming to a tumultuous climax, and he sensed the hard times coming to his family even as he was thankful to his Father for the grace already shown. With the strength of his Father, he would gather up his family and endure to the end. Mary would be a part of it all, as she was part of him, and he could not leave her behind.

In time, he rose, drew water from the well. They washed their clothing in the bathtub in the farmhouse. The clothes were hung to dry within the house—there was no breeze outside the house, and why alert any passing brigands? Refilling the bathtub water, they took baths in solitude in the cool, refreshing well water. Tim and Mat allowed water to heat in the sun and then shaved. Even Mary and Katie had the luxury of shaving legs.

They lounged as a family within the trees, backs against logs or standing trees. Tim, Mat, and Katie remained close to Mary. They wished her mind to be occupied with them. They knew her mind should not go inward, where the voice of Satan lay in wait. They could smell the fragrance of soap on their bodies, smell the fresh scent of laundry detergent on their clothing. Tim collected wood from the trees. Using a hatchet, he split much of it; the sun dried the wood's dampness and the punky wetness of rot. When darkness descended, he lit a small fire—the size of two hands. He had little fear of marauders at night in this desolate place. The land was so silent any movement could be heard for hundreds of yards, and he had his weapons. He thought drones would fly mostly over the populated areas, perhaps occasionally flying over the uninhabited regions to assure those in charge that bandit gangs had not formed.

Katie and Matthew remembered songs from the Camp. They remembered songs they had sung with the Smith kids and Emily, when the disc player had been working, and they'd had private worship services almost daily. The antiquated songs that spoke of Jesus and His redeeming love and saving grace. Tim moved to the side of brooding Mary, took her hand and held it in his as Katie began to sing plaintively and deeply, her emotion giving forth a tone that pierced the soul. She sang of her love of Christ and His love for mankind. Tim squeezed the hand gently, wishing to find Mary's thoughts and emotions. He sensed she enjoyed his touch and the gentle messaging of her fingers. She spoke. "Your daughter can sing."

"She's yours, too." Tim was saddened at the desire to divide what was whole, their family. He had watched her face as she spoke; the form of her mouth, her gentle, inviting lips pulled him into past memories, when they had been one, when they had a goal to move their family successfully through life, when there had been that deep need to love each other. He took her hand in both his hands, massaged her fingers, her wrist, her forearm. He interlocked his fingers with hers.

"You know I still love you with all my heart," he whispered.

"No, I did not know. It seems you left me for another."

"Who?"

"This phantom God you pursue, along with your children, Josh, and his disciples."

"That is a problem. I apologize that I left you behind in my pursuit. I should have brought you along. I just became overwhelmed." He kissed her on the cheek as she pulled away.

Her pulling away annoyed him. Life had been very tough—life and death concerns daily for Katie and Mat, for his family, which included her. Trying to make sense of all the struggles, pains, fears…no- terrors. Where had Mary been? Why hadn't she seen his need and strengthened him? She had simply disappeared as a mother and wife, watching it all. Tim reproached himself for his thoughts; deep down, he knew that Mary was not well. At some point, she had snapped, and he had not been there to bind her up. He had been so absorbed in himself and the kids that he had forgotten her. He admitted his sin to the Lord in contrition and remorse.

If only God would give him one more chance. If only God's overwhelming power would enter Mary, realign her, snap the brokenness into place, cover the wound with His love. Place His Presence over her, teach her of the Redeemer. Katie had finished her song. Tim and Mat clapped. Mary smiled and spoke. "Well done."

"Thanks, Mom." Katie wished to cry; she had sung it for her mother, hoping—praying—her heart's ache would touch her mom.

"Now, it's my turn," said Mat.

Katie moved to her mother's free side and sat beside her. She took her mother's free hand and held it. Katie kissed her mother's cheek.

"I'm popular tonight," Mary said aloofly.

"You've been popular every night since the day you birthed me," Katie said as she squeezed Mom's hand.

"Wouldn't have known it."

Tim felt his anger rise; Katie didn't deserve such a remark.

Katie ignored the comment. Mom was feeling unloved, abandoned, and she wanted to strike out and hurt in return. This wasn't a time for words. And it didn't matter that Mom's feelings were her own inventions and not reality. Katie nestled nearer her mother and listened to her brother's song. Her brother's passion was deep—he lived for Christ.

Tim was amazed at Mat's voice, the richness and manliness. His son was fully a man at sixteen, a man in wisdom, sincerity, fortitude, love, responsibility—true manhood, not the world's manhood of producing unloved children and holding a job. When the song was done, their applause finished, they talked about happier times. Tim told them of the days of their births, incidents from their childhood they did not remember. Mary listened and did not join the remembrances. Tim could see the pain underneath Matthew's happy exterior caused by Mary's withdrawal. He had a sadness for his mother.

Strange that his children had experienced humanity at its worst, and yet did not talk of the bad but only the good—only the few glimpses of goodness they had witnessed. No bitterness in their hearts. Their goodness and purity shamed him. He thanked God they had been spared the fate of their mother. He was a debtor to God for this. He owed God something, some act, some loyalty, but how could he express it? He wanted to give his Father all that he was for the love that had been shown him and his children.

When it was time to sleep, the kids insisted on being tucked in, as had been done when they were younger. Then, they prayed the prayer that had been taught them as children. After the formal prayer, as was their custom, they spoke to God directly, speaking of people, of events, of hopes. Mary listened from her seat before the fire. Tim stroked their foreheads, kissed them on their foreheads, and said good-night. He went to his own bed. Mary had been sleeping alone since Emily died.

He needed insight from the Lord into Mary's thoughts. He needed a plan to place gentle correcting thoughts into her mind. She had found the God who created emotion—who had emotion Himself. That had been a huge step, seeing God as other than a computer that made creation. God was also the artist Who formed not just the bodies of men and women but shaped their thoughts, their emotions by the world around them and the thoughts within. He gave them choices, courses of action. With the loss of Emily, perhaps Mary saw the artist as vainglorious, cruel, delighting in His own power to destroy and hurt—as if His creation belonged only to Him and not to the beings whom He taught to love others as themselves. In Mary's eyes, perhaps God was an adolescent kid who wanted it His way, who thought He had no need to obey His own rules.

Tim awoke in the stillness of predawn. A mist clung to the ground. He smelled the ashes of the fire, the punky wood. The robin was asleep in its perch on the nearest tree. The kids slept peacefully. He sat up in the trapped warmth of his sleeping bag, felt heat escaping, tucked in an end. The coolness surrounded his upper body. He looked over at Mary's bag. Mary was gone. He scanned the woods; no sight of her, and no sound. Why would she leave now? Here, in the middle of nowhere? What could be gained by leaving now? Had the sharing of food yesterday been the cause of her departure? Or had the talk of old times left her feeling guilty, bitter? Or with the death of Emily, did she feel a false freedom or false emptiness—as if her family did not need her? Tim remembered that he had had that feeling once—when they were rescued by Stasic. Or did she just want to hurt those who loved her?

He rose, searched her bag for a note. None. She had taken her ruck and rations. She had left the living picture behind; her most treasured object. He searched for her trail, and beyond the tracks of Josh's people, he found it. She was headed west along the mountain. Then, at the river, he knew she would move south toward Harrisburg. The predawn lightened the darkness; illumination was cast onto his thoughts.

She would attempt to sell the information on the coming gathering of believers to the Church's men. Yes, she would do this. Her children no longer meant anything to her; motherhood had died within her. She had no love for her husband. Mary was all that mattered to Mary. Mary's full stomach, Mary's warm clothes, Mary's home, Mary's appeal to men. No, it wasn't about Mary's comfort and happiness—Mary wanted to hurt her loved ones to prove the powerlessness of their God, to show them how much she hurt. She would never turn her family over to outsiders. No, she would turn them in fully convinced she was helping them, even as she hurt them.

He dressed quickly, placed the machine pistol in his ruck, then awoke Matthew.

"Stay here with your sister. I left the shotgun, right beside you. Don't let anyone approach. Your mother ran off. I'm going to bring her back."

"Okay." Matthew was wide awake.

"If I'm not back in two days, bury what little supplies remain and go to the meeting on the river."

"Okay." Matthew stared into his dad's eyes and wondered if he would see his father—or mother—again.

Tim moved quickly; his body felt strong, almost superhuman. He had been living at starvation level so long he had forgotten the sensations of health. The strength he had built up from the day of feasting would now be expended in the chase. He would reason with her, and she would return with him. What if she would not return with him? He did not have the strength to carry her. But he couldn't leave her. What if she were caught by the authorities and drugged and told them of the meeting by the river? Could he kill her? Could he tell the kids she had been attacked by wolves? What had happened to the woman he had once loved, who had been faithful, dutiful, self-possessed, optimistic? He moved determinedly down the valley, amazed at his speed.

From the end of the valley, on top of a barren ridge, he looked to the south. His view was blocked by the high mountain ridge that had ended at the river. He wished his eyes could turn corners. The avalanche-prone path around the mountain was boulder strewn and debris filled. It would be rugged and dangerous. He could discern the spot where Emily had died—the boulder that killed her had not rolled far. He picked up his pace, moving determinedly, developing a rhythm in his movement, seeming to dance around boulders, stones, trees and over crevices.

Far off to his left, he could see a sliver of the city in the distance. In the ruins of the city, he saw movement, reflections from metal, glass. Big machines working, pushing debris away, he guessed. What a scene of desolation. No trees, no greenness, no undestroyed buildings. Just rock, debris, the shells of buildings, dust trails rising lazily, the glimmer of water mirages on roads, the oppressive heat of the sun, vultures circling in a cloudless sky.

Looking down on the river road, beside the commuter tracks that once carried him to and from work, a figure in a brown jacket walked. Mary—appearing as a speck of brown indistinguishable from a deer or a wolf. She had an extensive lead on him; if he walked in pursuit, he would never overtake her. She must have left their camp within an hour of his falling asleep. If he walked, she would be at the first sentry post and under the authority and protection of the State well before he caught up to her. The Church was generous to informants and spies. He ran down the slope in pursuit.

He was upon the road, running at the methodical pace of determination, when he heard vehicles behind him. How long since he had heard so many vehicles? Since the rebellion, yes, since the convoy into the city. Were they coming after him? He turned to look behind. Coming from the east, dropping down from the high road by the mountain, military vehicles. Scout cars followed by tanks, moving at a cautious but quick pace. As the column lengthened, he saw trucks behind the tanks.

The base-gray vehicles, unpainted from the factory, all bore the symbol of the Church blazoned in scarlet. No time for paint or no money—or no need—gray was the color of the world now. The figures in the vehicles were dressed in the black uniforms of the Church, not the camo of the US military. He moved to the shoulder of the road, began walking. Then dodged into a debris pile and hurriedly covered his weapon with debris.

A scout car passed. His neck tingled in fear, the hairs standing on end. These men were well fed, had health and weapons, could do to him what they wished. Weak and powerless, he was at their mercy. He prayed they would not stop. The men in the first vehicle did not glance back at him. The exhaust smelled sweet in his nose. Something hit him violently in the back but did not knock him forward. Flat and heavy. He turned; on the ground was a food package. A soldier, a boy, in the second scout car, smiled goofily and savagely gave him the finger. Tim ignored the gesture, read the message attached to the heavy package. Compliments of the Church, promises of more food.

He picked up the package, began to run again, waving at the convoy as if overjoyed. He lost sight of Mary around the corner of a pile of ruins. She had been waving to the convoy, trying to get someone to pick her up. He hoped the men didn't have the lust to stop for her. When she had sighted him, she had begun to run.

The towering trucks hummed by on their cushions of air. So many trucks…what did this mean? These men, this food? He rounded the ruins of warehouses; Mary had collapsed along the shoulder of the road. The last vehicle, marked with a red cross, slowed but did not stop. He walked, dizzy from the run. He saw that she was weeping with an overwhelming emotion. He hadn't thought her capable of tears. Her utter distress wrenched compassion from his soul. She was speaking as she looked down upon the ground; he could not hear her words. The walk to her side seemed so long.

"Don't kill me! Don't kill me! Oh, please don't…please."

He crouched down beside her. "Why would I want to kill you, Mary?" Her own lips would condemn her or set her free.

"Because I stole the food; because I left you. Because I haven't been a good mother, a good wife. Please don't kill me. Please…"

He stood and momentarily lost his balance from dizziness. "Let's get up, beautiful. I still love you. Mat and Katie still love you…" He lifted her to her feet by placing his arms under her arms. Her body slipped close to his, he smelled her hair. The fine strands were still thick. He had loved to caress her head when they were dating; feel the fine hair between his fingers and pull on the roots and watch her smile in delight. He hugged her and felt her thin frame. He helped her from the shoulder of the road back to a pile of twisted tree trunks deposited by the flood. He spread his jacket on a damp trunk; he sat her down, straddling the trunk. He sat in the same fashion before her. They were hidden from any traffic passing on the road. He could never harm her. To protect his family, Josh, and his people, would she need to die? Please, Lord, give me the words, he begged. Would her death be the act he owed God?

He held her hands, his hands covering her two hands together. He looked into those eyes, haunted and in pain. The lips beckoned him to past memories of delight and oneness; the thin neck, the small and soft earlobes recalled a resting place.

"Mary, I love you more than the day I married you. You have been a fantastic mother and wife during the worst times Earth has ever known or will know. These have been dark days of fear and anxiety, but of hope and joy as well. Mat and Katie adore you and know how you have shaped their characters—optimism, loyalty, kindness, concern for others. Those are all traits that certainly didn't come from me." His words seemed inadequate.

"Jesus loves you. He is the proof that God loves you. God is a God of emotion, but no evil resides in that emotion. His character is pure goodness, and His emotion is righteous and good. He would not ask you to endure if there was not some great and overwhelming goal before us. You and I must bring our kids home, together, as partners…to that finish line…where there is peace and rest…and great and glorious will be the celebration. We are so near." His tears flowed freely. To lose his friend, his helper, his confidant so close to the finish. Her absence would ravage his soul—leave him lifeless.

"I'm tired," she said, her face flat, emotionless.

"So is God…in a sense. Tired of a humanity that flees from Him and seeks all that is evil. Those who wish to love Him have to live in this neighborhood of chaos. All He is doing is moving us to His new neighborhood, filled with people who love Him. The old neighborhood and its inhabitants will be destroyed. This is the appointed time in history. Fantastic as it seems, this is the appointed time. We must endure to the end. Come with me to your new home, it wouldn't be home without you."

"Very clever you are." She laughed unaffectedly. She was happy that he had pursued her. She still had power and worth. "I've been moved to so many neighborhoods in these past years—you know your audience." She grasped his forearm, lovingly massaged the warmth of his muscle. He watched her eyes sparkle like they had when they were in their courtship.

"But my cleverness is only truth," Tim said. "And Emily will be in the new neighborhood with us. You've seen what men and women are really like—just remember those times in the work camp."

"I concede." It was there that she had become a cunt, seen as a pleasure body—not as a person, not as a woman. Women had no value in that male world of carnality. It was there that she understood the world and humanity was sick and that she had lived in a fantasy world that didn't exist. Yes, destroy the world; but was there another life waiting?

Tim felt he had reached her analytical core, her soul, and in this moment, whether brief or enduring, the Lord was winning her heart. In this moment, when Mary was contrite, weak, stripped of mixed emotions, she was sincere. The Mary he had married was before him. Only if she could remain weak, broken. Only if the truth within her emotion could overcome the bitterness. He wiped her brow, removed her tears with his fingers. He spoke with deep sadness.

"Remember how we met, Mary? At church. I arrived late, and my regular seat in the back was taken. I hadn't known you existed. I sat beside you. Oh, you smelled of sage, wore that soft-blue dress. The sparkle in your eyes—kind, mischievous, knowing. I knew you were the one. When we first kissed, your lips invited me into your soul. Oh, you could kiss."

She was smiling, remembering with him; she stole a glance into his eyes. His eyes were dreamy, happy within a world of sadness. He continued.

"The first time we made love, I felt you give me your heart and soul, no holding back; you were innocent, tender, vulnerable. You trusted me.

You have always been a great mother, a great wife. So many years of happiness, Mary. Two wonderful children."

She looked directly into his gaze. "Kiss me, Tim. Kiss me like you used to."

She yearned for him and those times past when life was good. She had been a good wife, a good mother.

He kissed her, felt the smallness, the weakness of her lips, smelled her sensuous breath. His heart was breaking; he had so much more to say. He held her tightly, kissed her with the tenderness and love of the past times. He felt the return of his love and a yearning. He remained within the allure of her presence.

She spoke softly. "Do you know why I left?"

"No." He wondered why she needed to tell him now.

"Because I am not the same Mary. These times have ruined me, made me evil, cruel, selfish. I know what I am and cannot change. I can only bring you and the kids down, can only hurt you." She lied; she had begged God to give Emily life, and He had not. That's how much Daddy God loved His child Mary.

"Mary! You *are* the same woman—kind, loving, giving. Even as God is the same God—kind, loving, giving. The deceiver is casting a false narrative before your consciousness. He was a liar from the beginning. He projected his evil character and motivations on God, and in your bitterness, you let them in."

"Ah, the Satan narrative—in Satan, all evil lies."

"Yes, so simple. God allowed Satan his rebellion, and Satan wants followers. God allowed Satan to continue because God wanted humanity to willfully and purposely choose Him and His values. Like children who are of age at a divorce: Who do you want to live with, Timmy? The person who lets you stay up late, eat anything, and be nasty and evil to everyone? Or the person who sets standards of right and wrong?"

Mary chuckled. "My clever man, how you make the complex simple."

Tim laughed with a joy that had long been missing from life. The phrase *my clever man* had been used throughout their courtship. That one phrase given honestly, sincerely had bestowed upon him the confidence to pursue her.

Mary's voice now came without emotion and with a decidedly cold pragmatism. "Where is life leading in these final days? The authorities know we are murderers. The storm troopers who first came to our door had body cams. The computers used by the Church's men have our data in as the last entry."

Her change of subject sent apprehension through his mind. Had she been beguiling him? Letting him speak and pretending to accept his truth? Allowing him to bask in his insightful stories? Mary had a great cleverness that sometimes seemed to be cunning. What web had he fallen into? Her mind was still sharp, knowing the data was in the computers.

"Jones was to wipe out the data entry on the computers. She would erase the body cams if they had survived the grenade blasts."

Why was he so certain of Jones's thoroughness and loyalty? Mary wondered. Had they been lovers? "Kiss me, Tim. Kiss me like you used to, when life was good." She drew close to him, lifted his big hand with her small hands, placed his hand upon her heart. You couldn't erase body cams. She slipped his hand into her shirt, onto her bare skin. Her lips were upon his. The kisses were sexual; she wished to consume him.

She hadn't replied to his statement about Jones and the body cams. Why not? She hadn't shown sexual desire for him in weeks. Was it as she said: his cleverness and her returning heart? Or had she realized she had succeeded in her beguiling, and his defenses were down. What did she hope to gain? His hand slipped from her breast. He spoke as he leaned back from her, then slid a leg over the tree trunk seat and stood. His legs had been tingling, the blood flow ceasing, and he was afraid of the direction of her words. He saw something in her eyes, an inward look—she seemed to ask herself whether she had been caught.

"I'm tired, Tim. Emily took the last of my goodness, my caring. If the Lord whom you worship had raised her from the dead, I would still be with you. I pleaded with Him, and He was deaf. How much time and energy would it have taken almighty God to give her life? He would not do that for me? You and the kids can make it on your own; you admit your time is short. Go on without me. I don't believe life as we know it is coming to an end. This is just a dark age in the reign of humanity. There have been many. All I need to do is repent of my past contacts, go to a reeducation camp—at most—and receive the microchip. I will honestly tell them I don't know where you are. They won't waste truth serum on me. Food is pouring into the city. The Church has brought the rain. Look here!" She reached down to the ground; topsoil collected before the trunks.

"Life will sprout from this. Not from your invisible God, but from out of God. The God within man's intelligence. God, our helper. When your God does not return, you will find me waiting for you and the kids."

Tim's mind was scrambling for answers. Had all her newfound knowledge of God faltered on a disbelief that the end was near? Or because she just could not believe that humanity was depraved and worthy of destruction? Or was she denying that *she* was depraved and rebellious, with no spark of untainted goodness within? Or was it just simple bitterness that a wish had been denied and unfulfilled?

"Mary, how do you know the Lord hadn't saved Emily from a worse future? A disease unto death, or a horrible adoptive family, or a violent death at the hands of men? She's in a better place. Where we all will be very soon. Why aren't you happy for her? Why does your happiness need to be fulfilled over her happiness? Are you selfish in this, Mary? By my Lord, my God, Mary, can't you walk with us one more year? If the end does not come, we will give ourselves up as a family. You've got the grit, woman! You're an O'Brien—your culture, your people have survived conquests, famines, persecutions for centuries. You as an individual are the toughest woman I know. Stay with us. We love you. Will these others love you? Yes, they'll love to take advantage of you, rape you. You, yourself, know the hearts of the average citizen—think of the work camp. Men and women with their hands in their pants at every free moment, every filthy and domineering thought of the greatest perversity uttered from their lips. You've learned so much of character and the goodness of God—you *know* He cares. Trust Him and live in His world forever." His fervor was spent.

His children, they were the center of his life, they were his meaning. She had been the mother of the family, his children's mother. She would turn them in. No, she would get them back, that would be part of the deal. But the Church's men wouldn't honor such a deal. She was the fool. His persuasive words couldn't bring her back, his clever arguments couldn't bring her back. These things had not brought him to God. The Holiest Spirit of God set free at Christ's death had brought him home, in his right mind. How could he give her the Spirit of God Himself?

She saw his momentary confusion. "I'm standing up," she said. "I'm walking away. I don't have the strength to fight you. You would have to carry me back. Do you have the strength or the will? No…and it would be futile. Do you have the heart to kill me, your wife? Who shared your being, your bed, birthed your children, raised them? No. It is what you should do, but this Christ has made you weak. Good-bye, Tim."

She stood, arrogance and confidence in her eyes. Swung her leg over the trunk, her head high, and began walking.

A rage possessed Tim. Her haughtiness, her disdain for him and her children provoked his soul. The authorities would drug her, and she would turn in her family. She thought she knew him? He would snap her neck, the bitch. He wasn't going to place the future of his children in her hands. He would kill her now.

As suddenly as the rage came, it broke. Christ did not want her killed. What she thought of him or Christ meant nothing. Her thoughts were the thoughts of a warped mind, bent by weariness, holding to nothing but her own self-preservation. She wanted life so badly she would ruin, destroy the only meaning in life—love; Love for her husband, her children, and those people whose God made them kind and good. She was the weak one—throwing a tantrum at God, her Father, to spite Him who knew all things and loved His children with an ingenuous love and protected them with a piercing awareness. She was ruled by her flesh and her desire to live comfortably, secure in that flesh. That flesh that needed food, shelter, warmth. She was the marathoner who quit fifty yards from the finish when even crawling over the line would bring God's victory—not of man-made garlands, medals, and ribbons but of the imperishable honor of faithfulness. The heavenly hosts waited on the sidelines to aid and encourage, the invisible straining for her faith to make them visible.

He couldn't kill her. He did love her. It was his fault; he had not monitored her walk with the Lord. He had not given all she needed to succeed; he had started too late, given too little, and paused too often. Only the once-in-history event, the Tribulation of the coming end, had broken her. Her will died, and her flesh hurt, and she was human and unable to access the superhuman force of God. If she were to die, it would be by someone else's hand. If God wanted his family destroyed and the band of believers captured and killed, so be it.

He called to her. "Mary."

She turned and stared, waiting. If he was a man, he would come, bind her, and carry her back.

"It is not weakness to love."

She spit at him in the rage he had once possessed, turned angrily, and walked toward the city.

He remained by the tangle of tree trunks. Got on his knees, used the trunk, once a seat, as an altar. He prayed she would never reach the city, prayed she would die, or be disbelieved. Then he prayed that her heart would change, that God would reach into her heart and give her an understanding of it all. He prayed no one would drug her or molest her. Pray for your enemies, said the Bible. He had turned the other cheek. He had let a potential murderess walk, to do her evil. He had done this against all common sense, all earthly knowledge, trusting God.

Should he bind her and bring her back? Simply wait for her to be too weak to resist? He was at his emotional and physical end; barely out of sight, he saw her flag down a military truck and enter the cab. He bowed his head and cried. "Your will be done, Father God."

CHAPTER 28

Two hundred people had gathered on the gentle slope—a beach of gray silt deposited by the river flood. The silt was a mixture of the new volcanic ash and the brown sand flecked with coal dust of the old riverbed. The small beach area, within the recess of a semicircular indentation in the shoreline, was bordered by an ancient, towering retaining wall of brown sandstone, built unknown hundreds of years in the past. The massive brown stones, which once secured a railroad bed, broke their sameness with the arch of a bridge, under which a stream had once flowed into the river.

The solid stone wall had formed a barrier in the flood and was now thick with tree trunks, branches, the smashed hulls of cars, trucks, the remains of homes. The wall and debris secluded the alcove and directed sound toward the river. The massive, bare rock face of a heaved-up mountain ridge loomed above.

The modern canal bed, with its liner of plasticized cement, had been totally destroyed by the quake and washed away by the sludge flood of the recent past. Parts of the plastic bed had been wedged on the rocky ledges of the old riverbed, almost out of sight of the gathering's location and in the middle of the old riverbed.

The mountain seemed to hang over the bank below, promising rock slides for any disturbance of movement or sound. The highway that ran between the river and the mountain had effectively disappeared under debris from the upheaval of the mountain and subsequent avalanches. Only a one-lane road, excavated by military construction crews, cut through the debris field.

Early morning, and the splotched sun had made the beach sand burning hot. All heads were covered, long shirts and pants were worn. Sunscreen had become plentiful and was thickly applied. Exposed skin would blister, suppurate within an hour. Skin cancers had momentarily surpassed the plague as the leading cause of deaths. A hot wind blew from the west, from across the riverbed. On the eastern bank, the river as a moving, flowing entity had ceased days after the flood. Pockets of water sat in stagnating pools. A small trickle of water, from runoff percolating through the strata, came from the under the arch. The pool of water within the alcove, at its deepest, was five feet. A large flat rock sat within the small pondlike alcove. Fully ten feet above the water, it formed the perfect stage. A musician played a guitar. The sediment had settled; the water sparkled and was as hot as newly passed urine.

The view up the wide riverbed to the west and north, between the mountain ridges, was glorious. Water remained in the old channel, the wide channel, prior to the barge way. The fishponds and ag fields built on the old bed had been inundated, and the remains of their retaining walls still held captured water. On the western riverbed, a trickle of water still flowed from the Juniata River and the West Branch of the Susquehanna River, guessed Tim, as he had no knowledge of the new topography of the drainage basin. Sea gulls from the Chesapeake Bay swooped, called over the flatness. No one at the gathering knew the Chesapeake Bay was a silted, stinking dead zone, and no sea gulls would return to that once broad expanse of water. The alcove water lapped the shore of silt. The breeze from the west, though hot, was pleasant and clean, holding the smells of soil and wet wood.

Josh had stationed sentries on the bare mountaintops of successive ridges. The sentries searched the land with high-powered ocular devices for the forces of evil. The greatest accomplishment was the securing of a high-powered ocular device attached to a mini hovering drone. They could see for miles over the bare land, right into the city itself. The gangs had been bribed to leave the gathering in peace. The participants had nothing worth stealing. Only the Church, which was now the State, was to be feared. The one-lane roadway was essentially dead—no trucks moving supplies, no military patrols. What little north-south traffic existed used the highway on the west bank. Air vehicles were no longer feared; no one had seen even a drone in a year. Did spy satellites exist? Even if they existed and reported a gathering, the sentries on the mountain would see the forces coming.

Blankets had been spread on the hot earth or on the horizontal tree trunks. Josh had collected the food parcels that the military convoy had so readily thrown to citizens or simply dropped on the roadsides, and he had given each person attending a parcel. He had huge containers of fresh water for drinking, collected from the percolating mountain runoff and purified with a military-grade purifier his people had found. A latrine had been thrown together with blankets and plastic sheeting. Shoots of grass came from the silt; small and green, they gave false hope. Hunger had broken the suspicion of a poisoning of the parcels and water, and people ate and drank as they watched Josh eat and drink. The faces were boney, worn, and battered; the clothing, abject. The faces were hues and shades of black, white, brown. Loners, groups of twos or threes, nothing larger. Few intact families existed; few had been in existence before the troubles. What bonds held the little groups together? Family ties, emotional needs, love, friendships from work or neighborhood, gang affiliations, bonds of survival or familiarity, sexual lust, perversions?

Tim and his kids sat to the side, near the rear, facing the river and the huge rock—the height of a man, the size of a car—that was the stage. He noticed that paranoia and stress were dissolving as he watched. The good-naturedness of the people was just like before the troubles. It was good to be with people again and almost trust them. To hear the sound of live music delighted his senses. He reached over and tightened the opening to his pack. No need for anyone to see a weapon. With a start, he realized that his compulsive need to guard his weapons had told any thief present where the valuables were located. Katie and Matthew returned to the blanket with crackers and fruit punch and sat beside him.

Josh climbed the rock, spread out his hands for silence. In one hand was a Bible.

"Hear the word of the Lord!"

No preliminaries, like in the times before the troubles. Who knew how long this moment would last?

"Mark 8:34–9:1," he said and then began to read.

"'And he called to him the multitude, with his disciples, and said to them, If any man would come after me, let him deny himself and take up his cross and follow me. For whoever would save his life will lose it; and whoever loses his life for my sake and the gospel's will save it.'"

Tim heard the words and understood. Before, he would have said that everyone suffers in these times; it was a cross to be responsible for two children; Mary was his cross; life, these times had denied him every-thing—a future, a good job. This denial had been thrust upon him. But he was not everyone, and everyone was not carrying his burden. The Lord was looking upon him, not the world. He had come to the place of hurt from which he could not run. He was through with the world the moment he had denied the microchip. He was following Jesus; he was through with himself; his life had been lost; only the word of God was left to comfort, nourish Tim and his family. Christ had won, and he was thankful.

"'For what does it profit a man, to gain the whole world and forfeit his life? For what can a man give in return for his life?'" Josh read.

Christ was talking about the immortal soul. What does a man get for having the good things of earthly life, having his control, but losing eter-nal life? Or was it losing the truth of life, the true values? Why did a man have to choose? Why couldn't he have both? It had been God's design to make life—this world—the choosing ground. Would you obey deception or truth? God or the deceiver?

"'For whoever is ashamed of me and of my words in this adulterous and sinful generation, of him will the Son of man also be ashamed, when he comes in the glory of his Father with the holy angels.'" Josh continued.

This was straightforward. Tim wasn't ashamed of Christ or His words. He was safe on that. He hadn't felt much shame in his life—only as a youth, when he had been ashamed of his mother and father. They acted so boorishly that he didn't like his friends meeting them. Then, he realized they were the only two people on Earth who loved him…well, cared for him. Sadly, within the years of Tribulation, when the mind had time to wander, he had realized that they had never truly loved him. They had loved him for his athletic and scholarly accomplishments, for his belonging to the right group of people, for his popularity with the girls of his age group. All this reflected well on them—as if they had been responsible for the seeming glory that was upon him. God had known truly who he had been and loved him anyway. Where were his father and mother now? He had not given them a thought since the troubles with John and Gramps. Likely, they were dead. Another sin Christ had forgiven—he had not loved his parents.

Christ said He was coming with His angels, and this event was only a year or two away, if he lived to see it. He hoped he would.

From the rock, Josh read, "And he said to them, 'Truly, I say to you, there are some standing here who will not taste death before they see the kingdom of God come with power.'"

The kingdom of God must have begun with Pentecost for it to have come in the lifetime of those around Christ. Was the fulfillment of that kingdom truly coming? The previous passage said so. Christ couldn't be God if He contradicted himself. The kingdom had come already to the human heart, the individual, and soon it would come to the earth with Christ and his angels. As Mat had told him, the reality of the Bible and the Godhead would no longer be in dispute when the legions of angels filled the sky, and all beheld the Christ.

Josh stepped down; another speaker came. Tim wondered if the kingdom of God had come to his heart. Kingdom—vast, expansive, encompassing all that humanity was, did, and produced. No, there was no kingdom of God in his heart. Why wasn't the kingdom in his heart? How would he fit into this new order coming? Matthew and Katie had finished their food, were held spellbound by the words of Josh. The new speaker began. Katie glanced at her father. He didn't understand; she wanted him to know Jesus.

"Dad, man does not live by bread alone, but by every word that God utters."

He smiled. "Thank you, Katie. I live that now."

She guessed that had been a dumb thing to say, not right for the moment. She had to say something. Tim lay back, listened to the new speaker. It was good to hear a voice; silence seemed so much a part of life now. People were too worn to talk, had nothing on their minds but finding the next meal. Minds were so sick, motives so base, communication invariably led to troubles. He was falling into sleep, his arm intertwined in the pack straps. The weapons were security, of more value than gold. Gold was worthless now. He slept.

When he awoke, Katie and Matthew were gone. He scanned the crowd anxiously. He studied the blanket he was sitting upon; something was missing. A cup, a metal cup, belonging to Katie, used for the free fruit drink. Maybe she had taken it with her. He saw his kids in a group by the river. In the currentless backwater, people were being baptized. Katie and Matthew were next in line. She held no cup, nor was there a bulge in her sweater pockets. He looked around him, the faces all innocent.

Katie was about to pull off her sweater then realized the sun would dry it in minutes. Mat was deep in prayer beside her. He watched as Katie was led into the clear water. Three men and a woman were singing a song so old it must have been sung when the first settlers had come to this shore. "Come thou font of every blessing, Tune my heart to sing Thy grace; streams of mercy never ceasing, Call for songs of loudest praise. Teach me some melodious sonnet, Sung by flaming tongues above; Praise the mount, I'm fixed upon it! Mount of thy redeeming love."

Mat knew those settlers had had the same religion, knew the same God. Had the Holy Spirit filled them as he was now being filled? Time was no barrier to God and time had not changed God or the force, quality, character, of His Love. Mercy never ceasing. The Johnsons were among those first settlers. How many had truly heard and known God and loved Him? Mat's great-great-grandfather Jeremiah had known the Lord—and his great-grandfather Gramps, his uncle John, and his dad. And now he knew. They were all bound together, and they would meet in heaven. These feelings were not of blood and lineage, for Josh was as much his blood, his family. Any person in Christ was his family. It was the honor of having someone close, someone you trusted and knew, who had found the precious gift and carried it through the years, passing it on to a new generation, that was the blessing of his ancestors. The questions he would ask! They had carried Christ in their hearts. Mat carried Him, would carry Him through the final moments of this world. To think it would end soon, the long chain of truth—invisible yet tangible—of the greatest worth and yet worthless to the world.

The ages past had had their difficulties, yet this time had been designed to be the worst. There were no restraints on the stupidity of people. This was the difficult time to hold onto Jesus. Mat felt kind of honored—honored that he should be trusted to serve in the toughest of times, during the ugliest moment of history. This was like sports—like being in a must-win game when your team wasn't winning. The game seems lost, your side is injured, hurting, dispirited, and everything your team does seems to fall apart. You've got to trust God, know He wants good for you, and know that victory can happen in one play, one second. You have to pick yourself up, keep your mind on the basics, and perform and carry on. He might lose a play, but He would win this game. Matthew spoke quietly to himself. "God, give me the strength to be true to you and to all who went before me."

"Jesus sought me when a stranger, wand'ring from the fold of God; He, to rescue me from danger, interposed His precious blood," sang the congregation.

Matthew bowed his head, prayed for his sister.

Tim watched Katie go under three times. Her arms shot up after the final dunk, raised to heaven. He heard her voice carry over the water and earth. "Praise God! Praise God!" She eagerly waded to the rocky sandbar and hugged Matthew, before he too was led in. Three times he went under. No hands in the air, no words. Something was different about him in posture, mannerisms. Tim knew his son had been greatly affected by the experience and that the fluttering dove, the shimmering force that was the Holy Spirit—seen yet not seen—had consecrated, sealed, found a permanent home.

Katie hugged her brother again when he emerged from the water. She held his hand as they walked back to their father. Tim was touched by her love, her trust in her brother. Why hadn't the troubles touched her, made her bitter? How could she remain so pure, loving? Who could be against this God Who had created such love in a little girl? Or such love between a brother and a sister?

He had been justified in killing Simmons and his men, though the death struggles sometimes haunted his sleep. He would do all in his power to keep his children in this God, out of the world, out of the grips of the Church. Matthew seemed undisturbed by his part in the killing. Katie began running. Where did she find any spare energy on that starving frame?

"Daddy! Dad!"

She had taken his hand and was pulling him. Her face was pale, slathered in sunscreen. No, her face shone even under her broadbrimmed hat. A great, heartfelt urgency was in her voice. "Come on, Dad! Start a new life. The Holy Spirit is here! Jesus is here! He is!"

"No...no... no. I must remain here. Besides we were baptized by Josh, remember."

She saw him clutching the packs. Ah, the weapons tied him to the spot. Every thief already knew the packs contained something valuable, because of his protective movements. Thieves would suspect guns—something heavy—if he carried them, then deposited them by the river.

"That's not what can save you, Dad. It's Jesus who saves!"

Matthew was now by the blanket. He calmly sat, earnestly studied his father's face. He grabbed a towel from the pack and handed it to Katie to dab the water from near her eyes. They would not need to change their clothes; a dressing area had been set up, but the heat was so intense and the water evaporating from their clothes was cooling. They would be dry in ten minutes. Strange, Tim mused; Matthew seemed a wise old man, wiser than his own father.

"Dad, you should go," Mat said. "I'll stay here."

Tim relented to Katie's pulling, walked down to the water, her hand in his. Her smaller hand had strength, warmth; she eagerly watched his face for expression.

'Don't be afraid.'

He inwardly chuckled. She had no understanding of where he had been in his life. He had killed men with his bare hands, face-to-face; he had gone into combat and slain men by the score. He had conquered every life challenge. How innocent she thought him to be. This was pleasing to him. People were singing. The song was old, ancient.

"Just as I am, without one plea, but that Thy blood was shed for me, and that thou bidd'st me come to Thee; O Lamb of God, I come! I come!"

The man in the water spoke to him. "Do you wish to receive Jesus Christ as your Lord and Savior?"

"I do." His heart was fluttering—Lord and Savior? No? Yes? Of course, Yes. When a doubt would come, he thought of Mat, lost from him in the dust of combat. He could never repay the debts he owed to his God.

"Step into the water."

Tim followed the man. The water felt cool in that deep hole. The man spoke.

"This is the end of the old ways, the death of the flesh. Three times. Here we go. In the name of the Father..." One down. "The Son..." Two down, and water had slipped into his nose. "The Holy Ghost." Up, out of the water. He felt refreshed. Katie was clapping from the shore, then waded in—though her body was shaking from the coolness of the water and the strong heat of the sun upon the flesh—anxious to meet her father.

"See, Dad? What did I tell you?" She put her hand in his, led him back to shore. Matthew was still by the blanket, Josh and two others were by his side, talking. Tim had never seen his daughter so happy. He thanked God for her happiness.

Matthew searched his father's face, his spirit, as he approached. His father—where was he? Fully in or partially in or out? He could not discern. Josh sensed Tim was saved, had been before the ceremony, but was one of many who did not sense a presence. Nor was this feeling necessary. Obedience was what the Lord sought, for that was truly loving God with all your heart, soul, mind, and strength.

"Congratulations. I've got your son and daughter signed up to come into the city and hand out leaflets. Everyone's going," said Josh.

"No, not everyone," Tim said determinedly. "You'll be executed, tortured first. My kids aren't going."

"We won't remain until we are caught. This has been carefully planned. We know where the Church's men are headquartered, know their response time. We are concentrating on one zone, where we have permission, then we'll head out of town before the Church's men arrive."

"You've got to be dreaming! The Church is probably already waiting. Do you think your bribe can match the reward the Church is offering?"

"Tim, there are only a few years left, then the world as we know it will be gone. Years of utter misery. To die is to gain."

Tim held his tongue. He wasn't ready to waste his life—nor his children's lives—in the hopes someone would accept Christ. Imprisonment, torture, starvation, rape, degradation—that was the future Josh was gambling with. Hell, death was an easy thing. Yes, it was good to have Christ. Tim knew he had no love of mankind. Humanity had made the world that he and his family had turned their backs upon. The world, the flesh, and Satan. There were people left in the world who needed Christ, but subtle tactics—quiet, stealthy fishing—would lure them and enlighten them, not throwing heavy nets over the ship's sides, winches creaking, while calling to your crew. Even this open-air meeting was more than Tim thought safe.

Matthew had his vision focused outside their immediate group; he scanned the crowd along the shore, the rugged bank and mountain, the river. He had made this—the constant searching and studying—a habit since his paramilitary training. The enemy was always prowling. He noticed puddles, far out in the riverbed to the west, rippling as if the water was dancing, being vibrated. The ripples, the droplets bouncing, covered a circular area and moved toward shore, even causing the sandbars to vibrate. Earthquake? No, the entire river would be rippling as well as the earth shaking. Fish? The river had no such numbers. Besides, none had broken the surface. Wind? No, this pattern was of deep vibrations, not the wafting pattern of wind on the surface.

As the ripples advanced toward the alcove, touched shore, Mat was overwhelmed with a sense of dread. He grabbed his father and sister by the arms, began pulling them backward. "Let's get out of here."

His father stumbled; Katie fell. Mat fell backward, still clinging to them, tightening his grip. Josh and the others stood transfixed. Matthew pumped his thighs till they burned, dragging his family and himself backward.

The blank looks of Josh and his friends turned to painful grimacing as the earth vibrated, hummed, tingled. Mat felt his legs go numb. With a supernatural burst of strength, he jerked Katie forward. She, in turn, dug her heals into the ground, sitting, pulled at her brother's arm. He seemed glued to the earth. The entire assemblage was upon the ground, save for a few running figures upriver. She was outside the force. Matthew released his father, with his two arms free, Katie pulling at the scruff of his shirt, Mat freed himself. They pulled at their father, whose head had been outside the force field. He was so heavy, and weighed down by the packs, which he had grabbed at the first warning. They strained, felt him moving into freedom. His face was a mask of pain, he cried out in agony. Their father's cry released their desperation to God, their strength flowed from some unknown source, within or without them? Their father was free.

Their hearts pounded in fear, their strength gone, the three lay on the ground, looking into the invisible force field. Josh could not speak, though he saw his friends free. He tried to wave them away but could not.

"Let's go. We can't help them here." Mat was upon his feet, helping his sister and father to rise. He wished to stay. His priority was his family, and his father had yet to comprehend the fullness of Christ and be saved.

They ran downriver, stopped for rest after only a dozen yards, by a pile of logs. The effects of the force field clung to them. Their legs tingled, felt numb and weak. Everyone had heard vague rumors of the military's newest weapon and its use against civilians. As they gasped for breath in the shelter of the debris pile, they saw air platforms swoop over the mountain, land on the roadway above them. Black-uniformed soldiers carrying laser rifles and stun sticks ran from the vehicles.

"Let's get in the water, float downstream." Tim began to pull his family. Mary! Mary was responsible. He cursed himself for not killing her, for listening to Christ, to that weak side of his nature.

"No. Let's go to the retaining wall." Matthew's voice was firm; the safest place was close to the enemy. The river on the east side was just a collection of pools and puddles; no stream flowed between. A few big rocks, rock ledges, tree trunks, and man-made debris offered scant cover. Chances were that someone on the road, with the height advantage, would spot them in the open expanse of riverbed. He grabbed one ruck from his father, pulled out the sawed-off shotgun, slipped the pack onto his back.

They bolted, using flood-deposited logs for cover. Hugging the retaining wall, they could not be seen from above. Mat guessed a squad would come from the south, disperse as a wide net, and drive toward the north, capturing any escapees from the force field. Against the retaining wall might be a storm drain or drainage ditch to provide cover.

Matthew smiled when he saw the cement ditch beside the wall—two and a half feet deep and as wide as a man. Their chances of escape had increased. They moved south, downriver, in a crouch within the ditch, sometimes on hands and knees, hoping to outrun the pincer movement that would surely come from the south. Matthew, in the lead, saw the squad first. Troops were running down the steep embankment onto the gentle bank sloping into the riverbed. He heard the equipment jangling, heard curses. The black uniforms were so dark against the brown rock. The troops immediately fanned out, from embankment to river's edge. The family lay in the ditch.

They heard the men talking to each other, lewd comments of women and booty. The debris of logs, trees slowed them. The man nearest the embankment and their position was straying away from the wall as the wall had collected more debris. He had no desire to wade through the debris and fall behind the advance of his comrades. Matthew thought it likely the man hadn't seen the drainage ditch. If the man discovered them, he would be killed. Then Mat would shoot down the line of men with the shotgun. If he lined them up right, his first two shots might kill and injure many. He could grab their lasers if the lasers had no safety controls to stop their use by an unauthorized person. He would kill with his knife and his bare hands.

The line had moved even with them. A garbled comment came from the river end of the line of men.

"Fuck all of you," came a reply from the man nearest the family's hiding place. They heard the line move past.

Matthew raised his head slowly, warily; the line was closing in on the gathering. He saw other black-uniformed men already at the site. The line had no trail man; clumsy soldiering.

"Let's go," Mat whispered. The family moved in erratic swiftness, taking what the terrain allowed. They heard movement on the road above them—men in web gear and packs and vehicles were repositioning. Then talk and engines shut off.

The drainage ditch ended at a heavy sewer grate; the wall tapered off into the slope. The river and the roadway touched only a short distance away. They had to cross the road, head into the valley jammed with forest debris. Debris that had washed down the valley, destined for the river, till the high embankment of the roadway had been met. They were only a few hundred yards from the military vehicles parked on the highway. Matthew turned to his father, handing him the shotgun. He slipped his pack onto his sister's shoulders. He took the machine pistol from his father.

"We've got to cross the road. I'll go last. If we're seen, we'll split up. You and Katie go together. We'll meet at Gramps's house."

"Okay." Tim nodded in agreement.

Matthew knew if they were spotted, the well-fed soldiers would run them down—on foot or by vehicle. Who could outrun a laser once the forest debris was left behind? His mission was to have the forces pursue him. His father had yet to give his heart to Christ. The soldiers would rape Katie. Probably both would be killed. Dad must be given time; Katie would act as his guide.

Matthew snaked up the slope, peered over the edge of the roadway. The vehicles, large and ominous, sat blocking the one-lane road. The black uniforms caught the eye. Drivers sat on top of their vehicles. A group of men stood on the roadway talking, probably the leaders of the operation. He motioned Katie to come up. Her presence was beside him; she peered under the guardrail, up the highway. Her brother spoke.

"When the soldier looking in this direction faces upriver—away from us—go. I'll say when." He had no sooner finished speaking, when the soldier turned upriver.

"Go! Go! Go!" he whispered urgently.

CHAPTER 29

He heard his sister grunt as she straddled the guardrail. Her wobbly legs, bending under the pack, carried her across the barren cement. She dropped from sight over the far guardrail just as the soldier's head jerked back in their direction. Had he seen movement? Matthew prayed Katie would remain still. The soldier walked down the roadway, staring intently. He carried a sidearm, holstered. He hesitated, stopped.

"Go back, go back. You saw nothing," Matthew mumbled under his breath. The man began walking backward, not taking his eyes off the location where he had suspected movement. He raised his fist into the air, bringing his arm up and down, as he called over his shoulder. Matthew saw the driver in the first vehicle duck down into his vehicle. The gathered soldiers stiffened, had a heightened sense of awareness.

Matthew signaled his father. Tim was beside him, analyzing the scene up the highway. The man wasn't going to turn back to the vehicle but would wait for the vehicle to come to him. Matthew spoke.

"You've got to cross the road. The vehicle will stop at the soldier on the road nearest us. He will take his eyes from the road to climb on board. That is when you run. I'll hold them off."

"No." The vehicle was moving.

"Yes! Think of Katie." The man was grasping handholds on the vehicle.

His son was right; no time for debate or for good-byes. The man's back was turned. Tim bolted across the road. The climbing soldier was told by the driver to turn his head. The climbing soldier fumbled with his holster as he turned. Dad was off the road. Mat placed the laser sight on the man's chest, holding his fire. The man did not draw his weapon, the vehicle was now moving south, toward Mat, the turret scanning. A delay, a stop, occurred as men were rounded up for the pursuit and climbed aboard.

When the vehicle appeared ready to resume, Mat trotted across the roadway, paused, spewed a few bullets harmlessly over the vehicles, hoping to anger and divert the patrol. He remained on the highway till he saw their eyes lock upon him. He ran into the forest debris, where the vehicle could not follow, as if to outflank the armored column and to gain height on the vast mountain flank. Dad and Katie would be moving south into the valley of tangled dead wood and shrubbery. Eventually they would need to ascend the north flank of the next mountain.

As he dodged and climbed forest debris, he heard the engine gunned for a few seconds, then the vehicle stopped suddenly. The pursuers had left their vehicle on the roadway. Mat smelled the fumes of the engines. The vehicle should have circled the forest debris, sprinted up the bare mountain slope to an overwatch position, and waited for the quarry to appear. These soldiers were inexperienced, Mat realized. They had made no plans to track the others in the debris, if, indeed, they had seen them, and had concentrated on him. They had not used their advantage, the vehicle, wisely. He could see the vehicle and saw no one on the turret. The driver had wanted to be part of the chase. Mat saw black uniforms enter the debris, become slowed in the tangle. He bolted north, straight up the bare mountain, away from his father and sister.

They did not shoot, even when he sent more rounds over their heads. He had no wish to kill—that would only anger them and make his death more certain if he was captured. They wanted him for interrogation, torture. If they felt endangered by his shots, they would shoot to kill. With him dead, they would turn their attention to the possibility of more renegades. His father and sister were not yet safe.

In a very short time, his legs burned with fatigue; he was forced to walk. He paused twice to judge the soldiers' progress; they were gaining. He scanned the far valley and southern mountain for sight of his father and sister. How desolate were the mountain flanks of the valley—nothing but rock layers exposed and some fuzzy greenness where soil had collected and seeds had sprouted.

He could see for miles as he gained in elevation. In a draw, on the far side of the forest debris, he saw his sister and father, moving upward. No one was in pursuit. Only the lone vehicle was stationary on the road; either no reinforcements had been called or reinforcements were not available. All his father had to do was sit, wait for darkness.

Mat pushed his body. If he had been well fed, he would have outdistanced them. His legs collapsed near the summit. He could see far to the north, a land of steep ridges, brown, barren. The sky was empty of clouds and blue; the sun, hot. His mouth was completely dry; his heartbeat shook his body. He wished he could have led his pursuers farther. Strange, how the flesh wouldn't listen to the desire of his heart. His body had never failed him before. A forlornness came over him. He thought now of shooting to kill. If he wounded or killed one of them, the instinct would be to kill him. Death would be good.

Life hadn't been worth living for some time. The only reason he rose in the morning was because he knew God wanted him to live. Life on this earth held no promise for him, just suffering. He remembered before the troubles, when he had had dreams of the future and college; of excelling in sports, having a girlfriend, a car, an apartment. A career in geology, like his dad, traveling the globe to exotic places. How quickly life had turned to a world in chaos. He shook his head involuntarily at the strangeness of it all—his time of birth within world events, his life with two parents, his family connections with two Enslavers. And yet, the Lord knew he would be here on this mountain, facing death and torture. It was good then—the Lord was here, and anything was possible.

Better to kill as many of them as he could, then himself. If he was drugged, he would reveal the hiding place of his father and sister, Gramps's home. Under torture, he might talk. He hated to think of his flesh having that power over his mind and will. His heart ached for Katie; she needed to be protected from the world.

He quickly scanned the ridgetop, consisting of huge, elongated boulders, broken pieces of sedimentary layers, flat and sharp. In a cave-like opening, between two boulders, he hid. Two men came into view before he had time to settle in. They were moving directly to the opening, not yet certain of the object inside. He lined up the laser sight. Pulled the trigger. Nothing! He pulled open the bolt; the bullet was deformed and jammed. His fingernails, worn, failed to unseat the projectile. He found his pocket knife.

He heard them calling out in alarm; they split from his view. Vainly he worked on the bullet, even as they reemerged at the entrance and jerked and dragged him from his den, pulling the weapon out of his hand. A boot pressed down on his neck. He hadn't the strength to resist. Another man kicked him in the ribs. The men gathered around him. They stood like hunters around a trophy animal. They spit upon him. One urinated on him. They kicked him, taunted him. The humiliation was ignored as Mat concentrated inwardly on protecting his body. Their taunts seemed so pitiful; their kicks, stomps were savage. He failed to fully block a blow to the head. He was in a daze. Jesus had been taunted and abused, the Spirit reminded him. Mat felt the fullness of the Presence of Christ. He smiled.

"He's fuckin' happy about it!" A snarling teenager spit the words.

"Okay, let's lay off for a minute. Sarge is coming," said an older man.

The sergeant approached the group without a word. The group parted as the sergeant scanned the prisoner's forehead. The sergeant laughed. "We hit the lottery. A wanted man—accomplice to murder." They laughed in surprise and taunted the man within the ball of clothing at their feet. They congratulated themselves for capturing a high value target and speculated upon what rewards might be theirs.

Mat's hands were bound with plastic nooses. The supply of exploding cuffs must have run dry long ago. He was lifted to his feet. Someone spit on him, kicked him savagely in the buttocks.

He fell many times on the way down the mountain; his legs had no strength. He knew he must end his life before he was tortured. He was certain torture would come first; it was expedient. Drugging was done in the city, at military headquarters. On the highway, by the vehicle, a soldier with a holster approached. He held the rank of a master sergeant.

"Where are the others?" The man, in his forties, studied the face of Mat. The kid looked familiar. Where did he know this kid from? Ah, the kid from the Camp. Returning to the Camp after his captivity and near-torture experience, he had learned from the others that the kid and the older man who had saved him were son and father—a pair of their own. He had never bumped into either of them at the Camp prior to that and never saw them again after. Damn, the kid was a good soldier—and the good soldier had saved his life. But he did not owe him anything. Now the allegiances had changed. Attitudes changed with alliances.

Matthew shrugged his shoulders. "I only saw one man ahead of me. I don't know him." His voice quivered; he did not want it to quiver.

The master sergeant wondered if the "man ahead" had been the kid's father. The master sergeant's face flashed in anger, his open hand slapped and pushed into Mat's head. Mat fell to the ground. He had not punched the kid—he'd been taught to always leave room for an increase in force. "Fuckin' liar." He turned to a subordinate. "Get me the pruning shears."

He pulled Mat's head up by the jacket collar. "Know what we do with pruning shears?"

Mat said nothing.

"Aren't you of the *true vine*?" He had loved to present that line in the past, but now there was a kid before him who had saved his life—a kid who had risked all for him and the others—and they hadn't even known each other. They had worn the same uniform that day and that had been enough for the kid. The kid had not needed to get involved—he could have slunk away from the scene of torture, and no one would have been the wiser. Well, now they did not wear the same uniform. Now, through the computer file, he knew the kid was an Enslaver. The master sergeant had been trained to hate Enslavers through education programs and trained to love the true Church. It was all shit.

Mat recognized the reference to the true vine from the Gospel of John. The sergeant spoke mockingly. "I am the true vine, and my Father is the vine-dresser. Every branch of mine that bears no fruit, he takes away, and every branch that does bear fruit he prunes that it may bear more fruit." The words ended with a tone of utter bitterness and hatred. Matthew looked deeply into the eyes and saw rage. Then a bewildering softness came into the eyes. The man's eyes hardened again, and then softened. Mat knew two spirits were in conflict within the mind. Mat spoke. "You hate me? For what crime?"

The man stepped back, wanting to kick the kneeling enemy in the side of his head. He would not—he owed the kid something? He wanted that integrity of returning good for good? He didn't understand why he wanted that. Why should this kid receive a reward for simply honoring the uniform being worn at the time? Didn't his rescue of his teammates make his side stronger? The kid cared nothing for him personally. He slowly placed his foot on Mat's upper chest and shoulder and pushed him over.

"You sent us on a chase we didn't want to take. What do you have to say to that?" The sentence was shouted repeatedly as the patrol gathered, clamoring for the sergeant to kill the prostrate enemy.

What was this kid's crime? asked God of the sergeant. That he had risked his life and that of his father to save your life- Sergeant? No one would have known, had he done nothing. Why should I save your life on that day fast approaching-Sergeant?

Mat's mind heard the internal struggle. Who was this sergeant within whom mercy battled? One of his rescued men. A dizziness had entered Mat's mind.—he fought to remain in control of his balance. The man straddled Mat.

"The world loves its own," Mat mumbled, his speech slurred. The master sergeant said nothing. He knew Enslavers believed in a new world coming…and a judgment. But why should he give evil for good? The kid had saved his life. Wasn't that enough, simply on its own, whatever the reason? The small hand pruners were brought. Mat was propped against the side of a vehicle, the pruners placed before his eyes.

"Look! It's up to you how many fingers and toes you want to lose before you talk, but you will talk. Now! How many escaped, where are they going?"

Though dazed and weakened, Mat wondered why a squad wasn't out searching if the escapees, his sister and father, had such value? He was certain the master sergeant had not seen Katie. Either he just wanted an excuse to torture, or he hoped to uncover a larger group.

"One man, who I never saw before," Mat said. "He's probably hiding in the debris."

The sergeant's walk was stiff as he paced before his prisoner. The threat had not worked. In the past, he had taken fingers and toes. Only the last digits—the work camps and military wanted no impaired prisoners. But he could only bluff now; the rules had changed. Orders were not to torture until higher authority was given. The sergeant hated Christ and His followers and had tortured with zealousness. Still, he would not place the call to higher authorities for permission to torture this boy. This boy-man would go to the judge. Let someone else torture or administer the serum. Let someone else garner the praise and rewards for finding more Enslavers. Once he and this kid had fought on the same side, once the kid had saved his life. A smart kid would never have risked his life or his father's by boldly attacking a superior party. The risks had been immense. He would honor the kid's daring; that, he could do. Perhaps there was at least one more Enslaver running free. In time, he would be caught. They would all be caught and exterminated.

"One of you take him back. The rest of us are going to scour the debris field. I want one man on the mountain to the south."

Matthew kept his face a mask. His father and sister would be safe. If they had continued climbing, they were over the mountain. If they had remained in the draw, hid themselves well, they still might go undetected. These soldiers, though well fed and in excellent health, had already decided their day's work was done. He saw it in their faces when the sergeant ordered them back on patrol.

An air platform flew above them. Matthew noticed the round protuberance hanging from the underside of the nose, likely a heat tracer. His heart sank as the air platform began to trace out the pattern of a search grid. This was a thorough operation.

If his father and sister were within the search grid, they could only escape now by hiding in a cave or with a reflecting blanket over them. There was one in the pack. Would Dad remember to use it? Perhaps there were so many fugitives running that his father and sister would have time to escape the grid. Perhaps. He had to trust God, walk in faith. God, the power of the universe, wanted his father and sister to escape. He had to believe God would give them every opportunity to remain free. He had to believe God would even act supernaturally, outside the rules of earthly reality. He had to believe God loved them that much.

Beyond the vehicles, on the highway, a holding area had been established for the prisoners. As he neared, he saw they had been separated into three groups. All were bound, gagged, and still seemed to be woozy from the effects of the force field. He guessed a satellite had pinpointed the collection of people, a force field had been beamed down. He surmised that every person in central Pennsylvania knew of the gathering and would have gladly shared the location for a few packaged meals. Slightly off target, the beam had landed in the river and was walked into the gathering. It was that initial miss that had allowed his family's escape.

A table had been set up, men in black robes sat behind the table, an empty chair stood in front of the table. One group of prisoners sat before the table; the two other groups were to the side. One group on the side consisted of younger men and women. He thought they were to be spared. In the larger group, Mat saw Josh and his followers; these men would be tortured and executed. The group before the table, he assumed, had yet to be judged. He was placed with the group before the table, confirming his thoughts. A blindfold and gag were applied.

He waited as the day moved slowly on. His head hurt, and his stomach growled in hunger. No one had given him water, his tongue stuck to the roof of his mouth. He had heard the air platform slowly expand its search grid, till it had left his hearing. He had time to think of Josh and his group. He had seen all the faces of the people who had visited and shared a meal at Gramps's home. All would be tortured. Josh, of the 144,000, knew he would die a martyr on the day he knew Jesus was the Messiah.

The air platform returned when the sun had lost its warmth. He believed no one was added to his group. Had Katie and his father been killed? Or had they escaped? He knew they'd escaped, for the angel of death had not come with the premonition of death, nor had the Spirit as Comforter wrapped him in consolation. Mat slept. When he awoke, he sensed by hearing that only two people were ahead of him.

Then, finally, he was lifted to his feet, placed in the chair before the tables. His mouth gag was released. He heard the men before him on the keyboards of computers. He heard his name, whispered discussion. Then a formal, loud voice spoke.

"Matthew Charles Johnson, you are a suspect in the murder of four men, agents of the Church. You are charged with participating in an illegal gathering and resisting arrest. How do you plead?"

The voice was weary, strained. Mat had been listening to it all afternoon.

"Guilty," Mat replied firmly.

"Are you guilty of murder?"

"Yes."

"Where are your father, sister, mother?" A different voice spoke the last sentence. A familiar voice.

"Dead." Why wasn't he attached to lie-detecting apparatus? Maybe no one cared anymore.

"We know your mother is alive. Now, where are your father and sister?"

"Dead." How did they know his mother was alive? Dad said she had jumped into a military vehicle. Then it made sense: she had been turned in; the authorities had her.

Carl Stasic looked upon Matthew with an utter sadness. The body was boney, shaking from cold and weakness. The spirit in the boy was beaten. He suspected this boy to be an Enslaver. So what? Matthew had always been pragmatic, a realist. He could have had a future in the new Church. He had envisioned Matthew as becoming someone. After the rebellion, the amnesty, he had lost track of the Order members and their families as he struggled to keep himself alive. Carl knew this boy's sorry state was as much his fault as Mat's. He had no love of the Church, had fought it with all his being, but knew it was the coming reality. How could you hang a political tag on any sixteen-year-old kid? They clung to the opinion of anyone they admired; they had no ability to judge facts, build facts into a coherent world view, and intertwine a political system upon the whole.

He wondered if Mat was lying about Tim and Katie. They could have died; perhaps that was the prod that moved him into Enslaver beliefs. Tim was wily, yet who could escape disease or unseen assailants? If Tim and Katie were alive, they would have been at the gathering with Mat, whether they believed or not - a loyal bunch. The drone footage was not yet available for viewing. Stasic smiled. It was highly probable that Tim and Katie had escaped. One sentence could prove his theory —one sentence he could not utter. *The air platform killed your father and sister*. By Mat's reaction, he would know. In his weakened condition, Mat could not hide his emotion.

"So what do we do?" asked a member of the board to Carl.

Carl answered in a whisper to the men beside him. "We can't prove or disprove he is a murderer. Simmons and his men are dead; we can profit nothing from justice. He says he is guilty—but he wants to die. Can we prove he is a murderer, and is it worth our time? Even if he admits to the killing under the serum, we can't prosecute. Such admissions are inadmissible. Now, for being at the illegal rally, we can sentence him to military enlistment and earn a bounty."

Carl thought about profit. The small bonuses added up, made life better—food delicacies, alcohol, stimulants. He thought of two more people out there running free. Tim and Katie could both be caught and enlisted in a work program which would mean a greater bounty, plus a better-looking success rate. They'd soon starve outside the system anyway. Why shouldn't he make a profit? The friendship was past; and even as a friend, sometimes you had to help people by hurting them.

"Mat. This is Carl. Stasic." To his orderly, Carl whispered, "Take the blindfold off."

Mat smiled, heard someone approaching, felt his blindfold touched, removed, then sight. He blinked his eyes as they adjusted to the light. "I thought that was you." Carl was thinner in his face, and his eyes were worn and tired, less steady in their focus. A peace came across Mat's mind, the knowledge that Carl was about to lie.

"Mat. Your father and sister were killed by the air platform." Carl's voice was grave, sad.

Matthew smiled. "Carl."

"Yes, Mat?"

"Jesus is Lord."

"So I've heard, Mat. You should have remained true to the State. We could have used you." Damn, the boy was slick. That peace he had… he hadn't flinched. Maybe he hadn't heard. He remembered his first meeting with Mat in the high-rise, moving gear to a nonexistent car. "Mat, your father and sister are dead."

"I've told you that, Carl." Mat's mind desperately raced to his cover story as to how they had died.

Chagrin covered Carl's face. "You were a good soldier. We're giving you a chance to serve again, for a true cause. Good luck to you, Mat."

"Thanks, Carl."

Carl was amazed that Mat's voice held no bitterness, as if he was truly thankful. Men grabbed Mat's arms and led him to a waiting truck. Carl turned to his orderly. "See he gets some warm clothes and rations and uncuff his hands."

The men and women in the truck parted as Mat was thrown in. He noticed his arms were free. He guessed all the males were going to the Middle East. The women, they would become whores of the Church, serve in the military. That is what he guessed. One of the guards who had thrown him on board, threw him a ragged jumpsuit. In the thigh pocket was a ration. He thanked the Lord—Katie and Dad were free.

CHAPTER 30

The sun was hot, the clouds puffy and white in the clean, blue air. The air was so hot and dry it burned her nostrils. Katie squirted a small plastic container of synthetic lotion into her nostrils then used her pinkie to coat the inner membrane. She was in her morning hole, not far from their former warehouse apartment, on a slight ridge upon the slope of the first mountain. She liked to look down on the city from the heights. The city dwellers were always busy. She did not move—an easy task when you had no energy to move. Draped over her laid-back sitting/ reclining position was the heat shield blanket, muting her form.

She thought back over the two months since they had last seen Mat on the mountainside, fleeing his pursuers. The machine pistol shots had echoed forlornly over the vast mountain slopes and valley. The black uniforms of the pursuers had been stark against the naked stone heights. Seeing Mat so far away and being unable to help him had been tough. But Christ through the Spirit had been with him—a far better friend and helper than she could ever be.

They had waited at Gramps's house for three weeks, stretching out the remainder of the supplies in the cache. They had filled the cache with clean water from the well, using any available container they had, then buried the cache. Then, after filling every portable water container, they had returned to their old neighborhood. Dad said it would be as safe as anywhere else—and just knowing the lay of the land, the history of human activity was an advantage. Certainly, records might exist that they once lived here in the corner warehouse apartment, but they believed the authorities had greater problems than searching for *outsiders* as their type were now known.

She missed Mat, and she missed Mom. She knew they were alive; the angels had not told her of their deaths. Angels were punctual and conscientious, when not battling the enemy, and if your mind was fixed on Christ and the world was silent to you, you could most definitely hear. She prayed every morning for them and then again before evening sleep. She believed Mat had been captured, and she knew the beast needed bodies for his army—young, old, sickly, healthy. The beast paid bounties for bodies. The beast would march his army to the Middle East and Israel. This is what she had heard at the river gathering.

She studied the scene below her. The floodwaters and the ponds, puddles, pools left scattered over the earth, had disappeared over a month ago. The old riverbed was a swath of yellowing brown and faint green. The levee to the barge way had disappeared in the flood. The fishpond walls had been washed away; only massive tree trunks and boulders remained in the scoured bed, and the layer of silt that had birthed the greenness immediately after the flood. The bridges as well as many of their piers were gone. A pontoon bridge, placed over the once swollen river, lay on the stony bed.

To smell plant life in the air was to smell hope itself, dreams of a recovering Earth. False dreams, thought Katie. For the unredeemed, the end was near. The plants were living in the moisture still trapped between the hard bed and the soil and supported by morning mists. Katie was reminded of Jesus's lesson of the seeds scattered on different soil types. The sunspots covered almost a third of the sun. The heat was intense—probably 120 degrees every day. They had scraped a cave into the hillside, back and up the mountain slope from their corner apartment at the warehouse. The cave was their home during the day, and luckily, days had been shortened by the lack of sunlight. They continued to eat rations scattered by the Church the day her mother had left—the day of the convoy of trucks. Rain had come in insignificant spatterings since the deluge. She looked to the north. Thin patches of green clung to the mountain ridge. Some had already burst into flame. The greenness was good, even if there was no hope in it, because it spoke of the resiliency of God's creation. Only in Jesus was there hope.

They could see the city had been affected by the flood. Debris, ruins, shells of buildings had been washed away or scattered. Only the heart of the city remained, stubbled high-rises, government buildings. The capitol dome, once hidden by surrounding buildings, was now visible. Other blunted high-rises remained outside the central core, scattered about the city. Tim and Katie heard drilling, explosions; saw earth-moving, debris-bearing construction vehicles moving every day. They watched the toppling of the high-rise stubs. First, they saw the dust, the tilt and fall, and then the sounds of explosions came over them. Every day, dust rose in the air over the ruins. Help had come from somewhere—machines, manpower, and the money they could not see. Had the convoys of soldiers and the thrown food packages of that day announced the beginning of civilization's revival?

They intended to tour the city, walk the streets, when a dust storm came from the west and cloaked the earth in mystery. The storms were unpredictable, but she and her dad thought the storms always followed weather like this day—clear and sparkling. Perhaps tomorrow would be the day.

***

In the flat desert, Mat ran his eyes along the barbed-wire fence, running north to south. A desert of barren sedimentary rock sending shimmering heat waves into the air, the rock sprinkled with sand and desert plants, both in uneven patches. Blasting hot winds and the relentless sun pounded into his senses. He wore the desert uniform—gloves, jacket, neck scarf, facial mask, goggles, tight-fitting helmet—the new version with intersliding plates that covered the neck, forehead, and even the cheeks, nose, and mouth. The sign said *Egypt* in five languages. He had yet to break a sweat this morning. He had come to this place alone, a scout, riding a one-person rotor-bladed mount using solar energy as the main source of propulsion.

Behind him, perhaps twenty miles to the west. was a massive army of Federation forces. They covered a front of a hundred miles and their columns stretched for a day's ride behind them. There were units from North America and every nation south of the former United States— now officially designated as America. As there were no nations south of America, only warlords and their armies, the Federation—by bribery or armed incursions—had collected men and women to fill the ranks. African forces from every region of the continent were attached. Most were of Middle Eastern Muslim blood. They were followed in number by European white colonists, and lastly, black Africans, who had been affected by the plague to a devastating degree.

As he stared east, his eyes would glimpse at his recon panel. No drones reported; no enemy forces moving, though men could be hiding under heat shields in slit trenches—snipers, advanced scouts, scattered randomly over the desert. No electronic monitoring devices in operation. The screen recognized other scouts of the Federation to his north and south, all gathering at the border fence.

The end was up ahead—the end of earthly man's reign. Mankind had begun in the Middle East and would end there. So tidy, so fitting. Most likely, his death was ahead—and the transition to his new world. To be at the cusp of history, to be allowed to watch it end, filled him with a sense of wonder. His mind wanted to turn back to Katie, Dad, and Mom. He thought of his journey from his capture on the Pennsylvania mountaintop to this place; the commuter trip with his fellow conscripts to the New Jersey port. The seven-day ocean voyage. The decrepit ship and the unmoving, windless, fish-oil-glazed, red ocean of foul odors. Vaccinations, vitamin supplements, steroid shots, amphetamines, unending tasteless food bars given between meals and training. He thought the steroids would have long-term effects if they were to live a normal life span; it wasn't planned they would. Classroom training followed by physical training, twelve hours a day.

Conscripts who had urinary problems wore diapers; conscripts who couldn't keep their sexual appendages inside their pants wore electronic destimulators; medicines were scarce; females wore chastity belts; conscripts with mental quirks, learning disabilities, personality disorders were given injections for their problems or simply tranquilized. Hernias were repaired; appendixes, removed; bad teeth, pulled. Flat feet, curved backs, any deformity—ignored. No excuses, no deferments. Everyone would go, and the battlefield would decide who lived and who died. Some conscripts jumped ship into the smelly mass of rotting fish bodies and drowned.

Mat had had only two enjoyments. One was studying the dead ocean creatures floating on the waters in various states of decomposition—whales, octopi of fantastic size, sharks, oddities he could not attach names to. He had seen many crewless ships in various states of dilapidation float by—sailboats, yachts, fishing boats, cargo ships, cruise ships, destroyers. Once, half of a Russian submarine bobbed before him. Then at night, his last enjoyment: the heavens, a mass of shooting stars, comets, and blood-red moons.

Land. The discharge of troops and equipment of hundreds of ships to join the already tens of thousands of would-be soldiers in camps, waiting. A three-thousand-mile march across Africa; a moving training-and-conditioning course of periodic missile attacks, skirmishes with Muslim jihadists, and training accidents. Forced hikes, truck rides, destroyed homes, villages, towns, cities, and an absence of native peoples. Intense heat and glaring sun, rationed water. The bodies of suicides or soldier criminals hung by the road. It was noted by people of authority that Mat was capable of independent activity and possessed truthfulness. They designated him a scout.

When all thoughts of the present, or moving his body to point B from point A, or responsibilities and concerns quieted, he thought of Katie, Dad, and Mom and prayed for an easy end to their lives and his own.

***

Mary studied the delicate supports of the vaulted ceiling of the immense roof of the tent. The supports resembled spider webs in their sheerness. The white silken fabric of the tent seemed to match her flowing robe and that of the other handmaidens of the Prophet in color and fabric texture. Probably the material had been on sale - she giggled to herself then laughed aloud. She was doped up and it damned well felt good. She crawled away from the two foot high table into the nest of pillows behind her. The other handmaidens had already found their nesting spots within the pillowed room. One maiden had passed out with elbows and head resting on the table. Bill Smith came and pulled her back into the pillows.

Mary felt rivers of relaxation flow through her body, swirling into her pelvis and crotch and then moving down her legs. She marveled at her luck in finding Bill at a train station in Altoona, where her luck had seemed to run out only two days out of Harrisburg. The soldiers who had given her a ride had just decided to go AWOL, minutes before picking her up, and they drove west. They slowly began their advances with words. She thwarted their advances as she attempted to read who was the power person in the truck, not the highest-ranking man, but the one who would defend his prize and not share.

She had escaped the decision when a roadblock came into view, and the truck stopped as the soldier/boys decided their course of action. She jumped out and moved toward the roadblock. The truck swerved in an about turn. As guards at the roadblock entered their vehicle to pursue, Mary ducked into a lumber pile of sawed tree trunks that was stored along the road. She found a train station beyond the roadblock and no visible security. A long train was slowly pulling out, headed west. She pulled herself onto a flatcar. Watched the scenery of devastation move on by.

There in Altoona, where the train stopped, was Bill. She recognized him instantly, and he recognized her. He was a front man, he said, for Pastor Dave, whose audience had expanded through his traveling tent sermons. He was now known as the Prophet or, as Bill said with bitterness and cynicism, the Profit. Bill's family had all perished singly or together—she could not remember. Everyone had a hard-luck story.

Then there was Noreen and the kids, working for the Profit's show. Mary chuckled at her own cynicism. Pastor Dave seduced her as he had back in Harrisburg. Then, she'd had sex with him only two times. Now, it was ongoing, but she knew he would eventually tire of her just like he had the others. Noreen seemed not to mind. Nothing mattered to anyone anymore. Everyone seemed to be waiting for the other guy to do it—have a plan, create food, create jobs—then they would take what the other guy had by stealth or force. It was like a documentary from her youth, in which the lions killed the wildebeest, the hyenas took, by overwhelming numbers, the lions' kill, and then the insistent wild dogs—more aggressive and numerous—took from the hyenas. Everyone's goal in life was to have a full stomach, plenty of sex or drugs and a comfortable place to sleep. Her own conscience was dead. The drugs killed it, and that was okay.

***

This was the day to explore the city. The ash storm had come in the beginning hours of the new day; Katie felt underneath her baggy jacket, her hand touched the big knife. Dad had a knife also. He had sawed off the stock of the shotgun and had the weapon strapped to his shoulder, inside his jacket. She wondered if they would find food-ration packets on their journey. Many had been scattered randomly, bizarrely, the first day the ration convoy had come into the city. Punk-kid soldiers had thrown them just to be rid of them. The wolves could not smell the contents—by design—and the packaging was brown, the perfect camouflage to hide them from the very people who needed them. The Lord would provide.

"Ready, Dad?"

"Ready."

"Dad?"

"Yes, my Katie?"

"If someone—or a group—tries to rape me, don't get involved. I'll pull my knife and fight, but I don't want you dying for nothing. I can live with it. And I can die with peace and no regrets."

She wore baggy men's trousers, layers of clothing under her jacket that hid the burgeoning femininity of her form. Her hair was as short as a man's, her face usually dirty, the world of makeup was gone. Still, anyone within talking distance could see she was a young woman. At a distance her movements appeared feminine. But so did the movements of men—starved, weakened by disease, living in exhaustion, their manhood sapped by physical stress.

"Don't get close to anyone, Katie. From a distance, you can pass as a man." He thought of the sardonic humor in his thinking. Looking like a man wouldn't save her from rape; perhaps it might even increase her chances of being attacked by a gang. Although a lone man would think twice about confronting his equal.

"I will get involved," he said. "We've come this far with integrity, better to die with it intact. If I am attacked by sods, you run."

"Okay, Dad." She agreed with him to appease him. She would fight for him and gladly die.

They walked west in the darkness, past the location of the once populous row homes of paper, where they had lived. The homes had been moved into the heart of the city. They quietly and nervously passed through the rubble of homes and offices of the old city. When they sensed the old riverbed ahead, they turned south. The trick was to move either between the riverbed and the new river road, or between the railyard tracks. These were the physical barriers that would have sensors and collect criminals—or simply desperate holdouts from authority. Tim chose to move between the riverbed and the new river road. No movement was heard, no sensors seen. The dust was thick; they tightened their air-filter masks and googles.

They climbed up the steep bank of the riverbed where the riverfront park had once existed. She remembered the tall shade trees and their fallen stateliness after the great quake. On her back with a compound fracture, she had had plenty of time to look at trees. Their root balls left massive holes. From her hiding holes on the ridge, she had watched many of the trees sawed into lumber. Most had been carried away by the flood. Not enough manpower for the cleanup. Once there was lush green grass, a walking path; now, only hard sedimentary layers. The hospital had fallen, been scavenged of useful equipment and supplies and the debris hauled away. She never could have guessed at the course of her life from that day after the quake visit until now.

A line of lights, high in the air, taller than streetlights, shone at even intervals through the dust and darkness, north to south. She saw other lights shining, and intact buildings behind this row. From behind, out of the dust, a man came, passed close by them. She sensed he was searching for an opportunity to steal. Her father reached into his coat; the man stayed his course into the city. Other people were now seen—purposely avoiding others, moving into the city lights. That was the way people were now. If you saw people ahead, you set your course fifty yards to their right or left, however inconvenient. No one could be trusted.

They crossed Front Street. The dust storm suddenly stopped. More people could be seen in the city. With a sudden realization, Tim understood people were going to work—their occupations, their jobs. Organization, productivity, purpose had returned to a perverse and emotionally empty humanity. The dust was settling quickly, and more clarity came. He beheld the empty expanse to the east, north, south. The east was bounded by the glacial riverbank bluffs sitting half a mile or so away. This rise of land had been called the Hill since the city had formed hundreds of years in the past. Before the quake and troubles, this area had been dense with high-rises, so that you could only peer down streets and run your eyes up the towering buildings, never seeing the glacial river bluffs.

Demolition crews worked to the north, probably had been working till the dust-storm hiatus. They watched the huge machines gather up the debris and waste of a civilization and deposit it into the hauling machines. Tim and Katie moved north, skirting any construction or demolition activity. Across a rubble-strewn cleared area, they stopped to rest, watched a construction project. They felt more at ease as the number of walking people increased. They were just a part of the rhythm of the city.

It seemed trucks were dumping concrete rubble into the hopper of huge, wheeled mixer or furnace. Beside this great hopper, extended a twenty-foot-wide, rectangular, concrete form of perhaps fifty yards in length. The hopper moved at a snail's pace, and the form followed. From the hopper, a thick liquid was pouring into the form. Tim watched, studied. Then spoke in amazement.

"They're building a wall! Reconstituted, fast-drying concrete. It's a wall, not a building!"

"Around a new city?" Katie asked.

"Maybe. Let's take a closer look."

Ahead of the construction crew, they noticed the ground had been prepared for the wall. The wall would be poured into the rectangular form whose edges sat atop of the footing within the ditch. They followed this footing north through the band of cleared rubble, till they came to a gate. The gate stood alone, waiting for its flanking walls. Perhaps the plans for the gate's flanking towers had yet to be decided. Uniformed security guards sauntered by the gate; one group seemed on break, while another group watched an instructor at a cement podium before the gate. The podium seemed to have something of interest set within.

"Learning the new scanning procedures, maybe?" said Katie. "Once the wall is completed, we will never be able to enter."

They could see, past the gate to the east and north, the prefab apartments of wood product and two-story office buildings. And within and beyond this area, new concrete buildings were rising. "I'm going into the city, Dad. We have to know what's being planned inside." She was sure that once the wall was completed, no one would enter who didn't belong to the beast.

Tim knew the information might be helpful in the future. "No, we don't."

"You've got the weapon. Stay here. I'll only be ten minutes."

"We've got to stick together," he said adamantly.

"What if scanners pick up on the weapon?"

Tim pulled out the shotgun and placed it in a convenient crack in the concrete floor of the absent building they happened to be standing on. "So much garbage about…so few people. If we're not being surveilled by cameras, we're okay."

"Let's go, Dad—quickly." She wanted distance between the dropped weapon and them.

Katie's long strides carried her over the footing, moving east toward the center of the old city. She saw the prefabricated apartments beside the old high-rises; the high-rises were mounds of rubble. One building's summit had found great favor among the buzzards. New concrete buildings were rising beside the old and the temporary. Coming close to one foundation, they saw the buildings were to be constructed on giant pads underlaid with springs and ball bearings to withstand the movement of future earthquakes. Suddenly it seemed black-robed men were everywhere, computer boards in their hands, conferring with healthy, vigorous men in hard hats. The arms of the black-robed priests were always pointing, or their hands upon the backs of subordinates, in friendly inclusion and guidance. They saw saplings planted in cement containers, noticed drip pipes in the containers.

The trees had been brought in from some nursery where water was plentiful. They saw a tall drilling rig. A deep-water source must have been tapped. Water so plentiful shade trees could be irrigated? They came upon an empty pool that could only be meant for a fountain. New streets were being built; the sewers seemed designed to trap any rainwater that might fall.

Tim and Katie moved north, skirting people. No one seemed alarmed or disturbed by their presence. The intended size of the new city amazed them. They walked a newly built, empty street, already lined with the saplings in their cement planters. Sports fields of artificial turf dazzled with their greenness; a stadium waited for its grand opening. Everything was going up so quickly, in such an orderly fashion; the black-robed men were so numerous and businesslike and the workers so robust in their movements that they concluded the city was being raised on a standard plan. They guessed that the bulk of the priests and supervisors and skilled workers were a team that traveled throughout the devasted world, building cities.

A hospital had been erected; the World Church flag flew on the highest pole, and the Federation flag flew beneath it. Tim noticed the absence of the flag of the United States. They passed a newly built school, with children in uniform streaming in. The school's entrance was guarded by a storm trooper. Was kidnapping for ransom feared? Or child molesters? They saw no more storm troopers but identified what appeared to be a police headquarters by the flags flying and the military vehicles parked outside. Beside this building were Quonset-hut garages, wood-and-paper barracks, gray vehicles—troop carriers—and tanks lining up in convoy. Air platforms were parked in formation on a cement field. Did the military scour the countryside, rounding up stragglers, breaking up rebellions and gangs of thugs?

At the very northern end of the city, the wall had already been constructed. One-story, prefabricated buildings, long and deep, spacious, with sides open lined newly constructed streets. These were factories of the new industrial base of the economy. Within, men and women stood at long tables, and great spindles rotated. Large fans blew air through the building. Tim and Katie smelled fabric—uniforms, they thought; uniforms for the army, police, workers. They passed five more of these buildings, each with different machines, smells, clusters of workers. One emanated a smell they associated with military equipment, rucksacks, web gear. Another building had a gentler fabric odor, the spindles held brown, blue threads. They noticed many men and women were dressed in brown and blue jumpsuits. From the waste bin of another building, they were certain electronics were manufactured. One factory had piles of freshly cut lumber outside; it emitted the smell of sawdust and the whine of high-speed sanders, grinders, saws. Adjacent to these factories, crews were laying out the sites of new buildings, probably the next generation of factories.

At a huge factory sitting apart from the rest, rugged vehicles were moving crisply, methodically from the building to scrap piles of metal. Steel beams, many twisted and holding cement like gnawed flesh on bones, were delivered from the wreckage of the city. They could see shimmers of heat coming out of the buildings where the scrap was remelted. Beside the furnaces were railroad cars stacked with newly made commuter rails, chassis, military vehicle bodies. Signs warned pedestrians to come no closer. Railroad cars! Contact with other cities, commerce!

Tim turned suddenly to retrace their steps, realizing any camera watching would see two tourists or spies aimlessly wandering. Perhaps that was planned—a way to induce holdouts from the chip to want to belong to the beast and his accomplishments. Tim determined to walk a slightly altered route back to the shotgun. Perhaps they should not return for their weapon? Katie noticed that all the factories had cafeterias, and she nudged her dad in the side. Suddenly, they were forced to mingle with people coming from the buildings. No one paid them any attention. No one spoke. The faces were tired but clean, healthy, full—not gaunt. At a distance she saw a man leer at her as he approached from the opposite direction. He imperceptibly moved toward her side of the walkway. Tim noticed and placed himself on Katie's vulnerable side.

As if he'd been hit by an invisible electric shock, the man's eyes became confused, then pained. In utter fear, he moved stiffly past her. Katie sighed; Tim's tightened muscles relaxed. Was order being kept by artificial means, not only in this man but everyone? It did seem strange that these people living, working together were, just weeks ago, spewing profanities and insults and seeking pleasure in another's pain and sexual satisfaction in every passerby. Was this new behavior simply the result of having purpose and hope? Was it fear of law and punishment—the choice of coexistence or starvation? Or were these people still devoid of goodness and self- control being manipulated by some type of implantation, chemical or shock therapy?

Three-quarters of the people passing Tim and Katie were dressed in the new jumpsuits of either blue or brown. The other people were like them, dressed in worn, tattered clothing from before the troubles. All the faces seemed alike now; there was nothing human about them— no emotion, no fear. Why was the wall necessary? Who did the authorities want to keep out? Wolves, coyotes, a few lone stragglers like Katie and her father, living in the ruins? Any opposing force gathering in the countryside would readily be discovered by satellite. Was the wall to keep people in?

As Tim's mind trailed away from this first puzzle, another entered his consciousness. Where was the ag-related industry? Where were the irrigated fields, the barns of cattle? No plans to produce food, no plans to process food from the outside. Not even experimental fields, gardens; no fishponds, not even ground set aside for such things. All the food eaten now, the food fattening these pathetic people in new clothes, was coming from somewhere else by rail, a transportation feat in these times. Were the people eating rations, food stocks, from before the troubles? Or was there somewhere on Earth where food was being grown? In time, maybe, the black-robed priests planned to have ag fields surrounding the city. This city seemed built on a tenuous food supply.

As Tim and Katie neared their entry point, Katie realized the docility of the population might make talking to a passerby a possibility. What could she learn? Would the information be worth the risk of being captured? Decidedly not! A crowded intercity commuter car moved by. What was the source of power for this city? Solar, nuclear, thermal, wind? She turned her head and looked north to the high mountain ridge. The white wind-turbine blades were visible along the ridgeline even in the half-light. Construction of new units was extending the line.

Turning her head for her final look south, she saw movement against the southern portion of the wall; a train moved north against the gray backdrop. She had not seen the station on their walk; it was probably near the steel mill and under military guard. The train likely brought food into the city and the product of the factories out. The track nearest the city would be the opportune place to steal food. She hadn't seen a train moving in years. If she stowed away on a train, what city would she find at the other end?

They returned to their starting point. Tim studied the ground ahead, looking for the location of the shotgun. He saw no one in their immediate vicinity. No vehicles at a distance waiting, no cluster of people. The skies held no visible drones. Once he did collect the shotgun, they would be vulnerable, and resistance would be futile. He spoke to her. "If we are caught, do you want me to end our lives?"

"It doesn't matter anymore…we've both had enough. Yes, let it end."

Tim saw the odd-shaped piece of cement that had been his marker; it looked like an elephant but was only the size of a cat. Behind the marker, a man rose out of the flat ruins as if he had sprung from a manhole cover. He was dressed in unwashed rags. His body odor wafted to them.

"You're late!" he said angrily and then sighed with relief.

"I'm sorry. You just get out of the sun." Tim spoke with concern in his voice. Tim's eyes searched for the crevice and the sawed-off barrel and stock. He saw the gun.

"Now?" asked the man.

"Yes, before you burn," said Tim.

The man compliantly bent down, grasped the rim of the round opening, and stepped in. Then he dropped down and disappeared. Tim gathered up the shotgun, placed it within his coat, grabbed Katie's hand, pivoted, and walked away.

They walked north, following the footing for the wall that was to keep people in. When the wall stopped its northward run, and a right angle went east, they stopped. Continuing north would lead them home more quickly, but they saw what appeared to be another gateway to the east and beyond it, a small plaza area. Perhaps a statue had been erected. Their curiosity roused, they continued east.

A gate; a plaza; a statue of the very ordinary man known as the beast; the Federation flag; a large, empty, tiled pool with a large, empty, tiled bowl set above and within it, waiting for water. Behind the newly constructed fount, a semicircle portico gave shade to a large granite block with a smooth top. A black rectangular panel on the block was labeled PUSH. Katie had it pushed before Tim could raise an objection. A hologram appeared. A propaganda documentary began extolling the struggles of the beast to gain control of government and the Church. The plagues, earthquakes, famines, meteor strikes upon Earth, the sunspots were all natural disasters that happened by chance and could be best met by a world government. The subsequent wars were seen as mankind fighting for scant resources. Who could doubt the righteousness of the beast and all his actions?

The enemies of the beast were the enemies of mankind. Violent footage of political riots, wars, food riots appeared. Tim and Katie stiffened as the term *Enslavers* was heard. The footage was local. They saw people being nailed to crosses, three-dimensional figures; close-ups of nails in hands and feet, naked bodies with strings of flesh hanging. The faces were studied; they had a familiarity. And then there was the face of Josh, delirious, groaning in agony. The feet and lower legs of the people were sprayed with a liquid, and an electric match touched the liquid.

Katie turned away from the horror. Tim grabbed her arms and escorted her outside the portico, and they quickly began walking. The people were those with whom they had shared a meal at Gramps's campsite. These were the people who had organized the revival meeting and who had been captured. They were the redeemed, and they had died. Josh was dead, his mission complete. They had eternal life—they were absent from the earth at the moment but very much alive…and waiting.

***

Security monitor Jones watched her screens and focused in upon the north portico hologram. She saw the two outsiders watching the presentation. She had been monitoring them since their first contact with her cameras along the riverbank. Not till the hologram had she recognized Johnson and his daughter. Their reaction to the hologram clearly fit the *outsider/Enslaver* designation; the security computer program had clearly registered the two figures as security risks. It was clearly her duty to send units to pick them up for interrogation and eventually, reeducation or torture.

She'd known this day would come. The day she would be forced to turn in her own, her brothers and sisters—in the Lord. All fifteen of her previous suspects had simply been outsiders, fools and other demented types, who were reeducated and medicated by the State. She could not erase the computer's designation of *Enslaver*. Odd that she would save Tim Johnson and his daughter again, but decidedly good.

She sat. She inhaled deeply and exhaled deeply. Smiling thankfully, she mused upon her Savior's forgiveness of her once-sinful life—her life of rebellion and ignorance. His love and His kindness would bring her home. She had no tears for the world she would be leaving, only tears of gratitude—that the story of Tim Johnson had come into her life, the story of John and Gramps and Diana Rochembeau. She was curious to know how close she had been to John Johnson on that riverbank in Poland so many years ago. Strange how God worked; He was such a counterpuncher—every blow Satan threw, God threw one over the top, even harder.

She entered her virus data, which in the end, would lead to a charge of thermolytic-plastic heat cooking the entire system. Nothing could be undone now. She could safely walk away; no one could reverse the destruction. She was bound for heaven; that could not be reversed, as God was no liar. Where did she want to die? A place to take her poison pill. Ah… the rooftop break station. Sometimes there was breeze wafting through the pavilioned area. The view was stunning of the heaved-up mountain ridge she had always wanted to climb. She sort of dreamed of going to the top of that ridge, where the wind turbines turned. Probably was like standing on the top of the world.

She entered the elevator. Yes, she wanted to be outside in the heat, not in the cool of air conditioning. She wanted it real. The tiny female clerk from the first floor was inside the elevator. Jones looked at the woman and wondered…What the heck. "Hey, my name's Jones, monitor security. Anyone ever tell you about the wonderful saving grace of our God?"

The woman would not look at her; she seemed to stiffen in fright.

"It's okay. I once was like you…His name is Jesus Christ, the Messiah, the Anointed One, Emanuel. He conquered death and sent the Holy Spirit to give us guidance and everything else we need to have truth and peace and forgiveness."

The woman began to smile. Or was it a smirk?

"I was such a tramp, a low life…Do you want to hear more?"

The elevator door opened. The woman scurried away.

"I guess not," Jones said audibly. She began to think of her death. She had a sadness for the life she had led. No mother or father, then the rape at thirteen. What had kept her living? Must have been Jesus…must have been…for she had wanted to die, even had tried. Never had any kids. Always wanted to have one, but the men she met were scum. And life? She couldn't bring a kid into this world now that she saw it clearly.

There was nothing she wanted from this life. The important thing was He had come to her and wrapped His arms around her. There was a life ahead—a good life—without end. Those years from birth to Jesus would shrink each day she lived into eternity. He would explain it all once she met Him face-to-face.

The elevator stopped on the roof. No one else was under the pavilion; she turned to face the high mountain ridge. Even the heat felt good, and there was a breeze. How long would it take for security to come through the door? She opened her heart-shaped locket, kept in her pants pocket. She would scoop the tiny capsule out with her tongue—the capsule shell adhered to moisture.

She turned when she heard the elevator door open; two security men she knew—both spiritually empty and filling their days with sex. By their avoidance of eye contact with her, she knew they were coming for her. Even as they ran for her, the pill was scooped without panic and bitten into. She smiled as they were upon her. She collapsed to the floor, dead. Not wishing to waste a warm piece as shapely as Jones, they raped her lifeless body. And laughed when it was done.

Jones saw them as her spirit rose to the heavens. Soon they would never laugh again, these sad, sick men who would burn in hell forever.

CHAPTER 31

Katie sat in the sentry hole, within the doorway of their underground shelter, looking out into the blinding white heat of midafternoon. She needed sunglasses to peer out into the light, even though her sitting place was shadowed. Without shifting her position she briefly glanced outside with the oculars. A swirling breeze, as hot as any oven, brought her the scent of smoke. Exposed skin would burn in a matter of minutes in the light. Her mouth was dry—even with the small, rubbery piece of beef jerky she kept in her cheek. In an hour she would take a sip of water—water was very scarce—just one sip every hour. She adjusted the cushion under her boney rump, moved the shotgun nearer to her arm resting on the armrest she had dug in the side of the tunnel. The relatively cool dirt of the tunnel passed through the fabric of her shirt.

After their visit to the city, they vowed never to return. That had been a year and a half ago. Dad believed the hologram shrine had been a clever trap. Why they had not been caught was a mystery. Perhaps the trap had yet to have been connected to police headquarters. They remodeled their temporary, scratched-out hole into a cave home by working during dust storms, either in the day or night. Their new home was partially a metal packing container that had once stored a turbine awaiting shipment from the warehouse. They had dug an entirely new hole adjacent to their existing quarters, dropped in the container, and buried it flush with the original contour of the land. You could not stand in the container; they slept there and added shelves for storage. The original hole was expanded, and Dad actually framed a room within, with heavy planks covering the ceiling and floor. The walls were left bare soil and stone, just awaiting the right windfall of lumber to complete the project.

She liked living in her old neighborhood - the warehouse district. The field where Mr. Woodchuck had lived, where the dog had been eaten by coyotes, where the baby had been snatched, where they watched the heavens at night, brought back memories. She could see the foundations to the rows of paper apartments where once they had lived—where the officials of the government were killed and the storm troopers. The same location where the tent city had stood—where Mr. Bensen had carried her off, where Mat and Dad had fought in the rebellion.

Katie turned, took off her sunglasses, raised her ocular, looked down the short entranceway, only three feet high, at Dad. He lay on his sleeping bag, staring at the ceiling. He spent his days reliving his life. He shared many remembrances. He lived to look at the ideograph—the living picture Mom had always carried with her—of their happy family. They had a Bible, the old nonbattery, turn-the-page book. They discussed scripture and guessed when the end would come. They reminisced over their getting-their-ticket-for-the-Jesus-train parable—that phrase that explained it all; that engine that had carried their lives and propelled the world to its end. She shared with him scripture and had concentrated on those dealing with the Spirit of God—His Holy Spirit. He in turn showed her scriptures that were important, valuable, precious to him.

"Dad, look."

He saw the ocular aimed at him. "Any big pieces of food left between my teeth? I could eat a meal about now." He pulled his cheeks back to reveal more tooth area.

"I can't out-clown you," she said in mock stoicism.

She placed her sunglasses over her eyes, turned back to the entrance, and looked into the whiteness, then brought the ocular to her eyes.

Farthest in her eastern vision was the concrete retaining wall of the highway. Very little traffic had moved on the road, even after the debris—mostly cars—had been removed and bridges or ramps placed over fissures. The depression stretching from the hillside to the wall had once been lush with vegetation but now was scorched black.

It had rained three times since they had ventured to the city a year and a half ago. Nothing had been accomplished by the rain—the greenness that followed was scorched within a day. Sunspots still blotched the sun and had grown slightly in size. They had seen a few birds— sparrows, starlings—come with the rain, as if the birds were following the storms. Many chose to die where the water had once trickled from the retaining wall. She supposed they held memories of water or could smell moisture and came and found the promises empty. The small pond had returned once in the low point of the depression, right where the water had once gushed from the wall. Only mice, rats, an occasional owl or wolf prowled.

The whiteness suddenly turned black. She pulled off her sunglasses, could see dimly. She inhaled deeply, smelled the sudden coldness. No trace of the gasoline, tarry smell. Was this real rain coming? Storms came suddenly now, with incredibly violent winds that would knock a strong man down, push him along the ground like a piece of trash.

The wind came so suddenly, so loudly that the three-and-a-half-foot rounded entrance was like the pipe of a flute. Oooohhh, it sounded. She smelled that strange smell, knew that the fire, the red rain, the hail, the molten lava were coming. She rose, reached for the metal plate that acted as their door.

She stole a glimpse at the heavens, though the grit stung her face. Black as hell was the sky; the clouds created solid walls, had form, substance. Tornadoes twirled before the wall of blackness. She saw fire, glowering, glimmering, sparking and dying, in the blackness; small fires, millions and millions of burning pieces of debris, wood, lava. The hail was already pounding the earth, some of the ice balls black, some red, the size of a human head and larger.

She closed the door, gathered up her cushion and the shotgun, joined her father inside the container. The hail was drumming on the earth above them; she felt the coldness coming around the edges of the door. Tim turned on a small flashlight. They had plenty of batteries, having uncovered a supermarket's battery supply and a charger with a portable solar panel. Scavenging the old stores was pretty much wasted time now. So many people had scavenged; the government had even joined the enterprise, using earth-moving equipment. The original cache stored by their warehouse apartment was entirely gone. The bulk of their food came from the rail line into the city. A few items were found randomly on their night forays.

Tim moved his leg, felt the twinge of pain, a result of their last theft from the train. He had not told his daughter of the injury, didn't want her to become alarmed. He had been searching his mind for an easier way to rob the trains. The storm was welcomed simply because it broke the monotony of the days. He again reviewed the present robbery procedure.

The basic plan was simple: they had discovered two unused highway bridges, damaged by the quake, which bisected the rail line. Fortunately, these bridges were situated where the train slowed to a crawl, prior to its entry into the station. He would fall onto a passing car, open the shipping containers with bolt cutters, if necessary. Many containers were just hard-paper boxes. He would throw boxes of supplies off, into a depression they had dug. Hidden Katie pulled a hidden rope that covered the hole with a camouflaged blanket. At the second bridge, he would snag himself on a rope ladder, hidden by the bridge's support beams. He was out of sight by the time the rear watchman passed under the bridge. The rear watchman never saw him, due to the bend in the tracks. When the train had passed, they gathered up the supplies, carried them home. Simple.

Simple except that falling onto a moving train, climbing ropes, and moving around metal containers devoid of footholds was straining his nerves and his physical abilities. Yesterday he had hit his knee while seeking easily opened containers within the boxcars. Soon, the rail authorities would do something about the broken containers. Though, since he never had time to empty them completely, he thought it likely that train employees were taking the remainders and not reporting the thefts. Eventually someone in authority would see reward in halting the thefts.

They had built a surplus of food, enough for what he thought would be the three hardest months of winter cold, if a winter came. Who knew when the trains would stop running, or guards would be placed in the middle cars, or the containers would be booby-trapped or made foolproof, or all-enclosed cars would be used, or the bridges torn down, or drones used as escorts? He had to keep stealing, and each time he did, the risks increased.

Food was the least of their worries; the water situation was reaching critical. Water had been taken from the city's water pipe, which tapped into the natural flow coming from the concrete wall. He had chipped out a small hole in the concrete, taken his water, then plugged the hole with a bathtub stopper. The water inspectors who came weekly could not see the plug, nor would they ever notice a drop in water pressure. He had always insisted on keeping every water container filled and then refilling every day. Then, one morning, they had come to the water pipe, seen the dead birds littered before the small pond, and looked at the pipe outlet, where a drip around a joint had been used by the birds. The water had a reddish tinge. He guessed the brilliant and desperate scientists had seeded the clouds with chemicals to produce rain, and some unknown reaction or interaction had created poisoned waters. The city, evidently using their underground water source, had simply shut down the pipe. Perhaps, the rainwater could be percolated sufficiently to rid it of contaminants, or the poisonous effects might wear off over time.

They had gone to one-third their water ration, hoping the moisture in the few containered goods they found in the old supermarket sites would make up for the lost water. He had tried using the meltwater from the hailstorms so prevalent, percolating it through earth, through a water purifying system, to no avail. In two weeks they would be out of water, from both their water caches, including the retrieved farmhouse cache, and the water containers within their home. He had plans to scavenge a prequake distilled-water factory; even if they only found one overlooked container, it would help.

The pounding had stopped. The ventilation shaft carried the odor of moisture and oil.

"Dad."

"Yes, my dearest."

"Let's watch the sunset over the city tonight and the meteor showers. It's been awhile since we've done that." The volcanic ash in the air created beautiful sunsets; and the sunspots, auroras.

Outside they heard the long, drawn-out whoosh of air igniting by static electricity where the oil droplets were thickest.

"Let's start now, get in some foraging."

"Alright," she said excitedly as she reached for her army field hat with its wide brim, her gloves, her jacket. She stuffed a coat into her pack—the nights were cold—then the rations and a small canteen of water. Her knife was always on her person. She took her walking stick—an aluminum rod, five feet in length, one end sharpened to a point. This was her weapon and prod while scavenging unknown sites.

She was out the tunnel before he had fully risen. She hated being inside. The white light and heat had already attained its former strength. She looked to the south, where she saw the backside of the storm. Here, against the blackness and the rainbows, great flashes of fire could be seen—some moving horizontal to the earth, some rising vertically, some twisting—wherever the droplets had reached ignition stage. She could hear the sounds. Some exploded like thunder, others ripped along, like a tear in an old sheet. The hail that had fallen had already turned to vapor. The steam rose, hissing. In a minute, it would be gone.

She searched the skies. They had not seen an aircraft on a surveillance mission in weeks. Occasionally, air platforms would land and depart from the field she knew to be by police headquarters in the city. They were flying to known points, in straight flight paths, to other cities, she thought. They easily could have been caught by satellites, but most had been destroyed in the ongoing wars between nations. Heat-seeking or sound-detection drones could be picked up on the handheld warning device she now clicked to the *on* position. On their scavenging, they had seen no others like themselves, dressed in rags, living free. She thought everyone had received the chip, lived in the city, served the beast. What few people remained outside weren't worth the effort of collecting? Still, that policy could change; she always scanned the skies.

She could see and hear the construction vehicles in the distance, below in the city; antiquated types that dug and pushed, pulled, or scraped, and belched exhaust. She could hear demolitions sounding. The crews no longer worked the peak heat period of the day; too hot. The evenings knew full and double crews. She laughed to herself. How busy humans were—like little ants, absorbed in their efforts, not knowing the foot of God would make their efforts fruitless, pointless. People had always been absorbed by the unimportant; that's why the world had to be judged.

The city's wall had been completed; all the old structures torn down within; new buildings rising. Almost all the buildings outside the wall had been flattened and trucked away. An expansive catchment basin or reservoir was being built around the city walls—like a wide medieval moat. The canal, the new river channel, and levee were being repaired. Dad thought water was going to be diverted from the Great Lakes, sent through the Susquehanna River channel and deposited in the reservoir. The scientists must believe they could purify the water, for they had not stopped the project when the water turned red.

She looked down the depression to the water pipe coming out of the wall. A fluorescent sign warned of danger, contamination. Why did they bother with a sign when everyone was within the city and those outside were considered vermin? She remembered the faces of the men who had put up the sign, taken water samples. Under the canopy extending from their vehicle, they had taken off their masks and sun shields to do their tests. Their faces had been covered in sores.

Tim placed the metal plate carefully while arming the grenade that would guard their home. He smoothed out the powdery earth before the doorway so any animal or human print would be seen. They moved down the hill, through the debris of the warehouse, which had been thinned by the winds so only the heaviest containers remained, like children's blocks on a table. He feared the future when work crews would come and remove the containers for scrap or useful items. Workers would wander away on their breaks, searching for treasure. They gazed over the flat desert that had once been a lush field before their apartment.

"Remember the rabbits, Dad?" The field, especially at dusk, had always been thick with rabbits, back in the days of rain. "Remember

Mr. Woodchuck?" She laughed at the remembrance of the fat body waddling. Her father smiled faintly as he scanned the field, the ruins of the apartments where he had fought so hard and so many men had died. He spoke.

"Woody Woodchuck would have made a good meal—plenty of fat."

Katie smiled as she admitted to herself that Woody would have looked good on an outdoor grill. "Are you assuredly saved, Dad?"

"Yes, you know I am." He paused, wondered how he could convince her. "There's the place I lost Mat in the dust of battle." He pointed over the empty space to the ruins of the high-rises. "That's where I met God, my Father, my Dad who loves me." He had told her the story many times—the scary movies, the reassuring arm around his son, the desolation at having lost sight of Mat. The understanding that Mat had carried him through the day of combat. The realization that God had lost His son so that mankind would be saved. Jesus carried His own through the chaos of a perverse and fallen world. Katie always laughed and teared in joy, unfailingly.

"And you know I am dead to the world. That happened over there in our apartment, when they came to sign us up for citizenship in the world of the beast." He glanced at his daughter, saw tears in her eyes. "Rest assured, Katie, that if I die before you, you will see me again in heaven, for eternity."

Katie needed the assurance; she loved him and cared about him, just as he knew Mat loved him. If only Mom could lose her bitterness, could return to them…

* * *

Mary sat in a very comfortable porch chair; her stomach was filled with mashed potatoes, corn, and lean but tender roast beef. That had been her lunch. She had showered in the morning, and her clothes had been washed the night before. A living tree provided shade to the narrow, south-facing porch of the fan-cooled ranch house of her host. A slight, hot breeze sometimes stirred. Her host, Mr. Barnes, had last been seen at the barn, a good walk away.

Underground springs common in the region—somewhere between Pittsburgh and Altoona—had gushed with ten times the usual volume water after the massive quake of years ago. Fields were irrigated and pleasingly green; dairy and beef cattle lowed and bellowed in herds upon the pastures. A pipeline had been built and carried water to the remnant survivors of Pittsburgh. A second pipeline was being built to central Pennsylvania, to Harrisburg. A rail car as light as air and propelled by solar panels that also served as wind sails was running from Pittsburgh to Philadelphia weekly. Mrs. Barnes was in the home, awakening her children.

Mary thought of Tim. He would be shocked at the prosperity. The hope that the world was recovering and life wasn't coming to a close imbued all endeavors. Mr. Barnes said heat-resistant qualities were being identified in plants and animals, and genetics was creating life that could flourish. No poverty, no panic, just hard work. The churches were well attended, and the priests respected, and everyone was happy with the new pope and the new world order. She wondered if Tim lived. She closed her mind to her children; the ache was more than she could bear.

Mrs. Barnes came through the sliding patio doors. In her arms was one-year-old Emily and, holding her hand, three-year-old Amanda. Both with the blond hair of their mom.

"Hello, Amanda." Mary waved, and Amanda laughed. "Come here and let me hold you while Mommy gets your sister situated." Amanda came willingly, throwing her arms up for the lift onto the lap of the smiling woman. Mary made the snatch and grab, and Amanda was securely on her lap.

"Thanks, Mary. Sorry for the delay. The water was red. This morning it was clear and now suddenly red. Was it red in Pittsburgh?" Mrs. Barnes had also taken the opportunity to search Mary's meager travel bag. As the informal hostess for her parish and the county, she was often ask to host guests. Sometimes there was insufficient or dubious knowledge of these guests, hence the detective work.

"I don't know about now. I haven't talked to Dave or Noreen in days. Though they are scheduled to be here in another two days. It's just an algae, but the water might need treated."

Mrs. Barnes, or Emma, as she preferred, had Emily securely in the high chair and had shoveled a few spoonfuls into Emily to "prime the pump," a saying in vogue in that region. Emily took the spoon from her mother.

"Do you want to share any more of the past?" asked Emma. They had stopped the narrative at Mary's life in the paper house last night after dinner, sitting on the porch while watching the meteor show. The chip had been mentioned. The chip had yet to be offered in their area, but everybody was for it. Mary had hinted that her husband, Tim, had been against it. She had mentioned his odd views repeatedly, and this seemed the reason for her split from her family. But to leave her kids, their adopted Emily, and her husband? Emma needed to know more.

Mary thought back to last evening's talk, then began. "Let's just say we didn't get the chip. We ran into the desolate areas, a rainstorm came, there was flooding. My Emily was killed by a falling boulder. We lavished all our food on a wandering band of Tim's type, and then I left. Picked up by a group of soldiers, dropped off at a train station. Ended up in Pittsburgh, and by accident stumbled upon Dave and Noreen, friends from Harrisburg. He had been a leader of a small group of friends, of which we were part, somewhat related to the Church through dogma. They took me in. He does tent evangelism work for the World Church now." No need for Emma to know everything. This was a scouting mission to see what could be taken from the Barnes's, the region, and who would come to the Prophet's revival meeting.

"You have been through much. Here in ag land, our disruptions from the quake were minor; and as we were all self-sufficient, we just made do with what we had. No gangs, no starvation, no desire to break away from the Federation. We had no cash, no business due to disrupted transportation and markets, but that was temporary. People seemed a little freer sexually. It's always been like that here—too much boredom, and too many discreet places to rendezvous. But in hindsight, if the springs hadn't gushed water, we would have eventually starved."

Emma saw Mary fading away, staring outwardly as her mind relived the past. This lady wasn't balanced, she hurt inside; there was much more to the story. She came from a good home and had a delightful life until her husband's grandfather and brother had ruined it.

Mary watched Emma take the empty bowl of breakfast cereal from Emily who had been licking the inside. Amanda had long since departed Mary's lap and was playing in the pile of sand within the porch sandbox. Emily complained loudly and tried to grab the bowl back. Emily kicked her feet rapidly. But the bowl was hidden from sight. Mary knew Emily was finished; Emma knew Emily was finished; only Emily believed she had a hunger.

Mary saw the connection—why had it entered her mind? Was it because deep down, her subconscious was still on that hurt? Mary had not been done with her Emily, and God had taken Emily away. Mary threw a fit. Her irritation would never be satiated, and Mary would never see Emily again. Emily had been Mary's food—feeding her need to be wanted, to be important, to be owed. God had wanted Emily in her new home. God had need of Emily, and Emily had learned all she needed to learn from the deciding and testing place called Earth.

Yes…the memory of God's love. His peace came again to her. It had been so long. She had felt the peace when God had revealed His emotion to her, His love. He had revealed His love for her when He had given His Emily into her care. God was love, and He was emotion rightly apportioned and righteously displayed. He was superior to His creation. Mary was not the decider of what God was or is, but God was the Creator, Determiner of all He made, even Mary. God had loved Emily and was loving her still. Was it not better that God was loving Emily than earthly Mary, who lived on an Earth gone mad? Why couldn't Mary let go of Emily unselfishly into the arms of the Lord? Why couldn't Mary thank the Lord for the time she had had with Emily? Why, Mary? Why couldn't you?

"Mary. Mary." Emma shook the shoulder of her houseguest. Mary looked up in bewilderment into the eyes of Emma.

"Are you okay?"

"Yes, very much so! I took a little trip into the past…I'm sorry I worried you. And I am thankful to be with a person kind enough to worry."

"You're sure you're okay?"

"I'm better than okay." She smiled at Emma and touched her hand reassuringly. Why was she plotting to rob this good woman, who had opened her home and family to her? She thought of Katie and Mat. They were on this Earth, and they needed to be loved. Tim? She hated his independence and stubbornness. She hated the man, and she still loved him. He could never love her now, if he knew the things she had done.

CHAPTER 32

Tim and Katie moved into the ruins of the northern edge of the old city. The heat was intense within her clothes. The demolition crews would never come to this area; time was short, the city ruins vast. She looked at the bare mountain to the north, dull gray rock with patches of brown earth. She remembered when the mountain had been half as tall and fluffy with trees, a beautiful green forest had lain over it like a blanket. She saw a man-made wall on the cliff edge of the mountain, where the restaurant had once stood. Nothing remained but debris. A thousand feet above the ruins, the wind engines began. The glistening white wind propellers turned; each windmill evenly spaced along the crest of the ridge. More were being erected daily.

They had eaten at the restaurant a few times. Once, a young man had sat across the aisle from her with his family. She had thought him handsome. He was probably dead now, and certainly he had not known Jesus. Still, she would ask about him when she arrived in heaven. She had an entire list of people she would seek, from curiosity. Barb and Dan Jr. would be there, she was certain. She had a faint sadness for what could have been, but heaven, eternal life in heaven, was better than the sadness of the present. Mat had said they might live a thousand years on a new Earth, even be able to marry if they survived in their bodies to the end. Well, the redeemed would know when the time came. Whatever could have been will be surpassed by what will be—or it wouldn't be called heaven.

The earth began to rumble, then shake. They sat in the middle of the street. The earth shook violently. She began to hum; the shaking created a vibrato. She raised and lowered her pitch. She and Matthew had played that game when the quakes came. As kids, before the troubles and quakes, they used to thump each other's chests rapidly, listen to the goofy sounds that came out. Yes, she had good memories. Tim watched his daughter and laughed despite himself. When the quake stopped, they rose and continued their walk.

They saw a rat scurry across the street. They followed it into the rubble, hoping it would lead to a food source. They poked, prodded, pulled away debris. Something white caught her eye. She pulled away a metal cabinet lying on its side. A skeleton. A gold chain hung around the neck; a wedding band was upon the finger. Earrings lay on either side of the skull. The clothes were moldy, compressed, gnawed by rats and mice. Burnt-orange sweater, black slacks, well-made utilitarian shoes. Who was she? Had the falling cabinet killed her? Katie knew you could tell age, race, even number of children by the bones.

"Did you know Jesus, Ms. Corpse? Maybe I'll see you again. Maybe."

She moved the sweater and the rib cage within with the walking stick, discovered a blue blanket with the bones of an infant underneath. Katie unclasped the woman's necklace, took it as a memento of this woman and child she didn't know, but for whom she felt great sadness. She would return the necklace if this woman and her child were met in heaven. What a talk they would have.

Finding no food, they wandered on till they came to their favorite vantage point. They climbed four flights of steps; the remaining steps—the building—had toppled and been dispersed so thoroughly that it seemed never to have existed. They had a view of the old city, the new, the river, the west shore, and the mountain running west into the horizon.

Katie surveyed the vista; there was beauty even in destruction. Then she gasped in amazement. "Dad, the canal is full! I see a boat. Look! The reservoir around the city is filling!"

The water was red and about a tenth of the way up the sides of the catchment area. A day ago, the river had been empty. How these empty people clung to life, their accomplishments, even as their hearts were full of wickedness. No doubt they had celebrated their foolishness. She pitied them. Still, the view was glorious, the boat on the canal. The clear sky, the hot wind, the construction vehicles churning up trails of dust. The walled city looking like a medieval fortress, the new buildings within gave the appearance of castles.

Tim scanned the riverbank and reservoir with binoculars. Great Lakes water, he was certain. He watched the debris-remover crews miles away. The wind blew the dust to the south. He studied two vehicles that were stopped. Saw the two operators, men, front-to-back in embrace. The man in front had his jumpsuit down, the white flesh of his buttocks glowed. The motion spoke of sodomy. Another vehicle pulled up and a man got out, raising his arms in utter rage. The two men broke their embrace, climbed back into their vehicles.

He saw wolves working among the vehicles, waiting for rats, mice to be kicked up by the movement. So damn hot. His skin burned from the heat, even under his clothes.

"How many are left, Dad?"

"People? Thirty thousand at the most."

"Out of millions?"

"Yes; but remember, thousands are in the military and thousands have moved away." They knew Mat was in that number; they had seen his name printed on a wall with thousands of names as a tribute to those dutiful citizens serving their lord and their Federation.

He scanned again, to the north, and saw nothing living except vultures slowly circling south to their evening perches in the ruins. The sun was low in the west. A distant storm swept the western horizon, refracting the white light. The temperature was dropping dramatically as it did every night. Colors appeared in the west—deep reds, purples, yellows, oranges. He could see meteors streaking, just quick white flashes, the sky not yet sufficiently dark to reveal their trails.

Tim went back to his binoculars and the city.

"Dad, look!" Katie pointed to the west, to the place of the setting sun. Rising from the western horizon was a cross—of smoke, dust, cloud? She could not ascertain. But a cross, geometric; no fading lines, but sharp. The sun's setting rays shone around it as if it were solid. She stared at it till she realized it wasn't going to fade away. The clouds behind the sun glowed crimson. The breeze was cold; she put on her coat, took off her sunglasses. They ate their meal, drank their water. When she looked again, the cross remained. Now it shimmered like fire, had lost nothing in size. She remembered that the Jews in their wilderness wanderings had followed a pillar of cloud in the day and a pillar of fire by night.

"Strange, isn't it?" she said cynically, knowing this had nothing to do with her Jesus. Many would be deceived in the last days.

"Yes, strange."

The stars were visible, the meteors falling in showers. The trails were of green, blue, yellow. Sonic booms sounded as meteors hurtled into Earth's atmosphere. They saw one meteor crash into the old riverbed, saw flaming chunks rise from the impact. Still the cross illumined the western sky.

Lights suddenly appeared in the city; neat orderly rows of street-lights, lights around all the buildings. Individual light flicked on within the apartments. She saw the factory lights glow; people were working all shifts, producing for the war effort. They were about to turn from the scene and start home. Their hands were numb with cold, and no heat was trapped between their bodies and their coats; they had none to produce. They heard explosions, saw flashes of light from detonations; lights flickered. Figures were running from build-ings; vehicles were moving at high speed. They saw laser flashes and heard powder guns popping.

"The perfect world has its troubles," Tim said gleefully. He brought the binoculars to his eyes and scanned the city. He was glad suffering came to them. They deserved punishment for turning their hearts from God. Abashedly, he remembered when his heart was cold to God. He saw people shot. Some lay, moving in agony, on the streets, a hand raised, a knee bent, writhing. He saw fires in the factories. He watched a group of men attack a lone man. They brutally beat the man about the torso and legs with wrecking bars till he fell. Someone brought the heel of a foot down into his groin and pelvis; the man convulsed in pain as his pelvis broke, his scrotum was pushed into his stomach. A man beat his head with a wrecking bar till the skull flattened. By the postures, head and waist movements of the group, he suspected they laughed convulsively. He saw a group of blindfolded prisoners lined up; someone read to them. Charges? A sharp swordlike piece of metal was swung. He saw a head roll. Someone farther down the line fainted. The heads rolled like underinflated basketballs. He felt the cruelty, the human spirit in full perversity. He sensed the desperation of the blindfolded.

A breach was blown in the glistening white wall, people streamed out. Many were cut down by laser fire. The people moved toward the river.

"Let's get home. We don't want to run into these fugitives in the dark or be shot as fugitives. The police may get an air platform into the air."

They moved quickly, as much from fear as cold. Their breaths trailed into the night. The moving sky of falling stars, their weakness, the night shadows made them dizzy; it seemed they floated home.

***

Mat slid down the spine of a ridge that had been formed a day ago by the strike of two meteors, whose craters, a quarter mile wide, flanked the ridge. He thought it possible that one meteor had suddenly split in equal halves before impact. The sky was hazy with dirt and dust particles in the half-light of the spotted sun. He was light-headed from hunger and overexertion. He had been leading men for weeks, once the Egyptian border had been recrossed. Men had been dying from meteor and missile strikes, from starvation and dehydration and from unremitting enemy attacks.

He had been in the craters once and survived. He would go again into the valley of the shadow of death. He wished someone would tell him the name of this place. He would die in the valley, and he wished to know the name. Ah, God knew the name; that was sufficient. Why did armies clash on a piece of ground so choked with bodies? Why didn't one side or the other back away, regroup, slide off a flank? They were so locked into positions, they couldn't move, he imagined. Only God knew. Funny, how the stench of death no longer tore his stomach apart.

He heard aircraft overhead, explosions, sonic booms. None of the men beside him was familiar; all replacements. Or was he the addition to this company? He and a handful of men who had survived the first assault? Depended on your viewpoint, he supposed, or the designation on the headquarter maps. The heat, the exertion of the last months had shriveled him lean. He was almost a skeleton, and still the heat brought sweat. Heat like an oven. The earth shook constantly, the air vibrating with shock waves from the ordnance. Far, distant, near; the layers of sound piled up in his head.

He wondered about Katie and Dad, and Mom; were they alive? Did they see reports of the carnage on the electrascreen? Or had this whole war been censored? He hoped they had entered heaven. The desert sky, the desert flatness had been his theater. He remembered how he had praised the Lord, danced like a crazy man at the sight, while others cowered. Oh, so soon, it would all be over; so soon. He longed to be with his father and sister. His soul began to ache, a pain as real as a broken limb. The Lord stopped the pain. The last year had been hell; only the Lord had kept him alive.

His army had passed through the remnants of Jewish refugee camps in Egypt, then was diverted south to oppose the Indian Army moving north. His first combat had been clean, a sporting event, compared with his present experience. The Indian Campaign was characterized by rapid movements more like vacation excursions, technological superiority, victories. He had been a part of many good ambushes, behind-the-lines strikes on supply trains. The outbreak of a new strain of plague stopped all armies, stole away the joy of victory in the soldiers around him. Then the sun had afflicted them, burning human flesh after only minutes of exposure. The temperature climbed to near intolerable levels. The effects of the heat made worse by the necessity of remaining constantly covered. The trip back to the Middle East was wearisome, the road lined with corpses. They waited for the armies of the East, the Chinese, under the scorching sun. Each second was an eternity. He prayed for death.

From the continual distant booming of ordnance, he heard the distinctive whomping sounds of approaching concussions. He thought the north end of the ridge was being worked over. The explosions came rapidly down the ridge, toward his company. Through the haze he saw thousands of men running off the ridge. Men, pieces of men, equipment went flying through the air. He sat patiently for the Reaper. The explosions stopped. The ground his company occupied had not received a round. He saw men slowly raise their heads, begin the weary climb back up the ridge.

He wished that he had a friend. Jesus was good, but Jesus in Katie had been better. He missed his sister. He hadn't found a believer in the entire company. A few had claimed to be, but their spirits had been so warped by mental illness as not to be salvageable. Never having a friend through all this, just bodies beside you, with whom you couldn't even share food or water—against regulations, not that he wished to. Most, if not all of his company, were sexual perverts, mental cases, liars, thieves.

Discipline was severe. Desertion brought torture and death. The punishment for theft, death; disobeying an order, death; rape of other men (he had not seen a woman in months), torture then death. He assumed rape had become so prevalent, so disruptive to morale that the penalty had been made higher.

His officers, the administrators of justice, were brutal men. God in His justice had tormented them with open sores. The enlisted men of the criminal companies were free of sores. Matthew had assumed the beast's new microchips, used to mark his own, were causing unwanted side effects. The officers had been drugged to stop their itching, burning pain.

Starvation had taken a perverse course, and men were being eaten, cooked in roasters designed for whole pigs and cattle. The generals set standards for the flesh offered—no diseased or mutilated flesh, only the flesh of soldiers who had committed crimes and had been sentenced to death. The cooked bodies were offered to units who had excelled in combat. He had eaten twice and had no qualms. When one soldier volunteered, "It tastes like chicken," Mat had laughed hysterically till he could not stand.

He had no fear of death and welcomed its release. The course of his life was in the hands of God.

***

From a distance Tim could see that the door to their home had been blown open by the hidden grenade. Two forms lay near the door. He and Katie circled their home, saw no one else. They approached the forms, both dressed in the newly manufactured jumpsuits of the city. The man nearest the door had his face blown off. Katie was beside the other.

"He's breathing," she said hopefully.

"Watch him." Why did she care? She just couldn't let go of her compassion.

Tim dragged the corpse down the hill, into a depression. He then rubbed out the drag marks left in the powdcry earth. The vultures would have the flesh picked clean in one day. He would check for the microchip tomorrow. Sometimes the buzzards inadvertently ate the chips and flew them away. When he returned, the second man was sitting upright against the entrance way. Tim's shotgun was pointed at the man's chest.

"Don't kill him, Dad. Let's hear what he has to say."

Tim's first impulse was to shoot the man, but his curiosity as to life in the city and the fighting was overwhelming. The man had open sores on his face, minor shrapnel wounds in his legs. The first man must have shielded the survivor from the full blast. Some object must have hurtled back, causing a concussion. Tim saw a dented set of night-vision goggles.

"Keep your distance; we don't know if those sores are contagious."

Katie pulled a canteen from the man's thigh pocket with her gloved hands, placed the canteen to his lips. He drank; his eyes opened.

"Don't kill me. Don't kill me. You can have me; there's people who would pay ransom. We weren't going to rob you. Curious…that's all."

Tim smiled wryly in derision. "We won't kill you if you talk to us."

"I'll talk; only the truth, nothin' but the truth." The man gasped as he spoke.

Tim kept the shotgun aimed at the man's chest. He should search the man for hidden weapons; the sores deterred him. Katie would need to sterilize her gloves.

"What's going on in the city?"

"Some people are tired of half rations of food and water while others have full rations. Some people think the truth isn't being told about the water. Some people are tired of not having their sexual fun while others aren't denied. Some people want to go out and meet the prophet of God, the anointed one, who is coming from the west. That's what's happenin' in the city."

The man took the canteen and drank heartily.

"What prophet?"

"Are you blind too? You haven't seen the cross in the sky every night for the last week?" The man's face flushed as his anger rose at the stupidity before him. His fists tightened; the shotgun held him in check. He buried his anger. "Some people have had visions of a man who is God coming. He will return the Earth to the way it was. He's right over the river; right over there, waiting for some people."

"When will he be here?"

"Now!" The voice was raised in anger and impatience. "He's there now. And some people damn well want to go and see him."

Tim wondered at the occupation of the man before the troubles—unskilled, uneducated, blessed with a strong constitution and luck. You didn't have to be smart or educated to survive, just genetically hardy and lucky. The cross had been an impressive sight, the technology needed was state of the art. A technology *that* developed might be able to restore the Earth, he thought sardonically. Food, sex, favoritism, curiosity had caused the city to riot. This prophet was bringing it all to the flash point.

"Did *some people* win?"

"We'll know tomorrow. If the people come out and cross the river, some people did win."

The man wasn't going to be pinned to a side.

"How did you come across this place?"

"Chance. That's all chance." He was shouting again, the voice listening to its own sincerity. "We was lookin' for the water pipe, hopin' for some clean stuff. Cuttin' back to where we started. Got curious; that's all. We called out. How'd we know survivors were still out in the ruins? They said everyone was inside the walls."

"Is there a man named Stasic in the city?"

"Stasic? Yeah. Big man, runs the power plant."

Old Stasic was bound to rise to eminence. This man before him had to be killed. Tim had not killed Mary, and look what his weakness had done—it had doomed Josh and hundreds of others. He wasn't going to risk his daughter's life.

Katie spoke. "I'm sure my father wants to kill you; afraid you'll come back and steal the little we have."

"I swear I won't. I swear. I'm going to see the Prophet. Yes, I am."

"Dad, let him live."

Tim nodded his head in affirmation.

"If we see you, we will shoot to kill. I'll shoot you myself," Katie said angrily.

Tim thought her incapable of killing.

"I swear I'm leaving. I swear. The man rose slowly to his feet, hobbled stiffly down the hill. If the man had the microchip, the microchip could be picked up by satellite. The man would be recaptured in days or killed by an air platform, if he did not return to the city. If he were recaptured, would he use his knowledge of two outcasts as a bargaining chip? Stupid question.

"Dad, thanks."

"Sure."

"Dad, let's go see this prophet, then, once we're out of water, let's hop the train out, see where it takes us. We'll be dead in days if we don't find more water, whether we leave or stay."

"I would rather die in the comfort of my familiar hole, not providing amusement to a group of thieves and sods. But we can take a distant look at this prophet. The authorities, the Church must be in some confusion in allowing him to preach freely. They could have easily destroyed the man and his machinery with air platforms. Unless he is their trap for the malcontents of the new order. We still have hope for water at Gramps's farmhouse. Even if the well was empty when we cleaned out our cache. Could have been rain on the other side of the mountain."

She thought him correct about the prophet; a thing to ponder…a trap. She agreed that Gramps's house needed to be checked. "I'm going in." She was tired from all the excitement of the day. The storm, the barge way filled, the cross in the sky, the rebellion in the city, the captured man, the prophet. "Don't hurt that man, Dad. You gave your word."

"I just want to make sure he leaves entirely. The password is three—as in three in one. You keep the shotgun." He knew the man would double back.

Katie heard; she knew that without hearing the password, she was to remain inside and wait with shotgun pointed at the doorway. She crawled inside. Tim immediately moved downhill to the last sighting of the man.

He came upon the man resting against a container, bandaging his leg. Tim watched quietly, patiently; he had not been seen. The man rose, searched the debris, found a club. His limping shuffle moved him to the left and up the hill. He was flanking their cave with the intent of killing them. Tim moved quietly behind the track of the man, his knife pointed at the man's spine, and slowly gained ground. He heard the man muttering and cursing to himself. "Kill them, I will. The little bitch is tender meat." Tim sheaved the knife, pulled his garroting wire from his pocket.

With one step, the wire was over the man's head and tightening around the neck. The man was unconscious before he could bring his hands to his neck. He died with barely a gurgle as he lay on the ground. Tim pulled the man downhill by his feet; gravity lessened the effort necessary. The bulky-looking man could not have weighed more than ninety pounds. All clothes, thought Tim. His buddy had weighed more. When Tim's energy was spent, he stuffed the corpse in the nearest depression. He cut open the jacket, the shirts, for easier access by the vultures. Tomorrow he would move both corpses farther from his home, unless wolves or vultures had done the work for him.

CHAPTER 33

Carl watched the gates of the city open from the height of his broad office window. The crowd of people surged through. As a member of city council and a novice priest of the true Church, he had voted to give the people a forty-eight-hour pass. An anger seized him as his sores began to burn and itch. The damn political scene was so vague, so damn murky. Let the trash go; the good citizens would remain. That was harsh. He could understand some good people might want to see the Prophet. His mind turned to the riots of last night. Some good people had died.

The leaders of state government had conveniently chosen to defer the question of prophets and holy men to local government. He assumed the prophet currently approaching the city had political power or influence at the highest level. Was this prophet allowed to roam freely through the State purposely, as a means of identifying the discontented? Certainly, a satellite or drone was recording every citizen present. Or was this prophet part of another coup within the Church? In the end, what did he care? He was fed, clothed, had an apartment, women, power, respect—those things were life. Then why was he empty inside?

He was a smart man; he had played the political scene correctly. Quite a feat, after having been the leader of a failed insurrection. He had clearly perceived that the old God, conceived in the Judeo-Christian heritage, would give way to the new god of human achievement, sensuality. Subtlety accomplished. The ruler of the Federation and the world—the Antichrist—had supplanted Christ. Saying *Antichrist* aloud was a severe jail sentence. But in effect, he *had* supplanted Christ. Christ was only a word, an ancient word devoid of power. This ruler's political partner and cabinet member, a prophet himself—the false prophet, supplanted the function of the Holy Spirit. God? God, once the maker and ruler of the universe, was supplanted by the ruler of this world—the collective power of man and his life force, the one Christians called Satan. A total reversal! Amazing!

Amazingly, Carl had helped wipe out the last political undesirables, those who clung to the roots of the Christian religion. They had no place in the new world. What triumph he had acknowledged when Joshua and his band had been captured. What utter sadness he had felt in their torture and death. He had once aided the small band and seen them as allies. He smiled pensively as he remembered how he had discovered, through the drone footage, that Tim Johnson and daughter Katie had been at the revival meeting by the river with Mat, and that Mat had lied so perfectly. Mat's unit was in the Middle East. He wished he had had a son like that. His five sons were dead, hadn't amounted to much. He hadn't enjoyed the execution of Josh or his band, but the times were different—brutal. His survival meant everything now; God knew his heart and that was enough. Then, why was he empty inside?

Carl slipped a pill into his mouth. A medicine to help the itching, the pain. He was one of the privileged few to receive the medication. The word was a vaccine would be ready for distribution in a month or two. Why had Tim taken his family into Enslaver doctrine? He seemed so sane, so like himself: an achiever, a survivor. Ah…a part of him was an intellectual, one of those who built fairy-tale kingdoms in their minds, where all happiness and goodness resided. Then they lived by the fairy-tale laws and motives of right conduct and found satisfaction in that.

Carl turned at the sound of footsteps in his spacious office. He shivered in dread as the high priest and the mayor walked toward him. Young men, early thirties, no wives, no children, never talked of their pasts. They were odd fellows, completely odd. They came from nowhere, already endowed with power. He could not discern an accent, a geographic tell in their speech. There was no trace of a regional dialect or global accent. No hint of their origin was given by their vocabulary. No one had any recollection of them in city politics or business, or even as citizens. The internet did not even have their names.

They disturbed him deeply. He physically feared them. He sensed their great physical strength, not of muscle or hormones—not like storm troopers—but of some vast well of unlimited power constantly flowing within them. Their height and thinness and musculature seemed to speak of steel cables stretched tautly. He was reminded of his demolition machines—his debris clearers, using the old hydraulic or pneumatic systems. Even their movements and mannerisms seemed different, though he could not identify or put a name or description to that difference. Perhaps, it was that they seemed to be acting as men, performing a role. They didn't fit into this world. Otherworldly? He could almost believe it.

His mind was under great stress. He had been thinking strange thoughts. He even realized that he talked to himself—to Buddy, his other self. Maybe it was loneliness or a way to find clarity apart from himself. The sores were distracting and painful.

Intellectually the high priest and the mayor frightened him. They seemed to mockingly look down upon his intellect, his intelligence. He believed he could never measure up to their mental standards, that they had wisdom, thought processes, he could not fathom. He had never in all his life been in the presence of men or women whose minds were deeper or sharper than his. He had known people who were quicker, who had photographic minds, who operated from different paths of logic; but in the end, he had always gained equality of understanding, if not superiority. He could not best these men. He thought, when together in private, they laughed at him in arrogance and disdain. They seemed to communicate with each other without speech. They created a paranoia within him.

If all this was not enough, he sensed that they lusted for him, together. Just standing beside them, making eye-to-eye contact, he felt their minds were exploring the private parts of his body, and even his internal workings, spleen, liver, kidneys, bowels. He had handled homosexuals before, calmly denied them or forcefully denied them, but he had always had the power to do so. The power of money, prestige, politics, or friendship, but more importantly, physical power kept them in their place. He had been blessed with natural strength, and the hormone supplements had allowed him to retain if not increase his power, even as he reached seventy years. But these two had greater power; he sensed it, trembled, knew they could rape him at their pleasure or pull him apart with their hands like he was a loaf of fresh-baked French bread.

He had wondered if it was his imagination. Had he gone mad? Sex had never been mentioned, they never talked of their sex lives, never commented on a passing woman or man, never mentioned spouses. They seemed almost asexual at one level. He kept a retractable-bladed stiletto in his pocket from the moment he awakened to the moment he slept. He kept a shotgun by his bed. He never allowed a woman to sleep with him—didn't trust anyone.

He scanned the past years for an overview. People weren't what they were; he thought he had to include himself within this comment on humanity. Six or seven years ago, by his guess, things began to get strange. Seven years ago, he enjoyed one woman, the wife of the moment, as his partner, confidant. Now, it was group sex with three. He had to participate in the orgies of the Church hierarchy, men and women. He had allowed no one to enter him, but some had been on their knees before him. Eight years ago, he would have put a laser to his brain at the thought of such filth within his mind, let alone a physical act. Now, it seemed as nothing.

"Carl." The mayor smiled as he came up beside him. Even their voices did not ring true to human standards. Something mechanical in the tone, even when the inflections and vocabulary were human. And it seemed as if they had trouble slowing their thoughts to the speed of their speech. "Why aren't you overseeing this adventure?"

The high priest, beside the mayor, gleamed at Carl.

"Why should I?" He enjoyed being defiant, challenging their every sentence. He would like to kill them.

"To give us a report."

This wasn't an order, but it was wise to follow their suggestions. Did they truly wish to know? He doubted this; they probably had been privy to all the reports generated on this prophet. Therefore, the real reason was they wanted him out of the city…to assassinate him? To embarrass him for political, Church purposes? Or to have him absent when they did something sure to raise his ire? For all their haughtiness, they were amateurs at politics. Carl addressed the high priest.

"Is this prophet of your faith? As head of the Church, you should meet him."

For once he had them confused. If the Prophet was of their Church, then what was the point of his being, his roaming? If the Prophet was not, and they answered as such, then why was he allowed to roam?

"We wish you to watch our citizens, guard their safety to and from the Prophet's meeting."

"You didn't answer my question." He was tired of being subtle with these freaks. The priest answered. "In a sense, he is of our faith, though he is of no value to us, except as amusement for our people. And again, he is not of our organization, but he's no threat to our numbers. We tolerate him."

"Like you tolerate me?"

They said nothing. He sensed both were excited—not from fear; it was an excitement sexual in nature, but not sexual. Damn it! Why was he so confused?

"I'll get my coat and my driver and be on my way." Anywhere to absent himself from their presence.

***

The Prophet sat on a large boulder, one third of the way up the barren hillside. The vehicles of his caravan were parked in a semicircle at the side, and the base of the hill. Standing in small groups, close at hand, and yet separate, the disciples of his inner circle waited for his direction.

Behind the vehicles was the Prophet's tent, within were his women—perfumed, in silks, waiting for his touch. Mary lay within the tent, her stomach full, her body with curves and roundness restored, her mind lightly but happily drugged.

The Prophet's long hair and flowing beard were as white as his loose-fitting robes. His skin was tanned darkly, though he was a Caucasian. Around him, thousands were gathering on the flat land, once an ag field. The lone hillside and flat land encircling consisted of rock-hard base soil, small stones, an occasional boulder, eroded gullies. The sky was clouded with volcanic ash. The air was cool, the light subdued. The Prophet wished that it were finished.

***

Since dawn, Tim and Katie had watched the people stream out of the city. Tim thought he had seen Carl Stasic in a vehicle. Tim and Katie had followed the crowds, parallel to the procession, keeping a distance that would, hopefully, preclude them from air surveillance and ocular devices. They saw others like themselves along the fringe of the movement, scavengers dressed in the old clothes—ragged, dirty, emaciated. He wondered what weapons these people carried and became fearful. He was certain the authorities used the Prophet to collect people such as himself and Katie. He increased their distance away from the scavengers, but still he went on.

By noon, the people were gathered before the Prophet. Blankets were spread. Some sipped water and surreptitiously placed morsels of food into their mouths. No true meals were eaten—he guessed no one had food or they were afraid of theft. Tim noticed a great aura of peace over the people below him. No fighting, no cursing, no arguing. He was certain he had identified Carl watching from a vehicle. The day stretched into the late afternoon, and the Prophet sat on his boulder in meditation. Tim focused his binoculars on the Prophet, studied the man. He was certain he knew the man.

"That's Dave! That's Dave! Remember Pastor Dave? The estate, the swimming pool?"

"It couldn't be, Dad; that man is older. Dave had dark hair. Dave fled to the desert," said Katie flatly, hoping to bring down her dad's enthusiasm.

Tim handed his daughter the binoculars. "You know all the obvious answers to your objections. Just look."

Katie held the binoculars, which automatically stabilized. She pulled her eyes away after a long gaze, then looked again. "It could be."

"It is. Let's go down and ask him." Tim laughed crazily. Katie refused to respond to the absurdity. Nothing would change—even if it was Dave. Certainly this man wasn't proclaiming the Jesus they knew, for he would then have been an Enslaver.

The Prophet nimbly raised himself from his lotus position on the boulder. He raised his hands, waited for the gazing eyes to focus and the silence to become complete.

"You are thirsty. God will give you water."

His voice carried over the crowd, up into the ears of Tim and Katie, who were behind and to the side of the hill, on a gentle rise. The clarity and volume were unnatural for a man making no effort to be heard. The Prophet pointed to the gentle rise of land to his right. The eyes followed his outstretched hand. Patiently, they waited for something. But what?

Tim and Katie heard the gasps first, then the word *water* on hundreds of lips. In unison, the entire assemblage gasped, spoke of water. "Water! Water! Water!" Tim saw the growing stream of water coming from the earth. First a trickle, then a stream, then a gush. The water carried into the gullies, became a stream. People stood, cheered, clapped, hugged, danced, ran to the stream, buried their faces in the water, scooping water with hands, cups, any container they could find. People crowded along the gullies as the water branched into tens of channels.

The people moaned in relief; they prayed, they were on hands and knees, lay on their bellies, raised hands to the Prophet. Suddenly, utter silence, save for the gulping of water.

Tim bolted from his hillside position. Katie grabbed at him but could not stop him. She would not move—she would not be a part of the lie. She would remain apart. She would remain with Jesus.

She watched her father move to the end of the crowd; the people were so thick by the source of the water that he could not have forced himself through. She saw him bend down, drink with his hand, then lay on his stomach, pulling water in with both hands.

The water was so sweet, so pure. The sound of the water moving in the gully brought back memories of the happy times. He heard the thousands of people gulping, slurping, talking in low whispers to themselves of their deliverance.

As the people had their fill, they rolled upon their backs on the hard ground, they sat in utter contentment and peace. Throughout the crowd, single voices began to call, almost singing, "You are God. You are the Savior."

The Prophet listened with bowed head, as if humbled by their adoration. Soon the entire assemblage had hands raised, were following dominant voices who sang God's praises. On and on went the praise, seemingly forever. Till the Prophet raised his head. Silence. The Prophet raised his hands. The silence was heavy as if every breath was held, every exhalation ceased. Only the sound of the gushing water could be heard. The expectancy grew; it seemed it would break into shouts. But then the Prophet spoke.

"You are hungry. Eat." His arms spread out as if showing a table. His disciples carried boxes from the vehicles. Brown, foiled packages were passed through the crowd. The people ate, and they ate again. Each time they finished one meal; another meal was in their hands. Tim, on the fringe of the gathered, had a food box passed to him. He ate, enthralled, sitting in peace and contentment. His stomach filled with the meat—chicken by the texture, flavor, and bones. He read the package's listing of contents—quail. Where in the Bible had he read of quail? The people of Israel in the wilderness.

Katie watched her father. He had slipped no meal into his jacket for her, nor filled the small flask he carried with water for her. Satan had tempted her father, and her dad could not say, "Man does not live on bread alone, but on every word from the mouth of God." He had seemed solidly in Christ yesterday, solidly in Christ this morning. Water and food—the desires of the flesh. He sat for the longest time; she thought he nodded into sleep as his stomach digested the meal. She nodded in and out of sleep.

In time, he awakened, rose; and she watched him work his way to the front of the crowd, to the very stone that the Prophet sat upon. The Prophet stooped down and talked to her father for some time. Yes, it must be Dave for them to talk so long. The smile on her father's face said as much. Her father sat. He had always sought and cherished the company of men of repute. That was the world's hold on him. Now the Prophet— the devil's representative—had him. The world, status; the flesh, satiation; the devil, friendship. Dad could not see it happening.

He had left his pack with her and the shotgun. She would make no attempt to go down to him. On the hill she would spend the night, if necessary, hoping he would return to her. She would not go to him till morning, then she would plead with him to return with her. She sensed this was the Spirit's will. The Lord was showing Dad his weakness. The crowd, full of food and water, began to doze as the Prophet moved off the rock into his private tent.

*****

Mary watched the Prophet come into the tent, two of his latest favorites twined around him. He fondled them. He glanced at Mary, wondered if he should tell her that her husband was outside, gleaming like a child because he knew the "Prophet." The Prophet knew the story as to their parting. He wished to see the emotion upon her face as proof of the validity of her story.

Mary studied him. When he had just been Dave, his appeal had been overwhelming. His masculine form and beauty, disciplined from all but his wife, was unattainable, distant, and pulled at every woman's desire. She had slept with him twice then. Tim had never known; it had been good, and then it had rotted into remorse and emptiness. For the first month of their reunion, he had entered regularly. He was just a man now; she felt nothing for him. Only his body made love to her, and only her body responded. She was officially a cunt—this world's term of worth for her. She despised herself.

She had never acted upon that moment of revelation and clarity at Emma Barnes's home. She had rejoined Dave and Noreen, reported the prosperity of the Allegheny region, told them where the wealth was located, what was being preached in their churches. "Profit" Dave had come, fattened himself on the land and the willing women. Mary took just one pill to even her mood that day. One pill became many pills. Now, she felt only shame, disgust. Her stomach was full; her body bathed, clothed in fine linens; she had prestige, access to good drugs; and these things she had once wanted were like chains upon her.

Profit Dave had told her that her son was in the Middle East, her husband and daughter were still alive, wandering. She now wished to God she was with them. There was no love here, no peace; she was trapped in her flesh, she ached for her husband, her children. They were the best years of her life yet, those family years, and even the memories of those good days would die—as she would die for her sins. Tim would never want her back. What she had birthed, nurtured, and educated—her children—had eternal value and life. The thought had come upon her from nowhere. She wanted to see them again, to hold and love them.

The Prophet glanced at Mary. She excited him now that he had seen Tim. Her misery and unhappiness excited him. His power of knowing, of secretly shaming her with his knowledge, excited him. He knew she wished desperately to be reunited with her husband and daughter. She needed their forgiveness and love. He would love to penetrate her aching soul, make her hurt more. Make her hurt as he hurt for his sins. How had he come to this philosophical desert, where his hatred of love was his love and satisfaction?

She saw his desiring gaze and spoke. "A good crowd?" She had only been to one other gathering, near Altoona.

"Yes. Many people."

She knew by what city they had stopped. "Anyone among them that I would know?"

How she longed for a familiar face, an acquaintance, word of her daughter or husband.

"No." His own cruelty amazed him. He held her hand and led her into an inner chamber and was upon her. She cried as he loved her. Noreen, Dave's first wife, stood secretively outside the chamber's fabric and listened and wished it was she under the body of the Prophet.

CHAPTER 34

Katie awoke with a start in the middle of the night. For a brief moment, she glimpsed the angels standing guard over her. They all smiled at her in love and empathy. She was cold, her breath twirled from her nostrils. The heavens were in disarray, stars streaking everywhere. Planets exploding. A message had been dropped into her mind, a message from the angels. She swung the sawed-off shotgun around her. No movement on her ridgetop. Nothing on the barren hilltop of the Prophet's tent. On the flat plain before the barren hilltop, she saw the sleeping forms of the multitudes. Dim nightlights burned in the Prophet's tent and those of his disciples. What a strange silence was upon the crowd, illuminated by the night sky.

She wrapped the sleeping bag around her as she sat, watching the silent and still crowd. She saw a man moving through and around the prone figures. A blanket of thickness and size was over his head and around his body—he seemed to be studying the forms. She saw her father's form, curled up. The searching man was hovering over her father. Her stomach was empty, her body shook with cold. Why hadn't Dad returned to her at nightfall?

She jumped up suddenly, waving her arms purposely. The searching man saw her and concentrated his gaze upon her. He suddenly and quickly made his way out of the prone, quiet multitude, moving toward the Prophet's tent. She stuffed the sleeping bag into her pack. She was going home. She had seen enough of the Prophet. What had that man with the blanket wanted? She would tell her father about the man—tell him that she was going home, and he needed to come with her.

She entered the sleeping mass. They were so quiet—no snoring, no whimpering, no coughs, no tossing and turning as they sought to keep their blankets arranged upon them. The night was so cold. No condensed breath coming from nostrils and mouths. Dad had separated himself as best he could from the others. She bent down near his head. "Dad, Dad, wake up," she whispered. She shook his shoulder. His face was ashen white, his body stiff, his skin cold and waxen. She felt his neck for a pulse—cold skin; as cold as the night, no pulse. She touched other bodies around him; they were all dead, all ashen white.

Her daddy was dead—that is why the angels had come! She was not cold—the Comforter had His arms around her and like a blanket, shielded her; warmed her in her heart and mind. It had to happen sometime. The odds they would have finished the race together had always been a long shot. Katie stood, gazed at the tent of the Prophet. The man covered in the blanket was standing, watching her. He raised his arm and waved a broad wave. She waved back.

She wanted to take her daddy back to their hillside home. She didn't want him touched by strangers, thrown into the crematorium, where the smoke never ceased. Her dad's spirit was gone; she saw an empty shell, nothing more. She must leave his body and be content with his spirit in heaven. Angels had gathered around her; they were explaining to her it was best to leave. That it wasn't done. She didn't know what that meant, except that they referred to Jesus's coming for His elect, but she trusted. "See you soon, Dad." She smiled as she spoke, even as her eyes streamed tears, and moved quickly into the barren land.

Dad had failed his final test. Thoughts came into her mind. Jesus hadn't failed her dad nor had He failed her. Her daddy was sealed with the Holy Spirit—a seal so strong the world, the flesh, Satan could not break it. A man or woman could certainly not break the Spirit's protection, certainly not by the weakness of the flesh. God could not break His oath, and

Jesus could not be anything less than Savior, Redeemer. Yes, we would always fail, she thought, and God would never fail us. That's what the angels had been saying. We were incapable of earning our salvation, and we were incapable of keeping it even by our flawed dutifulness and devotion. "See you soon, Daddy." She laughed in delight at the kindness and mercy of her heavenly Dad—Father God.

Bill Smith placed his hand by his side and pulled his blanket tight. That must have been Tim's daughter, Katie, waving. He had heard they had never received the chip and roamed free. Mat, their son, was in the Middle East. Their mother right here, a drugged-out whore of the Prophet.

Katie looked back at the huge tent, saw another form by the Prophet's tent—someone dressed in a white gown and staring at her. Katie was over the ridge and on her way home.

***

Mary had come outside to clear her head. Too many pills, and yet not enough to hide her shame and regrets. Mary saw the form walking over the ridge and out of sight. She had seen the form bent down in the mass of sleeping bodies beside one figure. Her curiosity was aroused. So many people, so sound asleep. All came to hear the words of a liar, a man—not a god. She walked down off the hill to where the figure had been standing. By that man, yes; by that man, the figure had stood. Bill Smith had waved at the figure.

Strange that no one moved, rearranged blankets, coughed, snored. So deathly still. Emboldened. Mary moved closer to the isolated, sleeping figure. She could see his face clearly—ashen white. A meteor shower exploded overhead in a sonic boom. She knew that man. A familiar face. Where had she known him from? She moved closer…closer. No exhalation from the nostrils, no movement of the lungs. She was getting cold, hadn't expected to be out this long. She should go back. One more step.

She smiled broadly. Tim, her beloved Tim. A mental surge engulfed her of all the good times, the intimate moments, the triumphs of their lives together. Innocent, pure, good moments. Her heart leapt for joy as if all the evil between had disappeared, never existed. God had brought

483

them back together. God, she still loved Tim, still wanted him. If only he would forgive her.

"Tim, Tim. Tim. Wake up!" she whispered hoarsely, anxious to gaze upon him, and to have him hold her closely. She shook him by the shoulder. It would be alright; he would forgive her. She shook him again. So unmoving, unfeeling. Her knees buckled, she collapsed to the cold, hard ground. In utter despair, she realized he was dead. Her hands clutched his coat, she shook him in anger. She felt a hard rectangle within the coat, an ideograph, her living picture. She pulled out the rectangle, pushed the button. The six-by-nine-inch rectangle came to life.

She saw them together, after the birth of Katie, Matthew still a toddler. Back in the professor's house, back when life had been good. The style of the clothes seemed so quaint. Matthew bent over his sister and kissed her on the cheek. Matthew had loved his sister. Tim was beaming, so full of pride, confidence. He glanced at her. She saw the love, admiration he had had for her. She, so youthful, so willing to please him. They had been the perfect family. The perfect family. She watched the scene repeat itself, over and over. Each time, her resistance grew weaker.

That figure that had walked away from Tim? Katie? It was Katie!

Resolutely, Mary rose. It was all clear to her now. The so-called "Prophet" was a tool of the Church. The Prophet cleaned the scum from the new society, the new world coming. She had been too drugged to know she was part of an extermination squad—back in Altoona, thousands had come, and she could not remember their leaving. Her Tim, her foolish Tim, had hoped in a lie.

Bill Smith was beside her. They had shared the past good times—the cookouts, their kids swimming together in the pool. Tim had thought highly of Bill.

"Bill! What has happened here? My husband is dead."

"He is only sleeping now; soon he will be dead."

"What do you mean *sleeping*? What do you know? He always told me what a good man you were. How he thought you were special—kind-hearted and bold. Help him if you can. Wake him. I must tell him I love him. Oh, please Bill…not for me…for Tim…for the love of the only true and righteous God of this world, Jesus! Jesus, awake my husband! Oh God, I beg, I beg you!"

Tears appeared on Bill's face for his family that was no longer upon the earth. If only he could have brought his family back to life. Had Tim thought so highly of him? He believed Mary. That Tim had found value in him bathed his cringing soul in worthiness. He pulled a syringe from his jacket pocket as his blanket fell. He methodically exposed the bare skin of Tim's chest and sent the needle into the heart. "We must rub him, stimulate his muscles gently. We need to warm his body." He searched Mary's eyes.

"Take him to my vehicle," a voice boomed above them.

"Carl?" Mary was astonished as she turned and saw Carl.

"Yes, let's move quickly." Bill and Carl supported Tim, placed his arms around their shoulders. Tim's feet dragged upon the ground as they hustled him to the vehicle. They spread him upon the back seat of the luxury sedan. Carl increased the heat within the car and began massaging. "Go find Katie, Mary; she was on the hillside watching. Bill and I will watch over Tim. He will be fine. We will watch you and follow as best we can." Mary bolted from the car.

The direct path to Katie's last position was through the Prophet's tent. Mary strode to the tent; pulled out a tent peg. A homemade peg made of scrap metal, sharp and rigid. She stared at the electronic eye that guarded the tent. She was enveloped into the doorway folds of the tent and entered and then quickly entered the Prophet's chamber.

There was the Prophet, a naked woman on each side, asleep in his bed. Muscled, tanned, the perfectly handsome face. She could clearly see his ribs. He prided himself on his leanness. His chest was heavily muscled, dense over his sternum. She slowly, carefully aimed the stake two inches up from the bottom of his sternum and to her right. Then she thrust, her full weight leaning atop the stake. She felt the sternum compress, then the stake penetrated between the ribs. The sternum seemed to engulf the stake.

She moved the stake heavily, searching for the heart. She felt the heart tighten, spasm, even as he rose and struck her across the face. His women slid from the bed, drugged to a stupor. She strode for the veiled egress. He attempted to yell, hoarsely came the muted cry; blood bubbled and spewed from his mouth. People were rising. She ran as fast as she could over the hill toward Harrisburg.

She must see her daughter. She must beg for forgiveness. She must know that she was forgiven. She had become a hateful woman, had destroyed her family. Katie was all that was left to hold onto, all that was left of the good in her life. An overwhelming anxiety seized her mind. Bill Smith had lied—Tim was dead; cold as the night. Her slippers fell from her feet. The rocky earth of sandstone layers cut her feet. She fell and tore her robe. The cold grabbed her bare skin.

The cold was intense. The sonic booms, the meteors crashing to Earth, the stars moving and exploding, the hurtling comets at last filled her with dread. The world was ending! No scientist in this world could mend the heavens. She had to have that forgiveness from Katie before this world ended. She moved in the direction of their old apartment. The food cache was there; that is where Katie was going.

Bill Smith and Carl Stasic had watched Mary go back into the expansive tent of the Prophet. Bill tensed and grabbed the car door handle, ready to bolt. Carl stopped the massaging, grabbed Bill's shoulder, and applied the heaviness of his bodily weight. "What are you doing?"

"She's going to kill him." Smith was panicked.

"No, she is just picking up shoes and a coat. It's on the way. You need to help me with Tim."

Bill looked back at Tim. "He's dead! The antidote was administered too late. Even given on time, it only has a 50 percent success rate. Let go of my shoulder! She is going to kill my only hope." Bill broke free.

"What about friends—true friends?" retorted Carl.

Bill did not turn back. Carl began his massaging even more vigorously. He managed to place his hands on Tim's bare chest. He felt warmth in the skin; he saw a pulsing in the chest. He stripped Tim's jacket, shirt from him and began massaging arms, shoulders, back, neck, torso. Breath was coming to Tim's nostrils. "Yeah, baby. Now we're cooking. Keep it beating." Carl began moving the arms, bending them at the elbows, then flailing them in arcs over Tim's head. Carl bear-hugged Tim and lifted him up, up and down repeatedly. "Tim, speak to me. Speak, Tim," Carl begged, as he verged on panic.

"Enough," said Tim angrily, and then he spoke gratefully. "Enough."

Carl winced a laugh, pleased with his efforts. "Praise God, the Lord of Lords. I have never worshiped you till now. Where have I been, Lord?" His contriteness came from a deep shock and ache. You just had to keep trying when all seemed lost. You just had to keep trying. Take the sledge and pound, Buddy. Make the dust and chips fly. His life's motto had become an inner conversation with Buddy. But it was true; they were only people, and they all needed help sometimes. Stubborn help. Carl bundled Tim in blankets, moved quickly to the front seat, and drove, while quietly and patiently turning the car back to the trail of Katie and Mary. They were gone, over the dry hills. Best to cross the river at the bridge and intersect them on the east shore.

***

Bill entered the tent. No one seemed to have stirred. All in deep sleep from tiredness or drugs. He entered the inner chamber. The Prophet, once known as Pastor Dave, lay upon his silken, room-sized bed of cushions and pillows. It was evident he had tried to rise when the tent peg had entered. The stink of a final bowel movement had been the result. Little Davie has pooped his jammies, thought Bill. The tanned, healthy skin, the chiseled body, the overused sex organ had meant nothing to the tent peg and the woman enraged. Well, Bill, it is over. You had backed the wrong horse, bet the wrong spread. The full stomach and access to antibiotics and antivirals was over. It had been over when his family died—years ago, on the commune in the desert place of the Midwest. Life had died then, and there had been no shot in the heart to revive him.

Bill had no desire to continue. It was time to die—and pray the real and true God of creation would have mercy on his soul. Isn't that right? There was a true God Who loved us? No. No mercy existed in life; the word should not exist. Mercy? If the Enslavers were correct, this God had a new world waiting—a place where he and his family could live once again. How he had laughed and mocked those childish tales, even when Pastor Dave had spoken of them; and now he would have flayed his body with his own hands, poured salt into his flesh, eaten dirt, cried to God for a thousand years to enter the thought of that bright and hopeful world. God mocked him now, for he could see that place in a vision—in a reality. A great tree of life offering shade and coolness from the heat of hell. God never mocks, came a word. Such a wonderful wife he had had, such good and pleasant children he had led astray. The purity—the goodness, the joy that came from that sparkling vision of what was and could be. It was like champagne filling the bed of a river; the bottom of varied-colored stones glistening, and the tree on its banks so green and leafy that he could eat of the fruit, so sweet and luscious.

He could see his children—from the time of diapers, to the summer shorts and swimsuits, to the awkward years—and in every scene was his companion, his other half, the woman who knew his thoughts before he spoke them. He smelled the scent of her perfume, that sandy dry scent of desert blooms. Where were his kids, his wife? He had failed as a husband and as a man. He unclasped the small, circular gold container from around his neck; pressed a pin-sized protrusion; the lid sprang open. An ancient piece of jewelry containing a plastic vial filled with a clear liquid. No! Grab the vision and repent! It's never too late for God! "God, forgive me for my blindness, my ambition. Forgive me for leading astray my wife and my children—your greatest gift to me. I am so sorry, Lord!" He placed the vial into his mouth and bit down with his incisors. Bill Smith, who had always wanted to help others, who always strove to be more and do more, watched his body die—for just an instant—and then he was gone, falling through blackness.

***

Carl had passed the nexus point five times slowly. Carl could see Tim's eyes were half open; he looked sleepy more than drugged or comatose. "Say something, Tim. Let me know you're alive."

"Something," said the weary voice. "Something is some thing." From a man who had returned from the dead.

Surely, Katie should have passed by, if not Mary. He knew there were drones in the sky that night, and his driving would arouse suspicions. And even though he was Carl Stasic, a big man in the new town, he had an Enslaver in his car. The freaks he worked for—the mayor and the high priest—would read his mind and find Katie and Mary. He wanted to make this reunion happen as atonement for what he had done to Mat, for all the good times he had shared with Tim, for the sweetness of Katie and the loyalty of Mary. He had wanted to see his sons and daughters and had not. It left an emptiness.

He could not take Tim to the office; the cameras would pick up his form, would investigate with facial recognition, or read the invisible ID number in the skin of the forehead. The freaks were always stopping in unannounced. There was spyware in his office, which they thought he did not know existed. He could take Tim to his home…no, that posed the same problems as the office did. Besides, his home was a rathole with paper-thin walls. He basically lived in his office.

He knew where Tim was living. Well, the area near his old warehouse apartment. He had been privy to drone and satellite recordings. The dumb asses—military intelligence and the police—viewing them hadn't seen the signs of habitual movement, the patterns of life, or the odd pieces of debris that were, in reality, camouflaged forms. "Tim, listen good. Are you listening?"

"Yes, Carl."

"Get ready to leave this vehicle quickly. Get your clothes fastened. Take food and drink packets from that box in the back. Take them all if you can cram them in. Take the blanket. I'm dropping you off by the last rubble pile of the high-rise near your old apartment."

"Gotchya."

"Crawl out of the seat and into the building. That's the best I can do."

"Thanks, Carl."

Carl smiled, remembering when Mat had said those same words, *"Thanks Carl."* Mat sounded just like his old man. The car stopped, Tim rolled out and into the building, and Carl was gone. Back to the office.

Carl pulled his car up to the freight elevator in the underground parking area. His usual parking place. He felt tired but light of foot and contented of mind. Doing good always felt good. He thought of the vigorous rubbing that brought Tim back. How thin and weightless Tim was—just a shadow of himself, the wiry muscle was gone that had withstood the thugs that day they had met. Inside, Carl passed the employee gym and the wide and long community treadmill—fifteen people easily could walk or run, the groupings arranged by previous treadmill performances. Fucking running and going nowhere, just like life—his life. One day, the setting had been too high, and all had either fallen or been jettisoned from the back or had jumped off the sides.

A metaphor for life, he thought, as he entered the elevator. He had no cover story, if he was asked why he took such a curious route back to his office. *Just wanted to ride. Got a problem?* He sensed the story was coming quickly to a close, the story of his life. He had never seen his earthly life as a treadmill going nowhere. He had always believed God was life; it was God's world, He made things happen, and a man was to live and enjoy. The world had been a wonderful place. Now, now that it was all coming to an end, he realized that the Enslavers had it right.

The world wasn't wonderful; it didn't belong to God any more than the lives of the inhabitants of this world did. It was Satan's world, and men lived Satan's life upon it. The good people, with heart and patience, kept the treadmill going; and it was a victory just to do the smallest good—to encourage people, to give them a happy thought to think; to patiently endure while the malcontents came along on the ride for free.

The good people knew that God wanted accountability and responsibility; He wanted them to give kindness, opportunity to those around them, to treat others like they would want to be treated. So simple, and the world's people couldn't even do these basic things—they were dumb asses, lazy dumb asses, dead weight. "I pledge allegiance to the flag of the United States of America, one nation under God…" Yeah, he still remembered the ancient words. And even he had been duped—Carl Stasic, the sharpest thinker of his time, had been duped. The world wasn't good; it was evil. Life wasn't good if God wasn't the center of your being, because it was God—God, alone—who was good. There had never been a goal for mankind to achieve, not some heaven on Earth or some state of human enlightenment to strive for; the treadmill went round and round.

This Earth had just been a testing ground—who would love Him and who would ignore Him—a place to dig deeper into the mind of God. Who would choose Him? Tim and his family had found Him. Mat and Katie—just by looking at them, you knew they were different. And the Smith kids, Dan Jr. and Barbara; they'd had something—something good and unique. These Enslavers knew this world was all going to fail; their Bible had said so. They dug their foundations deep, with character and truth as their goals. They were simply waiting, enduring, taking pleasure in their God—not life—till that day when He returned.

Carl entered his office. He moved toward the bar. The hell with it; he needed to be sober—judgment was coming. Carl was ashamed of himself, of his life. He had never taken the time to know God…it had been all about possessions and power- for Carl. He changed course, went to his hidden drawer and pulled out his sawed-down shotgun loaded with buckshot. He loaded his pockets with shells. Four barreled and light as a feather; he could shoot singles or doubles. Just the appearance of the barrels frightened people. He grabbed an energy drink from his small refrigerator and sat on the couch against the wall.

"Well, Buddy, I think it's just about over for me. What do you think?" No answer came from Carl's imaginary self. A thought was placed in Carl's mind: Tim, Mary, and Katie likely needed food, water, maybe even blankets and medical attention. One last kind act might be significant in their lives; he would do it before he met the God of wrath that would so rightly punish him.

Carl heard his automatic door slide open and deep masculine laughter—the two freaks, the mayor and the high priest. They must have been waiting for him. Carl quietly placed the shotgun between the couch's backrest and the couch's seat cushion. He could tell they already knew he was in the room by the way their noses explored the room's scent. They smelled dirty bodies; maybe their sense of smell was so keen they knew who the missing body, whose scent clung to Carl's clothes, was. He must kill them quickly before they read his thoughts.

"I heard you talking to your friend. What have you two to report?" the mayor said with actual human mockery in his voice. He had heard Carl talk to his friend before. The standing men faced sitting Carl. Carl saw the beginnings of worry on their faces—dread—and then it dissipated. They didn't think he had the nerve. Well, he had the fuckin' nerve, and he pulled up the shotgun with his right arm—his finger on the trigger as he swung the gun over, close to the cushion. The high priest's leg swung around in a roundhouse kick. Cark had known it would come; he had seen the priest stage his body prior to the kick, knew the man's long, thin legs were his only recourse for self-defense. Carl touched two barrels to the priest's torso as the priest regained balance from the strikeless kick. Without a break in his motion, Carl emptied two into the torso of the mayor.

No launching of the bodies backward; just a black, wet mist billowing around the standing and bent bodies. He *knew* they hadn't been earthly! Carl remained in his seat calmly but quickly ejected the shells and loaded four more. He blasted the upper chests. As he rose he reloaded again, wondering if ingesting the mist would kill him. Black liquid was pooling on the tile floor. It smelled like blood. They weren't of this world. They had remained standing until he kicked a foot out from under each of them.

Still, their cognizant eyes looked at him. He pulled the dagger he had strapped to his forearm and cleared away their clothing. He saw muscle-fiber tubes, bands of muscle stretching from feet to lungs and necks, tightly packed and running vertically. The lung area held a long chamber and beside the lungs a long tube that he thought was a heart. Carl stabbed each man between the eyes and drove the dagger deep. Then he was gone from the room.

It was too late to help the Johnsons. Even to go near that area now would bring the authorities and an intensive search. "Well, Buddy, let's go to the Camp. Relive our finest days. A good place to die."

***

Tim opened another meal, his third, and was just as hungry as he had been for the first. He had managed to bring the entire box. Laying in and on rubble; feeling cold air pressing into sinuses through ears, nose, mouth; smelling and tasting the devastation of the times was business as usual. He was alive! Dead or as close as a human could come without actually being—and now alive. His body was humming with life from whatever concoction he had been injected with. He smelled the pulverized concrete dust, the lingering odors of human carcasses—likely just bodily fluids, the skin and bones carried away by coyotes, wolves, buzzards, rats long ago.

He must lie and eat and, hopefully, sleep before moving on to their underground home not so very far away. His only entertainment was thought. The thoughts in his mind, they were life—the proof that he was alive. How soon would it all be over—man's reign upon the earth; really, Satan's reign. That evil figure, who, for most of Tim's life, had only been a murky abstraction of what was wrong in the world. That evil figure who had wrested control of life from man and sent creation into turmoil.

Soon there would be justice and punishment. You couldn't crucify God's Son and expect no consequences. If Mat had died in the war, or had been captured and tortured, Tim's rage would have known no satiation. God had sent His Son to His vineyards, and the tenants had killed Him. Tim understood the righteousness of God's wrath, yet he could not understand the stupidity of the tenants—and he had *been* a tenant. Admittedly, Tim was a more conscientious tenant than those around him. Holding to a faith in a God he sometimes could not define, holding to rules of life that brought goodness and kindness to his family and to others. *Love thy neighbor as thyself...do onto others as you would have them do onto you.* More cultural norms that most people had not known existed yet, for the most part, followed.

Such generalities would not excuse humanity on the day coming. Everyone had forgotten the imperative to "love the Lord thy God with all your heart, soul, mind and strength." That was where the Church had gone wrong; that was where man had gone wrong; people ignored their Creator, their Dad, and with that gone, they were just unruly, self-centered, pleasure seeking, hateful brats. Worse, they were subhuman—a mix of man and animal—just creatures. Even animals had more integrity than they did. Animals were what God had made them…humans were not.

Even though he had seen the remains of tortured people, seen men tortured, seen starvation, brutal robberies, and assaults, he had no energy to hate. Probably God had no hatred. Probably just a duty. God fulfilled His Word. No empty threats to scare you into doing right. He would clean up the mess and reward the kids who listened to His voice. Just love God for who He is and not for what He gives you. Lying in the rubble now, in worn and smelly clothes, with a half-full stomach after three meals, with a family scattered, but with his Father, his Dad, Tim felt more peace and contentment than he had ever known in his prime, when he'd been loved by students, adored by his family, admired by his colleagues, and in perfect health.

Where was his Mary now…how could he open her eyes? Where was his Mat? Where was his Katie? God knew. God cared. And all would be well, because God was good, and He loved His kids.

CHAPTER 35

Mat crouched upon the slope. The air was thick with clouds, layers of smoke, dust, engine exhaust, ordnance vapors. He guessed the unseen sky to be a solid lid of clouds. No shining sun when the suspended layers of warfare's pollutants separated. Dull light was all his eyes had known for some time, like a perpetual dusk. Always oven-like heat. When the smoke and dust parted, he could glimpse, along the desert ridge, company after company, thousands of men, waiting to go over the top, into the valley.

His buttocks slipped, pressuring his heels, which began to slide. Bare rock, made slimy by decaying, bleeding, oozing corpses. Among the ooze were bare bones, wet or dried fabric, uniforms, gas masks, rucksacks, every imaginable piece of military equipment in some state of brokenness. Above this layer of war was another—bodies recently dead, whole, wormy, shrinking, bare skulls grinning as the flesh pulled away, and black, decaying flesh. Sitting on this layer were the most recent corpses, now bloated from the heat and seeming ready to burst out of their uniforms. Most of the bodies had tumbled down into the crease of the ridge. At one time, the whine of flies was louder than a man could talk; the stench was such that a man had to wear his gas mask. The crease had been shelled with rounds of pesticides and lime. The whine had decreased until a new generation of flies, fewer in number, had come.

Mat's slide stopped when his feet hit a solid ledge of rock. He sipped from his canteen; thought of forcing himself to eat. He couldn't. The valley over the ridge, for as far as the eye could see, was covered in this triple layer of dead flesh. Interspersed among the corpses of people were the corpses of mules, horses, even the camels of the adversary—the great armies of the East, China, India, and the Muslim nations of Asia. Burned-out equipment was mixed among the flesh, tanks, personnel carriers, covey launchers, artillery, scout cars, air platforms. Three generations of equipment, the modern air foils, the old combustion engines, horses, draft animals. Three generations of weapons, the laser, the powder, the bayonet and sword.

Ordnance booming at all points of the compass. The whoomping sounds of approaching concussions that would shake your heart, suck your breath from your lungs, and shake your legs out from under you came with the regularity of an assembly line or an automatic jackhammer. Lay in your concealing hole and hope. Listen for the throat-com whistle and go where you were ordered to go.

The haze of the battlefield began to break apart. Anxiously, Mat checked himself for exposed skin, then realized the danger from the sun had past weeks ago; perpetual gloom wrapped the Earth. A figure scrambled over to him. The face jaundiced, the eyes bloodshot, the teeth rotten, the cracked lips open in a foolish grin.

"I'm going to get you, my sweet. I'm going to plug that hole. I'm going to jump on your corpse and love you to death!" The face was contorted in ecstasy.

"Tell that to Jesus." Emotionless but confident was the answer. The true General—Jesus—was coming.

He knew the soldier, or rather, the personality within a soldier's uniform. He always gave the boy/man the same answer, and sometimes the man left in bewilderment, and sometimes the man cursed Christ with a hatred only Satan possessed. The man was a homosexual, a necrophile, and had taken a liking to him. Matthew had no doubt that if he did fall in combat and no officer was watching, this perverse creature would attempt to carry out his promise. And if given the opportunity, he, Matthew Johnson, would kill this abomination of the flesh.

Today, a dumb look glazed the man's eyes. He whimpered, scampered away as if fearing for his life. A whistle sounded, one long blast on the throat com. A collective groan rose from the parched throats of the weary soldiers. They rose to their feet and started for the crest. Their objective, a column of burned-out tanks, then a small rise of land further into the valley. What strategic value this had, he didn't know. Upon the crest, he looked out over the vast valley. The haze of war had risen, stretched like an aura from the valley's rim. He caught glimpses of movement—columns, men, machines, moving over the gore, pressing out the blood and serum of the dead like wine from a press. Tens of thousands of rats moved among the corpses, making it seem as if the earth moved. He had learned that Megiddo was the land's name—the plains of Megiddo.

***

Carl looked over the debris of the Camp. Every structure had been torched, all the single-family homes, the clubhouse, the command center. The pool had been pulled up into a heap. Human bones lay scattered about, white and forlorn; some still with clothing. It had been a place of hope, a refuge, the last gasp of people who remembered what had made their country good and great. He wished to be on the top of the mountain ridge behind the Camp. He wanted to see far, and he wanted to be closer to heaven.

He drove off road, headed straight up the mountain of soil and rock. Eventually, he would ruin the rotors, but there would be no garage fee; this was the end. It felt good to be climbing, gaining height. The silence outside the vehicle was good. Then, a rough bump, the rotors turning off kilter. Then, the odor of metallic friction, heat, a seizing, a jolting stop. Carl eased out of the vehicle. A gentle breeze blew from the south, offering a lessening of the pounding heat. He looked up to the crest of the mountain; the steepest ascent was yet to come, a half mile of sedimentary layers. There were openings almost like paths; it was doable. He looked west, east, and south. A brown vista with metallic reflections from buildings, roofs, solar panels, windmills, debris. The cumulus clouds had shaved bottoms and towered mightily into the heavens.

"Well, Buddy, I'm a horse of a man, but I don't know if I have the cardiovascular for this climb." This was the final trip—no future appointments, no job to go back to, just to die on top of the mountain. Just take your time, Carl. No rush, said Buddy. Carl exited his vehicle, and on hands and knees, he felt under his seat till he located the box strapped to the seat. He pulled an old-fashioned, leather-bound book out; he had never read it. Now, he had the time. He placed it in a coat pocket and began to climb.

Carl stood on the top of the world, so it seemed, as there was no greater height in central Pennsylvania. His hands and legs trembled. His heart beat rapidly, but his breathing was not labored. He had stumbled once, and his knee was scraped. His sweat stung the abrasion. His heavily perspiring body felt cold in the constant breeze. "I am home," he said to God.

He believed God heard him. He tried to kneel into a cross-legged sitting position, but near the ground of flaky, sandy shale, he tipped to one side and felt the hot rocks and dirt cling to his wet cotton shirt before he righted himself.

The elation of the view—the feeling of the hawk or eagle—the peacefulness and quiet were good. Clouds, sky, the blues and whites; the earth, browns and grays—colors were good. The breeze was good. The immensity of material that made the earth was incredible and awesome. God's creation was good. It was mankind that had ruined it all—those little three-pound masses of material tucked into those hard skulls; mobile on two legs of flesh, bone. Little demons from hell—twisting, turning, deceitful little minds attempting to escape their Creator's authority and love.

The burdens of his heart were so heavy. He thought of Mat. All he had done for Mat was to keep him alive a little longer—to suffer more. But Carl Stasic had collected a bonus, said Buddy. He couldn't remember what the bonus had bought him. Was Mat now dead or alive? Where was he in that dryness and destruction that was the Middle East. Where did his bones lie? He sensed Mat sitting in a pile of rubble, half starved, angry—with the enemy around him. Why didn't he try with more zeal and determination to save Mat? Why did he so willingly collect the bounty and send Mat away? He could have pulled strings; he could have saved Mat. The course of history would have been altered. Perhaps Tim, Mary, Mat, and Katie would be sitting here with him now. Why had he hunted Joshua as if he were a rat running loose in an immaculate home? The blood of that righteous man and his followers was on his hands. Carl winced as he remembered their torture. He had been responsible for their pain and their deaths. Oh Lord, forgive.

And his own family—where were his children, grandchildren, great-grandchildren? Why couldn't he have remained married to his first love? What had pulled him away? Yes, the twisted mass sitting within his skull. He was like all the others, the race of men: perverse.

And yet he had done some good. He had lifted people from poverty by creating jobs or just by bestowing money upon the needy. He thought of the little Asian woman with two preteen children who had lost her husband on one of his demo jobs, when the business was first starting. Carl had paid off her mortgage, found her a job in an office, bought the family clothes. The smiles on those kid's faces, the joy in the woman's heart. She had been the first. He had done the same for many over the years. He'd given people opportunity and watched them grow. He had kept businesses open that were only breaking even to keep people employed. He had started businesses that had meant nothing to him to give people jobs and hope. Nothing was needed in return; to want something from them was to degrade the goodness that life…no, *God* had thrown his way. Maybe that counted with God; maybe it did. But now it was only his sins that weighed upon him. He had killed God's people and heaped anguish upon their lives. He opened the book he had brought, called the Bible, and began to read.

***

Katie awoke from her sleep. The crevice she had wedged herself in was halfway between the Prophet's meeting place and her hilltop home. The crevice had been created by the runoff from the last significant deluge, back when they had lost their Emily. The sunlight had yet to pierce the sunspots—she was in that extended dawn—yet the heat was intense, and she covered her lower face with her bandanna. She wished she could have made it home, but the strength wasn't there. Daddy, Daddy, Daddy. she thought scoldingly. You just wanted to be important one last time; just wanted the curiosity satisfied. Dad was firmly in the hands of Jesus; Satan couldn't pry him loose, no matter how it appeared. For some time, the Lord had been preparing her for Dad's leaving. The Spirit's presence buoyed her in the belief that Dad had found and held onto what he needed to know—that Jesus was Lord. He was truth, and humanity owed Him its very existence. Dad owed Him everything, and her dad had fixed that idea permanently in his heart.

Crap! What was that swaying in the breeze? The figure of a person, seeming to move in her direction, barely discernable in the heat waves coming off the bare earth. Yes, the person was taking the same route she had taken. Surely, the wind would have carried her tracks away; it was just coincidence; it was just the easiest route if a person were heading to the northeast corner of the old city. Who would want to go there? Who had seen her traveling at night? Or was she visible in this crevice on the hillside?

Some loony from the Prophet's meeting? Someone to rob or rape her? Well, let that person come. That person would be getting weaker with every step closer. Katie felt for her knife. It would be quiet. She touched the sawed-off shotgun—the extreme backup. She waited patiently and studied the person as the distance decreased. A woman. An older woman. A well-fed woman, compared with the average. A barefooted woman who could no longer feel the pain in her bloodied feet.

Mom!

Katie was about to burst from her cover and run to her. Who was watching? Was this a trap? She let the woman come. Yes, it was Mom. Mom was on a course to pass her. Mom had appeared to look at the crevice and decided to go up the slope to the right of the crevice. Katie waited till her mother had passed, then slowly, cautiously scanned the area. She saw no one. Katie rose and began to follow.

Mom walked into an area of rubble. Katie realized Mom must have slept outside, weary with exhaustion, unless she had lost the track and wandered in the night only to pick up the trail again. When Katie was close enough to talk in a conversational tone, she spoke. "Turn around, Mom. It's me, your daughter. Do you remember my name?"

"Katie? Is it you?" Mom turned. Tears welled from her eyes. Katie looked into her mother's eyes and saw the heartbreak. Mom just stood there; and Katie went over and embraced her, rubbed her arms and back with her hands, moved the straggly black hair away from her face and kissed her forehead, her cheeks. The past swept over Katie as she remembered the soothing Mom scent of skin and hair, the warm breath of a mommy who made every pain right. "We're together again, Mom. Let's go home together, and we will talk."

Her mother's eyes lit with happiness. Her mother found Katie's hand and held it like she once did when Katie was just a young girl. Katie swung the hand. "It will be alright, Mom. You will see. Jesus loves us, Mom."

"I've got to get back to your dad." Her urgency ached with anxiety and dread.

"He's in a good place, Mom, and we will all be there so very soon," Katie patiently and confidently replied.

Mary ceased to worry.

***

The last artillery shell dropped. The ringing in his ears continued, yet softer in volume and intensity. Mat raised his head and saw hills and ridges, the flat valley, covered with the dead. He saw movement ahead—a hundred yards, a quarter of a mile, two miles, he could not orient himself, and spatial reasoning was not returning. He checked his pockets and his ruck—no rations. He sighted his laser at the nearest movement. The sight said two hundred yards, and the optics revealed the men to be Chinese; three, one wounded badly. Mat searched the bodies clustered near him; they were Federation forces. He found a hard rectangle in a hamstring cargo pocket, a ration. He grabbed the arm sleeve and turned the body to access the ration. The jaundiced skin, the rotten teeth—his wannabe tormentor, the necrophile. He smiled at God's justice and providence. He opened the box—beef stew and bread.

His mind went back to the dead woods around Gramps's home and the meeting of Josh and his crew. There, Dad had cooked beef stew. The best meal he had ever eaten—even surpassing the Thanksgiving turkey meals of his childhood. He wondered if Josh and his people were alive. He had seen them at the interrogation center. No, they were dead and had been tortured before they died; he was certain. Was Stasic "the informer" alive? The man who had lived bold and free…and then became an informer, a sniveling coward who kissed the hands of the men who killed his country…killed even the hope of freedom. Where was Jesus in the life of Stasic?

Mom, Dad, Katie? No need to speculate. He felt it in the air; time was almost gone. He laughed; they would meet soon, and all the answers would be revealed. The questions to the test had been given to him. He laughed, as it felt like the night before Christmas when he was a kid—total expectation; the hope that material dreams would come true, that mere material objects of play or learning would soon be presented to him. Just because it was that time of the year and the hope of the world had been born. Oh, how sweet was that expectation that something good would happen. Priceless joy. The true Christmas was coming—Jesus returning for His own.

Mat began to cry—in pity for the naïveté of the child he had been; in sadness for a Savior who deserved much more than humanity could give; in joy, contentment, happiness for Matthew Johnson, who had a God who was his Daddy and loved him. Times had been so hard, the worry, the anxiety, the hopelessness. He raised his hands to the heavens for the Christ Who would soon come; he assumed the pose he had seen so often on the battlefield of men who had surrendered. That is what you had to do: surrender when your hurt was overwhelming, when Satan was tramping on your neck, and despair was in your last breath. The overwhelming love of God could kill your enemies as surely as a high-velocity bullet. Overwhelming love could birth you into a new world, where they could not follow. He reached for the arms of his Savior.

He remembered back to that time when he had surrendered—he was just a kid—and Dad had told them they had missed the Jesus train. Dad was perfect; how could they have missed the train? Then he'd known that his sister—his friend—was his responsibility. Mom and Dad could fail again. He had to talk to God about this. On his knees, in the still of the night, he gave his anxiety and worry and his fear to God. Matthew Johnson had given his life away to God in the hope his sister would know no pain on Earth, that his sister would have eternal life in heaven.

He watched the enemy; the two were bandaging the one. Likely no knowledge of Jesus there; just straight, overwhelming communist doctrine, political hero worship, and racial superiority. The world Federation had much in common with those soldiers, but at least these Chinese had nationalism to raise the goose bumps and exhort their efforts. He should kill them now while they were out in the open.

Walk over to their dead bodies and see what goodies were in their rations and have himself a party. He had no officer or noncom over him. He sat isolated. He was the war, the Chinese trio were the war. He scanned the other pockets of movement farther away. The ridgeline movement could be an enemy mortar emplacement or artillery observation post. He would watch, for now; and if his communications gear came back up, he'd request a round on the three.

The day would be long; the stew would help.

***

In the shelter of the cave home, Katie and Mary sat, backs resting against a wall softened by pillows, their legs stretched out before them. They had eaten a morning meal prepared by Katie and now had warm tea in mugs by their side. The last water had been used. The tunnel doorway was open. A trip grenade wire was stretched across the opening. The shotgun was by Katie's side. Sound detectors were placed outside, near the door. They looked like rocks. Her handheld control panel would flash at the first and slightest sound. Mary had taken the living picture from Tim's possession when he had lain helpless and now was showing Katie the scene.

"Yes, Mom, there we are—you and Dad in your prime. Me, a diaper pooper; and Mat, on his way to adulthood." She joked. Mat had always been mature, it seemed.

"You know, Dad is alive…Bill Smith was giving him a shot." Mary's voice was vaporous and uncertain, it seemed to Katie. Was Mom telling her about a dream?

"We will seek him out, Mom, and see whether he pulled through. He was ice cold to my touch, and I think his body had been dead quite a while."

"Why don't you have hope?" Mary asked. "God is a God of hope."

"Our hope is different in this situation, Mom. We will see Dad in heaven, and that is only days or weeks, maybe months away. Then we will have a thousand years with him on Earth and an eternity in heavenly realms. It is less important that he lives to see Jesus in the air, returning."

"But the scripture said we had to endure to the end," Mary said adamantly.

"To the end of our time. Dad was and is fully rooted in God—we had talks. You know he liked to socialize, rub elbows with important people. He was always curious; he made a mistake in wanting to see the Prophet and getting pulled into the moment. Our sins are forgiven when Christ fully owns us. Temptations can't undo the new people we and he had become. Once God makes His decision to claim us as His own, the deal is done and can never be reversed. Not by man, not by Satan." Her heavenly Daddy held onto His own and the thought of that unimaginable, unfathomable love brought tears.

Katie sipped her tea, then gulped, realizing it was turning from hot to warm. She didn't want to use more heat tabs to warm it. Mary studied the scene on the ideograph: a family that did not know God. How strange. At the time, she thought she knew God. She had known nothing, and the little she thought she knew had been wrong.

"Drink your tea, Mom, before it gets cold."

"You sound like the mom here," Mary said, not unpleased as she followed her daughter's advice and example and drank her tea. "I did not know, God, Katie. I look upon the scene of the supposedly happy family and realize how deluded your dad and I were. Me, most of all. I have failed you, Mat, and your dad."

Katie looked closely into her mother's eyes, then spoke. "We need to talk about Jesus, Mom. I need to know that we will all be one happy family in heaven. Tell me what you know of Him now."

"I know He is God, and there is no other. He made us in His image, and that seemingly trivial thought is the key to it all. He is not a supercomputer, nor is He an *it* or a *she*. He is not simply logic and mathematical equations. He is emotion, fully apportioned and righteously displayed. Our emotion is tainted by our sin, so that we cannot trust it or live by it. We compensate with our logic, which is just as tainted as our emotion. His emotion created, gave the world life, and sustains life. His emotion is perfect, balanced with His logic, His knowledge. How can we comprehend Him? Where I am? I had a breakthrough in my bitterness at losing Emily. I saw myself as the child I was, throwing a temper tantrum, thinking that Emily was mine and He had no right to her."

"When was this?" Katie was pleasantly shocked by her mother's revelations. The Lord had certainly heard a daughter's prayers.

"Just months ago? I've lost track of time, between Pittsburgh and Harrisburg. Then the mind relaxers stole my heart away."

"The world, the flesh, the devil. Mom, the enemies. Your flesh cried for peace and ease, and you took the wrong way out."

"I know. Yet it was deeper than that," Mary said. "My mind's logic and clear thinking was twisted by emotions and falsehoods, so that even when I discovered a part of the truth, it could not hold under the assault. The Lord taught me something that has cleared my path—that my own mind wars against God's control of me. It does so by denying the utter purity of God's goodness. For if God is an admixture of good and evil, then I can be the decider of what is good and right for me. That is Satan's lie, for Satan must cling to my mind if he is to retain control. To know God's purity is to define the enemy, Satan." If Katie only knew what a sinner her mother was—a slut, unfaithful to her husband. A stupid woman who had helped kill thousands of innocents. She began to cry.

Katie was shocked at the depth of her mother's search and the wisdom in her words—wisdom Katie had never felt the need to formulate or even grasp, as she had always thought of God as pure goodness; that He could be some admixture was an alien thought. A more pressing concern was the end of the world. Did Mom have time to self-analyze?

"Does God have the right to end the world when He wishes?" Katie asked.

"Yes." The word came between the tears.

"Do you understand you are a sinner and have no right to demand eternal life?"

"Yes."

"Do you trust fully in Jesus's death on the cross to wash away your sins and open the portals of heaven?"

"Yes."

"Then we're going home together." Katie was excited; it was like being a kid and getting into the car for the two-week vacation at the beach. Expectancy of goodness and pleasure ahead—and adventure. Katie clasped her mother's hand firmly and shook it and leaned into her mother and kissed her cheeks. Mom was coming along on the trip that lasted forever.

"Is it that easy?" Mary asked mildly in protest. She had made her daughter happy, had answered her questions, and knew that, indeed, it was that easy. She wished to reward Katie for her caring and concern. She knew it was easy, wanted it to be easy, but her sins—and her guilt—were horrendous in their implications. She could not share the degradation caused by her sins with her daughter. "Surely, I must pay…I must do…something for the privilege of heaven. I don't deserve this."

"Yes, it is that easy, and you just needed to know that to make it complete. Our God is that good." A great weariness came to Katie; Mom looked tired too. "It's not about proving yourself through works aimed at God. It not about amassing knowledge of the Bible and God. It's about admitting you're from a fallen race and never wanting to belong to it again. Just in the privacy of your heart, tell Him you're done with that world, and you want Him. He paid it all with His Son's torture, degradation, and His suffering on the cross. He did it for you, Mom! He wanted to show you Daddy, our Father, our God. Just obey Him; that makes His heart glad. Let's take a nap, watch the star show tonight. Tomorrow will be another day."

The sound-detector panel was blinking the red warning. Katie grabbed the shotgun, pointed it at the entrance.

A voice came from outside. "Katie, it's me, Dad. Are you in there?"

In elation, Katie scrambled to the door on hands and knees, her face and mind wild with emotion. She stopped suddenly—it could be a trap, a voice recording; or her father could be outside with a knife to his neck, or a laser aimed at his heart. She turned back suddenly, retrieved the shotgun, and then returned to the doorway. "Listen well, Dad." She paused. "Three."

"I know what you're asking. Just give me a minute…my mind is foggy. Carl brought me back from death with an injection."

"Did he tell you about Mom?"

"No."

"She's here with me."

Was Katie okay? wondered Tim. Was this a trap? Concentrate…Katie was giving him the password challenge. "One. Three in One! Father, Son, and Holy Spirit."

Katie detriggered the grenade. "Come in, Daddy. I saw you dead—cold dead! I cannot believe this!" She retreated to the living quarters just as Dad rose from his hands and knees to hug her. They hugged each other for an eternity, it seemed. Katie cried. Through his tears, he saw a weeping Mary behind their daughter. His Mary seemed so small and frail. Katie, with eyes of mirth and love, looked her dad straight in the eyes. "You and Mom have things to talk about. I will be right outside, in my observation pit." Katie gathered up her jacket, gloves, hat, and shotgun and moved down the tunnel entrance.

***

Tim stared hard at Mary. This woman had brought unnecessary tumult, anxiety, sadness to him and the kids. He believed her to be responsible for Mat's capture, the capture of all of Josh's people and countless unknown citizens. Was Mat dead? Was he wounded? Was he a prisoner, being starved and beaten? Josh and his followers had undergone excruciating torture before being burned alive. How had Mary gotten here? Dave had not mentioned her, but he was no friend. Was she the same hateful woman? Or had new layers of falsehood and hate been added since last they spoke? Mary saw a hatred welling up within him as he spoke.

"Who did you inform?"

"No one, Tim. I got into a truck with a group of AWOL soldiers when I left you, then a train. I talked to no one. I couldn't turn against my family. I was a mess. I was bitter at God. I was bitter at you because of your damn faith was greater than my hurt. I was wrong about it all. Please forgive me. Please." She searched his eyes. Could he love her again? Did he want to love her? "I want to go into this next life with you and Katie and Mat. I want to be a good mom. I want to love you again, Tim. I was the problem…please, forgive me. Please."

"You couldn't turn against your family? You walked out on us when we needed you most." No response came. He stared and he glared, waiting for the pressure to crack her silence. Nothing. "You came back with Pastor Dave?"

"Yes…simply by chance, I met Bill Smith in the western part of the state, and he led me to Dave and Noreen. That's where I've been. That's where I failed you. He hooked me on pills…and he used me for his dirty life."

Dirty life? That was Mary's euphemism for unrestrained sex. Her strategy was to blunt the edge of her sins.

"That was the first time…for sex with him?" Tim remembered a time when he went to her workplace, and she was not there. He had set his trap.

Mary took a deep breath. She could lie…but she could not, because she had not been raised to be a liar. "Twice I had sex with him then. It brought nothing but shame."

"So much shame you went all the way across state to engage in it again."

"No, no, no! The AWOL soldiers let me out by a train station, and I went west. I was alone in a strange place, and I bumped into Bill Smith—he gave you the shot that brought you back to life. Dave was to give me a job, and then he made it easy for the pills to be before me. He weakened me then used me." Mary had slowly decreased the distance between them. She just wanted to touch, to hug him. He needed to feel her need for him. She needed his love and acceptance.

"Tim. He was killing people, and no one told me. He was a murderer. And I murdered him." She broke into sobs, and she crumpled to the floor.

Tim recognized the genuine hurt, the devastation. She had chosen her words not to deceive him but in an attempt to protect herself from herself. Mary had always held life as sacred. He knew what being associated with an organization that killed, with a man who killed, would do to her self-respect, her ego of vigilance and awareness. She had killed Dave? Incredible. New layers of guilt had been added to her, if true. "How did you kill him?" Mary had always held that their marriage was sacred, and their sexual bond of fidelity was precious beyond measure. How Satan had debased her, degraded her, and now laughed.

"I drove a tent peg into his heart. The night you died."

Unbelievable. Now his wife was a murderer? No—he had killed in combat and in peace. The gangster George had been kicked to death. She must hurt deeply. Her hurt was real, and whatever healing she could receive, he must be a part of it. But she had betrayed him; she was damaged and could only take from him his peace.

He was not perfect, and he had been damaged, and he had only taken from her in that damaged state. He must give back to her. He must soothe and heal her damaged places. He must provide validity to the goodness within her and within their God. He could not turn from her or punish her. She was his own flesh and blood. She had raised his kids and had done it well. He chose to love her. She was flawed, she had fought battles with God and with Satan, and now she needed to mend. The Lord had done so for him—stood by him, took him through times of pain and heartache, to the other side, and embraced him. He could do no less for Mary.

He propped himself up against the cave's wall, drew Mary into him. Rested her head upon his chest. Kissed her cheek. His leg lay upon something. He pulled from under him the living picture and pressed the tab. "Mary," he whispered. "Open your eyes. Look at our perfect little family."

She opened her eyes, wiped away her tears, and smiled as she watched her handsome husband, a loving and kind man, with his young children.

He held her tightly. kissed her cheeks, lips. "I love you, Mary—I always have, and I always will…an upside-down world…the deceiver as our enemy…cannot conquer our Father's love for us and our family."

Mary sighed. "I love you more than the day we married." She could rest in Tim; he was a man of faithfulness and love.

CHAPTER 36

Sunrise is coming to 666 Armageddon Way, thought Mat. The normal sunrise time before sunspots. He noted the Chinese trio was moving, and a fourth soldier seemed to pop up behind them. A messenger or the first of reinforcements. He still had no communications. He was being given his chance to be a hero—to fend off wave after wave of attacking Chinese. In a week's time, the only living witnesses to his struggles would be the rats. He would fight hard and make the enemy pay—for his life had worth, and his Lord had worth, and they, his enemies, stood for nothing noble or worthy. When it was done, when he had ground them into death, they would understand. He would join the long list of soldiers who did their duty and died, unknown to anyone but their Maker.

God was Mat's God, his personal friend, the only One who truly cared about the inside-your-head pain of living. Father God knew all about the human named Matthew. God had created the world, life, to bring into being Matthew Johnson. Hard to comprehend—Matthew Johnson was such a worthless creature. Hadn't accomplished much. He loved Katie, he loved Mom and Dad; his only accomplishment: loving them. He loved God and His son, Jesus, and the Holy Spirit. Was that all there was to life—to love? To protect those you loved and to help them grow to love? To love their God. "Love God with all your heart and soul, mind and strength." Yes, that was it, and it was more than enough.

He had endured to the end. He would be leaving soon—dying. He expected pain, prolonged or brief, he didn't know. What a place to have it end—three layers deep in rotting flesh, the smoke and mists of war acrid on the tongue and in the lungs. Just where God, through the Bible, said it would end.

A dark force stole over the landscape like a giant shadow. Mat felt an ominous foreboding, like the presence of a killer behind him. The stars were still visible; stars were falling like rain. He saw a sliver of moon, blood red; the earth began to shake.

As if one with the earth, hundreds of Chinese soldiers arose and at a calculated trot, began their sweep up the valley and toward his position. He rested his barrel on the helmeted head of the corpse that was his shield. He began firing—knocking them down in one long row. No one took cover; they just kept coming. They wanted to die…they were as tired of living as he was. He thought of Dad, Mom, Katie. Chinese whistles sounded. Return to positions. The advancing ranks were not returning; they were falling to their knees. Who was firing at them? The eastern horizon was brilliant with white and golden light in a narrow belt around the arc of Earth. Was this a normal sunrise? It had been so long since he had seen the sun rise.

Jesus was coming! Jesus was coming, something inside told him. This very moment, Christ was returning! Glory hallelujah! He said He would come, and He was coming this very day. Matthew, already on his knees, dropped his weapon, began ripping off his gear. He raised his hands, shouting, clapping. The enemy was watching him, wondering. The Chinese soldiers could not rise from their kneeling postures, they could not hold weapons. He saw them struggling and failing to regain their feet. He looked behind—an advancing relief platoon of Federation forces were on their knees, some with their faces to the earth. There was fear, anxiety, terror in their eyes. He was laughing. Yes! Yes! Yes! The filth of this world would soon be no more. As great as his elation, he had a sadness for the thousands around him who could not rise. Mat stood, his waving arms calling in the heavenly host.

The light was spreading over the earth, racing toward him. Brilliant, dazzling white, incomprehensible, filled with roiling clouds of light. No…not clouds…vast masses, hurtling toward Earth. Shadows were cast by the ridge, mountains, by machines and soldiers. Then the shadows disappeared. The masses were individual beings. Angels! Angels! The world had laughed at their existence. So many angels, the heavens were filled. Rushing through the sky. Trumpets? Glorious sounds! A million voices? Instruments? Vast legions of angels with the air whistling through their wings and the horns sounding. Oh, my Lord! My God! The sound of the horns announcing justice and righteousness coming.

Christ! Christ! Christ! In the center. A weapon in His hand. Eyes steeled for combat. Righteous was His anger. Righteousness, His strength! The world had spit upon Him. The world had beaten Him, made Him wear the thorny crown; the world had nailed Him to a splintery cross and mocked His pain. His body pierced with nails; His body shredded by bone- and lead-embedded whips. What a joke His people had been to the world. What utter foolishness they had been, ridiculed and mocked. How His people had been tramped upon, spat upon, treated as dirt under the feet of the strong, the intelligent, the knowing. Christ came now! In His glory! The God Who held truth and righteousness!

"My Lord! My Lord! Oh, my God! My God! My King! My Savior!" Mat fell to his knees upon the shaking ground, crying, unworthy to even look upon the feet of his Master.

"Katie! Katie! Dad! Mom!"

Mat was lifted up, off the earth, into the sky. He saw a lone Chinese soldier rise in the far distance. No one rose from the Federation ranks, save Mat, as far as Mat could see. He saw masses of men, women, children of Earth—the beginning of the gathering, the harvest—rising. Behind them, he sensed intense heat, brilliant-yellow light, as if from flame, engulfing the east. He was going home! He laughed joyously.

***

Katie awoke in an emotion of pleasant expectancy. She and Mom and Dad had just turned in, but she couldn't sleep; there was something she was supposed to see. She shook Dad's covers.

"Dad! Dad! Wake up." The Spirit was with her every moment, now that her dad had returned. No, He must have been with her always, but now there was no earthly distraction from His presence. Her little cave was peaceful and warm. Mom and Dad were in love again, within their covers. Christ had healed all the recriminations and hurts and brought out a love from deep familiarity, years of sharing and knowing each other. Katie gathered her sweater and made her way to the round, metal plate that was the door. "Hurry up, Dad, Mom. Dad had his coat on—not understanding the urgency, but he too felt the expectancy. Mary grabbed a shawl Katie had given her and collected herself behind Tim.

Katie normally listened for five minutes before detriggering the grenade. Five minutes when she listened for a cough, a scratching, mumbling, the movement of clothing, the shift of body position. Even when the sound detectors gave no alarm. But now—right now, it is safe! said the voice. It was the Spirit of God talking to her. This was Christmas Day. This was Easter Resurrection. This was the Day of Pentecost. The moment seemed safe, and she rolled the plate to the side. She sat and smelled the air for body odors of sweat or food stains on clothes, or wounds, or greasy hair. The air held only the scent of bare rock. Dad was silent. Knowing his daughter, he studied her demeanor and knew God was present. They moved out to the sitting stones, only feet away from the door, but from which they could pivot in their seats and see 360 degrees.

The sun was rising, but it was eleven o'clock at night. Where was the sun? There was only light! They saw the curve of the earth. For weeks, she had thought of Matthew in this initial waking time. Today, she knew for certain that he was alive. Dad had tried so hard to lead his little family to Christ and to keep them together and alive. He had come to know Christ—not as she and Mat knew Him, but he had come to appreciate His sacrifices and to know what it meant to leave the world, the flesh, and Satan behind. One slip up, one temptation—the water, the food, the people, and seeing Pastor Dave again had been too much to resist. God had remained faithful to His child and had brought him home. Mom was here; what kind of miracle was that? Huh? Huh? Think of that, Satan and you forces of evil! Her mother was right beside her! She loved her God and longed to kiss His face and feel His steady hand upon her shoulders. Where was Mat? Was he seeing this sky?

Katie's eyes scanned the city—the white walls glowing, the low roofs dull and gray, the streetlights flicking off. Katie pivoted to the mountain behind her—the great propellers of the line of windmills turning at a walking pace. They caught some yellowish light cast out by the sun. She saw vultures on their ridgetop stone perches, shaking out their wings. She looked to the west and saw the crease of the riverbed and the continuation of the high mountain ridge. She stood, the increase in height gave her a new vantage. "Mom, Dad! Jesus is coming."

"I know, Katie," said her mother. Her dad said nothing, for he knew.

"No, I mean He's coming *now*!"

"Yes! I see tiny objects in the sky, filling the sky, and they are coming our way—and the mass of light in the center?" Mom dropped the living picture, which had been in her hand. Dad was raising his hands.

"Glory, glory, glory!" were the only words he could speak, and his outstretched arms seemed to cast those very words into the heavens. Mom was hugging her.

"He who endures to the end shall be saved," Tim said to Mary and Katie. Where was his Matthew—his precious boy, who had become a man? Tim fell to his knees and wept uncontrollably for his missing son, and then he wept for his Savior, who was telling him that his son was alive and coming to him. "Thank you, Lord. Thank you, Lord."

They heard a deep horn resonating through the air. Katie looked to the east and up; something filled the heavens—little living things, moving, like her mom had said. An air hit them, filled with incense. The light was building in intensity, coming from all the objects that flowed, roiled; the horns were sounding—many horns. What was that bright object in the center of it all? Katie's body became alive, filled with strength. Happiness overwhelmed her. Jesus! Jesus was the object, and He was coming for her and Mom and Dad. It was over. The history of sinners was over.

What a glorious day! She reached up to heaven, she grabbed Mom, and they hugged and spun in a circle, jumping wildly. Christ was right before them, looking at each of them. They were gazing upon the face of Jesus.

He was grinning—he laughed, and they laughed. An angel took her by the arms up into the mass of the heavenly hosts, into the trumpets calling, the incense so clean and sweet. The host of angels was uncountable, swirling, unending, sparkling in light.

She saw others—humans—laughing and crying. Mat came from nowhere and hugged her tightly, and holding his hand was little Emily. Emily grabbed Mary's hand, and they hugged. There was a black man with a Semitic nose, crying with joy, and his wife and children. That was Burnell. Dad had told her about him, and she had never met him, but she knew him. She knew Tish and Tanya, Anya and Flo. She saw DC Jones and Dan Jr. and Barb. The happiness and joy was overwhelming.

Tim felt a force gather him under his arms. Jesus held him, hugged him, and spoke. "Good and faithful servant, you have brought your family home." Tim joined with Mat, and they hugged. Precious Emily hugged him, Mary, and Katie. There was Burnell and his family and DC Jones, Dan Jr. and Barb. A Chinese soldier who had tagged behind Mat was waving a Bible. Josh? Josh and his band were in their midst, hugging one and all. All were hugging and praising God, and no thought was given to those who were not present—these thoughts were hidden by the One who gave joy.

Tim saw his brother, John, and Diana, John's friend. Katie had Diana by the hand, and Emily by the other. Tim rushed toward John and crushed him with a hug and tears, for it was John and Diana and Gramps—where was Gramps? Beside him—it was they who had told him the truth about himself, that He did not know God and lived for the world, the flesh, and Satan. Their blunt but gently delivered words had begun his search for truth and life. Without them, his family would be dead in their sins. "Thanks, John…I thank you with all that I possess—and you, too, Diana."

Gramps nudged Tim. "What about me?"

Tim hugged Gramps. "And you, too, most of all—for only you understood the import of the times, the reality no one else could see." Tim knew Gramps was about to speak, and he knew what he would say. Tim spoke. "Yes, the Holy Spirit told you, but your heart was tuned to hear

His words."

While Tim and Gramps were talking, DC Jones approached John. An immediate insight was revealed to John. "The security guard at Van Ord's murder site. I walked right past you! So happy you are here!" The memory of the time came clearly to him; he saw it all but could filter the emotional pain from the time. "I am here because of you. Your trail gave me a glimpse of Jesus ahead. I followed, and here I am." John hugged DC Jones. He wondered at that time of stress and doubt when he had blindly followed the Spirit's call and walked in faith. Diana joined him. Life was finally good—and with his soulmate beside him to share life and God's Kingdom around him, the possibilities were eternally endless.

***

Stasic awoke from his cramped position in his rock lair; his constructed windbreak of gathered stones. His lightweight heat blanket of thin, woven metals fell from his shoulders. The Bible had been used as a pillow, not in disrespect, but in the hopes his sleeping mind would ingest the words. Fuckin' air platforms were shining searchlights on him. He jumped up, pointing his shotgun, but it weighed so much, it fell to the ground. He fell to the ground on his knees. The whole damn sky was filled with light, movement, angels—uncountable angels—and a white mass in the center. Incense flooded the earth; horns sounded, deep and resonant, sending shivers through his bones. He saw the mass of angels filling the sky; he saw Jesus bathed in brilliant light, upon a white horse with a weapon in his hand. He saw humans—there was Tim! He saw Mary, Mat, Katie, and little Emily, the Jennings girl he had rescued. Joshua and his band of martyrs looked down upon him, and others he did not know.

As quickly as they came, they moved west. The entire world must be covered with light, the sound of horns, incense, and movement. Then the heavenly procession arose, and a blackness descended—blacker than any night. No moon, no sun, no stars. Carl began praying—praying for forgiveness. He felt oxygen leaving the earth. He was too stunned to cry, too devastated to beg; detesting himself, he wished to die—he wanted the pain of hell to come, for he was too loathsome to live without pain.

He was falling into darkness. He would not stop praying. He needed forgiveness; then he could take the horrors of hell. He just wanted the Lord to acknowledge that Carl Stasic was sincere; he deserved hell. No one upon the earth deserved the pain more than he, and he would feel it for eternity. He saw the heat and flames that would consume the world even as he traveled deeper into the darkness. He prayed. He would pray through all eternity for forgiveness. Just forgiveness. He deserved no second chance. He wanted no second chance.

The God who gave the adulterer and murderer David, king of Israel, a second chance; the God who forgave the thief on the cross; the God who forgave Saul of Tarsus his murder of God's chosen ones; the God who forgave Peter his denial of Christ. That same God forgave the sins of Carl Stasic.

***

Mat stood alone; the others, of the redeemed, were together. The Chinese soldier had never learned English yet had no trouble talking to everyone. He had no friends, relatives from his native country. It did not matter. Tanya, Anya, and Flo had included him in their games as their parents watched. Mat had met Burnell, first name Thomas, and learned of the story of his meeting with Dad. Thomas was a good man. Perhaps they would work together in the future.

He did not know what world they stood upon. He heard vast rumblings and swooshing sounds underneath their domain—noise of cataclysmic proportions. Was this the earth being cleansed? There was talk of white robes to be handed out and returning to Jerusalem for Christ's triumphal return. They said Jerusalem would look exactly as it had when Christ had walked the streets.

He saw a lone figure beyond even where he stood. A figure cloaked in the white haze of this place. He began walking toward the figure, which cowered, lowered itself, and would look at him and then avert his eyes. Yes, a man. Carl? How had Carl come to this place? It did not matter. God had decided, and there was no error in the decisions of God. Carl had done Mat wrong, yes. But whom had Mat done wrong to in the confusion of life? God had forgiven him, and He forgave Carl.

Carl was ashamed—yes, that was what the posture said. Mat picked up his pace, began to stride, as he felt the unrelenting hurt and shame of Carl. He must comfort Carl, forgive, lift his spirit. This was a time of happiness, a time to marvel at the grace of God and His powerful love.

"Lift your head, Carl. No bad thoughts in heaven. The time of shame is gone." Mat extended his hands in a welcoming, embracing desire. "God has forgiven you. I have forgiven you. Now forgive yourself in the name of Christ's sufferings on the cross." Mat nimbly and gently placed Carl's arms around himself. Mat squeezed Carl, and felt the tears streaming from Carl's eyes, bathing his face. Mat seemed to be ringing a wet towel. Deep sobs shook Carl's lungs and frame. "I am so sorry, Mat."

"You are a new man, Carl. The times of shame are past." The Spirit was with Mat. "God loved you, Carl, because you loved your neighbor as yourself." Mat rocked Carl gently, with his arms around Carl. "The times of shame are past."

EPILOGUE

As the word of God promised, as the Messiah spoke, the world was judged. Those who sought truth, wished with all their being to live it, sought the face of God; those who talked to Him, argued with Him with respect and humility, had been born again, and followed His way. They had renounced the world, the flesh, and Satan. They were washed, sanctified, justified in the name of Jesus. They had walked in the Spirit and inherited the Kingdom of God into everlasting eternity.

Those born in their sin, who judged themselves gods and wished to be God; those who decided what was right and wrong, living in their lust, who spoke only to God to mock and curse Him, remained in their flesh, remained with their world, and remained with their deceiver. They had renounced the Father, the Son, the Holy Spirit. Those who had strutted in life now crawled as the world was consumed in flame, and their inheritance was eternal loneliness and pain.

As for the lives of those mentioned in this story, and the lives of all the redeemed since the beginning of mankind—they lived a thousand years of their eternal journey upon the new earth—the earth as it would have been had first man not sinned. Tim and Mary knew a love they had not thought possible in intimacy, oneness, and delight. They had one last child, a daughter named Hope. Mat married Barb Smith, and they had a family of eight. Katie found the boy of the mountainside restaurant, married him, and matched her brother's family size. Dan Jr. became their dearest friend. Tim's brother, John, in a resurrection body, remained with his truest friend, Diana, and they served the Lord together. DC Jones became a part of Joshua's band—those in resurrection bodies who delighted in the companionship of Christ and the delights of the new life. Burnell had his own child with Tisha, and the three girls of Tisha—Tanya, Anya, and Flo, doted on their baby brother. In time they, too, had families.

Carl Stasic, the last man redeemed from the earth, had chosen to spend the millennium in singleness, honoring God through the many tasks and jobs that came his way. Till, at some point in endless time, well past the millennium, the Lord gave Carl management work, within a company, that only he could do.